Date: 3/23/20

BIO BOCELLI
Bocelli, Andrea.
The music of silence /

The Music of Silence

The Music of Silence

Andrea Bocelli

Translated from the Italian by
Consuelo Bixio Hackney

AMADEUS PRESS

An Imprint of Hal Leonard Corporation

Amadeus Press
An Imprint of Hal Leonard Corporation
7777 West Bluemound Road
Milwaukee, WI 53213

Trade Book Division Editorial Offices
33 Plymouth St., Montclair, NJ 07042

Published in 2010 as *La musica del silenzio* by Istituto Geografico De Agostini

English-language edition published in 2011 by Amadeus Press

Printed in the United States of America

Book design by F. L. Bergesen

Library of Congress Cataloging-in-Publication Data is available upon request.

Amadeus ISBN: 978-1-57467-197-1

www.amadeuspress.com

I

I feel a slight but undeniable tinge of embarrassment at the prospect of trying my hand once more, after such a long time, at the writer's craft, an activity to which I had dedicated many pleasurable hours in my youth.

My embarrassment stems mostly from the lack of any justification or pretext for such an endeavour; at that time my writing was almost entirely confined to school assignments, although occasionally I would write letters to distant friends, compose small poems, or indulge in other similar adolescent pursuits.

My intention now – if this can be a sufficient excuse for a man of my age to suddenly take up the pen – is merely to use some of my free time, to flee from the perils of idleness, and to tell the story of a simple life.

I confess that my main worry is not so much that the unfortunate reader might soon yawn over these poor scribbled pages. He can choose to put the book down at any time and not give it another thought. Instead it is that I feel myself observed by two eyes that read my thoughts while I write. They are the eyes of an old man with a kind face, an understanding expression, and that hint of a smile of one who is so familiar with the human comedy as to react to its vicissitudes with a sense of weariness and detachment. It is no longer possible to read the face of such a fellow whose passions have been extinguished forever by the inexorable passage of time and by the tenacious strength of his intellect. And yet that serene face, illuminated perhaps by the fire of ideas, seems to judge me severely. Beneath that gaze I feel ridiculous and intimidated and realise that I am incapable of doing anything, while only a moment ago I was presumptuous and deluded like those students who believe themselves to be custodians of absolute truths merely on the strength of a few philosophical notions they picked up at school. With the passing of time I seem to detect a touch of irony crossing the features of the old man. So then I ask myself: why is he not indulgent with me as he is with everyone else? Why does he take me so seriously?

The reader, who may by now have guessed the identity of the kind old inquisitor, will know that his implacable gaze is always there, looking over my shoulder, at every moment of the day, and is at the root of my every action or decision.

II

Here I am in one of my many cells: a room three metres square with two small armchairs, a basin, a mirror, a small table, and a fitted wardrobe. The space is illuminated by a single, small window looking out onto the street. It is two o'clock in the afternoon, and I will have to stay here until late this evening. In a while they will come and call me for a rehearsal, after that for make-up; they will bring me some water, a cup of coffee, the usual things. And so it is to trick time into passing that I begin this story. The computer is on. Now all I need is a subject.

I feel the need to detach myself from the task, but it is hard to do. I pace up and down the room in search of memories, feelings of nostalgia, and affection for distant people and places, and suddenly a small boy in shorts makes his way into my thoughts. He is thin as a rake with sinewy, slightly bandy legs covered in cuts and bruises. He has pitch-black hair, regular features, and a cheeky smart-aleck expression which could be more or less likeable depending on your point of view. If you don't mind I will talk to you about him because I know him well enough to allow myself free rein to comment on, or even judge, every aspect of his life, his ideas, and his most important decisions, and I can do this serenely with the benefit of hindsight.

I think I can safely describe him as a normal young boy, even if he is a little out of the ordinary as a result of a life which was also

3

somewhat uncommon for certain reasons which are by now quite well known. I therefore refer to his being normal in the sense that he presented a more or less equal measure of virtues and defects, and I also say normal in spite of a rather serious physical impairment, about which I will rather reluctantly but necessarily have to say something. I will do so but only after having given a name to the protagonist of this story.

As one name is as good as another I will call him Amos. This was the name of a man towards whom I hold a deep and infinite debt of gratitude and to whom I owe much of what little I know. It is his way of approaching life that I have attempted, with meagre success, to use to mould my own. It is also the name of one of the minor prophets: perhaps this is another reason why I like it and why it seems an appropriate name for a young lad who, as I was about to explain, had limited sight until the age of twelve, when he lost his sight completely as a result of an unfortunate mishap. On that occasion it took a good hour or so to spill all his tears of fear and dismay and a full week to get used to his new circumstance. After that, I would say, Amos put it all behind him, and in doing so he was also able to help his friends and relations to forget about it too. And this is all that needs to be said on the matter.

Instead, when it comes to describing Amos's character, it is necessary to be much more specific to allow the reader to judge freely whether, or to what degree, it may have influenced his destiny.

His mother frequently and tirelessly describes the difficulties she faced in bringing up her vivacious and impulsive first-born son. "You couldn't look away for a second without him getting up to one of his tricks!" she says. "He always loved taking risks and the sense of danger. One day I looked for him and he wasn't there. I called and got no answer. I looked up and saw him standing on the window-sill outside my bedroom window. We lived on the second floor and he was not yet five years old. But to help you understand what I went through I will tell you this story." And so she continues in her Tuscan accent, accompanied by her large gestures and great agitation. "One morning I was walking along a wide avenue in the centre of Turin, holding Amos by the hand and looking for a tram stop. I stopped at the first one I found and was just distracted for a moment while I looked at a shop window. When I turned round I felt my blood run cold. My baby was gone. Desperate, I looked everywhere...he was nowhere to be seen. I called out. There was no reply! I don't know what made me look upwards but I no longer knew where to look...and would you believe it...there he was. He had climbed up to the top of the post at the tram stop..."

"But wait! That's not the end of it!" she continues, interrupting her interlocutor's gasps of astonishment. "As he was not a good eater from the start, I would have to chase him all over the place, holding his bowl of soup in order to get a spoonful into his mouth...on the tractor, on the workers' motor scooters...everywhere!"

If the listener displays sufficient interest in her story, Amos's mother, Edi, visibly pleased, indefatigably adorns her monologue with even more elaborate detail which, while generally true, barring a few exceptions resulting from her irrepressible love of the dramatic and the paradoxical, does not always benefit the economy of the narrative.

I particularly recall the astonishment and sincere emotion of one elderly lady in response to Amos's mother's description of her little one's problems. "He was only a few months old..." she recounted emphatically, "when we noticed that he was experiencing a strong pain in his eyes. He had beautiful blue eyes...Shortly after that we were given the bad news. The doctors diagnosed a congenital bilateral glaucoma, a disease that invariably leads to total blindness. We immediately raced from one doctor to another, from specialists to healers. I am not ashamed to admit that we even tried that route. Our ordeal led us to Turin, into the hands of Professor Gallenga, who was a luminary in his field. We spent entire weeks in the hospital there. Little Amos would be operated on frequently in an attempt to salvage at least some residual sight. We would arrive tired out from the journey but above all prostrate with fear and uncertainty and shocked by our impotence in the face of the unjust destiny that was wreaking havoc on our poor child...My husband would leave the following morning and I would stay with Amos. The professor was very understanding. He gave us a room with two beds, and I soon got to know the doctors and nurses (which proved to be invaluable especially in the years that followed as Amos became increasingly boisterous). They even allowed me to bring a little bicycle onto the ward so that he could let off steam a bit."

Suddenly the elderly listener, visibly perturbed and moved, interrupted, exclaiming, "You cannot imagine how I feel for you! Forgive my curiosity, but did the child suffer from these painful eyes for very long?"

"My dear, if you only knew...we could not calm him down! One morning though, after a dreadful night spent vainly seeking some form of relief, the little boy suddenly stopped crying. It is hard to describe what one feels at moments like that. It is a sort of profound gratitude addressed to everyone and no-one in particular; it is a blessing for an unexpected moment of peace which comes in the midst of a terrible storm...I tried to figure out the reason for that sudden calm and fervently hoped that there was indeed a reason for it so that I might identify it and make use of it from then on. I observed, reflected; I tried to think of everything but failed to draw any conclusions. All of a sudden I noticed Amos turn on his side and press his little hands against the wall by his bed. A short time passed, I cannot recall how long, and then I became aware of a silence that I had not noticed a little while earlier in that room, and then, just then...Amos started crying again. What had happened? What had stopped happening? Had that sudden silence perhaps upset my son? I was in turmoil once more but just a little after that Amos calmed down once again. He pressed his hands against the wall just as he had done before. In the grip of a tension that I can't begin to describe to you, I listened and made out the strains of music coming from the next room. I leaned over and concentrated harder. It was music I did not know, probably classical music or music...what do they call it?...chamber music...I really could not get it; it was not something I understood...But I felt inclined to believe that my little one's tranquility really depended on that music. It was a small hope which filled me with joy, a joy as great as my suffering, such joy as I have probably never felt since then and which perhaps you can only feel when you have paid the price of such profound pain. I think then I rushed to the next room and immediately knocked at the door, and I was invited to come in by a man who spoke with a foreign accent. I plucked up courage and tip-toed in to find a patient sitting up on his bed, resting against, or more probably slumped between, two pillows arranged to support two strong shoulders. I remember his muscular arms and the hands of a manual labourer; I remember seeing an open, smiling face and his eyes wrapped in bandages. He was a Russian labourer who had recently lost his sight as a result of an industrial accident. A small record player was enough to keep him happy. I remember a lump coming to my throat and feeling profoundly moved...

"I don't know how I found the strength to overcome my emotion, but I do recall that I talked to him for a long time; I told that good man about what had just happened and asked his permission to bring my son to his room occasionally. His friendly welcome, his pleasure in being able to be useful, and his extraordinary spirit of human solidarity which was both simple and great are all things which I will never forget! I don't know how much that man actually understood, as his knowledge of Italian was limited to just a few words, but he realized he could be of assistance and he offered me his good will." This is the way Edi describes how she discovered her son's passion for music.

III

I have often experienced an uncontrollable desire to provide a new definition of music, in order at least to say something a bit different about this noble art, to which I owe an infinite number of hours of enormous pleasure as well as a fair number of hours of really excruciating anxiety.

During nights when I cannot sleep, in an attempt to give shape to random thoughts, I quite often get involved in contorted reflections which are the product of days of overwork. I think. I think long and hard, with the sole outcome, at times, of finding sleep, but never anything original, nothing of importance from a philosophical or artistic point of view. Music, even without my own definition, remains rich in all that has already been said and written. And so I use this poor page of my exercise book as an outlet upon which to spill the most trivial, most ridiculous notion in the world, something that has already been exclaimed a thousand times: "For me music is a fundamental need, like love; above all it is my destiny, as inescapable as the passing of time."

I found this thought in a short diary of Amos's, an old diary which contained a few of the little poems he would occasionally write, from his earliest childhood, as well as curious, random thoughts, such as the one I have quoted above only because it is useful for the purpose of what I am about to tell you about him.

On the other hand, it often happens that it is precisely those things that are thrown down haphazardly, distractedly, almost involuntarily, and without any importance being attributed to them that best describe a character and provide the best snapshot of the writer's inner truth.

Amos's mother's account of how she discovered her son's love of music triggered a cascade of gifts from his relatives of all manner of things which had to do with the world of sound. Amos received toys which could reproduce simple tunes, music boxes, and, eventually, a wonderful record player with his first record, an LP of songs which he liked well enough and which stirred his curiosity but did not fire his musical passion.

One day, at the end of a moving story told by an old uncle of his about the life and singing career of a recently departed, world-famous tenor, Amos expressed a determination to hear a record by this new hero, the legendary Beniamino Gigli. When he heard that voice, Amos felt such a strong emotion that his uncle had to extend the story and in the end was compelled to add a number of additional anecdotes of his own invention in order to satisfy Amos's excited childish imagination. It then required several of that inimitable tenor's records to placate his curiosity and his sudden feverish enthusiasm, and this was followed by demands for more stories about other new singing heroes.

Amos insisted that his most recent favourite should always be depicted as the best; as is so often the case with children, his passion would be ignited by his most recently discovered idol.

And so it was that the first recordings by Giuseppe Di Stefano, Mario Del Monaco, Aureliano Pertile, and Ferruccio Tagliavini found their way into the Bocelli household. Then Amos's uncle told him about Caruso. He did this with his usual eloquence and all his passion, assuring his nephew that he had really been the greatest singer – the one with the most powerful voice, the clearest and longest notes – and the most revered by lovers of opera. So it was not long before the first record by Caruso arrived and with it Amos's first disappointment. The little boy, who knew nothing about developments in recording techniques, found that voice which sounded as though it came from the bottom of a jar, that tone which had been largely rearranged by the rudimentary recording instruments of his day, was not at all to his liking. In his view Caruso's voice could really not stand up to comparison with the noble and imperious tones of Del Monaco or the sweet and passionate voice of Beniamino Gigli which had so impressed him.

Young Amos would eventually revise his opinions of the great Caruso but only after many years and many extraordinary events which form the basis of this story.

One morning Amos was alone in the courtyard of the house, lost in thought as he walked back and forth from the garage door to the gate leading onto the road, occasionally humming pieces from the arias that he knew. Suddenly he stopped, having heard the unmistakable steps of his "Tata" (the familiar name he used for Oriana, a girl who had been present when he was born, who worked as a domestic help in his house, and to whom he was very attached).

Oriana was coming back from running errands at the local shops. As she opened the gate she saw Amos coming towards her, and with a maternal smile, she called him to let him know that she had something important to read to him. She had just spotted it in the newspaper she had bought for his father. She quickly put the shopping away in the house and then came out again, holding the open newspaper.

"Listen carefully," she said before she began to read, carefully pronouncing each syllable. "Franco Corelli amazes at La Scala in Milan".

Amos was eight years old at the time. He knew about La Scala of Milan but nobody, not even his uncle, had ever mentioned this wonderful singer to him. "Who is Corelli, Tata?" he asked as he ran after her. Oriana began to read the article which described the first night of *Gli Ugonotti* in which the famous tenor had astonished his audience with a distinguished performance, displaying a very powerful voice – a true "bronzo" – rich in harmonies and, above

that art which is capable of captivating, beguiling, and touching even those spirits most hardened by the trials of life.

Oriana and Amos listened, almost stunned. They were overwhelmed by an entirely new emotion, and the little boy saw his nursemaid cover her eyes while the tenor, with incomparable sweetness, sang the lines "Oh, giovinetta bella d'un poeta non disprezzate il detto, udite, non conoscete amor? Amor!" This last word was a cry of passion, a very high and noble cry, in which the strength and beauty of the voice merged, leaving them breathless with admiration.

Still today Amos loves to describe that moment which was so important for him, and he does it with such passion as to leave no doubt of his sincerity. Nor does he forget Oriana's own excitement. Probably, in listening to that voice, she received the gift of a dream, a hope; she found a drive, a new energy which made everything easier for her. It made everything more tolerable in her modest existence, which may have been full of dreams but was without great excitement. Perhaps at that moment Oriana felt happier than she had ever felt in her life before, because a voice is also able to perform this kind of miracle, and perhaps her soul was enriched in some way and acquired a new nobility by hearing that "del mondo, anima e vita è l'Amore..." (Love is the life and soul of the world...).

IV

I have just realised that I have not yet given Amos a surname. From now on I will imagine that he belongs to the Bardi family as for the moment I really cannot think of anything better. However, I do solemnly promise the reader who has sufficient patience to read this story through to the last page that I will set out the reasons which have led me to give an invented name to a person who really exists. I also think that at this point I should tell you something about Amos's family, his home, and the folk he grew up with. After all, if it is true that each one of us is nothing more than the sum of our experiences and our knowledge, as well as, obviously, our own nature, then I have a duty to introduce to you the people who have loved and guided him and have shared his trials and his suffering.

If I were a real writer I would probably not resist the temptation to describe the places where Amos spent his childhood in minute detail too, if for no other reason than for their objective beauty which is typically Tuscan, pure and natural, or at least this is how it seems to my heart. But I will not give way to the temptation to indulge in descriptions which a simple map and a fine day out would render entirely superfluous. I will only say that in September 1958 Amos was born in La Sterza, a small hamlet bordering the village of Lajatico in the province of Pisa, about halfway between Volterra and Pontedera.

In broaching the subject of his home, a mysterious, complicated mechanism in my mind recalls "La Signorina Felicita", that delightful verse penned by Guido Gozzano, in which the poet brilliantly depicts a large house deep in the countryside. This was where the Signorina Felicita lived, a typical home of times gone by with "bulging, twisted, and worn window grating", rooms which were too large and full of old knick-knacks, hundreds of near useless objects, and yet alive... a living, breathing space thanks to the simplicity and hard work of those who occupied it: the domestic servant battling with the clattering crockery, the Signorina herself with her knitting needles, her mending on her lap and her subtle skirmishes, and her kindly father who, towards nightfall, would often surround himself with "all of the local political grandees..."

I don't know why, but Amos's house, which was situated right on the main road linking Sarzana to Valdera, in the open countryside, and was as big as an enormous capital L measuring twenty-five by twenty metres, overlooking a broad gravelled area at the top of the drive, overshadowed by two very tall pine trees, with one side of the garden flanking the road surrounded by the L-shaped building, and a tower with a turreted top floor... I don't know why this solid stone construction, probably dating back to the end of the nineteenth century, should always remind me of that famous poem by Gozzano. Entering by the front door one would find oneself in a small hallway with doors on each side leading to the kitchen on the right and to a dining area on the left. Straight ahead a glass doorway led through to a second and larger hall with more side doors, the one on the right leading to a large drawing room, which the family would use as a dining room for special occasions and where Amos would listen to his gramophone, walking around the table interminably and stopping only to change the records. The door on the left led instead to the storage and utility rooms. Amos would refer to the first of these as the dark room. In effect it was a windowless room in which there was a clothes-stand and an old wardrobe, a real *refugium peccatorum*. Straight ahead were the stairs leading to the upper storey with the bedrooms, the bathrooms, and other rooms which were hardly ever used, two of which served as an attic. Then there was a part of the house on the ground floor which could only be accessed from outside. In these immense rooms the Bardi family stored most of their agricultural machines: two "hothead" tractors (a Landini and an Orsi) and a gigantic threshing machine. Amos loved to go into those store rooms, to turn the huge pulleys on the threshing machine, and to let his imagination roam, thinking about all the mechanisms that these set in motion. There were also innumerable smaller agricultural tools: spades, hoes, gadgets of every sort, all objects of fascination which provided Amos with hours of entertainment.

Grandma Leda, much loved teacher of at least two generations of local children, who had given up teaching shortly after the birth of her grandchild, and kindly Oriana had their hands full trying to keep Amos and Alberto, his little brother, in check. They were inseparable playmates with other children from the neighbouring houses, and together they formed a veritable bunch of hooligans, at least as Grandma Leda was concerned, for this is how she would refer to them in her moments of exasperation. The poor woman could not bear seeing her flowers crushed by stray footballs, or having to put up with the strident protests from the passers-by who would be struck by a variety of missiles identifiable as having provenance from the Casa Bardi: stones slung from catapults or shot from small toy rifles and powerful jets of water from a hose which Amos's father, Signor Sandro, used to water the flower beds and, in the summer months, to wash down the yard in front of the house so that the family could eat outside. When no adults were around the hose would be used as a weapon against passing cars or, worse still, against two-wheeled vehicles...But after eight o'clock every evening, Amos's parents, his grandfather Signor Alcide, and the elderly aunt who had always worked with her brother-in-law so that her sister could carry on teaching at the local primary school would draw up an account of the misdemeanours carried out by the boys that day, under the command of Amos who was the oldest, and the originator and author of the most unpredictable pranks. Then they would all threaten exemplary punishments if this or that offence were ever to be repeated, but, as we all know, the liveliness of certain children frequently wins over the adults' severity, and that's as it should be.

Dottor Comparini, now retired but previously head of the local Financial Police and an Italian army colonel during the First World War, was probably Amos's favourite uncle – the one who had already sparked his imagination with the occasionally over-embellished stories of the lives and professional careers of the most famous opera stars of the century. Every summer Signora Leda and Amos would take a few days' holiday in Antignano, a small seaside village in the province of Pisa where the Comparini family, comprising Uncle Giovanni and Aunt Olga, lived. These relations, who were actually Amos's father's uncle and aunt, Signora Olga being Amos's grandmother's sister, were devoted to the Bardi family. During the Second World War they had taken Sandro, who was then studying for his diploma to qualify as a surveyor, into their home, and he had lived there for the entire period of his studies. When they were at the Comparinis' house, Amos enjoyed going to the beach every morning accompanied by his grandmother, who never let him out of her sight for a single second, but the time he most looked forward to was the late after-noon, when his uncle would call him upstairs and Amos was finally allowed to go into his study, which was full of fascination and mystery. In the military order of that room were to be found more than five thousand books and various objects which were treasured by the inhabitants of the house as well as by Amos himself. He would stand staring in wonder at an old mortar shell, defused of course, or the wild boar–skin mat, with its splendid, menacing head, perfectly embalmed. This is where his old uncle would let him listen to his records and where he would read to him and tell him endless stories which Amos loved and would listen to in rapture, saving all his questions till the end. Sometimes the ladies would also be called to take part and then those family gatherings of times past – with Uncle Giovanni reading and explaining, the ladies occasionally passing some brief comment or being moved by the stories – those gatherings filled the little boy's heart with an indescribable joy which Amos still retains clearly distilled in his memory today and which triggers in him a gentle sense of nostalgia.

Sometimes Uncle Giovanni would also tell Amos long stories about the war which he had lived through in the front lines, and these stories would fire Amos's imagination to the point that he began to dream of joining the army.

So Amos's uncle "enlisted" him, as a private, with the prospects of promotion which depended upon his good conduct and, more generally, on evidence of his progress in the most varied fields. Thus Amos soon rose through the ranks of lance-corporal and then corporal. On one occasion, when Uncle Giovanni was visiting the Bardi home towards Christmas time, he promoted him to the rank of sergeant. Shortly after that, upon demonstrating that he had learned the first letters of the alphabet, which Amos's grandmother had taught him using a large blue felt pen, Amos achieved promotion to sergeant major, and the first time he signed his own name earned him the rank of marshal. Meanwhile the moment for Amos to leave for boarding school was drawing closer. This was a solution which his parents had reluctantly accepted as the only way to provide their boy with the benefits of a specialized school which, thanks to familiarization with Braille, would later enable him to rejoin the mainstream school system with other normal, that is to say perfectly sighted, schoolmates.

His imminent departure stirred his uncle to feel a moment of compassion which resulted in Amos's further promotion to chief marshal. On the day he left for school, Amos was read a letter sent to him by Uncle Giovanni which bore the news of yet another promotion to battle adjutant. So Amos left home, nurturing the hope that he might soon return with the rank of captain: a rank which he would achieve upon gaining his first good marks at school.

V

On the morning of 20th March 1965, the car was parked in the driveway of the Bardi home, ready to leave. It had been loaded up with everything Amos would need and would soon be on its way towards Reggio Emilia, where young Amos would remain until June. After a thousand hesitations, which had already caused the little boy to lose a whole year of school, a special school in that city had been chosen for him. The moment of departure would be very hard, but it was very important for Amos to attend that school. It was a school where blind and visually impaired children learned Braille; they studied geography using special maps in relief and benefited from all the appropriate facilities and equipment available to help overcome their learning difficulties.

As much as Amos's parents tried to cheer him up, encouraging him to think about the new friends he would make, the games he would play, and the new things he would learn which he could then teach his little brother, the atmosphere remained extremely tense throughout the long journey. His father especially found the idea of leaving his son 150 miles from home quite impossible to bear. His mother tried to put a brave face on it. She knew she was doing this for her son's good, and nothing, not even her maternal feelings, would have prevented her from doing whatever was necessary to ensure that her son would be able to face life on an equal footing with everyone else.

When they pulled up in front of the Giuseppe Garibaldi Institute in Via Mazzini, Signor Bardi let his wife out and went to park the car; then he got out, unloaded Amos's suitcase, took him by the hand, and led him through the entrance of that dilapidated building. A porter accompanied them to the cloakroom, where they left Amos's suitcase and then showed them to the dormitory where the new boarder was to sleep. It was a dormitory with ten beds, which Signor Bardi considered too many. Then the porter led them into another dormitory where, to his dismay, Signor Bardi counted sixty-four iron beds and an equal number of bedside tables of the same material and colour. At this point he could hardly restrain himself from expressing his criticism of the levels of hygiene pre-sented by such an environment, but he had to think of his son's education. That was the most important thing. "Children get used to anything," he thought. But when he went into the bathrooms he saw three stand-up toilets, three small, dirty, smelly cubicles, and nearby a double row of basins with only a cold water tap. He shuddered at the sight and felt his heart freeze at the thought that he would be going back to his comfortable home without his little one who was condemned to remain in that horrible boarding school far away from all the people he loved. At that moment his heart was engaged in a violent battle with his reasoning, but Signor Bardi swallowed hard to drive back the tears and overcome his pain and concern. He mustered up the necessary strength and forced himself to carry on.

The porter then introduced Amos's parents to a cleaning woman they met in the hallway, and after asking her to show them around the various other parts of the building, he took his leave, having expressed the hope that he would soon find little Amos perfectly at home in that new community.

The good woman, whose name was Etmèa, showed the little group into a large room which she described as "the recreation room". Signor and Signora Bardi cast their gaze over the large, bare space which was well lit by enormous rectangular windows and had an upright piano against the wall and a television set. Just in front of them they saw there was a small wooden stage. "That is for the school plays and the end-of-year prize-giving ceremony," explained Etmèa, having noticed her visitors' curiosity. Then she invited them to follow her up a large staircase. Two flights up they found themselves in a long corridor on each side of which were many identical wooden doors, all facing each other at regular intervals. "These are some of the classrooms," she said. "There are others too which are smaller. They are through there . . . " she said, indicating a small staircase with a little doorway at the end leading to a narrow corridor. She then turned back and went down the stairs again to the ground floor, where she showed the family the three courtyards of the Institute. The first of these, to the right of the main entrance, was called the "small courtyard" and was, in effect, a small space paved in cement which was located practically at the centre of the building. It seemed to be a perfect square upon which many windows opened, providing light and air to the upper storeys. In front of the "small courtyard" and to the left of the main entrance was the "middle courtyard", which was similar to the first one but a little larger and was surrounded by a cloister supported by cement columns with a square base. This portico was particularly useful during rainy days in winter. At the end of the cloister, a large sturdy door opened onto a vast open area of beaten earth which was divided into two almost equal parts by a row of tall plane trees, which would cover the ground in dry leaves in the autumn, crunching under the footsteps of passersby. At one end of this huge space, which the boys called "the big courtyard", there was also a small bowls pitch. That part of the school raised Signor Bardi's spirits somewhat. He would check his watch from time to time, shooting furtive glances at his wife.

Later that afternoon the Bardi family left the school. Amos's parents, who had planned to remain in Reggio Emilia that night, took their son with them to prepare him gently for the separation. They ate at a small trattoria in the city centre and then went to stay at the hotel "La Storia". Amos slept in his parents' bed just as he occasionally did at home, without yet fully realizing what was in store for him or quite grasping how much his life was soon to change.

The next morning Amos was taken to the Institute. His mother left him with a teacher and promised him that she would come back to see him at the end of the morning. The teacher then accompanied him to a classroom where a number of children were already sitting at their desks. Amos was to spend the rest of the school year with them.

He sat down and the teacher introduced him to the boy next to him. His name was Davide Pisciotta; he came from Ravenna and was the oldest of eleven brothers. Soon after this Amos was given a lump of modelling clay. It was the first time he had ever handled the stuff, and he did not immediately understand what the teacher meant when she asked him to break off a small piece and make it into a stick. The classroom was a bit chilly and initially the clay was quite hard to mould. After a few minutes Amos began to feel tired, but, sensing that he was under the watchful eye of his teacher, he did not stop until he felt that he had completed his first duty. However, his teacher declared herself dissatisfied: the stick was not smooth enough. Amos felt rather offended but carried on with his task in silence.

Every hour a bell would ring, and at midday the children were asked to rise and follow another teaching assistant who would lead them to lunch. For Amos the most difficult moment was approaching: the moment when he would have to say goodbye to his parents. He found them in the corridor separating the classroom from the refectory, and he stopped there while the other children, famished, proceeded to lunch. Amos's parents gave him some words of advice and then kissed and hugged him, but as he moved away from them he started to cry. His mother then sent her husband off to get the car while she accompanied Amos to the refectory. She took him to his place and said goodbye once more. Amos clung to her arm and squeezed it with all his might. He felt a strong hand grip him by the elbow and pull him back, and at the same time a voice was saying something to him and his mother's arm was gradually escaping from his grasp. Then he managed to grab a finger but his sweaty hands were not able to hold on. He lost that too, and for the first time in his life he felt alone in the midst of so many people, abandoned to his fate. He despaired and shouted for his mother as foals do when they are taken away from the mare to be weaned, but then he calmed down, sat back down, and began to swallow a few spoonfuls of soup. After that he was brought some boiled meat with salad, a dish that he really disliked. He raised his hand as he had been told to do whenever he needed something. Someone immediately lowered his arm and asked him what he wanted. Amos timidly replied, "I don't want this meat." But the same voice retorted, "You will want it and you will eat it. Go on!"

With a lump in her throat, Amos's mother quickly bid goodbye to the staff who had accompanied her to the door and then ran to join her husband.

He was sitting in the car waiting for her, hidden behind an open newspaper. When she opened the door she realized he was sobbing desperately. She hugged him and together they tried to comfort each other. Signor Bardi, who had also been to boarding school as a boy, had always said that he wanted to spare his children that experience, but he had not been able to do so. On the other hand, this was the only way their little boy would be able to learn to read and write like all the others. Only this way could he grow up to be a man who could face life with courage and wisdom.

On the way home husband and wife began to recover some peace of mind. The gaping void left by their son gradually began to be filled with tentative feelings of hope, fleeting moments of optimism, and a vague sense of satisfaction that, with great determination, they had succeeded in doing what had to be done for the good of their boy, at which they even managed a tender smile.

all, enthralling his audience with his superlative high notes. The journalist described how the opera house had erupted into a tumultuous applause mixed with almost hysterical shouts and repeated entreaties for an encore.

When she had finished reading the article Oriana remained still for a moment with the newspaper in her hands. To Amos she seemed absorbed in some secret thoughts of her own, but then he saw her close the paper and lean over towards him. He heard her whisper, "…And he is really handsome!" Then she added, "You must ask them to give you a record of his; I am curious to hear his voice too…"

So a few days later the first Corelli record appeared in the house. It was Oriana herself who had gone to look for it and given it to Amos, displaying, moreover, an unusual interest in knowing what he thought of it.

Amos immediately rushed to the old turntable, turned it on, set the plate in motion, and turned the arm with the needle towards the outside which he then delicately placed on the new 45 record; there was the orchestral introduction to the recitative of the "Improvviso" from *Andrea Chénier* by Umberto Giordano, and finally a voice insinuated itself into the pauses and reached the listener unaccompanied. The lyrics of the "Colpito qui m'avete" came to him in a voice which was completely different from all the others. It was a big and extremely vibrant voice, full of feeling and holding an indefinable suffering, which spoke straight to the heart. The singing was full-voiced, free, and spontaneous, sweet in certain moments, fierce in others, but always authoritative and dominating. The "Improvviso" is a wonderful piece, but it requires an artist who can really identify with a character like Chénier, a poet whose drama unfolds in the very complex setting of the French Revolution. The singing line must be elegant but at the same time convincing and decisive.

Chénier, the poet, treats the theme of love understood in its broadest sense. Corelli, in that recording, seemed instead to be treating the theme of his love for his own art, the art of singing –

VI

On 1st October the following year Amos found himself seated at his school desk next to Davide again. He was beginning the first grade.

Before coming back to school after the summer holidays he had won yet another promotion from his uncle Giovanni, which he proudly announced to his schoolmates. His teacher, Signorina Giamprini, was a woman of about forty who had renounced matrimony in order to dedicate herself completely to teaching and to caring for her elderly mother. Although she too was visually impaired, she had been highly recommended to the Bardi family for her quite exceptional competence and her impressive enthusiasm for her work. She controlled the class with ease and nothing escaped her notice. From eight in the morning, when the children came into the classroom, until the ringing of the last school bell, she would roam along the rows of desks, making sure that everyone paid attention to her explanations and that no one was resting their head on the desk and sleeping. That year Amos and his friends began to study Braille. They were given a rectangular-shaped, wooden case with slots into which fitted small wooden pegs, which, according to their arrangement, simulated the shape of the various letters in Braille. Later the children would learn how to recognise the same letters represented by tiny dots made by

perforating the paper. Their teacher was indefatigable and succeeded in transmitting her extraordinary energy and enthusiasm
to her pupils. Often she would organize competitions which got
everyone excited and improved the general performance of the
class, but she never forgot those who struggled to keep up, paying
them special attention and occasionally allowing them a small
advantage to help them in those competitions which they would
otherwise never have had a chance of winning.

Signorina Giamprini was extremely devout. She possessed the
gift of an unshakable and authentic faith which to some made her
seem somewhat sanctimonious. Every morning, before lessons
began, she would ask the children to recite a prayer, and they would
say grace before lunch. She already started to teach the children
about the Bible in the first grade, and she told the stories with such
passion that her charges would listen to her with rapt attention,
occasionally interrupting to make comments or ask questions.

Many years later Amos remained convinced that, independent
of its religious significance, knowledge of the Old Testament was
of fundamental importance in the education of children, because
it helps to understand life, one's fellow man, and the history of
different peoples and cultures. No one who has a good knowledge
of the Bible can be completely surprised by anything and will
always benefit from an extraordinary inner strength and resilience.

That winter was extremely cold and it often snowed. Amos
would go out into the courtyard with his friends, and they would
all have fun throwing huge snowballs at each other. Perhaps this
also explained why he was often ill and would then spend time in
the school sick bay, where Signora Eva would keep vigil over her
patients and nurse them day and night with dedication and affection. Amos very much enjoyed being ill so he could stay tucked up
in that warm nest to play and chat with his fellow patients, far
from the strict regime and duties of his normal school days. Quite
early every morning the nurse would wake up and turn on a large
radio that broadcast relaxing melodies. The children would wake
up but remained snuggled up warm under the covers, awaiting

their medicines. The food was also better than the regular fare dished up in the refectory, so the young patients were always sorry to be declared well enough to resume their normal school routine.

In the spring things improved greatly: the mild weather meant that the children could spend much more time in the open air, and in the small courtyard they could organize great games of "legnetto". The "legnetto" could be a tin can or any old piece of wood, but it was used exactly as though it were a football and it assumed the same dignity. All the boys were crazy about this game, and they would identify with their football heroes when they listened to the matches every Sunday on their small transistor radios. Every so often the older boys would come up with an expertly homemade "legnetto", a real luxury item, skillfully fashioned from an empty shoe polish tin onto which they fixed a round piece of wood. That simple entertainment almost always took up the whole of their recreation time. Occasionally Signorina Giamprini would organise an outing to the countryside. She was keen to ensure her charges came into direct contact with nature so that she could explain many things which in a classroom remained totally abstract concepts and therefore difficult to fully understand. On these occasions they would invariably end up visiting the house of a dear friend of hers called Orazio. He was a saint of a man whose face had been completely disfigured as a result of an explosion and the ensuing fire. He had also lost both of his hands, and yet, to all who knew him, he was the very picture of serenity or even happiness. He was a simple and pure soul, and he too was supported by an unshakable faith from which he knew how to draw strength and courage. He would smile happily when surrounded by all those children and willingly display his gymnastic feat, the candle trick, which involved standing on his head with his feet pointing up in the air. There was something about him which was attractive yet awkward at the same time, like a vague irony in the face of life and its small everyday problems, combined with a sort of inexpressible, benevolent compassion towards his fellow man who was so much more fortunate than he. In short, Orazio was one of those characters one never forgets.

Before going back to school, in the late afternoon, Orazio's family would insist that the whole class come into the small kitchen where the children were invited to refresh themselves with homemade cakes and a drink. Then it was time for goodbyes and promises to return soon.

The next morning at school was always dedicated to observations on the previous day's experiences. The class would talk about flowers and leaves, animals, and farming, to ensure that the children would not only commit everything to memory but also think it all through and assimilate everything through the fundamental filter of their intelligence.

As spring arrived the teacher announced that the time had come to begin to learn how to write properly. One morning, instead of the wooden case, the children found a rectangular, metal object on their desks along with a metal strip and a stylus with a wooden handle. Signorina Giamprini showed them how to fix the sheet of paper onto the tablet and how to place the strip at the top, and she made them all note the double line of rectangular spaces on the strip, explaining that it was possible to make up to six perforations in each one of these. Then she asked everyone to begin practicing by making one in the first space on the right, up in the top right corner. "This, children," she announced, "is the letter A . . . " The children thus began writing, from right to left, later removing the page from the tablet and turning it over so that they then read it from left to right.

When the time came to learn numbers, the young students received a small plastic case and a tin box containing a number of little cubes upon the sides of which the numbers could be read in relief. In Braille these are distinguished by a "sign" which precedes them and by one of the first ten letters of the alphabet, starting with "a" which stands for 1, to "j" which stands for 0. Then there was a smooth face which served to indicate a comma, which in Italy is the sign used to precede decimal numbers.

Arithmetic presented a real challenge for Amos. Adding up sums, in particular, was a real torture for him. He really had a hard time grasping the concept of numbers being carried over. He found it easier to memorize the sum of two numbers rather than calculate the numbers according to the method that Signorina Giamprini was trying to teach him. It was his mother who eventually removed the mysterious obstacle that was holding Amos back from the world of mathematics. Amos was tucked up in his little bed, recovering from a nasty fever, and he unburdened his anxieties to his mother about going back to school, where he would have found himself having to struggle once more with the arithmetic problems that everyone else knew how to solve except him. Edi sensed her son's apprehension, fear, and shame, through that mysterious and invisible connection that is the maternal bond, and she managed to accomplish a kind of miracle. After patient, loving explanations and numerous examples the mystery was somehow suddenly unlocked as if by magic, and Amos finally understood. From then on arithmetic became one of his favourite subjects.

VII

In third grade Amos became interested in the basics of geography and particularly in history. His imagination began to carry him away. During break times he would often spend time alone, and as he paced up and down the hall or in one of the three courtyards, he would let his imagination run free, daydreaming about the adventurous life of prehistoric man and wondering what it would be like to live in a pile-dwelling like the one he had built in clay following the precise directions of his teacher. Or else he would imagine himself driving a Greek chariot just like the one he had given his parents during the Easter holiday, which he had made himself from cardboard and polystyrene, cutting it out with a fretsaw and then covering it with raffia. It was a long and patient endeavour and he was quite proud of the result.

Those were the days! At the beginning of May the children were given coloured T-shirts and shorts, and in the school courtyards, in the gentle warmth of the spring sunshine, they could already breathe in the atmosphere of the approaching holidays. The knowledge that they would soon be going home filled the children's hearts with such excitement that their happiness infected the teachers and assistants, who became more lenient and indulgent.

Amos had already learned how to keep track of the countdown to the holidays... Soon he would be hugging his parents, his grandparents, and his little brother again. He would see his friends, who were waiting to fill him in on everything he had missed and for him to regale them with tales of the curious life he was leading in places which were so far away and so different from their own world. Just thinking of those eagerly awaited moments would fill Amos's heart with indescribable pleasure. It was a pure joy which only children who have experienced the pain of separation from their parents can know.

May is a special month, especially in Italian boarding schools, where, thanks to the novenas and the songs dedicated to the Madonna, the children get an extra half an hour or so of recreation time to spend with their friends.

Amos's voice had already come to the attention of his friends and teachers, so if there was a solo part to sing it always fell to him. Nor did he hold back when singing in the choir sessions when he would enjoy hearing his own voice rising above all the others. And so it was that someone decided he should perform for the end-of-year ceremony, after the middle-school play. This would be the first time Amos would sing before a real audience, without any piano or other accompaniment, alone on stage in the recreation hall where, for important occasions, many rows of folding chairs would be set up and everyone would gather together, pupils, masters, teaching assistants, and other staff making a total of more than two hundred people.

The end-of-year ceremony was undoubtedly the most eagerly anticipated and exciting day in the school calendar. Events would kick off in the morning with prize-giving for all those who had come top of their class or who had won some other distinction. At lunch everyone would be allowed a glass of wine and a portion of dessert, which was almost invariably chocolate pudding. In the afternoon preparations would begin for the evening performance, which was the high point of the day and for which no time or effort was spared.

The leading roles were always carefully assigned to the most talented actors, and to appear on stage was considered a privilege that everyone aspired to with ill-disguised excitement.

Amos was not one of the prize-winners and felt a deep sense of humiliation; singing in public was a risky undertaking, but it could prove to be a way of really making his mark.

The play that year was nothing to write home about. It was about a somewhat dysfunctional family – a father who was a drunkard, a mother who made vain efforts to reform him, and four children who did not get on with each other. The actors entrusted with this task struggled to hold the attention of their audience, which sat through the performance to the end, watching with scant interest, occasionally chatting and offering faint applause.

Eventually it was Amos's turn. By this time he had been waiting in the wings for at least fifteen minutes, torn with anxiety and excitement. Just before going on he heard a voice calling for silence, and it seemed to him that there was also a hint of inappropriate laughter from the audience. He heard his name called and felt a strong hand on his shoulder pushing him forward, through a small gap in the curtain, onto the stage.

A constant murmuring from the audience came across as a clear indication to him that in reality his performance meant precious little to anyone, and while this disinterest was mildly upsetting, it also helped to give him courage, so he took a deep breath and began to sing.

He heard his voice ring out clearly throughout the large hall. "Che bella cosa è 'na 'jurnata 'e sole..." He sang the first phrase of that most famous song all in one breath, and when he paused to take another, he realized, to his astonishment, that a great hush had fallen across the room. For a split second he thought he had forgotten the words, but he breathed deeply and carried on. When he reached the first high note, on "Ma 'n'atu sole...", he was met with thunderous applause. Amos felt revived. His heart, which until a few moments ago had raced with fear, was now beating with elation... That had been his first real applause. He attacked the finale in full voice and sustained it with all his might to the very last of his breath, and before his voice faded, he was literally overwhelmed by a deafening, tumultuous applause. It was a real triumph or, perhaps it may be appropriate to say, a sign of his destiny.

VIII

Summer that year was very hot. When Amos and his friends played football out in the courtyard of his house they would be bathed in sweat. They would take turns to cool off standing under an outside tap at the corner of the building and would all gang together to protect each other from Amos's grandmother and Oriana, who would hurl harsh warnings at them, fearing for the children's health and despairing over the fate of their flowers, which would invariably end up crushed by a stray ball as it bounced away from the goal-mouth, or, to be more precise, from the gate which led onto the road. After the game the children would sit in the shade of the old arbour, from which hung heavy clusters of fragrant black grapes, and everyone would have something to say to explain their victory or defeat.

On one of those afternoons Amos began to tell his friends about something which immediately captured their attention. A few months earlier he had met a beautiful girl at his school who had come to visit her brother Guido. Her name was Eleonora and she had become very popular with everyone. "I let her chat with everyone..." said Amos, "but I noticed that she was always coming close to me. At a certain point I began to sing something and she came and listened. After that she introduced herself, and we spent the whole afternoon together talking about ourselves, our families, the things we liked. She was very shy but I encouraged her...!"

37

Amos was so taken with his own story that he didn't even realise that he had embroidered the tale with details which were entirely the fruit of his lively childish imagination caught in the throes of his first infatuation. He was truly lovestruck. Guido's sister, Eleonora, had been to visit her brother and had indeed been much liked by everyone, especially Amos, but either due to shyness or to the fact that her attention was quite understandably more drawn to the older boys, Eleonora had really only noticed Amos on one brief occasion when, in the middle of a group of friends, he had decided to sing something. The rest was entirely imagined. He had long fantasised about her, dreaming of taking her by the hand, wooing her away from the others and winning her heart. Nothing of the sort had happened, but Amos liked to think that it had and to persuade his little brother and his friends of it, so they now listened to him in rapt silence, avidly curious. No one interrupted him, no one asked questions, this being a subject matter which was new to all of them and rather mysterious. Each of them formed his own idea of a girl with a kind face, blue eyes, and a friendly, good-natured smile. As Amos's story developed, enriched with an abundance of detail, the image he conjured up became so clearly defined that she turned into a sort of ideal. By this stage all those boys wished they could meet Eleonora, so convinced were they that they too loved her. They would all have been kind, brave, and sincere with her, and they would all have begun to learn the art of courtship, which basically consists in knowing how to present the best of yourself while carefully concealing the worst.

At home, meanwhile, the household was buzzing with activity, preparing the dinner to celebrate the end of the harvest. At about eight o'clock all the men would arrive who had been working with Amos's father, cutting the grain, gathering it into sheaves, stacking it into great ricks, and then feeding one sheaf after another into the mouth of the huge threshing machine, which finally separated the wheat from the chaff. From another opening positioned quite low down on the side of the machine, solid bales would spew out which would then be stored in barns or delivered straight to the mill. Occasionally Amos had helped with the harvest too, in his shorts and vest, an outfit which seemed specially designed to cause him maximum discomfort and put him off the task very quickly due to terrible attacks of itching caused by the sweat, dust, and insects. That evening was the culmination of a year of work in the fields. There would be loud talking, jokes, and laughter, and Amos would undoubtedly be asked to sing. That was the price to pay for being allowed to stay up late. They would all dine outside, under the arbour, which he loved to do, and perhaps he would even get to drink some good, simple wine.

During the moments when Amos paused in his story, while he concentrated hard to dig up more memories and to conjure up more fantasies, he would hear the voices of the women who were busy with the preparations in the house, discussing the seating order and the amounts of food required – all sweet memories of a childhood which may well have been difficult in some ways, but which was happy and rich in the single thing which is most important in a child's life: love.

That evening the young singer was the centre of attention once again. Everyone had something to ask him, something to tell him, or memories with which to entertain him, because country folk are simple and generous, and being deeply attached to their land and their origins, they feel an instinctive tenderness towards a child who is forced to spend most of the year far from his home and loved ones. Towards the end of dinner there was another emotional moment when someone said some words in remembrance of Alcide, Amos's grandfather, who had died the previous November. This was the first harvest without the man who, in the company of other farmers, often used to refer to himself as a poet of the land. Grandmother Leda was very emotional, and Amos's father's eyes glistened with tears too, but it was just a brief moment of sadness. Edi, Amos's mother, delicately changed the subject, and everyone agreed that, at least for that evening, the book of the past would be closed.

When Amos went to bed, happy with the evening's events, he never imagined the surprise that awaited him the following morning. Grandfather Alcide had died some seven months earlier, at dawn on 4th November 1966, at the time when the overflowing river Arno had flooded disastrously into the streets of Florence and other local towns. However, a few days before he passed away, after having asked for his young grandson to come home from boarding school so that he could see him one last time, he had expressed a wish to give Amos a horse which would be suitable for a child to ride around the countryside. Amos's father, who had witnessed that promise, had sworn to himself that he would fulfil the dying man's wish, so, a few days before Amos came home from school, he had gone to Miemo, a small hill town not far from Lajatico, in the middle of the woods. There, on the Baldacci estate, where the forest rangers still worked on horseback, he had chosen a fine, docile mare, a small trap, and a child-sized saddle. One of the rangers had agreed to deliver the horse to the Bardis' farm where she was immediately lavished with food and attention. Amos's father could hardly contain his excitement and swore everyone to secrecy in order not to spoil his son's surprise.

After the dinner with the farm workers, Signor Sandro had decided to devote the whole morning to his son, taking him to meet the horse which he had named Stella. Amos was still fast asleep next to his little brother when he heard his father's voice calling him with eager excitement. Surprised to have been woken in this unusual way, he dressed hurriedly, grabbed a lightning breakfast, and left with his father for Poggioncino. He had been up there at the farm only a couple of days earlier but had stopped in the yard where the workers were busy with the threshing machine. In fact, this time when they got there he was struck by how quiet it was, in such sharp contrast to the frenetic activity he had encountered just a few days before. There was no one at Poggioncino except for his maternal grandfather, Ilo, who was waiting for them behind the old farmhouse. The ancestors of the Bardi family had first occupied this house two centuries earlier when, having left

The Music of Silence

their tenancy as sharecroppers on the farm owned by the Corsini princes, they had bought this property with their savings. Amos threw his arms around the neck of the old man and kissed him. He was happy to see him, as he was particularly fond of Grandfather Ilo, who in turn carefully cultivated this special attachment by regaling his grandson with thrilling tales of war, hunting, racehorses, dogs, cars, and everything which excited his young grandson's imagination. A few years later he would talk to him about politics and women.

With his father and grandfather on either side, Amos set off towards the corner of the house where there was a small stable which had been used as a tool shed for some time. A few days earlier his father had it cleared out so that it could be put back to its original use, and the mare had been settled in there. When they reached the door Grandfather Ilo went into the stable, and to Amos's astonishment he re-emerged leading a horse by the halter.

"This is Stella," he announced to the boy who watched, entranced. "She is good; you can stroke her." Then he began to give him advice. "Never walk behind her; she may take fright and kick. You must always stay to the left of a horse, like this, see?"

Meanwhile Stella had put her head to the ground and had begun to graze at the blades of grass between the stones. Speaking in a soft voice, in the tone of one who knows about such things, Grandfather Ilo added that this was just the right sort of horse for a child. In effect the Avelignese horse is a breed achieved by crossing an Arab stallion with a female pony originally from the Avelengo region. This crossbreed produces a small, very sturdy workhorse which survives well in all climates and, most importantly, is of docile character. It had been Grandfather Ilo who had advised his son-in-law on this choice, and he was now very proud of it.

Soon Beppe arrived too. He was a farm worker who lived in the house at Poggioncino, and he joined the group as they gathered round Stella, who was first carefully groomed and then hitched to the trap. The harness was perfect. Amos's grandfather inspected it, congratulated himself on his purchase, and then adjusted it to fit the peaceful animal, which let him do everything while contentedly nibbling at the grass every so often. After about a quarter of an hour she was harnessed up and Ilo climbed onto the trap, called Amos to come and sit next to him, and cracked the whip. Stella broke into a trot.

The pony and trap went down the driveway, turned to the left, and proceeded along the road between the adjoining properties leading to the point where the waters of the Era and Sterza streams meet. Stella had been born at the source of the Sterza and so had already been along this route a few days earlier when she had changed owners.

The workers labouring in the fields, who observed the scene with curiosity and amusement, saw two glowing faces: the delight of that moment had completely removed any traces of concern left on the old man's features by past experiences, suffering, and worry; Amos's face was the picture of innocent hope and faith in what the future might hold.

IX

Like all grandfathers the world over, Ilo doted on his grandchildren. He had seven of them, who were all very fond of him too, and he was always at their service acting as driver, games companion, sage, and oracle. However, he had a soft spot for Amos in particular, as, being a great opera lover, he would become very emotional whenever he heard him sing. Every time Ilo went to visit him he would urge him to stand on the second step of the fireplace next to the kitchen window and beg him to sing for him. Amos almost always obliged and, knowing his grandfather's preferences, would often launch into the celebrated aria from *Cavalleria Rusticana*, "Mamma, quel vino è generoso".

Oriana was another enthusiastic fan of these unusual performances and would support Ilo in his efforts to cajole the budding singer to abandon his games and take on the role of the theatre actor.

As Amos's performances became more confident and convincing, so these requests became more frequent and the audiences larger. Often, when the family was together after dinner, before deciding to retire to bed they would try to persuade Amos to grant them a song. It was a pleasant and relaxing way to end a hard day's work. Occasionally Grandfather Ilo would bring along some sceptical friend who invariably went home surprised and impressed.

Everyone in Lajatico knew or had heard rumours about the voice of the young Bardi lad, that boy "from whom Nature has taken with one hand and given with the other". Amos even began to receive timid requests for him to sing in church at the end of Mass or during wedding ceremonies. So it came about that soon young Amos performed his debut at the parish church, singing Schubert's "Ave Maria" before a young bride and groom and a small group of wedding guests and curious onlookers.

At the end of that childish and amateur performance many members of the congregation had tears in their eyes, moved especially by the contrast between the voice they heard and the sight of that small boy, between his natural gifts and his physical impairment...

Gradually, however, the idea that by singing he could draw others towards him became more and more firmly rooted in Amos's mind. Singing started to become a need for him from which it was impossible to flee, an inescapable reality, as much a part of him as his own features reflected in the mirror or his own shadow on a sunny day.

In any case children love attention and Amos was a child like any other. It was not, after all, so hard to grant the requests and accept the praise of friends and relatives. Showing off and arousing admiration seemed to him a game like any other. What is more, he had overheard his parents discussing the possibility of enrolling him for music classes. This was an idea that appealed to him a great deal given that until then, at school, he had been forbidden from even approaching those beautiful pianos which, tantalizingly, he would hear played every afternoon by some of his older companions. Only once had he secretly succeeded in touching the keys for a few minutes.

So it was that, at the end of that summer, when he went back to boarding school, Amos had the pleasant surprise of being called, along with a group of others, by Maestro Carlini, the piano teacher, and after a brief introduction they began the first music lesson.

Soon Amos and his friends learned to read, write, and sing the notes of the scale. If truth be told he found it a little boring, but he consoled himself with thoughts of when he would finally be able to sit at the piano and start to play. This happened a few days later. Alone in the class with the teacher, Amos was finally asked to place his hands on the keys and to move his small fingers over the first five notes of the scale using both hands, from low to high and vice versa.

After a few minutes Amos felt his wrists and the back of his hands begin to hurt, but he persevered, fearful of incurring the displeasure of his teacher, who in the meantime was writing something of his own, completely ignoring his student. Eventually Amos was asked to stop, granted a few seconds pause, and then given another exercise to tackle. He would have liked to play in his own way, the way he played the organ in his village church after Sunday Mass, but obviously that was not allowed, so he meekly followed his teacher's instructions.

Although his dedication to his studies was not great, Amos did feel a certain excitement when, for the first time, he was able to play a little exercise from the Beyer method. He repeated it dozens of times, dreaming of when he would play it for his parents or, who knows, perhaps even for his friends from the village who had probably never even seen a piano up close before.

One morning Signorina Giamprini made a surprise announcement to her pupils. After the ten o'clock break she took a number of cases out of a box and distributed one to each of the children. Inside each of them was a recorder. She then showed them how to assemble the instrument and how to hold it in the correct way. She advised the children who took piano lessons to seek Maestro Carlini's help and expressed her hope that everyone might succeed in playing something for the sheer pleasure of producing a sound from the instrument as well as, she pointed out, to keep idleness at bay.

After a couple of days Amos could already play various simple tunes on his recorder, thus establishing his reputation in the school as one of the more musically gifted students.

He kept his recorder in the drawer of his bedside table, and at night, when he was in bed, he would take it out and examine it, as though fearing he had not quite explored its full range of possibilities. That instrument exerted an inexplicable fascination on him, as if it possessed some magical property.

Of course he could not play it there, in the silence of the dormitory, but he simulated the movements, opening and closing the holes, until sleep overcame him, forcing him to put it away.

Amos had always held or stroked something before going to sleep. It was a habit that he felt helped to ward off his feelings of home-sickness, at least partially.

At that time Amos was finding it increasingly hard to get to sleep. He would hear the indecipherable whispering of many stifled voices which were probably confiding secrets, telling stories, experiences, inadmissible thoughts... and muffled laughs. From time to time the assistant on duty would get suspicious and sneak in to tell someone off, and then for a while the dorm would be plunged into complete silence.

It was precisely during one of those nocturnal discussions that Amos learned from the boy in the next bed, whose name was Ettore and who was a little older than him, that babies were not brought by the stork or found in the cabbage patch, nor even, as some had suggested, produced spontaneously from the mother's belly.

When Signorina Giamprini, with her admirable intuition, began to sense that some mischievous disinformation might threaten the innocence of her charges, she decided to hold proper classes on sex education. Beginning with the sixth commandment, she then broadened the discussion to the purely scientific aspects. After briefly referring to sexual relations, which she dealt with delicately and poetically, she went on to describe the encounter between the most fortunate sperm with the ovum and the formation of the zygote. She talked about chromosomes and the infinite number of possible combinations between them and described the development of the foetus to the moment of birth, raising great enthusiasm and interest from her students. Several days of lessons were required before Signorina Giamprini felt she had acquitted her duty as a Christian, at which point, persuaded that she had safely swept away any risk presented by trivializing or sinful influences, she decided to shelve the subject.

For Amos it was a great victory to be able to catch his parents by surprise and bring them up to date with his complete knowledge on a subject about which his father and mother had always been at best evasive and vague, when not downright misleading. Now he knew everything that they knew, and so it was only right that they should begin to treat him as a man and speak to him adult to adult. After all, he had always wanted to seem older than he was, to do what the grown-ups did, and to share in their discussions. The fact of being treated as a child had always been perceived by Amos as something slightly humiliating, because he did not feel himself to be a child at all.

X

Eventually that school year came to an end, and the day arrived to say goodbye to the teachers, to the assistants, and to discipline. The children went back to their families whom, in some cases, when the distance from home was too great and the financial resources too limited, they had not seen since the previous October.

Amos waited impatiently by his little bed, his suitcase packed, for a bell to ring and the porter on duty to holler, "Amos Bardi is wanted in the hall". His heart beat faster each time he heard the bell ring, but he had to wait longer than usual because his parents had been stuck in traffic on the motorway between Florence and Bologna. They finally arrived at lunch time. By that stage Amos's impatience was stronger than his appetite, so they set out immediately to go home. Amos wanted to get back in time to see his friends, maybe to go for a quick ride on the bike, and to see Stella and take her out of her stable to eat a bit of fresh grass. Basically it would have taken a forty-eight-hour day to tackle even half of his plans.

But when he got home he found only his grandparents and his little brother, who were waiting for him anxiously, and his other playmates were out in the fields with their parents lending a hand. Never mind, he would see them the next day; he, in any case, was in seventh heaven. It is impossible to describe the feelings of a child who has just come back from boarding school after months away from home. It is an extraordinarily sweet sensation, a honey even bees do not know how to make, an incomparable sense of peace, an infinite, indefinable, childish delight which can cast into oblivion all memory of the pain caused by the separation, the hours of profound melancholy, the discipline of the school, the envy of friends, the incomprehension of the teachers... The joy of coming home is well worth the high price paid in suffering at the moment of departure.

Summer that year was very hot and Amos could not wait to leave for the beach with his family. They would be staying with one of his father's aunts, Signora Eugenia, who had an apartment in Lido di Camaiore. But to enjoy that paradise he had to wait until August and it was still only June. For the time being it was just a question of organising things to do in the countryside.

One morning his friend Sergio, who lived just nearby, came by to show him his latest invention. It was a new catapult, undoubtedly more powerful and accurate than all their previous devices. Sergio had found a particularly well-shaped forked branch. He had stripped it and sawn it to the right size. Then he had gone in search of an old inner tube and with scissors had cut two strips about forty centimetres long. He had fastened one end of these to the two ends of the fork, the other end to an oval-shaped piece of leather, slipping them through two small lateral cuts and finally tying them with a strong, thin thread. Having completed this job Sergio immediately ran to his friend, recently returned from school, to give him that precious object as a token of their continuing friendship. Then the competitions began. The boys would take up positions standing in the middle of a circle traced out in the stones of the Bardi courtyard; then each one would aim his catapult and shoot a stone at one of the two pine trees which, impassive as ever, submitted to this assault and continued to shade the competition ring as though complicit in that innocent boyish game.

On 1st August the Bardi family finally left for the seaside. Aunt Eugenia's apartment was spacious, but it had to accommodate two families and so became quite crowded. Amos shared a room with his aunt Vanda, who was not his real aunt but a cousin of his father's whom he affectionately and respectfully addressed as aunt, as was the custom in his family. He felt a special admiration for Aunt Vanda, probably due to the fact that before going to sleep at night she would entertain him with stories about the most bizarre topics. Sometimes she would talk to him about animals. For example, she would describe the terrifying voracity of the piranha fish or the ferocity of the moray eel, thus setting his imagination on fire. On other occasions, Vanda, who taught literature in secondary school, would tell Amos one of Verga's stories or recite some poetry, explaining the meaning of certain words to him which did not yet form part of his vocabulary. In fact, Amos was soon to go into the fifth grade, and so he often asked her for all sorts of information: how difficult the exams were, the most common exam questions, the percentage of pass marks, and so on. Ever the patient teacher, Vanda tried to satisfy his curiosity and at the same time took the opportunity to improve his knowledge of grammar and logical analysis, and to provide him with the basic notions for an understanding of contemporary history. Amos was not a keen student, preferring life in the open air and the company of his friends to books; nonetheless he listened with fascination to Aunt Vanda, who would sometimes carry on talking until late at night, when they would finally be overcome by sleep and their voices would be replaced by the deep, dark soughing of the sea.

When Amos woke up in the morning he would be alone, his aunt having already gone out. He would call his mother, ask her for his breakfast coffee in bed, and she would systematically refuse this request in order to coax him out of bed. After breakfast Amos would go out to the Buon Amici beach club, which he particularly liked because it had good equipment: as well as the see-saw and swings which all the beach clubs along that carefully tended coast-line had these days, there were also rings and a trapeze. Amos loved to hang onto those rings, which were held by two ropes, and get into a vertical position with his feet up in the air and his head down. What exhilaration he felt in those moments...! Obviously his old aunt Eugenia and his other relatives would be afraid that he might hurt himself, but this merely increased his excitement because, it has to be said, like so many children of his age, he too was quite a show-off.

Often he would run off to look for Raffaello, the lifeguard, who would give him a large seashell, put it to his ear, and say, "Listen, it's the sound of the sea!" Raffaello had strong arms and muscles like a weightlifter. Amos was greatly impressed by his virile strength and liked to feel those sinewy arms with his little hands. He wondered what it must be like to have the physique of an athlete and dreamed of being a boxer, a wrestler, or a karate champion. So in those days Raffaello was his favourite, the living symbol of vigour, courage, and virility. Furthermore, that was also the year in which Raffaello taught Amos to swim. By arrangement with Signor Bardi they would meet at the beach at seven o'clock in the morning. He waited on the shoreline for father and son to join him and then set out in a little boat heading out to sea, rowing vigorously. When they reached the buoys he stopped, put the oars down, and tied a rope to the rowlock. Raffaello very dexterously knotted the other end of the rope around Amos's waist. Then he invited him to throw himself into the water, but Amos was overcome with fright and refused. After some fruitless entreaties, Raffaello decided there was nothing for it; he picked him up and, without further ado, flung him into the sea. A second later Amos found Raffaello beside him in the water, and with no time to transform his fear into tears, he focused on bringing some order to his movements. Raffaello issued precise instructions in a calm voice, and gradually Amos felt his alarm turn into pleasure. His father meanwhile looked on with satisfaction from the boat, occasionally proffering some words of encouragement. Soon Amos was able to move his arms and legs as instructed; in short, he had learned to swim. The mission was accomplished. He swam freestyle, breast stroke, and, later on, also backstroke.

That year the beach club was holding a swimming competition, so it was important for Amos to make progress, and Raffaello was always on hand to give him proper lessons or to provide occasional tips and show him the tricks of the trade. When Amos set his mind to a competition he really worked hard, as he hated losing. For him every defeat was a humiliation which brought him to tears and made him lose sleep.

The beach holiday was due to end on 18th August, and all in all, Amos was not unhappy to go home, where he would always find something new. In place of the old woodshed and the so-called "dark room", a new corridor was being built leading to a small studio. The work was well underway: the corridor was ready and the plastering and the flooring in the studio were done.

By 1st September the new rooms were furnished. Amos discovered a new pleasure: that of sitting at a desk, surrounded by books, pens, and notepads. He almost felt a desire to study – something entirely unfamiliar to him.

The day he had to go back to school on 1st October was the last time he would be going to that place so far from home, so it was less sad than usual. Next year things would be very different. He would be going somewhere much closer to home. He would have much more freedom to move around as he pleased and much more free time. So it was with these hopes in his heart that he said goodbye to his parents and prepared to face the fifth grade and the exams that would conclude that chapter of his life.

XI

"Oh Lord forgive me, I repent of my sins; by sinning I justly deserve your punishment..." with this prayer Amos and his friends began the new school year. They recited it all together, standing with their hands joined, each one at his place, and Signorina Giamprini prayed with them as she patrolled around the desks. Immediately afterwards there were greetings and hugs. There was a strange cheerfulness veiled with nostalgia for the memories of the summer and apprehension at the challenges presented by the school year that lay ahead.

As soon as they were seated the teacher proceeded once again with explanations of the Holy Bible. She began with the Book of Genesis and carried on lovingly narrating the story up to the description of the creation of Adam and Eve. The children enjoyed her passionate rendering of those exciting stories, so they would all listen quietly and attentively, only occasionally interrupting to ask a timid question. Signorina Giamprini would later expound on the life of Abraham and his son Isaac. She also spoke, more concisely, about Ishmael, first born son of Hagar, who was the handmaiden of Abraham's barren wife Sarah.

The children spent hours wondering at Jacob's adventures, and they loved Joseph with his life of tribulations and wondrous episodes. They learned the names of the twelve tribes of Israel by heart, and during recreation, they would even challenge each other to remember episodes or names from the Old Testament which they had been taught during those long lessons.

This was the last year that Signorina Giamprini would teach that class, so she gave her best efforts every morning to ensure that none of her charges would encounter difficulties when they went on to the middle school next year. Her intention was that by the end of the year they should have mastered the basics of algebra and started some logical analysis, and being a nature-lover, she would often go back to the subject of photosynthesis. She wanted the children to love plants and animals and was concerned that they should learn to have a lifelong respect and admiration for all that the good Lord had created.

The children would listen to their teacher's explanations of geography with their fingers following the relief maps of the various continents. She meanwhile would pass from one desk to the other to check that they were all paying attention to her correctly so that gradually they would acquire a clear understanding of the shape of the world.

She still organized outings to the countryside and kept up a correspondence between the class and some German families, with whom they would keep in touch by exchanging tape recordings. Her pupils would record poems, songs, and talk about this and that, and in return they would receive tales of the daily lives of those distant families told in their uncertain Italian. The children would talk about their schools and their games. On more than one occasion Amos recorded some songs, and all his school friends would later recall how once, while he was in the middle of a Neapolitan song, a particularly high note caused the microphone to break, and the recording had to be sent off to Germany incomplete.

Children in the fifth grade occasionally had the privilege of an extra ten minutes or so of recreation time in the evening. This made it possible for Amos and his friends to have much more contact with the students in the middle school. It was from them that our hero heard for the first time about a quite extraordinary drink which conferred amazing power to the drinker's muscles as well as a frightening degree of aggressiveness. The potion was achieved by dissolving an aspirin into a glass of Coca-Cola. Armed with this information, it only remained for Amos to find a way to get hold of an aspirin without having to report a fever or any other particular indisposition. He summoned up the courage to go to the infirmary where, for the last few days, a young nurse was substituting for Nurse Eva who was unwell. He complained of a bad headache and asked for a thermometer. Once he had it under his armpit he waited for the girl to attend to other patients and then started to rub the tip of the thermometer with his hands, taking care not to overdo it. If the temperature did not rise enough he would try again the next day. It was better not to risk being caught out. When the nurse came back his heart was beating like mad. Inspecting the mercury level she announced, "Yes, you do have a slight temperature, but it's nothing serious. Go to bed, cover up well, and tomorrow you'll be fine." "But my head hurts," protested Amos. "Couldn't I at least have an aspirin?" After a moment's hesitation the girl agreed. She found the pill and gave it to him with a glass of water. Amos pretended to hesitate and be reluctant to have to swallow it. "Well, are you going to make your mind up or not!" said the young nurse. Just then a child's voice called her from the other room, and her brief absence was enough for Amos to sneak the tablet into his pocket and, upon her return, to show her that his hands and the glass were empty. He hurried away from the infirmary and went straight to the drinks dispenser where, with a hundred lire coin, he bought a small bottle of Coca-Cola.

After he had drunk the potion Amos had the impression that his head was spinning a little, but it was probably nothing more than his imagination. He ran to join his friends to tell them about his adventure, and he thought he detected a greater respect and admiration on their part, as well as a good dose of curiosity of course.

Then he went to look for Antonio, the older kid who had revealed that secret to him, and when he found him, he immediately told him what he had done. Antonio listened and then gave him a clap on the shoulder, saying, "Well, it has to be said that you were very brave and clever, but don't do it too often because once it is dissolved into Coca-Cola, salicylic acid, or aspirin as we know it, effectively becomes a drug which is very bad for you."

Antonio had adopted a paternal attitude towards his young companion, who was now feeling somewhat disheartened and disappointed. His stunt had not brought him any discernible benefit and may even have been dangerous for his health. He said goodbye to Antonio and went to bed where he soon found himself bathed in sweat. His heart was beating faster than usual, making him anxious and preventing him from sleeping. When he woke the next morning he felt fine. He jumped out of bed, got ready quickly, and tried not to think about what he had done the previous evening.

In fact, Amos took great care of his physical fitness. He was rather obsessed with bodybuilding and loved physical exercise. So at boarding school he felt as though he was trapped in a cage. Perhaps for this reason he was particularly thrilled at the news that the school was soon to hold an Olympiad for its boarders. There would be athletics, gymnastics, soccer games, and many other events. Everyone was excited and could not wait for the great day.

The Olympiad began on a splendid day in May which bathed the Emilian countryside in an almost Tuscan light. That Sunday morning all the boys and their assistants gathered in the great courtyard for the opening ceremony. The head of the school, Dottor Marcuccio, gave a speech declaring how pleased he was with the new initiative, as he considered the values and practice of sport to be of fundamental importance. He urged everyone to be good sportsmen to the end and concluded wishing everyone a good time. Now the games could finally begin.

Amos took part in almost all the competitions and even won a few medals, but he did not get through the preliminaries for the high jump and dropped out of the marathon which involved running along the perimeter of the courtyard.

The following Sunday there was the soccer game. Amos was to have played in midfield, but instead he replaced the goalkeeper, who had suddenly fallen ill.

The score was one all when Amos had to make a daring move against the opposing centre-forward, who just at that moment took a shot at the goal. The ball hit Amos on his right eye, which was the one that allowed him to see light and colour. When he got up off the ground he noticed that his vision was blurred, and a gnawing pain forced him to withdraw from the game and go to the infirmary, where he was immediately given some eye-drops. A few hours later the pain and redness began to worry the young nurse who, after consulting the assistants, decided to call Amos's parents.

The next day Amos's mother arrived on the first train and rushed her son to Dr Bruno at the hospital in Reggio. He had been recommended to her by Professor Gallenga, whom she had managed to contact before she left.

After a brief examination of the eye, Amos was made to lie down. The doctor explained to his mother that it was absolutely imperative that he should block the haemorrhage produced by the impact of the ball; then he went up to the boy, reassured him gently, passing a hand through his hair, and called the nurse. She stood opposite him, and together they placed some tiny leeches between the eye and the temple of their young patient. By sucking blood in that area the leeches would help to normalize the blood pressure within the eye.

In effect it was not long before the little creatures became so enormously bloated that they had to be replaced with new ones. Amos could only feel some itching but no pain. His mother meanwhile struggled to control her horror at the sight of this operation. As he took his leave of them the doctor expressed his hope that it might be possible to save some residual eyesight, but he made no attempt to conceal his anxiety.

Amos went back to school with a bandage over his eye that prevented him from seeing anything. This new state of affairs made him reflect on the fact that he might really lose his sight completely. He would have to prepare himself for this eventuality. If that were to be the case, at the Institute he would be transferred from the category of those who were partially sighted to those who had no sight at all. This thought made him feel anxious in a way he had never experienced before.

He tried talking about it to a few of his schoolmates and found that this made him feel better. From that moment on he tried to acclimatize to the idea, just as one has to learn to get along with a new schoolmate who is not particularly likeable.

When the bandage was removed Amos realized that his sight had almost completely gone. He could barely distinguish the light from the lamp and experienced a sense of loss and bewilderment. He hoped that slowly things might go back to the way they were before, but that was a vain hope.

In the meantime the school year drew to a close and everyone went home for the holidays. In spite of everything Amos was happy, unaware of what was in store. One morning, when he raised his eyes up to the sky, towards the sun that he could feel burning the top of his head, he realized that he could no longer see it. He was gripped by a combination of fear and desperation. His eyes filled with tears and between sobs he called out to his mother. She ran to her son and embraced him in a desperate effort to spare him the anguish of that terrible moment, but although for some time she had been expecting to have to face this painful experience, she too was overcome and burst into tears. Amos had never before known his mother to cry and those tears touched him deeply. He would have liked to console her but he felt lost and helpless. There in that desperate embrace he now felt alarmed and horribly alone. He was almost twelve years old and had only just finished elementary school. The summer holidays had only just begun. What would he do at the beach? How could he play with his friends? And how would they behave towards him now?

At home, even though they tried to talk of other things when they all sat at lunch together, he found the atmosphere oppressive. Occasionally there would even be awkward silences, and you could hear the flies buzzing as they sought refuge in the Bardis' house, which, with its thick walls, was always quite cool in summer. After dinner Amos went to lie down for a while, and his mother, who did not want to leave him alone, followed him and lay down in his little brother's bed next to him. Edi had a question for her son which she could not bring herself to ask. She wanted to know what his eyes could see now. She wanted to know if the light had given way to darkness, to a darkness which felt like a source of fear and torment, to the darkness against which they had fought so hard. She could not bear the idea that, after so many sacrifices, so many hopes and countless journeys to Turin, her son would now be condemned to a life in the dark. She buried her face in the pillow and began to sob.

"Why are you crying, Mamma?" asked Amos, sharing her intolerable pain. His mother did not respond right away as she was almost choked by her tears. Then, summoning up some strength she asked quickly, "Do you see only darkness now?"

"No, Mamma," replied Amos timidly.

"Then what do you see?"

"Everything and nothing," he replied. He paused a moment and then continued. "I see what I want to see. I see my room, the cupboard, the beds, but I see them because I know they are there."

His mother could not quite grasp what he meant. Then, thinking back to her first meeting with the headmaster of her son's boarding school, Dottor Marcuccio, who was also blind as a result of an accident, she remembered that he had explained to her that darkness was a visual sensation and therefore a prerogative of those who have the gift of sight. "The blind," he had pointed out emphatically, "cannot see darkness, just as the deaf cannot hear silence, which is an auditory sensation, the antithesis of sound; that's all there is to it." At the time Edi had not dwelt sufficiently on those concepts because Amos could still see then, and in her heart she had hoped that he would always continue to see. But now those words came back to mind with their full significance and helped to comfort her somewhat. Moreover, she knew that there was nothing she could do other than to look forward and help her son as she had always done. Now more than ever she would dedicate all her physical and psychological strength to helping him; she would always encourage him; perhaps all was not lost.

Amos could not bear his mother's distress. He had never seen her so upset and in a way this made her almost unrecognizable to him. Suddenly he jumped up from his bed and ran to his parents' bed where he found his father stretched out but without his newspaper. He lay down next to him, put his arms around him, and in no time at all, fell fast asleep.

XII

Amos stayed in the house all day. That evening he ate dinner with no enthusiasm and then went straight to bed. He had hardly done anything at all and yet he felt tired. Tired of thinking, tired of his gloomy sadness, tired of all those insoluble problems he had been dwelling on all day, and tired of that forced nonchalance with which it seemed everyone treated him now; the overattentiveness, the kindness, the tenderness – he was tired of everything. He wanted to carry on being the same person he had always been in the eyes of others, and he was already beginning to understand that, to achieve that objective, he had to start by convincing himself that nothing had changed and that nothing would change thereafter.

That was the summer of memorable decisions and events.

The next day his parents broached the subject of his transferring to the Cavazza Institute in Bologna where he could attend the normal secondary school with sighted kids and make use of the educational support of the Institute, which provided specialized teachers and facilities to meet all the practical needs of the boarders. He would also be able to attend the conservatory, which had a special section within the college itself for blind students to study music.

However, this decision was a very difficult one to take due to the fact that for over a year student demonstrations had been causing considerable problems within the Cavazza Institute. There had been student occupations and violent demonstrations, and one morning the director of the Institute himself had been found dead in his apartment. It was said that he had hanged himself as a result of his inability to withstand the psychological pressure caused by all those serious events. The standard of the middle school in Amos's old school was poor, more suitable for those who wanted to pursue a vocational training, but how could a parent leave a child in the midst of the confusion that reigned in the Cavazza Institute with an easy conscience? This was the first opportunity Amos had had, since losing his sight completely, to demonstrate to himself and to others how strong, brave, and responsible he could be. He did not waste it, and at lunch one day he resolutely announced that he intended to move to Bologna. There he would enjoy greater freedom; he would learn how to move around the city without being dependent on others; in short, he would begin a new life. That sort of adventure, that unknown, and perhaps, in his parents' estimation, dangerous world, now fired his imagination, and something mysterious gradually began to replace his fears and uncertainties. Something inside him began to come to life again or was at least reawakened.

After the harvest Signor Bardi accepted his brother-in-law's invitation and took his family to Lido di Camaiore. Amos was worried about how his cousins would react now that he was completely blind, but he was surprised and relieved to find that they carried on as though nothing had changed. His three young cousins, especially the oldest boy, were likeable, independent, lively, and generous, and Amos always enjoyed spending time with them, particularly at night, when they would have hushed conversations in the bedroom until they eventually drifted off to sleep.

One morning Uncle Franco came back home from the beach, talking to his wife about the possibility of entering their nephew for a singing competition to be held at the Caffè Margherita in Viareggio. The winner would qualify to take part in the Festival of Castrocaro Terme.

Amos heard his uncle say to his wife with some excitement, "I will take him onto the stage and go and help him off at the end. But just imagine people's reactions when they hear him!" His uncle anxiously waited for his brother-in-law and his sister to come back for lunch, and the moment they came in, he rushed to meet them and started to explain everything that he had at first read in the paper and subsequently heard directly from the owner of the Caffè Margherita, where he had gone in person to get all the necessary information. He reported all of this with huge excitement to the assembled family. Amos listened and became increasingly apprehensive the more his uncle went on, talking about the size of the audience and about the orchestra which was to be directed by no less than Maestro Maraviglia, who was Luciano Tajoli's personal conductor.

So it came about that at exactly five o'clock on a baking hot August day, the young singer found himself auditioning in the presence of Maestro Maraviglia. If the audition went well he would take part in a first round of the competition. The winner would then go on to the finals.

"What would you like to sing?" asked the maestro, rather surprised to see such a young candidate. Amos replied that the only songs he knew all the way through were "O sole mio" and "O campagnola bella", the latter being a piece which his grandfather particularly loved and would often ask him to sing.

Young Amos was not used to performing with an accompaniment and initially had some trouble figuring out when to start. He also had difficulty adapting to the tempo required by the maestro. Nevertheless, half an hour later he was dismissed with an invitation to return the following evening for the competition.

As he approached the Caffè Margherita, with his father's hand resting on his shoulder, Amos suddenly felt burdened with a responsibility that made him feel quite ill. He found his hands were freezing and he was in a cold sweat. Behind him followed a procession of all his relations who seemed to him as excited as when they watched a soccer game on television. He suddenly felt

that he was the protagonist of an event for which no one had prepared him in advance. He clenched his fists, thinking that now
there was no escape: he had to sing and win if he was to avoid the
shame of defeat, causing disappointment to himself and everyone
else.

He sat at a table and waited for his turn.

The competition was judged by the customers in the café, who
received a voting slip showing the names and corresponding
numbers of all the contestants with each order.

Amos was lost in thought when he heard someone say his name
on the microphone. He pulled himself together, got up, and
accompanied by the uncle who had anxiously awaited this
moment from that first day, climbed up on stage, brushing past
musical instruments, microphone rods, and music stands and
trampling over large tangles of electrical cables. Eventually he
reached the right place, where a technician rushed to adjust the
height of the rod supporting the microphone, which was far too
high for a boy of his age. A few minutes later he heard the orchestra
launch into the introduction to "O campagnola bella".

His voice was a surprising tenor. It was robust and vibrant and
immediately amazed the audience, which burst into applause at
the end of the first strain. Amos smiled, pleased and encouraged,
and went on to sing with even greater vigour until he reached the
finale, which he belted out in full voice and held with all the
strength and length his breath would allow. Those skinny little
legs, that slight body, and his thin neck all seemed in such total
contrast with that voice, and this violent contrast provoked an
almost hysterical response from the audience. The applause and
cries continued as Amos made his way back among the tables to
return to his place. He was somewhat bewildered but visibly
happy. That warm reaction encouraged him; the affection which
he felt supporting him made him feel proud and full of hope for
the future.

At the end of the evening, after all the voting slips had been
scrutinized, Amos was proclaimed the winner and awarded a

silver margherita. This prize entitled him to take part in the final which was due to take place on the last Saturday in August.

For all the days that followed, at the beach and at home, no-one in the family could speak of anything else. Everyone had something to say, describing their impressions, reporting comments heard from neighbouring tables, and above all their thoughts turned to the finals. The young singer was kitted out with a new suit and a fine pair of shoes; he had his hair cut and at last the long-awaited Saturday arrived. Amos's mother went along with him to the afternoon rehearsals after which she tried to persuade him to lie down a while to rest. At dinner time they ate hurriedly and in a state of excitement following which everyone rushed to get ready, creating havoc in all the bedrooms and bathrooms.

By about ten o'clock Amos and his father were already close to the Caffè Margherita, which was surrounded by a large crowd of bystanders and late arrivals who had not found room to sit.

When the café owner spotted Amos he went to greet him and led him to the place he had reserved for him.

After about fifteen minutes the first contestant went up on stage. He was a big blond kid of about eighteen with an easy manner, who immediately found favour with the girls. He was followed by a girl of about thirteen or fourteen, who was very vivacious and sang confidently and in tune. The audience fell for her charms and applauded her enthusiastically.

Amos nervously awaited his turn, going over the words to his song under his breath. That evening he would sing "O sole mio", his *pièce de résistance*, but in reality he felt himself growing faint from nerves. Besides, an annoying stiff neck was preventing him from making any sudden movement. He realized his hands were icy cold and his heart was racing. Soon it would be his turn, and he really hated the idea of getting up onto that stage and facing the competition. By now everyone was counting on him to win. How would he deal with his own disappointment and that of all his supporters if he did not win after all? He had to win at all costs but for the moment all he could do was hope.

He was absorbed in these thoughts when he heard someone pronounce his name and felt his uncle's hand take him by the arm. With a few words of encouragement he was led towards the steps leading up on stage, passing through the tables packed with people applauding.

When the orchestra struck the first notes of that most famous of songs, Amos breathed in deeply, clenched his fists, and fighting his own heart, which was beating so hard as if trying to crush his breath, he began to sing in full voice.

Suddenly everyone was silent and stopped what they were doing: those who were drinking put down their glasses; those who were enjoying an ice cream put down their spoons; even the waiters stopped for a moment and turned their heads to see if that voice really came from a child, from such a slight boy, from such a small chest... Meanwhile, having reached the end of the first verse, Amos took another breath and gave it all to the high notes of "Ma 'n'atu sole" and was submerged by a hurricane of cheers and applause. At this point the young singer felt encouraged. He had the impression of having regained possession of his own will and succeeded in conquering his nerves and so managed to feel more relaxed. By this time he had won over the crowd, who were almost drowning his singing, so loud and so insistent was their applause. When he reached the finale, he squeezed his fists in determination again and, feeling as though the veins in his neck would pop at any moment, launched out over that festive audience with one last, real cry of passion, hope, pride, liberation, and perhaps even of rage. The audience was overwhelmed, surprised, and thrilled. It exploded into a deafening roar like the one that rises from football stadiums to greet a winning goal.

Amos thanked the audience and, stepping down from the stage, found himself surrounded by a crowd of people stretching out their hands and congratulating him. Some women kissed him, but for the young singer it was not a pleasant sensation to feel his cheeks damp from sweat perhaps, or tears or Lord knows what. He wanted to wipe his face dry with his hand but felt embarrassed.

He wanted to get back to his table and eventually succeeded. He hugged his parents, sat down, and thought that, all things considered, he had not done a bad job. Even if he did not win, at least his honour was intact.

The competition went on for another couple of hours. At the end they awarded the prizes. The presenter approached the microphone holding a sheet of paper and began to announce the results. He calmly read out the number of votes for the fifth place, then for the fourth. Third place went to a girl from Siena who had struck Amos as being particularly good. After announcing the winner of second place, the presenter paused for dramatic effect. He then said something which had nothing to do with the competition, and finally he relented and invited young Amos Bardi to join him on stage to receive the well-deserved gold margherita. A young lady came up to Amos, shook his hand, and pinned the small jewel to his jacket. Then she smiled, wished him great success, and left.

This is how Amos won his first singing competition. He had every reason to feel proud of himself. However, unbeknownst to him, from that time on, certain small illusions, certain apparently innocent dreams, began to take root in his childish mind, and like woodworms, they began to work invisibly, conditioning, or at least influencing, his future. The complex equation which pointed towards the destiny of that child, who had already been accustomed from the age of twelve to singing solo, "outside the chorus", depended on other factors such as luck.

XIII

On the first of October of that year, Amos, equipped with his gold margherita award and his world of memories, hopes, and dreams, stepped across the threshold of the Cavazza Institute of Bologna, where he encountered a situation quite unlike anything he had imagined.

His parents helped him to hang his clothes in the wardrobe next to his bed in the dormitory. Then they all went back down to the ground floor and said goodbye. It was time for lunch, so he went straight to the refectory where, to his surprise, he found a quarter litre of wine set by his glass. He drank it, or rather, he gulped it all down, even before finishing the soup.

He was the youngest, or perhaps it would be more correct to say the smallest, boarder at the Institute. In fact, an exception had been made in admitting him, as the minimum age for enrolment at the Cavazza Institute was fourteen.

The school rules were briefly explained to him, and he was given some advice and information. The next day he went out at about seven-thirty with two school friends who had spent the last five years with him at their last school and, like him, had transferred from there to Bologna and now found themselves in the same class. Without anyone accompanying them, the three boys made their way along Via Castiglione, under the porticoes, towards the San Domenico Middle School in Piazza Calderini. This was the school that had been so highly recommended to their parents.

They were quite excited by their small yet important undertaking. After consulting the relief map of the city they cautiously crossed a few small streets, bumping into and knocking over the odd moped which was carelessly parked under the arcades by the students from the technical and industrial institute on the way. Eventually they reached Via Farini where they turned left, walked for another two hundred yards or so, turned left again, and finally arrived in front of the main door of the school. There were already a number of students gathered there, and others continued to arrive in dribs and drabs.

The janitor met Amos and his friends and hurriedly showed them to their classroom. For the first time the three boys were sitting at desks in a mainstream school alongside other kids who were not visually impaired. In fact, the Cavazza Institute had decided to close its own school and let its boarders attend the normal city schools as a result of the strong pressure which the student movement had exerted on the local administration and the education authorities during the period of the student protests.

There had been some resistance to that decision, above all from the teaching and non-teaching staff who risked losing their jobs as a result of the closure of the special school for the blind. But the general feeling of the students that emerged from the meetings and study groups of that period favoured the complete integration of the blind in society, starting from the middle school, promoting access to new forms of employment in a variety of different fields which had until that time been considered unsuitable.

In the end the students had their way. All in all, for the public administration the closure of the school for the blind and of the associated branch of the music academy represented a considerable savings as well as sparing of a great many organizational difficulties. By 1971, when Amos arrived in Bologna, the battle had already been won. For the past two years, all the boarders had been regularly enrolled in normal state schools, and the people of Bologna had become accustomed to seeing the blind students of the Cavazza Institute wandering about their city and would occasionally assist them when they were crossing the street or considerately stop their cars to let them pass ahead of them.

So Amos and his friends would roam around the city, venturing ever further as they became more familiar with it. They would go out on Saturday afternoons and only return just in time for supper. As for Sundays, they would sometimes stay out for the whole day, taking a sandwich for lunch or perhaps eating at a schoolmate's home.

It was a very different experience from the quiet way of life at the school in Reggio Emilia, where everything was measured and planned and nothing out of the ordinary ever happened. In Bologna every day was unpredictable. The boarders at the Cavazza Institute were fully involved in the student movement, which at that time was fighting to revolutionize the whole of the school system.

In the evenings, after dinner, Amos often found himself attending long meetings, study groups, or general assemblies, where he would listen with fascination to political discussions and learn about people and events he had never even heard of before then. Sometimes, thinking about his family and his friends, he felt as if he were dreaming or living on another planet. Then he would shake himself and do his utmost to blend in, to fit in and summon up enthusiasm for this new approach to life. This, after all, was not so difficult for him given the adaptability and curiosity which are typical for boys of his age.

In early December some events occurred which were so extra-ordinary that they imprinted themselves indelibly in Amos's memory. These events unsettled him and caused many of his early certainties to crumble. Due to a fierce disagreement with the Cavazza Institute's administrative board, which as usual had no intention of giving way to the students' demands regarding some fundamental changes to the internal rules, the number of meetings intensified so that they were even called in the mornings during school hours. After three or four days, at the end of an interminable general assembly attended by all the Cavazza students and others who were friends of theirs from the university, a decision was taken towards midnight to occupy the college for an indefinite period. The staff on duty at that time was made to leave, and picket lines were established at all the entrances. Amos, full of excitement and admiration for the student leaders, thus experienced his first night entirely without sleep. He had been allocated to the picket that guarded the back door, the one that gave onto the courtyard. It was freezing cold so everyone had covered up as much as possible to try and keep warm. The shift lasted an hour and a half but to Amos it seemed an eternity. When he came back inside he met one of the students from another school who offered him some grappa. In all honesty he didn't really like it, but partly due to the cold and partly to feel more grown up, he gulped it down. Then he went to join his friends in the dorm, and together they tried to imagine the possible developments of that extraordinary situation.

At about four in the morning the boy in the next bed took a small cassette player from the bedside table, and they all listened to songs by Fabrizio De André, a singer Amos particularly liked for his warm voice and his colourful and racy lyrics, which were pretty outlandish for the time.

The occupation continued for three days. They were three days of complete anarchy; whoever wanted to sleep slept, whoever wanted to go out went out, at whatever time of day or night...

Amos went out to stock up on cigarettes, cigars, and pipe tobacco. He didn't really like smoking, but he didn't want to be different from the others, so he smoked without inhaling to avoid coughing, and having that cigar or cigarette between his fingers made him feel more self confident.

Sometimes he also bought bottles of wine. Now that was something he did like, and during the days of the student occupation he drank quite a lot more than he should have.

After the occupation, life went back to normal. The students did not get everything they wanted, but the compromise reached had persuaded them to suspend the agitation.

The following Sunday Signora Bardi went to visit her son and found him changed: more distant than usual and less happy to see her. She looked at him carefully and noticed that he had something written on the palms and the back of his hands. She took his hand and read some names: Karl Marx, Mao Tse-Tung, Ho Chi Minh... Rather alarmed, she felt entitled to ask her son for an explanation.

With the earnest air adolescents have when they feign indolence but in reality have a burning desire to express their ideas in order to impose their personality over others, Amos started to explain that in those first months in Bologna he had learned and understood things that until then had been carefully concealed from him.

"You and Pa," he began, "or perhaps it would be better to say *we*... are bourgeois, rich, or moderately rich, people, who live off the backs of the proletariat, exploit their labour and swan about in furs and jewellery... who can afford fast cars and all the world's luxuries. I don't think this is right."

His mother felt hurt, so she responded forcefully. "You'd better take note that I wake up earlier in the morning than your father's workers, I work more than they do, and I have more responsibilities and worries... and we are not as rich as you think. And what is more, your father and I have always worked honestly without stealing a lira from anyone else... just you remember that!"

Amos pondered for a moment. His mother was not wrong. He had heard her himself rising early in the morning, coming home late at night, working ceaselessly, looking after everything and everyone, always there at her husband's side. So where did the truth lie? Who was he to believe? And for the first time in his life he felt the discomfort of one who claims to have certainties to proclaim to the next man but then cannot find them, one who seeks truths that do not exist or worships idols that prove to be false... A tangle of thoughts, memories, feelings, passions, and muddled concepts flooded into his mind, and he felt bewildered. He could find no convincing reply and so let the matter drop to avoid the risk of being defeated by the strength of his mother's reasoning.

They went to lunch in a small trattoria and then took a walk in the city centre, but there was something between them that was driving them apart. Something was breaking that tie, that understanding that had always bonded mother and son. There was something wrong. In his heart Amos felt a sort of inexplicable mistrust of his family, but over the last few hours he also felt also a silent hatred for all his school companions to whom he had opened his soul, inebriated by the force of their ideas and their experiences. Now he felt alone and uncertain in a way that he had never felt before.

Oh bitter adolescence, oh youth when blissful unawareness, oblivious serenity can so inexplicably give way to unease, loneliness, sadness...

In the days that followed, Amos began to feel different from his friends, or else it seemed to him that his friends were different from him. There was no longer that agreeable sensation of reassuring companionship which had made him feel so bold and strong. Now he felt that they were distancing themselves from him, and at times he thought they were talking behind his back and keeping secrets from him. A cloying melancholy afflicted him for the rest of the day.

He was accused of being a bourgeois, a daddy's boy, a reactionary masquerading as a worker out of pure opportunism...

One evening, in the small room where Amos and his two classmates did their homework, an argument spiralled out of control and ended in blows. When Amos felt the pain of a punch in the stomach, he doubled up, tried to breathe, then he lowered his head and hurled himself at the boy closest to him, hitting him full in the face. The boy fell, and Amos threw himself on top of him while the third boy rained blows on his back. Amos gripped his victim's ear with his teeth and bit hard until he felt the nauseating taste of blood in his mouth. Only then did he let go. This fight lasted several minutes until someone came into the room and pulled the boys apart. But the episode created an irreparable rift between Amos and his friends which increased his solitude, his doubts, and his nostalgia for that world which had never betrayed him, even though he had been the one to distance himself from it – that far off, ever faithful world in his own beautiful Tuscany that waited lovingly for him, so full of tender promise.

He needed to confide in someone but did not have the courage to do so, and at night, before going to bed, he paced along the corridors of the Institute smoking one cigarette after another, counting the days and hours left before the end of the school year. To make matters worse, his report did not bode well: maths, in particular, was a problem. He had been falling behind and could not find the incentive to recover.

But however things turned out, Amos had determined to leave that school. Next year he would enrol in a local school so that he could stay at home with his family like most boys of his age. He had communicated this intention to his parents on the phone, and they had reacted favourably because the continuing troubles at his school were causing them to worry more and more each day. But this decision was not without its own risks. Would Amos have been ready to deal with the difficulties presented by a mainstream school without the supporting structures, the specialist teachers, readers, and equipment that made it possible for the blind to have access to all the learning that is normally acquired by means of images? The Bardi family pondered this dilemma and feared that they might be making an irreparable mistake, failing to take account of problems which might seriously obstruct Amos's progress. Amos instead seemed obstinately resolute and quite sure of himself. He was as determined as ever and nothing would change his mind. To all this should be added that in those very days there had been a new wave of student protests in Bologna that would soon to turn into a long and entrenched occupation of the Cavazza Institute.

Amos was present at the general assembly when it was unanimously decided to occupy the Institute, and in spite of all his misgivings, he experienced these new events with the same excitement and enthusiasm as before, with that spirit of adventure adolescents feel when they face situations, when the element of novelty and risk gives them a sense of being important, bold, and pure in their dedication to a cause.

It was one o'clock in the morning when all the staff were evicted and pickets were set up at all the entrances. Amos wandered up and down the halls of the Institute, breathing in that heady atmosphere of subversion and freedom. In his hands he held his packet of unfiltered "Nazionali" which he would light from time to time, never putting out the stub until it burnt his fingers.

For two days he didn't even go to the school. The fight for the definitive closure of the conservatory within the Institute and for a significant increase in the level of student freedom fired him up. One night Amos had been selected with five other boys to guard the main entrance. He sat at the porter's table and began to chat with the others. The board of directors had threatened to call in the police if the occupation was not brought to an end soon, and some members of the riot police had been spotted in the vicinity. As a result the students on picket duty were more jumpy than usual, uncertain of how the situation would develop.

Towards ten o'clock the bell rang, and one of them opened the small window the porter used to check who was outside before opening the door. A firm voice said, "This is the police. I have orders to end the current protests immediately."

"And so?" responded the bold young man.

"So you must end the occupation or we will be obliged to enter by force."

"I will relay the information," replied the boy, immediately closing the small window.

One of the members of the picket line jumped up and ran towards the staircase to go and warn the central committee assembled in the games room on the first floor, while the others stayed at their post awaiting instructions. Some of them hoped that in the meantime they would reach the end of their shift, while others, Amos included, hoped to be able to stay there where the main action would take place.

A few minutes later the intercom sounded. One of the boys picked up the receiver to reply.

"OK," he said and hung up. "Orders are not to open up for anyone."

"Very good," thought Amos to himself. "So there will be a fight soon," he said out loud. Then he sat on the porter's chair in place of the comrade who had answered the intercom. There was nothing for it but to wait.

In the two hours that followed the police rang at the door another four times, demanding the suspension of the occupation by making imperious noises through the small hatch.

Around one in the morning there was another ring. Piero, one of the members on picket duty who was also sitting at the porter's table, responded in a stentorian voice. "Again! Who is it?"

"Police!" came the reply.

"So what do you want?" answered Piero.

"We have received orders to enter. Open up or we will be forced to break down the door."

There was a moment of silence. "Here we go," thought Amos, excitedly.

He took the receiver with his left hand and pressed all the numbers on the intercom at once with his right hand, issuing the peremptory order to all those who answered from every part of the building. "Everyone come down. The police have issued us an ultimatum." In his adolescent breast beat a chaste and innocent revolutionary's heart.

From the porter's lodge they could hear the sound of many feet coming down the main staircase, and soon the leaders of the student protest were lined up in the entrance hall.

Amos got up and joined his companions in the front lines while the noise of voices, footsteps, and objects being thrown or roughly moved became louder. A thunderous crash against the main door startled them all. For a moment everyone froze. Then another blow came, similar to the first, which echoed around the hallway of the school. Shouts and curses were heard. A third and decisive blow brought the door down and the riot police broke in. They immediately clashed with the students. These included many political activists from the university who had come to lend reinforcements to their battle and party comrades occupying the Cavazza Institute.

Young Amos found himself disoriented in the commotion. He would have liked to punch, bite, fight, and show all his courage and bravery. But against whom? In the midst of all that confusion he could not make out who the aggressors were and, then, realistically, what could he do against men twice his size and trained for conflict. He was just beginning to take all this on board when a blow to his chest, perhaps from someone's knee, totally winded him. He was bent double when he took another blow on his back. He was overcome by shivers and a sense of impotence and fear brought tears to his eyes. Gathering up all his energy, he tried to make his way through his comrades to escape from the mêlée and reach the stairs, but it was not easy. He heard a voice on the megaphone rise over the general fray. "Do not put up any resistance. Everyone is to go to the main hall for a general assembly."

The noise died down and turned into a general muttering, a dark grumbling. Then, rather suddenly, the students began to retreat and left enough room for people to make their way through to the meeting place. With shaking legs and a growing pain in his back, Amos bumped against this and that person till he finally reached the stairs. He grabbed the bannister like a drowning man grasping a line to a lifebuoy, raced up to his room as fast as he could, and collapsed onto his bed. A few minutes later he felt himself shivering with cold, so he got up again, hurriedly undressed, and then buried himself under the covers which he pulled right up to his nose.

He fell asleep almost immediately but did not rest well. Every so often he would be woken by a shooting pain in his back which would bother him every time his troubled dreams caused him to toss and turn.

When the bell rang in the morning, he decided to spend the whole day in bed as he had a bad pain in his back. The duty assistant made him lift his pyjama top and confirmed that he did indeed have a large bruise there. The nurse was called who agreed with the assistant that the boy should be allowed to stay in bed.

"A haematoma like that is bad, especially as it means you cannot lean against the backrest of your chair," said Nurse Dedonatis with a smile. Nurse Dedonatis liked Amos and occasionally engaged him in conversations about opera and the great singers.

Amos felt a bit calmer. He began to daydream about his plans to leave the Institute as soon as possible and how he would enrol at a local school at home for the next year. With these thoughts he drifted off to sleep again.

He woke later that afternoon starving hungry and with his back in terrible pain. He got up, moving very cautiously, placed his feet carefully on the floor, and dressed slowly. He went down to the ground floor and found that the Institute had gone back to normal. The adventure was over and yet it had left its mark on him: a vague sense of oppression and disappointment, a weary resignation which, as the hours passed, transformed itself into a new hopefulness. Just as a convalescent regains his strength in the space of a few hours, so his spirit of optimism was quickly restored, transforming hope into dreams and dreams into real joy. It was the joy of imagining himself at home once again, finally in control of his own life: a new life.

It was in this state of mind that he received an unexpected visit from his father. Signor Bardi had been on his way home from a business trip to the small town of Treviglio where the tractor factory that he represented in his province had its head office. At the last minute he had decided to drop by and see his son and check how things were going. He had the porter call him and took him to dinner in a nearby trattoria. When they were at the table he started to answer Amos's many questions asking for news from home about his brother and his friends. Suddenly, however, his tone changed and he said rather solemnly, "Did you know, the men in the workshop have gone on strike?"

"Why?" asked Amos with a certain agitation.

"They were claiming a large salary increase and a reduction in their working hours. There was a very long meeting in my office during which Mario, whom you know very well, speaking on behalf of everyone, accused me of exploiting the workers."

"Couldn't you give them a raise?"

"Certainly not as much as they were asking. There is not a lot of money to be made from the workshop."

"So what's going to happen?" asked Amos impatiently.

"So I proposed to them that we all set up a company together, that way no one would feel exploited anymore, and by working for themselves, everyone would give their utmost, to the benefit of one and all."

There he stopped, raised his glass, and took a sip of Lambrusco.

"What did they say?" asked Amos, desperate to know the outcome.

"They thought about it for two days; they discussed it, argued about it, and then decided not to do anything!"

"Why not?"

"Perhaps so that they can continue to work less than I, to risk less than I, and to complain more than I."

Then Signor Bardi changed the subject to avoid giving the impression that he gave too much importance to the matter. In the meantime, however, the message had been imprinted indelibly on Amos's memory, changing his ideas just as a hammer and chisel, used artfully, change the shape of a stone.

When he took him back to the school, Amos's father noticed something new in his son's demeanour, a new understanding that made them both happy.

When they said goodbye it was with a real spirit of camaraderie that rejuvenated the father while bestowing an air of unusual maturity on the son. For a while any trace of filial subordination was erased from the relationship between father and son.

However, on his way home, Signor Bardi was assailed by worries. It pained him to think of the risks that his son had to face at that boarding establishment, but then he thought of the difficulties that

Amos would have to face if they did make the decision to bring him home and enrol him at a local school, without the support of a specialist facility for the blind. The drive home on the motorway was through a blanket of thick fog and the journey seemed interminable. At the Altopascio tollbooth he mechanically handed over the ticket, paid, and found himself again shrouded in the fog of the Padule.

When he reached Bientina the visibility began to improve, and by Pontedera the fog had lifted. As he approached his home, that road, which was so familiar to him, put Signor Bardi in a better mood which finally turned to joy when he found his wife still up waiting for him, anxious to hear his news about their boy.

XIV

By now it was late spring. Signora Bardi was always up very early in the morning; she would go straight to the window of her room, open it, and look out at the ears of corn growing in the field on the other side of the road. One morning her husband caught her in that contemplative moment and asked her what she was thinking. His wife moved back from the window sill and answered with a smile. "When those ears of corn are ripe Amos will come home, and for the harvest we will all be together again at last."

"I expect he will have to repeat some subjects this year." Then she frowned and warned, "But no one is to touch that grain until he is back home." Then she smiled at her husband and began to get ready.

Signor Bardi waited for his wife to go down to the kitchen for breakfast; then he would get up and join her.

Meanwhile, in Bologna, Amos was getting ready for school. It was another of those mornings when tiredness would get the better of him, and he would probably end up with his head on the desk fast asleep. The previous evening he had found a way to sneak out after dinner. He had gone to the Da Ciro bar, downed a couple of glasses of wine, bought himself a packet of cigarettes and a box of Tuscan cigars, and then he had come back and settled down by himself to listen to music on his new cassette recorder.

His friends were being increasingly distant towards him, considering him to be a daddy's boy, a bourgeois, and therefore alien from their concerns for the proletariat, their political commitment, and the class war in which they placed a blind faith and all their hopes.

Amos tried to adapt his behaviour and his language to fit in with his friends, but smoking, booze, and cursing were not enough to restore that bond, and so at night, in his bed, he would make the sign of the cross and ask God's forgiveness for his sins, promising to behave better starting from the next morning. He had just turned thirteen and felt very alone, but what was worse was that he felt ill at ease. He already felt a distinct lack of those certainties that usually make the lives of adolescents so carefree. His brief existence was complicated by seeming contradictions, by concepts and ideas which were so distant from each other as to render them totally irreconcilable and lacking any point of contact or convergence. This was why he felt an indefinable malaise, which he interpreted simply as a longing to go home, to his own environment, to the bosom of the family that loved and protected him and restored his lost strength. Back home, in effect, there were people who possessed a precious heritage of unshakable, irrefutable certainties, in which they placed their hopes and from which they all drew their courage and their peace of mind. Instead a curious destiny seemed to force him to consider everything with mistrust, to ponder and question everything, even, at times, the clearest evidence. This was tiring and depressing because it went against his impulsive and instinctive nature as a teenager. But Amos had not yet encountered Seneca. He had not read *De Vita Beata* (On the Happy Life) and so did not know that "people prefer to believe rather than to judge" (*unusquisque mavult credere quam iudicare*).

One day, many years later, he would read that passage and understand that the suffering and unease of those days constituted the true, solid foundations upon which he would build his whole life, and they were the sole basis for the strength of character which would see him through the trials that awaited him.

In the meantime he was counting the days left to the end of the school year. His grades did not concern him greatly; he knew he could not expect much. He would make up for his negligence during the summer, but after that everything would change.

At last June came and with it the end of school. Amos failed maths. It was his first real academic failure but his parents did not make a scene. Practical as ever, their main concern was to arrange some extra lessons during the summer holidays so that he would be well prepared for the retakes and be able to face the next year at his new school without too many difficulties.

The first thing to do was to find someone to help Amos with his studies. One morning Signora Bardi brought home a young woman called Manola, who she introduced to her son, explaining that she would be there to support him for the whole year and that they would start that very morning with some maths revision. Manola was a girl from their village who was at university in Florence and close to graduating. She was kind, polite, and very determined.

They immediately hit it off and began working in the studio of the Bardi house. Summer had already arrived, and the warm air would waft in from the open windows, bringing with it the sweetish grassy smell, the birdsong, the distant noises of the farm machines, and occasionally the voices of the men working in the fields. It was a gentle atmosphere which often distracted Amos from his main task. But the time passed quickly and pleasantly, and after a couple of hours of work Amos would run outside to call his friends, jump on the bike, and pedal off down the dusty country lanes, coming home later all dirty and sweaty. "Look what a state you've got yourself into," his grandmother would cry out. "You're a right mess!"

Amos would not even hear her. He would fill his lungs with that air smelling of wet dust from the courtyard which his father had just hosed down. Then he would run into the kitchen where the women were busy preparing dinner.

He was never still for a minute, and his grandparents would fret about his health. "You'll catch your death if you go around all sweaty like that. Calm down a while! Look how good your little brother is!"

In effect, his little brother, nicknamed "Pace Santa" ("Holy Peace") by his parents to emphasise how different he was in character from that wildfire Amos, would sit quietly at the table, bent over an exercise book with a pencil and rubber. He would have to be called repeatedly to get him to join everyone at the table for dinner. Alberto really was naturally inclined to study and his grades were excellent. In this regard he was the family's pride and joy. He was an introverted, quiet boy and meticulous to the point of obsession, but he got along very well with his older brother who was so different, so impulsive and extrovert, and always ready to debate and argue. Even at dinner, Alberto would eat silently and very slowly. The food was always too hot for him, and he would only just be finishing his first course when everyone else had finished. After supper he would often fall asleep in front of the television, and his father would carry him up to bed. Amos, on the other hand, was never tired in the evening, and he would have to be cajoled or threatened to make him go to bed.

In August the Bardi family went to the beach. That year they were all particularly excited as Signora Bardi had bought a beautiful apartment, and they were going to stay there for the first time. In a state of excitement and pride, Amos's mother had announced to him, when he came home from school, that the apartment had cost a full ten million lire, the whole of her savings which represented years of work and sacrifice, but she was sure she had made a good investment and was visibly delighted.

Amos had to carry on with his studies to be sure of passing the resits in September, so it was arranged that a maths teacher would be waiting for him on the beach every morning. Her name was Eugenia. She was unmarried but lived with her sister, who had two children of the same age as Amos and Alberto and a husband who had been described to Amos as a truly special man, both for his noble birth as for his charm and intelligence. Amos later had the opportunity to concur with this opinion. In fact, Dottor Della

Robbia soon substituted for his sister-in-law and, with great zeal and enthusiasm, dedicated his free time to teaching Amos the rudiments of Euclidean geometry and mathematics. He was particularly good at inspiring passion for that subject which, on that beach and with that teacher, became almost a game. Whenever he noticed that his pupil was getting tired, Dottor Della Robbia would interrupt the lesson and teach him how to play chess instead. He had won the regional championships as a university student, and now he transmitted that passion to Amos, who made great strides in the subject every day. He enjoyed alternating the geometry of that fascinating game with the scholastic geometry which Dottor Della Robbia would explain by drawing shapes in the very fine sand on the beach.

Amos had a boundless admiration for his new tutor, so he forgave him that degree of exaggerated self-regard which is typical of those to whom things come rather easily and who enjoy popularity and the trust of others without really ever being aware of the reasons for their success. Amos listened to him, enchanted. He loved the way his tutor would debate brilliantly and win arguments on the most varied of topics and tried to assimilate everything he said and please him by being industrious, alert, and intelligent. Dottor Della Robbia also excelled in physical activities. An excellent swimmer, he was also familiar with the martial arts, having practiced them in his youth. In short, he seemed to be the living embodiment of the precept *mens sana in corpore sano.* Amos's desire to emulate him grew day by day so that the lessons were a pleasure rather than a sacrifice, and he applied himself with diligence in order not to disappoint his tutor and, importantly, to ensure he did well in his exams.

By the end of the holiday Amos had certainly changed. New words had found their way into his vocabulary, Latin expressions which were not always used correctly; he made quips and wisecracks at the expense of those present or not and displayed an ostentatious self-assuredness. While on the one hand this may have made him seem less likeable, on the other hand, it undoubtedly helped to pull him out of the dejected state which he had been struggling with for a while before. Above all, he was well prepared for his exams which he passed with flying colours to the great joy of his family and the pride of Dottor Della Robbia, who immediately accepted the Bardi family's invitation to join them for a brief holiday in the country with his children, Gionata and Francesco-Maria, and his wife, Giuseppina, who still adored him like a new bride after many years of marriage.

The Della Robbia family arrived one Thursday evening. They quickly deposited their bags in their rooms, refreshed themselves, and came downstairs for a sumptuous dinner to celebrate Amos's exam success and the end of his time at boarding school. For the occasion, Signor Bardi uncorked some of his best bottles of wine, and everyone sang their praises. He was justifiably proud of the excellent quality of the wine as he had always personally tended to its production. The children were also allowed to sample it, and by the end of the evening everyone was feeling joyful and without a care in the world.

The next morning the children slept late and no one was up for breakfast. After lunch Dottor Della Robbia suggested a game of chess. The boards were set up on the tables, the pieces arranged, and a small tournament began.

At sunset, the children asked to go to the farm to see Amos's horses. They took the steep, shorter path which allowed them to avoid the main road. At the top of the hill, just a short distance away from them, was Stella, tethered in the middle of a field with her beautiful, black foal. He had been born a few months earlier and was called Fulmine.

Amos was eager to show off his courage and skill with horses. He approached the horse confidently, took hold of the rope, and followed it all the way to the stake, from which, after some effort, he managed to untie it, and then turned to the children who were watching from a distance. Stella followed him obediently, occasionally stopping to graze. Her foal followed her, jumping around gleefully, intoxicated with the feeling of freedom in that open space. The children walked on, crossing the farm road until they reached the group of houses. Stella went along too, but the foal stopped in the field, uncertain whether to follow his mother or to remain in his own little heaven. Suddenly he decided to follow too, just as a car appeared, travelling at great speed. The driver slammed on the brakes but it was too late. Poor Fulmine was struck in full, and as he fell, his back leg became trapped under the wheel of the car. When he struggled to get up it was apparent to everyone that his leg was broken. As it is practically impossible to reset a horse's bones, his fate was sealed.

Crying and sobbing, Amos ran with the others to call for help. His parents soon arrived and arranged for the children to go home. Then they called for someone to come and take the poor young animal to the slaughterhouse, where a few hours later a pistol shot would put an end to his suffering.

That evening at supper Amos could not hold back his tears, and as they fell into his pasta, he was amazed at the general indifference to that loss. His foal was dead and everyone seemed to have forgotten about it already.

Some days later, Amos and his brother were taken to the Mascagni conservatory in Livorno by a friend of their mother's, to enquire about enrolling for the piano course. Amos's brother wanted to study the violin. They both had to take an aptitude test as the courses were vastly oversubscribed – 610 applications were many more than the conservatory could accept. But Amos came first in the rankings and Alberto did well too, coming ninth. Alberto soon began studying with his usual zeal and commitment, very proud of his new Chinese violin. Amos instead proved to be strangely lacking in interest or motivation. The Braille method also presented some practical difficulties for both Amos and his teacher, who nevertheless, convinced of his pupil's talent, did everything he could to get the best from him.

At the start of the school year, Amos found himself with two new challenges to face: the middle school in Pontedera and his music studies at the conservatory in Livorno where his mother would take him and Alberto twice a week. Being fairly indolent by nature, Amos would usually end up practicing his music in the car on the way there, under the stern and astonished eye of his brother, who disapproved of such slack habits and was always perfectly prepared.

XV

At his new school Amos found a very different atmosphere from the one he had left behind in Bologna. No one there spoke of politics, of independence from parents, or of drugs; instead they talked about sport, holidays, and matters relating to the school. Often they would plot schemes against the teachers and plan ways of avoiding tests or playing truant without being found out and punished. To Amos all this seemed rather childish, and he found it difficult to fit in completely at first, in spite of the fact that everyone seemed to be very welcoming from the start.

Pontedera is known all over the world as the place where Piaggio manufactures scooters. It was here that Amos attended secondary school, living at home with his family like all the other kids. Although it seemed rather odd to him to leave home with a lunch box and a bit of change to buy a hot chocolate, it did not take him long to adjust to these new ways and to set aside the memories of his recent life at boarding school. A life which had certainly tested him and forced him to grow up before his time, as a result of his desperate hunt for affection and values, for what was simple and real and more in keeping with his age and his background.

His teachers quickly came to like him and tried hard to help him settle in. The boy who shared his desk was top of the class, and I would say that he considered Amos to be almost like a new project. He had guessed that the teachers had entrusted Amos to him so that he could look after him and intended to fulfil that duty with his usual, legendary diligence. For his part, Amos did everything to try and fit in as best he could. He considered it to be an important task which would earn him the respect, and perhaps also the benevolence, of the teachers, which was something important to him.

Consequently the two boys were almost always together. During recreation, during gym, music, or art lessons, when Amos would mould shapes out of plasticine or clay. When they had work to do in class, Pietro would check the dictionary for Amos too, without passing him his own translations, however, for fear of getting caught and punished.

Behind them sat two lively and enterprising young lads whom Amos soon came to like and admire. One was called Raffaele and the other Eugenio. Amos particularly took to Eugenio, whom he thought very open and extrovert, similar to himself in character and sharing his own approach to life. Eugenio was always ready with a joke and had a sense of mischief which Amos found attractive. He was also a formidable runner and would encourage him to do open-air activities.

In no time Amos had settled in so well that he felt almost as much at home when he was at school as with his own family. Professor Caponi, who taught music, was especially fond of him and did everything possible to have Amos with him, even stealing him away from other lessons, which was something Amos relished. He even wrote a song for Amos to perform at the year-end celebration, organized by the principal. On that occasion Amos stunned everyone with Radames's aria from Verdi's *Aida*, with a piano accompaniment provided by the professor, who was so proud of his pupil and his astonishing performance that he was almost beside himself with joy.

When he finished singing Amos found himself surrounded by a crowd of his schoolmates. He felt many hands searching for his own, grabbing him by the shoulders and pulling his jacket.

Eugenio, at his side, took advantage of the situation by chatting up the prettiest girls.

A few days later school ended and Amos had achieved good exam results. He had also done well in maths, which was thanks to the good efforts of his good friend Dottor Della Robbia.

The holidays that year were truly memorable ones, not so much as a result of any exceptional event as for the total, and peaceful, absence of drama which, for Amos, was a novel enough experience in itself.

His father had begun remodelling the house and had created a small studio for his son from the place where he had previously kept the farm machines. He had split up that big barn area to provide a small boiler room, a laundry, a wine cellar, and the study for Amos, which got its light from a window that opened out to the pergola where, already in August, magnificent bunches of Isabella grapes gave off a delicious smell. The birds would be attracted by it, and wanting to feast on that nectar, they would approach the open window suspiciously, peck at a grape, and fly away chirping happily.

Amos was overjoyed with his new den. He would sit at the piano, play something, and then stop and listen to the sounds that drifted in from the countryside like a magic symphony. Sometimes he would be so enraptured by those voices of nature that his own music would seem discordant to him, as if it were breaking the enchantment.

In that room, which the shade of the arbour kept quite cool even in summer, Amos would spend the early hours of the afternoon, reading, playing music, or listening to records, always pacing up and down with his hands behind his back – a habit he had as a result of his total inability to keep still whenever he listened to music which completely transported him. Occasionally a friend would drop by. Eugenio was his most frequent visitor, as he liked to train around the half deserted by-ways of that beautiful and silent countryside, dragging his friend along with him. To tell the truth Amos was not that keen on those strenuous runs, trying to keep up with his athletic friend, who would regularly wear him out. What he really loved was the time they spent in the den together. Eugenio liked to read and he was happy to read aloud: short stories, poems, and the lives of famous people. He also enjoyed digging out writings of a more explicit nature when Amos would close the door and Eugenio would read in more hushed tones.

In August, the Bardi family went to the beach again, staying in the apartment they had bought recently, which was proving a great success. It was quite a large apartment on the top floor of a brand new three-storey building about three hundred yards from the sea just off Via del Secco in Lido di Camaiore. The boys had a room with a wonderful terrace overlooking the sea, and their parents' room also had a terrace which was south-facing. Then there was a spacious dining room, a small kitchen, and a bathroom. In short, it was a luxury that the Bardi family would never have been able to dream of until a few years ago. But the family business had been doing well thanks both to the extraordinary economic boom of those years and to the hard work put in by the Bardis, who had never stinted in their efforts and always worked together from dawn to dusk as a perfect team. Amos's father was a prudent, shrewd, and competent man who was well-respected by his clients and colleagues alike. His wife was full of fighting spirit, blessed with a sharp business sense and a gregarious and outgoing nature. In just a few years they had transformed poor Alcide's humble mechanical workshop into an important commercial enterprise where it was possible to buy or repair any kind of agricultural equipment. Now they could afford to spend almost the whole month of August in their own apartment by the sea, relaxing and enjoying their by now teenage children and those last years of family life spent all together.

Amos started playing chess again with his tutor and with many other children at the beach club who had been infected with the chess bug. He would get some exercise by diving into the sea with the Della Robbia children and would swim out as far as the buoys.

Afterwards he would take a cold shower to wash the salt from his body.

Day by day he felt his body develop a new strength and energy, which made him feel more self-confident and even slightly narcissistic. It was an intoxicating feeling which increasingly spurred him into challenging both himself and others, taking needless risks, even risking his own life, as though this in some way served to give life a fuller meaning.

One afternoon he found the Della Robbia children on the beach with some other kids, all looking out at the sea, which had been very rough for three days. The waves were almost reaching the first row of umbrellas. Amos immediately had the idea of diving in and trying to swim, letting the waves pass over his body. He suggested this to the other children, and after a moment's hesitation the Della Robbia children accepted the challenge while the others refused. The three of them walked forwards, jumping with the waves; then once the water was up to their chests, they threw themselves underwater and began to swim with some difficulty. At a certain point Amos heard the older of the two boys shout out for help. His younger brother was in trouble...Perhaps the boy was caught out of his depth in a current which prevented him from getting back to shore. He was swimming but in a disorderly, desperate way, and he was not progressing towards either the shore or the other two boys. Amos swam as fast as he could, and when he reached the place where the voice came from he felt the younger Della Robbia boy's hand frantically grab his shoulder. Amos went under but quickly re-emerged. He tried with all his might to swim to shore, occasionally reaching down with his feet hoping to touch the sand. There was nothing. He was rapidly running out of strength, and they were still more or less in the same place in the water.

Amos was gripped by panic. Then he heard the voice of one of his two friends calling, "Help!" He tried to be calm and stopped swimming, concentrating only on keeping his head above water, and then called out to the older brother, who was a good swimmer.

The boy told him that the lifeguard was putting the lifeboat into the sea. Amos was overcome by fear and shame. He tried to swim again in a last desperate burst, using all his remaining energy, and after a few seconds, when he felt for the bottom, he found it, dug his toes into the sand, and raised himself upright. Something like joy brought tears to his eyes. He turned to call his friends. They too were now safe. The current had carried them away from the dangerous hollow in the seabed and back to shore.

If nothing else, that experience taught Amos a greater respect for the sea, and perhaps a fragment of prudence also began to take root in his proud and high-spirited character: a character that always pushed him to prove to the world how brave and clever he was and which at times made him a rather insufferable show-off. On the other hand, Amos hated having others worrying about him all the time or protecting him the way people protect the weak. He could not bear the fact that there were many people who still could not accept his normality and as a result acted in an altruistic and over-solicitous manner towards him to make themselves feel good and perhaps to win admiration from others. He felt entirely capable of doing everything that other kids of his own age did. He did not want to be treated in a special way and would do anything to assert his right always to be treated and judged by exactly the same standards as everyone else. "Be careful there"; "it's too dangerous for you"; "wait let me help you" – all these attitudes infuriated him and made his eyes sting with frustration. In the face of such concern he would lose all sense of danger, risk became his only life-line, and regardless of everything and everyone, he would deliberately throw himself into doing whatever he was being dissuaded from. This was why he was fascinated by horses, rough seas, racing downhill on bikes, weapons, and anything else that could constitute a bulwark against that excess of concern for his condition, a condition which in his heart he accepted without any difficulty, providing others did not make it weigh on him.

"One doesn't give charity to those who do not ask for it," thought Amos at times, caught between anger and desperation.

"Let them mind their own business. When they come riding with me they fall immediately; when they swim with me they are always afraid and make me go back to shore and then perhaps claim it was for my sake, with an attitude combining understanding with a sort of pity towards me."

This is how Amos would give vent to his feelings with his close friends. Then he would withdraw into himself, and he developed an extraordinary strength of will which enabled him to bulldoze his way forward, tackling every obstacle head-on, convinced that he had to do better than everyone else in order to be considered their equal. This thirst to learn and to improve, and the results which he achieved, gradually convinced him that every cloud has a silver lining. And day by day, with every obstacle overcome and goal achieved, an increasingly conscious optimism took hold of him.

Amos's teenage years were lived intensely, and he became increasingly convinced that life was a mysterious and fascinating journey during which you encounter ideas, become attached to them, and then these ideas become confused and drown in the sea of experience from which other ideas then emerge, leading to other experiences and so forth... After every year we are different from the person we were before, at times unrecognisably so, because every tiny episode contributes to this change. So we are all nothing more than the sum of our own experiences and knowledge.

Amos had by now left the whole boarding school experience behind him, and he had changed a great deal since then, even though nothing from that time had been lost. He had simply stored it away, in orderly fashion, with the care of one who does not want to waste anything because sooner or later everything has its use.

XVI

That October Amos and his classmates went into the third grade of middle school. At the end of that year there would be exams, and then the time would come when they would have to make important decisions. Some of them would begin work immediately, but the majority would carry on with their studies at various other schools in the local area. Amos had solemnly vowed to quit the conservatory, but he had promised his parents that he would continue to study music privately. The truth of the matter was that he could not stomach the idea that a blind person should necessarily be limited to working as a masseur, a switchboard operator, or, as his destiny seemed to be requiring of him, a musician. No! He would do something else. He would prove that it was possible for a blind person, or at least for him, to do anything he set his mind to.

Amos had been struck by something a friend of his who was learning English had said. "Where there is a will there is a way." He thought this English saying was more precise and elegant than its Italian equivalent: *volere è potere.* Nothing that he ardently desired seemed impossible to him, especially those things which others deemed beyond his reach.

So he asked his father for a horse that was faster and more lively than the Avelignese breed which he had always ridden, and after much hesitation, his father decided to buy him a medium-sized, pitch-black mare with a white stripe on her forehead. Amos's father had relented out of concern that his son might otherwise lose that great passion for horses which his dear grandfather had wished to instil in him before he died.

He had instructed Beppe, the man who looked after the animals on the farm, to be extremely careful and prudent. "Never leave him alone with this animal, and for the first few times, make sure you hold the bridle while he mounts; I wouldn't want her to play any nasty tricks," he said to himself, with the typical tone of someone trying to make amends for an error which has already been committed. The mare was named Andris, and Amos would go and visit her every day. Although he was wary of her excessive high spirits, he would go up to her with firm resolve, his heart beating hard in his chest, and, with Beppe's help, mount her. But riding Andris he discovered his limitations as a horseman. He was aware of the fact that he could not impose his will on the animal to make her go in the direction or at the pace he wanted. He felt hardly more than tolerated by her and in certain cases even rebuked if he exaggerated with his heels. She would react to his entreaties with threatening tosses of her head, even occasionally kicking or bucking. Frightened, Amos would grab her mane and try to calm her down with his voice. Fortunately she responded well and would then stop to nibble at the tufts of grass at the edge of the road.

Amos's relationship with Andris became increasingly important with every day that passed. She helped him to mature, to feel more secure and at ease; she made him love the challenges and goals he set for himself and to relish his achievements. Amos's horse influenced his character and personality in a very positive way.

Moreover, through horseback riding Amos was always in touch with nature, and he became much more consciously aware of his deep love for the countryside: those far-off sounds of the farm machines in the fields, the singing of the birds, and the silence all around him profoundly affected him and calmed his spirit. It all seemed to have been created for him, to give him peace and joy.

He breathed deeply, inhaling the fragrance of aromatic grasses, ripe fruit, orchards, manure, and must. Sounds and smells penetrated his very being and nourished him, infusing him with a sense of intoxication, of blessedness and physical energy. He felt grateful, although to whom he was not sure, but he felt grateful for the gift of life.

He even went willingly to school, where he was now completely at ease among students who were far removed from the acrimony of politics, or pseudo-politics. His new companions were sincere in their friendship and helped him in the most natural and spontaneous way.

His teachers, for their part, were proud to have a boy like him among their students for this gave them the opportunity to try out new and stimulating teaching techniques which they could then discuss with colleagues, friends, and family. So, besides the music teacher, who really adored Amos and had given him an A in his school report, his literature teacher was also particularly fond of him, possibly as a result of his curious predilection for poetry and an interest in fiction which was rather rare amongst those students. Signora Bonini, who taught French, would often speak to her friends about Amos. At first she had been worried about him, but he had proved to be a real treasure and had a genuine talent for languages. "He has an extraordinary musical ear which enables him to master the correct pronunciation with great ease," she would gush excitedly. Amos knew and loved some French operas, such as Gounod's *Faust* and Massenet's *Werther*, and delighted in committing to memory such famous arias as "Salut, demeure chaste et pure" or "Pourquoi me réveiller". When one day Signora Bonini spoke about *Andrea Chénier*, Amos's imagination was fired. He was gripped by curiosity and wanted to know the original text that the French poet had written in his own blood on the cuffs of his shirt, just hours before his death.

At home over lunch he recited those verses to his parents rather smugly, proud of his mastery of that erudite work which only he had taken the trouble to commit to memory while the rest of the class yawned and waited impatiently for the bell to ring. He instead had listened to those verses, immersed in his own world of distant memories, of sensations which would remain with him forever, and he had repeated them feverishly so as not to forget them. After the French lesson he had noted them down, and then at lunch, in a deliberately mournful tone, he began to recite them as though to himself. "Comme un dernier rayon, comme un dernier sourire animent la fin d'un beau jour, au pied de l'échafaud j'essaye encore ma lyre: peut-être est-ce bientôt mon tour".

He paused briefly and then translated the words. He noted a certain admiration in his parents' faces, but no one, in that moment, could share his profound emotion, because he alone was able to trace those lines back to the notes of Umberto Giordano and to the masterful performance by Franco Corelli, which had so struck and thrilled him some years ago when Oriana had given him those first records by his favourite tenor. While Amos recited those verses in French, in his mind he could hear Giordano's music, Corelli's voice, and the verses of the aria all ringing out together. He was immersed in a world of his own. He tried to imagine himself in that period in history, an age when people fought and killed one another with such ruthlessness and life had such little value. His imagination raced and he lost his bearings. He was eager to know more about the French Revolution and asked everyone he could about it, but he only received fragmentary and disconnected information. It felt to him as though the answers to his questions were given to him half-heartedly while people were thinking of other matters. They disappointed him and brought him back from his daydreams, returning him brusquely and sadly to a sense of reality. Amos went back to being the rascal, the wag who was always ready for a joke and a laugh. An inexhaustible source of mischief who was "always up to something" as they would say at home when describing his boisterous nature.

Meanwhile exam time was relentlessly approaching. A good performance would see Amos through to the upper school and bring an end to the years of careless abandon which, in reality,

Amos had never really fully experienced for himself. Nevertheless, he looked to the future with optimism and faith in himself as well as in others. Every morning, with his satchel slung over his shoulder and his typewriter, he would walk to the bus stop with his younger brother, just like a proud soldier full of happiness and hope.

He would climb on the bus and almost always go and sit at the back with the older boys. There he would silently listen to their conversations, with a detachment which denoted neither disdain nor lack of interest, merely an impression that their feelings and their world were different from his own. It was as though there were something preventing him from fitting into that world completely, nor was he really interested in doing so.

He would get off the bus in the main square at Pontedera, and a brisk walk would get him to the school courtyard, where many of his classmates would already be assembled. Sometimes they would skirmish briefly, the odd scuffle helping to ward off the cold and damp of those winter mornings. After the physical exertion he would feel more inclined to sit at a desk for five interminable hours.

When the last bell rang, awaited by all with eager anticipation, he would be one of the first to reach the gates, with the boy who shared his desk and Eugenio, but then he had to stop and wait for his brother, who would always be one of the last to arrive, slow as he was at organizing his school bag, putting everything carefully in order, and paying his respects to the teachers before finally making his way out.

Amos's teachers were pleased with his general performance. He approached his exams feeling reasonably confident and passed with a respectable "distinction", while two of his friends, one being Eugenio, earned the plaudit of "outstanding".

But it was a good result which placed him in the top five of the class, so he considered himself pleased and enjoyed the unexpected fuss that was made of his success at home.

The time had come to make the most important decision: Amos had to choose the direction his life would take and then seriously commit himself to it. His father came into his room one morning a few days after the end of the exams and, finding him still lying in bed, sat down on a wooden chest and talked to him about his responsibilities. "It's time for you to make some choices. There is no time to lose, think it over carefully, make a decision, and then you can enjoy the holidays," he said in a calm but serious and resolute tone.

Amos knew that in theory he was free to choose the school that he wanted, but he was also aware of the fact that he was expected to go to the secondary school and after five years receive the classical diploma. Everyone in his family felt that was the right path for an intelligent boy inclined more towards the humanities than scientific subjects.

Amos thought about it but he felt somehow driven by destiny to follow that advice. It was almost as though he had a mission that required him not to disappoint his parents. He soon put any reservations aside and announced his decision to his father: he would enrol in the classical Lyceum in Pontedera where he would study Greek and Latin, sacrificing his music studies, becoming a "man of letters" and thus fulfilling the hopes that had so often been expressed, but never imposed, by his family. This done he cleared his mind of all those thoughts and dedicated himself entirely to organising his holidays. These really were carefree days. He would spend half of the time in the country and half at the beach as the Bardi family had taken to doing every year. The family's apartment in Lido di Camaiore, while not large, was cosy, comfortable, and intimate. After dinner in the evening Amos loved to go out onto the balcony overlooking the sea and to take deep breaths of that salty air and listen to the sound of the waves when it was rough. In fact, the rougher the sea the more calm and tranquil he seemed to feel in his soul, but this was not matched by what he felt in his veins. Something was beginning to shake his body out of a sort of torpor, troubling his dreams at night and setting fire to his day-dreams whenever he listened to music and paced up and down in his room. He walked, reflected, and dreamed, trying to understand what he was feeling. For some days a pale, sweet face with regular features kept insinuating its way into his thoughts. It was the face of a young girl just coming into bloom. She had long, blond hair and bright eyes full of the joys of life.

He had met her at the beach. His friends could speak of nothing else and would follow her everywhere, unable to take their eyes off her. Amos had idealized her and now imagined her to be as perfect internally as she appeared externally: an angel from heaven. The angel, however, gave him no sign, no particular attention or kind gesture that might permit a hope to flower. She was respectful enough, but perhaps that was only out of consideration for his condition. Amos understood all these things but he did not think about them. Alessandra had a boyfriend, so Amos was not the only one to entertain vain hopes. Anyway, he thought, things could always change one day, and in the meantime he thought about her constantly, tormented with anguished feelings.

She was Amos's first love and he was determined that he should do something – something different from what others did. So, lying on his bed, with his bedroom door locked, he began composing some verses in rhyme, which he thought he might be able to deliver in secret to his fair angel: "Oh, mia fanciulla dai capelli biondi, bocca ridente e occhi giocondi..." (Oh, my young maiden with golden hair, smiling mouth, and joyful eyes).

He put together a dozen or so of these rhyming couplets and then began to plan a strategy which would successfully deliver them to her. Initially he thought the best thing might be to recite them to her in person, but he realised almost immediately that he could never do that. What would he have felt if she had started to laugh or made fun of him? No, it was better to give her the hand-written poems, he decided, but to whom would he dictate the poems and confess the name of the recipient?

In the end Amos decided to do nothing. He would hold the poems in his heart, like a secret. The thought of this first secret of love made him feel the blood rush to his cheeks. He jumped up off his bed and went to his tape recorder. "Best to distract myself with some music," he thought; then he pulled open the shutters that gave onto the balcony to let in some light and air. As the spools of his old Saba tape deck began to turn, he began to pace up and down his room with a sense of lightness and hope in his heart. He may not have had much of a chance with Alessandra, but life still smiled on him. He felt healthy and strong and happy to be in the world, surrounded by his friends and family, and to play his part, whether as protagonist, second lead, or extra, in whatever role the comedy of life would assign to him.

XVII

August passed quickly and the holidays came to an end, along with any hopes Amos still harboured concerning Alessandra. The feverish desire to embrace her, to kiss her lips, to establish an intimacy with her, would remain an unrealised dream, its secret only revealed in a few childish verses in rhyming couplets.

He tried to distract himself by thinking of all the new things he would find at home. While they had been away the builders had been working almost uninterruptedly. They had created a splendid large, rectangular room with a fireplace open on all sides in the centre. Wrought iron firedogs were supported by an old millstone with a square base about eighteen inches high off the ground so that it was convenient to light the fire or cook on it.

Amos's father had also promised him a billiard table for this room. It would be placed under the big window that looked out towards the back of the house.

The last section of the old shed that had been used as a store room had been sacrificed to create this room. By now almost all of the house had been restructured to meet the family's changing needs. Amos's father liked to transform it gradually and to see it become more and more elegant and functional. After all, he had studied to become a property surveyor and took huge pleasure in carrying out projects on his own house. It was the house where he had been born and where his sons were born, so for obvious reasons, he was deeply attached to it. When Amos stepped into the new room for the first time he felt a surge of excitement. He opened the door cautiously, with the slow deliberation of a poker player eyeing his last card. He went in treading softly, then bent down to touch the perfectly tiled terracotta floor and approached the fireplace, feeling greatly impressed by the originality of its design.

Suddenly, Alessandra came into his mind. He felt a pang in his stomach, and then his imagination began to work planning a large party to be held right there in that room. Alessandra would be there at his side along with all his other friends. It was really the ideal place for parties, and Amos's father would surely be happy for his masterpiece to be used by his sons.

With this in mind Amos turned and left by the side door that led into the garden. The builders were still working there, completing a small arcade supported by square columns of reinforced concrete. The columns still showed the traces of the irregular lines imprinted by the planks of wood in which they had been cast before the cement was completely dry. He leaned against a column to reflect, and for the first time, that big country house felt to him like a villa, a real villa. Along with the affection he had always felt for it he now felt a new respect for it. For a moment his sense of pleasure and good fortune at being able to live in such a house drove away any feelings of despondency or suffering.

Wheelbarrows were arriving with fresh mortar and dark red tiles for the floor. The lively, industriousness of the builders around him made Amos feel healthily energetic and transmitted an indefinable urge to do something useful too, to be able to share the satisfaction which he was sure he could guess was expressed on the faces of all concerned: workers and family members alike.

"How's the voice then? Let's hear something!" said one of the men, setting down his heavy barrow and turning towards him, relaxing his arms down by his sides. Amos smiled and took a few strides across the garden to stand in the shade of the palm that stood in the centre of that small lawn. From there he turned towards the arcade and in full voice, his veins standing out on his neck, he began to sing "La mattinata", the celebrated aria by Leoncavallo. "L'aurora di bianco vestita, già l'uscio dischiude al gran sol..."

The builders stopped to listen to him, pleased at this moment of diversion and the short rest it afforded them. Even the foreman, an indefatigable worker who usually never stopped, put down his hammer and trowel to listen.

After the last high note they all praised and thanked him and then, as they got back to work, started discussing the decline of modern music. They all agreed that these days songs were not as beautiful as the ones they used to hear when they were young.

"Even at the Sanremo Festival," said one, in a strong Tuscan accent with a precise local Volterran inflection, "you can't hear a decent song." Then, turning to Amos, he added, "Why don't you go and teach those clowns without a voice what it really means to sing!"

It wasn't the first time Amos had received this kind of reaction, but he enjoyed being the centre of attention and the focus of such respect and admiration.

He went into the house from the back door through the kitchen, and as he was about to open the glass doors leading to the first hallway, he heard voices that he did not recognize coming from the breakfast room to his right. He stopped, curious to hear what was being said. Just at that moment the door to the room opened and his grandmother, somewhat surprised to find him there, invited him to come in.

He was introduced to a young couple. "In two weeks' time they are getting married," explained Amos's grandmother, "and they would love it if you would sing at their wedding."

Amos did not know what to say so he just smiled. The young man intervened, addressing him and then looking at his fiancée as though to ask her tacit confirmation of everything he said. "You see," he began, "we all admire your voice; we even have a tape of you singing. Someone in our town gave it to us. He had recorded you when you came to sing in the theatre up there, and we always hoped you might sing at our wedding!"

Amos was silent. He was certainly not very keen to accept that invitation, but nor did he have it in him to decline. In the end it was his grandmother who spoke up and begged him to consent. Amos smiled once more and shyly said, "OK."

The following Sunday, dressed in his finest clothes, Amos went to the church half an hour before the Mass and the wedding ceremony was due to begin. Passing the altar, he reached the choir, where the organist was waiting for him to go through a quick rehearsal. Soon the guests began to arrive, while the bride and groom, as so often happens, were a little late, slightly holding up the start of the ceremony.

It had been agreed that, during the Eucharist, Amos would sing a piece that reminded him of his brother's first Communion. On that occasion he had sung "Vieni fratello". When the wedding vows had been exchanged, the newlyweds and the witnesses went to sign the register; he sang Schubert's "Ave Maria".

The guests were greatly moved by his singing, and after the ceremony Amos shook many hands and kissed several elderly ladies. He bade the young couple farewell, and after having received a gift from them, he went home with his parents and his grandmother, who never missed church on Sundays, even if unwell.

Later that afternoon his friend Francesco Andreoli arrived from Bologna with his wife. Francesco had graduated in Classics and taught in a school in that city. They had met when Amos was at the Cavazza Institute and he had become fond of him. So he had accepted an invitation from Amos's parents to spend a few days in the country at their home, where he could teach Amos the Greek alphabet and the first rudiments of that language, which he would soon be studying for the first time at his new school in Pontedera.

So while in certain vineyards the harvest had already begun and the good smell of newly pressed grapes filtered through the open windows into the houses, Amos spent that hot and luminous

September trying to put his mind to Greek. It was a real struggle as his instinct was to rebel against that forced sedentary activity. The air wafting into his study was rich with sounds and smells, but rather than calm him, it excited him and increased his burden. However, out of respect for his friend and the efforts he was making to help him, Amos tried to contain himself and even to display some interest in that ancient language that he had heard so often praised by his parents and relatives in their attempts to persuade him to study the classics.

At the beginning of October, full of hopes and good intentions, Amos, with two of his classmates from the previous year, entered the classical lyceum for the first time. He was pleased with his choice and prepared to give it his best efforts. Unfortunately, as a famous Italian film director used to say, "we often have many plans for the future; the sad thing is that they rarely coincide with the plans the future has for us." Things did not turn out as Amos and his parents had hoped. All because of a young teacher who spent about twenty hours a week teaching Amos's class Italian, Latin, Greek, history, and geography. Signorina Mistri did not welcome someone like Amos, who needed special attention and teaching methods. She was irritated by the fact that he could neither read her explanations on the blackboard like all the others nor consult the dictionary by himself.

Signorina Mistri did not spare her words in making this perfectly clear to Amos himself who, from the first day, felt humiliated and discriminated against. She would be perfectly capable of calling on Amos in the middle of a lesson and, without mincing her words, saying, "Now I would like you, or your mother, to explain to me how I can possibly send you up to the blackboard to write and translate this sentence like all the other students."

Amos would remain silent, blushing with embarrassment and filled with shame. His optimism and strength of character were powerless. He could do nothing to counter the misguided zeal of this ambitious and presumptuous woman for whom teaching was the only reason for living and who judged people only in terms of their objective potential. She measured everything in terms of her own ego, which was so overblown as to be almost pathological.

This woman sowed terror amongst her students. From the moment she entered the classroom until she left it the most complete silence reigned. No one dared whisper to a neighbour or pass a note, and the atmosphere was so stressful that during her tests some students even felt ill. Amos went to school every morning feeling increasingly sad, resigned, and alone and very soon began think he simply could not make a success of this. During classwork the teacher would call him to sit by her desk so that no friend could help him to look words up in the dictionary, and she would demand that he ask precise questions indicating the exact nominative form. But did she perhaps not know that when one knows the exact nominative form of a Latin or Greek word, often one also already knows its meaning? And that looking words up in a dictionary generally proceeds by trial and error?

After a couple of months Amos's psychological state was in tatters, and to avoid the risk of failing, he was forced to resign himself to the idea of giving up that school and transferring somewhere else mid-term. He was profoundly mortified by this state of affairs and sorry to let his family down, but at a certain point he realized that he had no alternative, and he surrendered defeated in order not to lose a year. It was, in this sense, a surrender, but with the honours of war.

Amos's friends and family immediately got to work and succeeded in arranging a swift transfer to another institute in the same city. It was not easy to obtain a transfer after the school year had already started, and valid reasons had to be presented for such a request. This only added to Amos's humiliation when he was already feeling crushed by his first real defeat, but he swallowed his pride and accepted whatever had to be done to go to the new school. His spirits were low and his enthusiasm for studying completely lost, but at that moment, this new school represented a new chapter in his life, and it meant he could put behind him an extremely painful experience which had only served to teach him how much ignorance and fanaticism can hurt a fellow human being.

Amos was fortunate to have understanding parents and also the sympathy of his classmates who, tacitly or openly, expressed a support and kindness that he had not really noticed until that moment. But his feeling of defeat remained. No one could get rid of that and he considered it a real blot on his existence. All his dreams were crumbling like sandcastles; it seemed they would always be thwarted by limitations, disappointments, humiliations, and bitterness, and his future looked bleak. At least this is what Amos felt and thought when he left his friends, discussed his future with his parents, or walked through the door of the new school from which he expected nothing good, nothing from anybody, nothing at all.

Entering an open gate in the courtyard of that old building, which the local authorities had designated for the training of those who wished to pursue a career teaching in nursery or elementary schools, Amos heard a soft but happy sound of voices, mostly high-pitched and squeaky, and, from a classroom on the first floor, a pleasant voice of a child which reminded him that this school offered music lessons.

His mother rang the bell and a middle-aged woman appeared. She was short and fat and seemed out of breath but smiled cheerfully and let them in. She called for the principal, then patted Amos's head, wished him well, and went back to her janitorial duties.

Not far away, a young girl had stopped on the stairs to look at Amos. Although she had never seen him before, she had probably heard about him. As soon as she saw the principal, she turned and fled, light as a gazelle.

Amos was escorted into his classroom and introduced to his new classmates who seemed pleased enough at this new arrival and glad of the interruption to the morning's routine. Then everything went back to normal, and the literature teacher was able to resume the lesson.

As the bell for the last period rang, Amos panicked. He knew he had to move to another room for the French class, but he didn't know whom to ask for help or where to go. He got up like all the others, left his desk, and tried to give an impression of calm which he did not feel at all. Several of his classmates had already left the room, others were gathering up their belongings, and he was totally resourceless, not knowing which way to turn or how to avoid obstacles and embarrassment.

He was trying to figure out what to do when he felt a firm, strong hand on his shoulder. A calm, masculine voice which seemed beautiful to him – full of warmth and good will – said, "My name is Adriano. Would you like to come with me to the French lesson? I'd like to talk with you." Adriano took Amos's arm, guided him down the corridor to the next class, and showed him where to sit. In those few minutes a bond was forged which was so strong and pure that it was already possible, without exaggeration, to call it true friendship.

Meeting Adriano changed Amos's life. First of all he very quickly restored his good humour and his faith in himself and others; then he transformed his physical appearance, advising him to abandon his elegant clothes – Prince of Wales check trousers, camel coats, and white shirts with starched collars – and took him shopping to buy some jeans. He also succeeded in showing Amos how to avoid certain movements and gestures that were typical of the blind and which it had never occurred to anyone, even at home, to attempt. With his new friend's help, in no time at all Amos already seemed a different person.

Adriano was a lively boy who was always ready for a joke and good at thinking up fun ways to pass the time. He was always cheerful, frank, and forthcoming with everyone: he was the guiding light among his friends so that in his circle no one dared do anything without first hearing his opinion, and his quips and witticisms would always be repeated so that they became part of the public domain.

One day Adriano and Amos went to a bar for a coffee. One of the other friends in their group joined them and started to tell

Amos all sorts of things he knew about Adriano: escapades from his childhood which had done the rounds in the town and caused much hilarity.

"One morning," recalled the friend, "Adriano saw a horse tied to a cart full of stuff, ready to be unloaded in a warehouse near his house. He was struck by the enormous size of the horse's penis. He ran home, grabbed a small pistol that he kept hidden in his room, positioned himself as to be carefully concealed from view, took aim, and shot the horse right in the penis! Right there! You can imagine what followed. The horse was enraged, reared up, and upset the whole cart. You should have heard the cursing of those men who had no idea what had suddenly caused the animal to go crazy. And he..." continued the boy, pointing with a deliberately exaggerated gesture at Adriano, who smiled in acknowledgement of his misdeed, "...he ran home and told his mother not to open the door to anyone who might come looking for a boy in a striped T-shirt and went and hid under the bed."

They all burst out laughing, along with a number of other kids who had also come over to listen to the story.

"Another time, but this happened some years later, when he was a good bit older," continued the narrator, enjoying being the centre of all that attention, "he was with his good friend Giuseppe. They met a team-mate of Giuseppe's outside the town, and the two of them stopped to talk about soccer in their usual way. Adriano, as you know, is not particularly keen on soccer (being instead a great volleyball player). He listened patiently for a while but then spotted a grocery store, so he removed himself from the conversation, went into the shop, bought something, came out quietly, moving up behind Giuseppe's friend, and cracked an egg over his head!!" Further bursts of laughter. Amos was doubled up and had tears in his eyes from laughing so hard.

After their coffee, the two friends left the bar to go back to Adriano's house where they were going to study for the next day. Amos was sure they would not get much work done together, not with someone like Adriano who was so lively, so keen on life in the open air and physical activity. All of these things did not help make Adriano into a model student. He had already had to repeat a year at his previous school and was in danger of failing again. But Amos knew that academic success is not always the best measure of a person's worth, especially not in the case of someone like his friend. While Adriano might not have been able to tell you what Quintilian had to say about the education of children, he certainly had a keen understanding of his fellow man and was a master of the art of friendship. The only ones who did not like Adriano were the teachers. In fact, they alone did not fall for his irresistible appeal. They did not appreciate the fact that he laughed at everything and everyone, even himself, and never took anything too seriously. They misjudged his apparently superficial and nonchalant ways, forgetting that sometimes the most serious things can only be said in jest, if they are not to seem boring, pretentious, or pedantic.

In fact, Adriano's life would really deserve a book of its own to describe it, being so rich in interesting episodes that are characterized by constant elements such as paradox, absurdity, and irony – frequently present in all of our lives but rarely in such a concentrated and significant way. However, here I will just say that even back then it was apparent that whatever road he chose to travel, no environment, no uniform, no profession, no temptation or corruption would ever have been able to remove the dignity and the extraordinary frankness that had, already then, made him such a fine person.

Amos was never to forget that big hand, slender and firm, resting lightly on his shoulder, offering to help him without asking anything in return. He always felt huge pleasure every time they met up and would greet each other with an enthusiastic handshake.

Adriano was also very popular with the girls. Blessed with a strong, athletic physique, he was clean-shaven with regular features and a kind, good-natured expression and certainly inspired feelings that were based on physical attraction but were also expressed in the form of an almost maternal tenderness. Deep down, however,

Adriano was a shy person who fought his insecurities by assuming a boisterous attitude, so he never took advantage of these situations, seeking refuge instead in platonic relationships that were full of poetry and grand ideals but sadly lacking in all the other aspects of true romance.

The most important of all these platonic relationships was with a girl called Barbara who sat in the front row in their class. Adriano had been particularly taken with her from the first and he had really fallen for her. She, however, never paid him much attention, largely due to the fact that he had never really declared himself but also perhaps because she was more attracted to older boys. Adriano suffered a lot as a result of these unrequited longings, and confiding in Amos, he spoke of her in the most flattering terms, so that Amos ended up falling hopelessly in love with her too. Amos immediately confessed these feelings to Adriano, and together, in an atmosphere of total loyalty, they began an assiduous practice of innocent courtship. Barbara was flattered by these not unwelcome attentions, but she had a twenty-two-year-old boyfriend who would often come to pick her up from school and take her home by car. So the boys' chances with her were fairly minimal; even so, they liked to nurture those hopes and spend time building castles in the air.

Barbara was small and had dark hair which she wore in a page-boy style. She was pretty and quite shapely, but it was her luminous and expressive face that was most beguiling. She was always smiling. She had large eyes and an intense gaze, a slightly retroussé nose, and dimples in her cheeks which were more in evidence the broader her smile. This is how Adriano had described her and this is how Amos imagined her. They both loved her with a love which was totally chaste and pure in both words and thoughts.

One afternoon, at Adriano's house, Amos was surprised by his friend. It was after one of their usual conversations about Barbara, extolling her infinite qualities and considering what might be best to do or say to please her, that Adriano rose, quickly left the room, and returned with a guitar that he barely knew how to strum. He sat down and told Amos to pay attention. Amos was sceptical but prepared to listen.

Adriano pulled a plectrum from the pocket of his shirt and began to pluck the strings, producing a chord of A minor (one of the few he knew), after which he began to sing a song Amos had never heard but which sounded sweet and full of feeling. When it was finished, Adriano explained with some emotion that he had written it himself for Barbara. Amos could hardly believe it but was sincerely touched and asked to hear it again. Then he asked to write down the words so he could take them home and sing them to himself, over and over again in his head as if they were his own:

"Mi ricordo quella notte sulla spiaggia,
illuminata dal tuo sguardo verso l'infinito..."
(I remember that night at the beach,
illuminated by your glance towards infinity...).

Was it a dream or had Adriano really spent a night with her at the beach? Amos wondered. The picture conjured up by the song seemed so poetic to him and so true! Barbara's look really could light up any darkness. He was also struck by the simile that followed:

"Come un gabbiano sperduto
cerca l'azzurro del mare,
io, nei tuoi occhi l'amore".
(As a lost seagull
seeks the blue of the sea,
so I seek love in your blue eyes).

Those simple words surged from a lovelorn, wounded heart just like his own, and he identified completely and lost himself in them, producing a shiver of emotion.

"Bravo, Adriano," Amos thought, unable to understand how such a delicate artistic vein could exist in a person who lacked even the most rudimentary knowledge of music. He felt a sense of admiration for his friend, but no envy, as this had no place in their friendship. From the outset Amos idealized this relationship and would do anything to protect it, unhesitatingly and unquestioning, with the almost fanatical zeal that teenagers often feel.

XVIII

Despite the significant changes Amos had made with his cooler clothes and more relaxed demeanour, his relationships with the opposite sex remained an unresolved problem. In fact, although he was blessed with looks which could hardly be described as displeasing – Amos had grown to be tall and slender, had very dark hair and quite regular, strong features, broad shoulders, narrow hips, and long, muscular legs – he could not attract the attention of his female classmates, especially those he was interested in. Forcing himself to analyse the situation, he came to the conclusion that the problem must lie in some sort of behaviour of his own. He was vaguely aware of being somewhat clumsy and awkward in his overly eager attempts to please, and then his disability did not help.

It was a case of resigning oneself to the situation; perhaps the best thing would be to focus all his attention on other things which in time, he hoped, would make him more interesting, more sure of himself, more of a man. But for now what he could not figure out or accept was the amazing success with girls enjoyed by certain other guys of his age. These unattractive specimens seemed to him totally vacuous, disagreeable, insensitive types who were totally incapable of pursuing an ideal, and yet he would meet them around Pontedera or elsewhere arm-in-arm with some of the most striking girls. With their absurd posturing he could not imagine how they could have won the hearts of those sweet girls. "What a strange comedy is life," he thought, as he struggled to grasp the rules, the mysterious means by which everyone moves around the stage reciting their own part. The more he tried, the less he understood of the world, losing himself in the labyrinth of his thoughts, intentions, and hopes.

Amos suffered without, however, despairing: a strange, indefinable presentiment prompted him to be strong, to have faith, and to be optimistic. And he appreciated everything he had: the affection of friends and family, well-being, the progress he was making... "All in all," he thought, "I have nothing to complain about. There are so many who are worse off than I." Then he forced himself to not think about what he was missing and to minimize every problem, every difficulty, every obstacle...

True, the thought that Barbara turned her attention to others made him feel ill, but he knew how to explain it to himself. After all, Adriano was in the same boat, and in this sense, "a trouble shared is a trouble halved", as the saying goes. Then he could always hope and dream of a platonic love which he could describe in his own mind to his own design.

Every morning he would wake up eagerly with the idea of seeing Barbara soon and being able to speak to her; a kind gesture, a glance, or a word from her would be enough to plant a dream in his heart, a hope that he would nurture for days and days. Usually he would dwell on these things while transported by his favourite music which also helped him to withdraw into himself and remain alone with his own thoughts.

One afternoon he was in his room listening to a tape of *Cavalleria Rusticana* and reading a poem by Gozzano at the same time, when he felt a sudden uncontrollable urge to compose verses for Barbara, just as had happened long before when he was pining for Alessandra. This time though he did not dream of reciting them to her but of keeping them to himself for his own pleasure. He closed the book, switched off the tape recorder, took his typewriter out, and poured out the following words:

...To leave everything and run far,
far from the gaze of people,
from this life of mine made of nothing,
to flee, holding you by the hand.
And then to find ourselves as though by magic
conquered by the same desires,
overcome by the same sincere feelings,
lost in a tender folly:
to love each other there! Crazy for you
to cover you with kisses first chaste and then less so,
to seek your skin beneath your clothes
and spoil you with wanton caresses.
But the dream lasts a moment and vanishes
and I remain the foolish dreamer
who believes in the fable of love;
that enchants, deceives, then ends...
Who knows from where the sound of a sad bell
reaches me to announce the evening;
I am alone and you are more distant than that bell
and my soul despairs. Is it mere cowardice or
melancholy?
What vice-like grip afflicts my heart?
What is this anxiety, this battle,
that unleashes in me with such fury when I think of you?
And quickly inflames my senses
so that suddenly I crave your kisses, your smile
and my desire grows?
Dismayed I wonder if you think of me
or who you carry in your heart;
and as one day dies, another comes,
I know that mine still yearns for you.

After the last verse Amos realised that he had not thought of a
title. By writing he had experienced a dream, he had put his hopes
and desires into verse, and all in all, this seemed to auger well for

the future. The title hardly seemed to matter at this point. Nevertheless, he went back to the top of the page, where he had left an ample margin, and wrote there the first thing that sprang to mind. *Sogno* (Dream). Then he tried reciting the poem out loud to see if it sounded right. Of course it could hardly compare with Gozzano, but he was quite pleased with what he had produced and felt that he should be indulgent with himself. He folded the paper, hid it between the pages of his encyclopedia, and went out for a breath of fresh air.

It was sunset, a spring sunset. The air was mild, and the light sea breeze carried the delicate scent of nature awakening from its wintery sleep and dressing in its festive bloom. Amos breathed it all in deeply and could feel a new energy flooding through his whole body, which turned into a need for physical movement, a need to think and transmit his thoughts to others... He felt the need for a friend to help, an enemy to fight, an idea in which to believe and one to reject; his soul felt the need to *do* something, to *achieve* something which later he would be able to contemplate, with the satisfaction of one who can say, "This is my work".

He began to run and reached the nearby house where his childhood friends lived. Sergio, one of two cousins with whom he had spent all his early years, was there, busy dismantling and reassembling bits of his Vespa. The two boys conferred briefly; then Sergio washed his hands, and they set off together towards the village on that scooter, which was only licensed for one rider, with no specific plan but, let's say, in search of their fortune. And if what happened next to Amos could not exactly be called fortune, it remained nevertheless in the category of those events that one remembers for the whole of one's life.

Once they reached the piazza Sergio parked his Vespa. Then the two headed towards a small youth club set up by the village kids themselves in a small two-roomed apartment with a tiny bathroom. In the first room was a counter, which had originally been in the village café (luckily this had undergone a refurbishment and so had disposed of it), a number of small tables with chairs, a pinball

machine, a television, and a fridge for ice cream: in short, the basic
requirements for a bar. In the second room there were only some
couches and armchairs and a stereo system. The two rooms opened
onto each other through an arch; the only barrier to this passage
was a curtain which was only haphazardly attached to the ceiling.
Anyone wanting to enter the other room would pull the curtain
aside and pass through without being able to knock. As a result
whoever entered would often become an involuntary witness to
one or more couples whose privacy was guarded only by the semi-
darkness of that room and the volume of the stereo system.

Amos climbed swiftly up the small external stairs to the club,
which he knew from memory as though they were the steps of his
own house. He went in and immediately realized they were organizing something. A boy approached him, greeted him, and told him
that it was still possible to sign up for the chess tournament. There
were a good number of people there and an air of great excitement.

Sergio, who had never been particularly interested in chess, left
Amos and went to the sports club, saying he would pass by later
and give Amos a ride home in time for dinner. Amos signed up for
the tournament and then went to sit at a table with some other
kids who were already playing to test their skills.

A girl came up to him, placed her hand on his, and greeted him
cordially, introducing herself as Antonella. He would have liked to
have invited her to sit next to him, but the table was full and so
she remained standing. Amos got up and gestured that she take his
seat, but with total nonchalance she gently turned him around and
sat on his knee.

Assisted by the relaxed atmosphere of the tournament and the
discussions about chess, Amos managed to act with an ease and
spontaneity that he didn't know he possessed. He talked about
opening gambits, game plans, and final moves, of the strategy and
philosophy of the game, and she pretended to be interested in all
those abstract concepts, but while he spoke he could tell that she
was observing him, and there was something strange about the
way she kept close to him. This was a new sensation for him which

gradually distracted him from his disquisitions and threw his senses into a state of physical turmoil.

Suddenly Antonella got up from his lap and went into the next room. She turned on the record player and arranged a stack of records to fall automatically onto the turntable so that the music played without interruption; then she sat on a couch to listen.

Antonella was a pupil at the local secondary school. She was cheerful and clever but had never tried to be anything other than a country girl, never affecting any behaviour or way of speaking other than those of the world in which she had grown up. She could not be described as a beauty. She was short, with a few extra pounds and large breasts, but she had an attractive face which expressed her irresistibly friendly good nature. She was dedicated to her studies, and she had always done well academically, but she also knew how to enjoy herself. She was unpretentious, frank, and open-minded. She liked boys and they flocked to her, attracted by her femininity and sensuality. Many in town had courted her with success; even so she was not the butt of jokes or gossip, in fact the contrary was true, and she was respected as those who know their business are respected.

After five or ten minutes, Antonella went back to Amos's table, stopped in front of him, and looking straight at him, she asked him to follow her so they could listen to some music together. Amos had a moment of hesitation but she grabbed him by the hand and pulled him up.

When the curtain closed behind them they sat down on a couch and Amos, who was already visibly embarrassed, started to chatter about whatever came into his head. For a while she listened to him patiently; then suddenly she came closer to him and, with her face almost touching his, said, "I like to listen to you, but I would prefer to look at you, if you would only keep quiet for a minute." Then she kissed him. It was a long, deep kiss. To Amos it seemed to go on forever.

As the evening went on the kids were leaving to go home for dinner. By eight o'clock there was no one left.

When Amos shook himself from that kind of dream and asked Antonella what the time was, she glanced at her watch and answered with a laugh, "It's nine o'clock. Why, are you hungry?"

Amos was not hungry but he was worried about his parents who would have been, and probably still were, out looking for him. Yet, it was such an extraordinary situation that he felt strong, courageous, and ready to face any problem.

He tried to take stock of the situation: although not everything had happened, what had happened was still considerable, and that meant a great deal to him. After that experience he felt different. Now he felt like a man.

He moved the curtain aside that a little earlier had closed behind him and in doing so opened before him a new world, a sensual paradise, which up till then he had only just heard about. He went behind the bar and took a bottle and two glasses; then he opened the till, paid, and sat at a table with his new friend.

"What sort of feeling is this?" he asked himself. All he knew was that it was a very different kind of love from the one he felt for Barbara. It was less ideal but more concrete.

Amidst all these thoughts he also regained a momentary sense of reality and wondered how he could track down his friend Sergio. In fact, Sergio had been told of these developments and had wisely called Amos's home to advise his parents that their son would be delayed in the village later than expected for the chess tournament and that he would also have stayed out for dinner.

In reality Amos ate absolutely nothing that night; he was not hungry and there was not even time. The kids were already gradually coming back to the club, and soon after that the tournament began. Amos's first opponent was not a major problem for him. He was a big, tall lad who had just had dinner and must have eaten abundantly. He hardly knew the moves and in barely half an hour he had surrendered. As the other game in that round ended quickly too, Amos had to play a second game. This time his opponent was one of the best players. He was a medical student who had almost completed his degree, and he dedicated himself quite ruthlessly to chess. Amos had already challenged him several times, and the odds were not stacked in his favour. What is more, he was feeling distracted and poorly motivated. His mind kept being drawn to the events of the day, and a sort of physical and spiritual satiety made him feel withdrawn and distant from what was going on in that room. He played the opening he knew best with the King, but after about twenty moves he made a silly mistake and lost a piece. When he realized that the match was effectively lost he got up and sportingly offered his hand to his opponent, said goodbye, and left with Sergio to go home.

In other circumstances he would have felt dejected and demoralized at this defeat. Tonight he did not even give it a thought. He couldn't wait to see Adriano to tell him about that day and talk about the experience he had had of which he felt immeasurably proud. Apart from anything else, he felt he had gained significant ground on the others; he had taken a very important step forward towards what could be called "normality" – his own normality being something of which others, not he, seemed in his view not always to be entirely convinced.

He got home excited but exhausted. His parents had already gone to bed. He raced up the stairs but, before reaching his room, heard his father's voice saying, in a stern tone, "What kind of time is this to be coming home? What state will you be in tomorrow morning?"

Amos didn't answer. He quickly undressed, got into bed, and pulled the covers up to his chin, and then he fell into such a deep and calm sleep that not even dreams found a way to disturb him.

XIX

The old aunt who lived in the house and who had always been especially fond of Amos, spoiling him with fuss and attention, had been preparing a more nourishing breakfast than usual for him based on eggs and milk, on the basis that springtime was a testing time for young people and that the only way to cope with the demands of school was to be fortified with some zabaglione and a good boiled egg to start the day. Amos would devour everything in no time and then, with his little brother, who could not face such a heavy breakfast early in the morning, would run to the stop to catch the bus which fortunately was always late. After about an hour he would finally be at his desk in the front row of class, where the teachers insisted he sit so they could keep a close eye on his boisterous behaviour and his lack of interest in certain subjects. In fact, Amos had a clear preference for the inflections of nouns and adjectives, the conjugations and paradigms of Latin verbs, and for history, and precious little interest in geometry or algebraic equations of the first degree. As a result, although his aspirations for studying the classics had ignominiously gone up in smoke, his natural inclination still tended much more towards literary studies than any of the sciences. He was much happier to translate a fable by Phaedrus, an essay, or a section of text from the *Aeneid* or the *Odyssey* than to consider the correct application of Pythagoras's or Euclid's theorems.

All in all those few months spent at the school studying the classics had turned out to be an excellent investment, allowing him to shine in literary studies at the Institute. However, he had fallen behind in mathematics and geometry compared to his new classmates, so at the end of the year he had good marks in most subjects but had to suffer the indignity of being failed in mathematics and consequently resigning himself to the prospect of another summer under the shadow of numbers and formulas, just as had happened three years earlier.

He felt mortified and disappointed, but once again he put his best face on the situation, and his family did not make a fuss.

Dottor Della Robbia was going to help him as before, alternating lessons with chess games, and Aunt Tilla – an old aunt of his father's who was a retired secondary school teacher – would see to the rest. Amos had to work hard and was quite fearful about the retakes, but as had happened the previous time, he passed with ease, and this work stood him in good stead as he never struggled in mathematics again, and it saw him through to his secondary school diploma. All of this was also thanks to the good efforts of a cousin of his father's who, from the following year, took him into her home and cared for him like a son. Her husband, a teacher of physics and maths, took a strong liking to him and really bent over backwards to help him with his science studies, while her sister-in-law, Aunt Vanda, who was single and lived in the same house, was a literature teacher and so her patient support was mostly to help Amos to study Latin. At the beginning of October, when Amos started the second year of secondary school, he was totally settled, happy, and outgoing. By now he had almost totally forgotten his boarding school days, and they had not left any lasting mark on him. Perhaps unconsciously Amos was trying to recover lost time. He tried to be the way a boy of his age should be, something which in the past he had never managed.

He got on well with all his schoolmates, and being what they would call a lad from a decent family, he was good company who was also well liked by all their parents and relations, and as a result he was frequently invited to dinners, teas, and birthday parties...

Aside from the usual minor difficulties which are typical of all adolescents, this was a particularly carefree period of Amos's teenage years, during which love, embodied by Barbara, played the role of the "cross to bear", while friendship, embodied by Adriano, was the "blessing". Together they represented the two most important aspects of Amos's development into an adult. They were two different reasons for living, two different causes for thought which produced two different and opposite effects. Barbara may have appreciated him; perhaps she recognized some of his good qualities: she had demonstrated her esteem for the first time when she voted for him as class prefect. So she esteemed him, but she did not love him. Amos would have greatly preferred her love to her esteem. Adriano instead was close to him in exactly the way he wanted. Sometimes he was the inspiration, at other times the completion, of Amos's thoughts, opinions, anxieties, and most intimate concerns. Amos could be sure that he could confide in Adriano about anything with the certainty that his concerns would be understood if not always shared. Adriano undoubtedly represented the epitome of success in terms of human relationships, and this was something that one could be proud of for the whole of one's life, if only for the seed of trust in one's fellow man that a friendship of this kind plants in a soul. In fact, once that seed takes root and develops, it never tires of bearing fruit, and its benefits soon translate into long-lasting serenity and inner peace.

Those who believe in friendship and have faith in their fellow humans usually present themselves to the world with such a positive and open demeanour as to immediately attract an amiable and respectful response from others and immediately quell any doubts. This leads their relationships to develop along the perfect tracks of correct and friendly behaviour. Faith is a precious charisma that leads to happiness: so a blind man is happy who has faith in the space that surrounds him, as is the deaf man who has faith in the harmony that accompanies him. A man who has faith in himself and in his fellow man is happy and thanks every day that passes.

This, at least, is what Amos already understood then, albeit in a rather confused fashion. Later he would make sense of the concept that, through his own personal experiences, became almost a philosophy of life for him, a creed, which he would never regret and which he would always hold dear. What is more, as he matured, Amos gradually became convinced that while every man distinguishes himself by his own qualities, all men resemble each other in their defects, which may be more or less pronounced in each individual but are universal. This thought directed Amos towards tolerance and understanding, to take a long and tortuous road which forced him to restrain his compulsive and passionate nature but which was rich in wonderful surprises.

When Amos thought about these things, he remembered his kind teacher and the long hours she had spent explaining the Gospel stories; all those things he had listened to half-heartedly, sometimes feeling quite bored, had gone to strike root in some well-guarded part of his memory and would now occasionally resurface, each time enriched with new and deeper meaning. Sayings like "Why look at the mote in your brother's eye when you do not see the beam in your own?" (Matthew 7:3) brought back the voice of his first teacher as though he had just heard her the day before. Moreover, every time he heard empty arguments or senseless offence being voiced by friends or acquaintances for the sole purpose of imposing their own opinion, or when, completely alone, he would think back calmly to previous discussions of his own, he would laugh at himself, at his own exaggerated behaviour, at his own excessive zeal or anger.

However, he sensed that he still had a long way to go because his character was hard to tame, and perhaps time alone would not be sufficient, nor the memories of his teacher or the experiences of daily life. Probably in that period Amos was seeking something in which to believe, a model to pursue, or someone to emulate.

It was during this period of his life that something very important happened which constituted a decisive turning point in his spiritual development. The young student who helped him with his reading and his homework every day had taken her degree and then decided to marry a local boy and leave the area. This left Amos with the task of finding a new reader immediately, as the year of the exams for the final diploma was soon coming up. There was no time to waste. On the other hand, it was not easy to find a bright, capable, and willing girl like her who would get to know Amos quickly and understand his difficulties and needs and who could master his particular way of learning. Everyone in the family was concerned and tried to think of who might be able to help, asking around and seeking information...

In the course of a long, sleepless night a solution to this dilemma presented itself to Amos's mother in the name of Ettore. Ettore had retired only a few days earlier from his position as director of the Banca Popolare Agricola of Lajatico. Everyone thought this was too early a retirement for a man of his age and energy, and she immediately saw her idea as being a clever solution albeit an extremely complex one to implement.

Ettore was a unique individual, endowed with exceptional human and intellectual qualities and still healthy and strong. He was fifty-five years old but looked a good ten years younger. How could such a lively and energetic man, so full of life, plentiful interests, and good-will, be forced into idleness and left to wander around the village? But with him one had to be prepared for anything. Moreover, he was someone who was happy just to hold a book in his hand, and he loved to go out into the countryside and woods looking for mush-rooms or snails or simply contemplating the wonders of nature. He had travelled practically all over the world with an insatiable thirst for knowledge and experience; his wife had followed him every-where with the same enthusiasm. Now he would have more time and even more opportunities to organise trips to distant lands.

He was an odd fellow! When the management of the bank had informed him of its intention to promote him to director he had calmly accepted but refused the corresponding increase in salary. Instead he had asked, with a few simple words not lacking in irony which was a feature of the way he approached such situations, to be allowed to retain the title of simple bank employee. There are never problems in accepting the sacrifices of others, so his request was soon accepted to the benefit of the bank and the satisfaction of its chairman, who had cheerfully observed, "He will therefore be a first among equals."

Ettore had immediately changed the subject with his inscrutable smile, which could have so many different meanings, while the chairman of the bank, only a little taken aback by his curious request, had not let such a good opportunity slip his grasp.

Ettore was really a man outside the norm, in every way, but no one had a word to say against him. Quite the contrary: in fact, everyone respected and admired him for his capabilities and also for his generosity in advising and helping anyone in need. Amos's mother was ruminating on all of this while she lay in bed, and she wondered anxiously if that unassuming man, who was apparently so timid and solitary, would have accepted the idea of lending a hand with her son's studies. The more she thought about it the more convinced she felt that he was the right man for the job, but she couldn't figure out how to go about asking him. Too elaborate an approach might ruin everything, she thought. It would be better to take a simple, direct approach without too much fuss.

Signora Bardi addressed a brief prayer to the good Lord, switched on the light, and glanced at the clock: it was six in the morning. She felt curiously restless so she got up, dressed, and went down to the kitchen. As she was trying to put some order to her thoughts, she remembered that she had an appointment with a client up at the farm to talk about the purchase of a tractor. So she had a quick breakfast and then jumped in the car and headed off towards Lajatico.

When she reached the central piazza, she checked the time: it was nearly seven-thirty. She turned right onto Via Garibaldi. The bar was already open, and she saw several children going in and others coming out with their mid-morning snacks ready to take to school for break time. She spotted Ettore walking briskly in her direction, holding a short pencil stub in one hand and a crumpled piece of paper in the other.

She watched him and wondered whether it was an opportune moment to stop him. She had a moment of indecision and overtook Ettore, but further on she changed her mind, slowed down, reversed, and went back to the piazza. Ettore was lingering in front of the newspaper kiosk. Signora Bardi parked the car, got out, and caught up with him just as he was emerging with a couple of newspapers under his arm and his nose buried in the open pages of another.

She greeted him, and he distractedly returned the greeting, but when he realized that Edi Bardi had something to say to him, he closed the newspaper and prepared to listen.

"I need your help," she said. Ettore smiled and she continued, "My son is taking his final school exams this year, and the young lady who was helping him is leaving us to get married..."

Ettore blushed and, taking a step back, he made an embarrassed gesture..., "So now you would like..."

Amos's mother took the initiative and interrupted him resolutely. "Yes," she said, "I am quite sure that you are the only person who can help us out of this predicament. Of course," she added, "you must give us an idea of your fee."

This last pronouncement which, as always, sounded rather clumsy and inelegant, had the effect of shaking Ettore from his train of thought and threw him into further confusion so that he instinctively retorted, "If you so much as mention such a thing to me again, Signora, you will force me to abandon the project."

Could this perhaps mean that he had accepted?

There was a moment of silence. Then Ettore, having recomposed himself, said with a smile, "All right, we can give it a try, but don't expect too much, as I really don't know if I will be up to the task."

He glanced at the newspapers and then said, "I will be at your house today at five o'clock. Does that time suit you?" He said goodbye, turned, and walked slowly towards the church, immersed once more in his reading.

Perhaps for the first time in her life Edi Bardi forgot about business. She went back to her car and rushed home to tell her husband about what she considered a victory. Her maternal instinct told her that this latest development could represent an important stroke of luck for her son.

She found her husband on the doorstep, ready to leave the house. She made him follow her inside and sat down. She insisted that he also sit and then, with the enthusiasm of a schoolgirl, proceeded to tell him about her sleepless night, her plans, and her encounter with Ettore. He listened with interest and when she had finished declared that he was really very surprised. He knew Ettore well; in recent years, as a member of the bank's board of directors and later, as vice-chairman, he had had frequent contact with him. He confessed that he might have laughed at his wife had she consulted him about the plan.

"But are you sure you understood him right? It seems very strange that he should have accepted, being such a reserved fellow, to the point of seeming rather misanthropic to those who don't know him well!"

"You never change!" she answered, a bit annoyed by her husband's scepticism. "You always doubt everything. Just you wait and see!"

"But I can't imagine that he'll last! With your son's character! He'll be off after half an hour!"

That is what Amos's father said, but one could see the joy and satisfaction on his face at that excellent piece of news so early in the morning.

Eventually they decided to go out together, but they talked all day about Ettore and wondered what Amos's reaction would be when he got home from school. Ettore and Amos had always known each other, but their contact had been minimal, and it was difficult to predict how things might turn out between them. "Whatever will be, will be ... it will be either very good or very bad," Amos's father would say, laughing every time he caught a glance from his wife or when he bumped into her rushing around some part of the shop.

"It will be fine!" she would reply, displaying her characteristic optimism.

That day at lunch, the whole Bardi family was present for once. They waited for the boys to return from school, and as soon as everyone was sitting down, Signora Bardi announced to Amos that Ettore, the director of the bank, had agreed to help him with his studies, at least until the end of the exams.

Amos took the news calmly, almost with a degree of indifference that no one would have expected of him. "Better this way," thought his mother to herself.

After lunch his father rose from the table and asked him to follow him into the breakfast room. "Are you happy about this?" he asked, and then he launched into a sort of speech in praise of Ettore. "You don't know him well; he is a rather strange man but undoubtedly exceptional. Just think, he only had a limited education and yet became director of the bank in our village, and when he took part in meetings with the directors of all the most important banks, he would almost always listen silently, but whenever he spoke everyone would listen to him with great respect, and no one dared to contradict him, knowing that he would never say anything unless he was absolutely sure of it. And he can read and write in at least six languages I think. In any case he certainly has a good command of French, English and Russian...just imagine that! Russian must be so difficult. And he gets by in Spanish and German too...He reads all the time about all sorts of things so you never catch him uninformed on any subject. It may seem incredible but it's true. He is a man who may be reluctant to say what he knows, but he always knows what he says...At elementary school he was a pupil of Aunt Leda's, and she always spoke of him as an extraordinarily gifted child, which is even more surprising when you think that he came from a very humble family: his father was a bricklayer and his mother a maid. He comes from the most dire poverty, but a man's destiny is closely related to his intelligence and ability, which Ettore has in abundance. But he is not very sociable. He is a fellow who prefers to keep his own company, and I think he has to be accepted the way he is. So try to behave yourself with him. Who knows, perhaps this time your mother has come up with a really good idea!"

He laughed at his gentle teasing of his wife and added, "And be very careful how you speak with him. If you say something wrong you will make a bad impression because he knows everything. Just remember that." And then he stopped. Amos had heard that description which had both reassured and intrigued him, in silence and without interrupting. "I get it," he said. Then he got up and left the room with his father. A few minutes later he was on the phone to a friend with whom he chatted about this and that and immediately forgot about Ettore, exams, and homework. That is just how he was; he knew how to bury away thoughts and worries until the moment came when it was absolutely necessary to deal with them.

XX

Ettore arrived ten minutes early, parked his Fiat 500 under the large pine nearest to the house, and rang the bell. Amos had been waiting for him to arrive and went to open the door while his parents looked on.

Their meeting was simple and informal: a handshake, then Ettore greeted the other members of the family and immediately asked to be shown to Amos's room in order to understand precisely what needed to be done.

Amos showed him his books and the tape recorder on which Ettore was to record his voice so that Amos could carry on with his studies by listening to him reading even when he was by himself. The director smiled. "I have never read out loud in my life, but I will try. I will do my best." Then they were left alone. The study door closed behind Nonna Leda, who was the last to leave the room, after having left a tray on the desk with two cups of coffee.

Everything worked out in the most natural way. It was just a part of normal daily life which was to mean a great deal to Amos, and not only to him.

After having exchanged pleasantries, Ettore opened a history book, while Amos prepared an eighteen-centimetre-diameter reel on his tape recorder which, as he explained, could record for sixteen whole hours thanks to its four tracks and double speed.

"Well, we'd better start to fill up this tape then," said Ettore and immediately began to read the first chapter, which was all about the Congress of Vienna of 1815.

He read, not without hesitation but without interruption, for more than one hour; then suddenly he closed the book and asked Amos to stop the tape.

"It would be a good idea at this point," he said, "to talk a bit about what we have read, to see if it is all clear or if I can help you to understand anything that has escaped you."

In reality Amos had not been paying close attention, and soon Ettore realised that he would have to explain everything all over again from the beginning. He did so with patience and enthusiasm, without expecting anything more from his student.

At the end of the scheduled two-hour period of study, Ettore got up and promised to return the following afternoon at the same time. Crossing the breakfast room to leave, Ettore spotted a chess board on a small table. "Do you like to play?"

"Yes, I am a *passionist*," answered Amos, proud to be able to reveal his skill at the game. Ettore gave a hearty but good-natured laugh. He looked at him, still laughing, and said, "You may be a passionate enthusiast, but I don't believe you belong to the order of passionist monks!" He started to tell him about that order, its founder, how it all developed. He spoke about various events and the passionists who had distinguished themselves, and Amos was stunned by his erudition and, feeling totally disarmed, let Ettore exhaust his subject in that curious, slightly laborious way of his. He had a way of expressing himself that gave the impression of a furious intellectual activity, as though all those ideas and concepts were crowding around the inner workings of his mind where the process of selection of things to say takes place, fighting to make their way out. Amos laughed although he felt slightly wounded and embarrassed by his error.

He was immediately reminded of what his father had told him just a few hours earlier. And to think that he had spoken so little and tried so hard not to say anything foolish! He vowed to be even more vigilant, but above all he felt an immature desire to catch Ettore in a mistake and to even up the score somehow. He very soon realized that would be impossible, as it was not a match between equals. Although he would have given anything to be able to reverse the outcome, Amos would regularly lose any arguments with Ettore and be forced to retire in humiliated defeat. Whenever Ettore could not persuade his young pupil with words alone and Amos dug his heels in and refused to concede, he would calmly get up from his chair, scan the bookcase, and pull out an encyclopedia or sometimes a dictionary or a book of essays, open it, and, smiling, show Amos his error. Then he would replace the book and not speak of the subject again. Amos would be taken aback by the way his tutor shelved his victories without ever taking the satisfaction of mocking him. Ettore never gloated over his triumphs, but in this way he won Amos's admiration for him day by day and with it his profound sense of gratitude.

Ettore taught Amos to question everything, dismantling every certainty, every preconceived notion, every form of youthful fanaticism. He sowed in him the seed of doubt, which at first provokes anguish and bewilderment but later turns into an intoxicating and joyful freedom. Not only does doubting help one to grow, above all it frees one from the unbearable slavery of needing to be right at all costs. And so gradually Amos began to feel a sense of equanimity and peace which he had never felt before. He also felt stronger and more courageous because that sense of peace provides a unique bastion which gets stronger each time it is attacked and cannot be overcome if not by the conscience that placed it there and thereby has knowledge of all its secrets.

From Ettore, Amos never received praise or signs of esteem, and yet he felt for him an affection that rapidly grew, fed by that extraordinary strength and dedication which his improvised tutor employed for the general good.

One day, during a walk along the river, Ettore said to Amos, "It takes great strength to produce both good and evil, but to do good requires more of it because good is to evil like building is to destroying, and the former is much more demanding than the latter. Good and evil are in the hands of the powerful, but those who do good are stronger even if often they don't get noticed and work in the shadows. Always remember that humanity advances on their shoulders."

Amos would never forget those words.

He listened and knew that he shared those ideas. He absorbed them and made them his own and was pleased at the favour with which they were received every time he repeated them to others.

He also felt that he seemed to be growing in the estimation of others in a way he had never dared hope.

Increasingly often he found that people would ask for his views, wanting to have his opinion on the most diverse range of topics, and by some arcane mechanism of the psyche, this made him feel more useful and more self-assured.

In the meantime, the exams were coming up, and Amos was beginning to feel increasingly anxious. Ettore intensified his tutorial sessions, and they would last up to as much as four or five hours every afternoon, and eventually he even started coming on Sunday mornings. However, he tried to help his young pupil to keep things in proportion. "These are things one must take seriously, we both agree," he would say about the exams, "but don't make them a matter of life or death. There are many more important things in this world, so work hard, but don't get too wound up about it all!"

Amos was studying as hard as he could, more than he had ever managed before, in spite of the springtime, the thousand distractions, his many interests, horses, music, records, and his love for Barbara...

At long last the day of the much feared exams arrived. These started with a written essay, a test which Amos felt was his strong point. He went to school with his typewriter and his school bag. After the register had been called, he was shown into an empty classroom so that he could type at ease without disturbing the other students. A teacher came to dictate the titles of the exam topics to him and then left, wishing him good luck and closing the door.

Amos then read the titles carefully once more and then calmly decided to tackle the essay on pedagogy, which was based on a passage from Quintilian on the importance of the "competitive spirit" in children during their early years of schooling.

He considered that many of his classmates would have fallen in with the thinking that was fashionable at that time and, above all, in line with their teacher's ideas, which gave priority to the group over the individual and favoured the school that aimed to "*form*" rather than "*inform*", that encouraged cooperation rather than competition and prepared its students to integrate into society rather than exclusively extolling the skills of the individual.

Instead, Amos decided to tackle the subject boldly and write what he really thought, setting out his ideas on the subject with moderation but resolutely, relying on the heartfelt honesty of someone acting in the spirit of common sense.

He began by setting out the general argument relating to the fundamental importance of the relationship between student and teacher. Moving beyond the theories of John Dewey, the Montessori method, the principles of Boschetti Alberti, and the work of others, he stressed that this was a special and intimate relationship which aimed to single out the natural inclinations of every student and enhance, guide, and optimize them.

It followed that the spirit of competition was fundamental and essential, as it fuels human will, fires the imagination, and develops the mind and its creative gifts. With competition comes an absolutely right and morally unimpeachable desire for success because whoever strives to win always gives the best of himself and sets goals that translate into benefits for the common good. Whoever strives to win understands this, and his objective is not to avoid defeat but, very simply, to let his own freedom to express himself in the best possible way triumph, thus becoming an example worth emulating.

Amos believed in what he was writing. The essay flowed easily so he did not even need to make a good copy from a rough draft. He finished early, got up from his desk, and left the classroom to ask for someone to come and collect his paper. He went out to the square where his mother was waiting for him, anxious to know how he thought he'd done.

Once the written exams were over, Amos concentrated his studies on the subjects he was presenting for the oral tests. He had chosen philosophy as his main subject and hoped that history would be chosen for his second one. His hopes were not in vain.

As soon as he heard his name read out he went into the exam hall. He was in such a state of nerves that he feared he would not be able to control them, but he sat down, clenched his fists, breathed deeply, and waited for the questions.

He began by talking about the great German philosopher Immanuel Kant, and then the questions moved on to Marx. Amos had written a small thesis for his teacher on Marx's essay *Wage Labour and Capital* earlier in the year so he felt touched by fortune and responded to the question with surprising ease.

When it came to the history test the entire examination panel was struck by his meticulous preparation for the subject, which went far beyond a superficial reading of the textbooks. Ettore had read the ideas contained in the books to him, but he had added much more of his own initiative, providing Amos with the benefit of his vast knowledge of that subject and his real life experience spanning periods of both war and peace. His recollections of life during the fascist period and during the Second World War had so captivated Amos that history became his favourite subject.

At the end of the oral exam, the president of the examining committee handed Amos back his written work, congratulating him on his excellent essay upon which the professor who had read it had not even made a single mark with his red pen.

Amos emerged triumphant from that classroom and from the school, to which he was never to return, and waited confidently for his results.

He had to wait several days, but in the end the results were posted on the notice board in the entrance to the school: Amos got the highest possible grade of sixty out of sixty. Exultant, he immediately phoned Ettore to share the good news. Ettore let him speak, then laughed and said that they had really gone easy on him. "Forty," he said, "yes, maybe you deserved a forty, but not more!" But it was obvious that he too was very pleased. Still it was no time to rest on one's laurels. It was time to look ahead and think of the future in a practical way. The very next morning Ettore turned up at Amos's house on his moped at ten on the dot with his nylon bag containing a couple of books and a newspaper.

"So have you decided what you want to do?" he asked Amos without wasting a moment.

"What do you want me to do? I will enrol in the foundation law course and then, if all goes well, proceed to the law faculty. That way I will have plenty of time to think about my future. After all, there are many lawyers in my family as you know, and everyone has always expected me to follow in their footsteps. I was still a child when they started telling me that I would be a lawyer when I grew up, and perhaps, with time, I started believing it a bit myself. Then came the diploma. If these exams hadn't gone so well who knows, I may have seriously concentrated on studying an instrument. I might have tried to complete my piano studies."

Ettore made no comment. Instead he offered to go to Pisa with him to help with all the formalities required for his application for the law foundation course, all of which was accomplished over the next few days. In order for Amos not to waste his mornings lazing in bed or idling about the countryside, Ettore also suggested to him that they should leaf through the newspapers together, which was a habit Amos had never acquired till then. A few days later they also started reading one of the great masterpieces of Italian literature, *The Leopard* by Giuseppe Tomasi di Lampedusa.

Amos loved that book, and in the sticky heat of that summer, he felt a renewed interest in literature, which he had forgotten since the times when his uncle Comparini would read to him. On those quiet family evenings his old uncle, who so loved the world of literature, would insist that the television, considered by him a "cumbersome and irksome guest", was kept switched off.

By now Ettore was reading aloud with greater ease than had been the case a few months earlier, and he never tired of adding comments and explanations. It was blissfully peaceful to listen to him. The time flew by and when Ettore left, Amos would feel a sense of emptiness and solitude. Then he would think back over what they had read, and it seemed to him that he was experiencing a kind of spiritual growth. This was demonstrated by his greater facility of expression and above all by the fact that he had many more things to say.

Amos went on to read and love the Russian classics. He began with Gogol, devouring his famous *Dead Souls* in no time at all. Then he fell in love with Dostoyevsky. Reading *The Brothers Karamazov* and, especially, *Crime and Punishment* made him feel like a different person. After this he threw himself voraciously into Tolstoy and finished *War and Peace* in a few nights. He told his friends about it with enormous enthusiasm and was stunned to find that none of them had read the whole book, and many had not read even a single line of the novel.

In the meantime he had started to attend the law foundation course. He found the afternoon classes neither demanding nor particularly interesting and described them to his friends jokingly as a real waste of time, just like military service, but this course would lead to the possibility of taking a degree in law. For now it meant he had a lot of free time without too much to worry about so he could spend it having fun with his friends as well as reading and indulging in his usual pastimes.

It was around that time that one Saturday Sergio took Amos out for a ride on his new motorbike to Marica's house. She was a girl Amos had heard a lot about. Sergio had met her at the vocational institute that year, and she told Amos she hoped to find a job as a secretary.

She was tall and slim, with long chestnut hair that framed a sweet face with near perfect features. Her legs were so long she could have been a catwalk model. But what really struck Amos, thanks to the advance information provided by Sergio and others, was Marica's voice, which was soft and persuasive, calm, and very feminine: the voice of a siren.

Amos stayed with her as long as possible, and when they said goodbye he took the opportunity to invite her to his house to listen to some music. He asked her a few questions and established that her knowledge of music was scarce, and what was worse, she had little interest in it. Even so, Marica accepted his invitation without hesitation, and on his way home Amos was excited, partly from the pleasure of that unexpected response and partly from nervousness at not perhaps being able to find suitable ways to entertain, surprise, and conquer that young beauty.

Up until then, for Amos, affairs of the heart had never been straightforward, so he was rather astonished that such a popular and, at least apparently, rather superficial girl – a fact which, however emotionally involved he might have been, for reasons of objectivity he had to concede was true – could have accepted his invitation with such enthusiasm or be interested in him in any way. He could not have imagined that Sergio had been so altruistic as to describe his friend's family, their property, their horses, and all sorts of things in a way which enhanced Amos's prospects and probably sparked her interest. On shaking hands with Amos Marica had found him kind, polite, and mature. Observing him closely, she had also thought him a good-looking boy and was not troubled by the fact that he could not see her. His friends would have doubtless talked to him about her; they would have also described her, and this gave her a pleasant feeling of nervous excitement.

That night, in her little room full of girlish clutter, Marica had tried to imagine Amos's room and the living room that Sergio had described to her in scrupulous detail, the comfortable sofas where he might invite her to sit, where he might hold her hand...

A few days later Marica kept her promise. When Amos went to open the door he was genuinely surprised to find her on the doorstep, but she wasn't embarrassed at all, so Amos soon also felt quite at ease. He took her into the kitchen and introduced her to Delfina, the woman who had replaced Oriana when she got married, who now helped the Bardi family with the housekeeping and of whom Amos was also very fond.

Then he invited her into the living room and asked her to sit down. He began to play a record of Italian pop songs and sat down next to her, where they remained for almost the entire afternoon.

When they came out of that room they already shared special secrets, sadness at having to leave each other, and the desire to see each other again as soon as possible.

Marica became Amos's first girlfriend. He introduced her to his friends in this way, and she was welcomed by them with great warmth. Everyone was pleased to see Amos with a girlfriend at parties and whenever there was any kind of get-together, where previously Amos would have turned up alone.

At the beginning of the summer when Amos passed his end-of-year exams, which were nothing more than a formality, they were still a couple. Several months had already gone by, and their relationship was beginning to be important to both of them: they could both attribute to that love affair many of the sweetest and, in a way the most illusory, experiences life offers.

They spent the whole summer together. They saw each other every day, and Amos threw himself into the relationship with all the fervour of his impetuous character. He was never tired of holding Marica in his arms, and she was not averse to being the object of such desire. They loved each other, or perhaps it would be truer to say they desired each other and placed no check on their mutual attraction.

In November Amos, who had enrolled at the Law Faculty according to plan, found himself attending lectures with his old friend from school, Eugenio.

They had both decided to begin their university careers by immediately plunging into the most complicated of the six first-year exams: private law. Ettore had the onerous task of explaining over and over again all the basics of the subject, the elements of contract law, commercial papers, and the laws of inheritance.

There were important texts to study, which seemed interminable to Amos and impossible to study in sufficient detail to avoid risk of failure under questioning.

Throughout this entire period he had moments when he felt seriously disheartened, but Ettore was always there ready to encourage him and to convince him that, in such circumstances, it was not one's memory that mattered but rather one's ability to reason out the concepts. "What counts," he would say, "is to understand the thinking that has guided the mind of the legislator; memory can betray one if it is not supported by the force of reason. And remember..." he laughed, "*ignorantia juris neminem excusat*, and if no one is allowed to plead ignorance of the law, you who are enrolled in the Law Faculty will have even less cause to do so." He would preach in this ironic, teasing way and then add seriously, "You may not get the same high marks as someone who has memorised every word of the text and probably not understood anything – but of what importance is that? What counts is to understand and to move on."

During the breaks in this work Amos would tell Ettore about the books he was reading, and it was at this time that Ettore introduced him to the French literature of the nineteenth and twentieth centuries. So having passed his first major law exam, without either special distinction or any cause for shame, Amos began to read and love the French authors, starting with Flaubert and going on to Guy de Maupassant, Zola, François Mauriac, Honoré de Balzac, Jean-Paul Sartre, and many others.

He read and discussed his impressions with Ettore. He would ask for further recommendations, and with every book he would become more and more passionate about literature and less and less so about the law studies he had embarked upon but to which he now applied himself sluggishly and with flagging enthusiasm.

Through the novels he seemed to better understand the deeper meaning of life; with his law studies he dealt only with purely theoretical problems so he could not project beyond these to capture their essence, their practical meaning.

In spite of this he managed to pass the exams in political economics, Roman law, public law, and civil law without too much effort; more willingly and with the highest possible grade, he sailed through the exam in philosophy of law, a subject which, compared to the others, he found alive and more intellectually stimulating for one who strove to progress and broaden his horizons. He decided to refer back to this subject when some time later he would have to start working on his degree thesis.

He had completed his first-year exams, and in the meantime Marica had graduated and had found work as a secretary in a furniture factory. For the first time in his life Amos felt a secret jealousy which he did not even dare confess to himself. He understood that he could not stop Marica from working but even so he suffered, thinking of all the men who would approach her and ply her with attention. What if she succumbed? Amos really could not bear the thought.

Easily guessing his new anxieties, Ettore would tease him. "So you are an old-fashioned man then!" he would say, and tried to cheer him up. "How can you step out with such a flashy girl at your side and imagine that others should ignore her! And then, aren't you just like all the others when you meet a beautiful girl who is already spoken for?" Amos did not respond but his whole being was in the grip of jealousy and rebelled at the situation.

One Saturday afternoon Marica seemed a bit different from usual. They had decided to go for a walk by the river, and she was very quiet and serious, perhaps even sad. Suddenly he grasped the nettle and asked her why. After some resistance she admitted that an episode the day before had greatly disturbed her.

"I was in my office," she began, "and just before finishing work my boss came in. He sat down in front of me and talked about a couple of admin matters of no great importance, and then suddenly he asked me if I would have dinner with him. As I didn't answer, and I have no idea what he must have been thinking, after a moment he quickly added that he wanted to talk to me about work and make me some very interesting offers. I immediately replied that my parents were expecting me at home and would not have allowed me to come home late, so then he offered to call my parents himself. I was very embarrassed and after thinking about it for a moment I told him that we could get something to eat at the bar across the road after work. He glanced at his watch, then he said that I could consider my work finished for the day and that we could therefore go there together right away. At the bar we sat at a little table, ordered a drink, and then, to cut a long story short, after complimenting me on my skills as a first-time employee, he confessed to having fallen in love with me from the first day. He said that if I went out with him he would turn his business into a limited company with him and me as sole partners..."

Amos could feel the blood rushing to his cheeks. "Such lack of style too," he thought to himself, but held himself in check. "So now what are you going to do?" he asked brusquely.

"I was waiting to talk to you about it to ask your advice, to hear what you think."

Amos replied, "There's nothing to think about! There's only one possible option: go in to work on Monday morning and resign."

"I had thought that too initially, except that I would be a bit sorry as it is my first job and I like it, and I was earning money..." but her voice broke and she began to cry.

Amos took her in his arms, held her tight, and tried to console her, without, however, changing his mind: Marica should leave that job without regrets. She would surely soon find another even better one.

"Anyone who sets their mind to it with determination will always find some good and honest job, and you are not lacking in determination, my darling. Why be so sad?" he said.

Marica attempted a timid protest, but in the end she dried her tears and promised Amos she would do as he said. They quickly returned to Amos's house, and Marica only left once she was sure that he was calm and serene once more. On her way home, though, Marica regretted having to quit her job. After all, the prospect of owning and running a company had tickled her fancy and flattered her vanity. Yet her love for Amos was still strong, even without considering the fact that marrying him would have been far from disadvantageous...

Nevertheless, this episode had left an indelible mark on Amos. Marica's story had severely dented his security, and he began to do what is most damaging and dangerous in a relationship: he began prying into his partner's private life. He besieged her with questions if they spent a day apart, wanting to know who she had met and what had happened, all of which Marica found hateful and intolerable.

After having successfully passed the commercial law exam, Amos and one of his university friends decided to take a brief holiday at his parents' apartment at Lido di Camaiore. He said goodbye to everyone and left for the beach, where he stayed until the beginning of the following week.

When he came home there was an unpleasant surprise waiting for him. Over the weekend Marica had met a boy who had invited her to go out dancing. As her boyfriend had gone away without her, she had accepted, and now she had fallen in love with her new friend and had no intention of continuing her relationship with Amos. Thus abandoned, Amos acknowledged the situation and did not make a scene, but in reality he suffered a great deal and for quite a long time found it hard to come to terms with it.

XXI

This proved to be the beginning of one of the saddest periods in Amos's life. He was quiet and became a bit of a hypochondriac, he hardly went out with his friends at all, and when he did, he spoke only about his ex-girlfriend and his hopes of winning her back. In short, he bored them with endless repetitions of the same old story.

He had become accustomed to having Marica around. Her presence had become so familiar that he felt completely at ease when she was there. Always by his side, she had helped him in a way which was more natural than he had felt with any of his other friends. What is more, he was not feeling particularly fulfilled by his studies, and even his relationship with music was undergoing a kind of crisis. He was experiencing a conflict which probably had its origins several years earlier during his adolescence when his voice had broken. It had changed over quite a short period and even prevented him from singing for a few months. He had tried to recover the use of his voice but had really thought that he would have to give up singing opera and resign himself to singing some popular songs as well as his friend Adriano's almost invariably autobiographical compositions. At that time he believed that he had lost the one thing that set him apart from everyone else, his best, most distinguishing quality. To make matters worse, he was also suffering particularly badly from an allergy which normally affected him in the spring but also occasionally at other times of year. A little dust was enough to make him immediately start sneezing and for his eyes to water, and he suffered from an unbearable itchiness which nothing would alleviate.

He underwent a series of tests which confirmed he was allergic to various substances including grasses, cat fur, and various types of pollen. The doctor also suggested that he stay away from horses to avoid contact with hay. So Amos would have had to give up his great passion, the horses which meant so much to him, to which he devoted so much time and energy and which afforded him that rather wild and masculine lifestyle which he loved.

All these things had happened over a period of time, but now they had all come to a head, making him suffer and above all disorienting him. Life had already accustomed him to difficulties and sacrifice. Was this perhaps his destiny?

At times he felt disheartened, discouraged, and defeated, but it did not take much to lift his spirits: a kind word or gesture, a good idea and his optimism and exuberance would spur him on again. His mood would immediately change, and he would force himself to believe that life was after all an amazing mystery and that sooner or later it rewarded those who loved it wholeheartedly. So then he would react by setting himself goals and would not rest until he had achieved them.

Two of his greatest passions, singing and horses, seemed to be impossible for him. This really was too much. He could not and would not surrender to such privation without a fight. Before he gave them up he would try everything possible.

In his diary Amos wrote some thoughts which help us understand his state of mind at that time. "I had dreams that I jealously guarded deep in my heart, and even those have been dashed against the wall of reality. They have shattered into a thousand pieces, but I have bent down, gathered them all up, and now, with infinite patience, I will put them back together. I will restore them to their old splendor, and I will give them wings so that they may learn to fly and little by little rise up to the heavens, perhaps even soaring over that wall to reach that place over there where dreams come true, first in the shape of ideas, then plans, and finally turning into concrete reality."

So with the help of a few remedies and soothing treatments Amos continued to ride his horses; indeed he went more than ever before with an almost fanatical commitment. He resumed his piano studies and also became interested in electronic music. He bought an electronic drum kit and decided to look for a place that might hire him as a pianist. This would be a good way to pass the time between one exam and the next and to earn his first pay cheque. It would provide plenty of opportunities to meet people, and above all it would allow him to keep faith with his music, or, more precisely, not feel that music had abandoned and betrayed him. The scheme really did offer a great many benefits, and all in one go.

The first opportunity soon presented itself. A small piano bar, the Boccaccio Club, asked him to substitute for the pianist who usually played for them but who was going to be away for a few days.

Amos quickly learned a number of pieces by heart and went to meet the owners to start his first job. He soon realised that he really enjoyed this work. He played peacefully while the people drank, chatted, and only very few of them bothered to listen to him or, more importantly, to judge him ... He could play and sing whatever he liked, and only rarely did anyone request a specific song. Every once in a while girls would notice him, come up to the piano, and talk to him, showing a certain interest in him which Amos revelled in. He would shyly study them as they placed their glass on the piano and, to affect an air of composure, would immediately light a cigarette. In reality that smoke bothered him a bit, but he put up with it out of kindness and quite willingly if he found them to be charming and friendly.

His work ended in the early hours of the morning. When he had finished Amos would rise from his piano stool with aching wrists and a painful back, but feeling satisfied and happy. He would not feel sleepy, so he would go to the restaurant area with some friends and order some pasta, some wine, and a coffee. Sometimes he would go into the small adjoining room where the owners, along with their friends and customers, often organized gambling tables. Just to soak in the atmosphere of that spectacle, which to him seemed quite crazy, Amos would occasionally place some bets himself and end up going home after daybreak. He would have time to catch two or three hours of sleep and then Ettore would arrive for their reading session or to go through some legal textbook with him. Dead tired, Amos would then swear to himself that in the future he would come home earlier, but the next evening, after work, he would again feel wide awake and change his mind. That is how things went for a few years up until the day of his graduation.

Sundays were the only days he could sleep in, and Amos would usually stay in bed until early afternoon, even skipping lunch. Eventually he would get up and go to the farm at Poggioncino to see the horses. If the weather allowed he would saddle the mare and ride around the countryside.

It was on one of these occasions that he heard a voice call out to him as he was approaching the old mill. He tightened the reins and the horse stopped, twitched her ears, and listened carefully, just like her rider. There was the voice again, and this time, in the silence of the countryside, he clearly distinguished a female, or even better, an angelic tone, calling out to him.

Amos went back a little way. A young girl came up to him. "My name is Gaia," she said. "I live here but you don't know me because we've never spoken. I called you because I'm crazy about horses and I would love to try..." She stopped and smiled.

Amos jumped to the ground, held out his hand to Gaia, and then asked if she would like to ride with him. The girl, who seemed very young to him, immediately said yes and began to laugh happily. "Wait for me here," said Amos. "I'm going to take the saddle off and come back. I'll be really quick..." and he galloped off at top speed, pleased to be able to show off his expert horsemanship.

After less than fifteen minutes he was back. Gaia was there waiting for him.

Without dismounting, Amos slid back a little. Following his instructions, the girl grabbed the mane, leapt up nimbly, and managed to get on the horse's back. He helped her to settle into a position well forward over the horse's withers. With a gentle touch of his heels the mare moved off slowly, almost as though fearful of losing her precious cargo.

They passed the old mill and took a path that ran along the edge of the woods and led to an abandoned farmhouse which belonged to the Bardi family. Amos rode with confidence, but that slender feminine body held between his arms, the dishevelled hair that tickled his face, and the cheerful voice speaking to him began to seriously distract him.

He felt a tenderness along with a warmth that soon turned into a burning flame; his senses were ablaze, fogging his mind and demolishing his willpower.

When they reached the isolated farmhouse, Amos was intoxicated with desire and suggested to the girl that they dismount to allow the horse to rest a while.

They jumped to the ground, and he deftly pulled a rope from his large raincoat pocket, unharnessed the horse, and attached the snap-hook of the rope to the halter and hitched the other end to a bell on the wall with a sailor's knot. Then he invited Gaia to follow him up the outside staircase to the first floor of that abandoned house.

Gaia followed him without demur; she did not seem at all embarrassed. They went into a large, empty room. Amos took off his raincoat, laid it on the floor, and invited the girl to sit on it next to him.

First they talked about horses and then about all sorts of other things. Amos stroked her hair and occasionally brushed her warm cheeks with the back of his hand. He took her hand and squeezed it between his own, and then suddenly he took her in his arms, drew her towards him and kissed her.

When Amos came back to reality he couldn't figure out how much time had gone by. He jumped up, remembering that his horse was only tied with a very old rope. Trying to regain some composure, he offered some confused apologies and rushed down the steps towards the bell. He found the bell right away there on the corner of the building where it had been hanging for so many years. He also found the rope ... but the horse had gone.

He felt a rush of terror. To have left his horse there like that had been completely irresponsible. She could have run across the main road and been hit by a car or a motorbike. The snap-hook was still intact, which meant that, with a sudden jerk, the animal must have broken the ring of the halter, and even if he could find her it would be difficult to catch her and put the bridle back on. "Zara! Zara!" He started to yell her name out though he knew full well that, not being an obedient animal like a dog, she would never have responded to his call.

Amos knew that startled horses usually galloped crazily back to their stables where they hoped to find their oats and a well-earned rest. He clasped his hands and offered a prayer to the good Lord, who until that moment he had completely forgotten, and then he called Gaia, who immediately joined him, blissfully unaware, as fifteen-year-olds are, and felt a sudden sense of irritation at her attitude! "We must run home!" he said, grabbing her by the hand and dragging her away.

When they reached the old mill, Amos, who by this time was quite worn out, stopped and called the owners who lived opposite and had transformed the mill into a chicken farm. The wife came out breathlessly and told him she had seen the mare come galloping past. "She must have seen something cross her path, perhaps a snake or who knows what, because she stopped dead and then, terror-struck, wheeled back and jumped into the meadow here behind the house. My husband tried to catch her, but as soon as he got close to her she would run away, and her halter was broken too. Let's hope she is still there."

"We certainly do hope so," Amos thought to himself and ran with Gaia towards the meadow.

Zara was not there anymore but Amos found her not far away, near the entrance to the farm. She was peacefully feeding from a bucket full of grain which was probably intended for the chickens.

Amos thanked heaven for his good fortune. He approached cautiously and Zara raised her head and looked at him, unsure whether to flee or stay; then she plunged her nose back in the bucket. Amos managed to get both of his arms round her neck and slowly and calmly passed the reins over her head. With some difficulty he also managed to insert the bit and so could finally relax.

That night at dinner Amos had plenty to tell his family about his day. He knew that his adventures would have met with general disapproval for the risks he had unjustifiably run, leaving his horse tied to a bell, but especially allowing a young girl to ride bareback with him. They could have fallen and hurt themselves... quite apart from the gossip they would have given rise to had anyone seen them going towards the house in the woods. It was such an isolated spot, anyone curious could have followed, spied on them, and then blurted everything to Gaia's father...

His family did not hold back their admonishments and really hauled him over the coals this time, but Amos was glad to have unburdened himself as, for someone as extrovert as him, it was always difficult to keep unnecessary secrets.

It was also a good opportunity to talk about Gaia, who by now had found a place in his heart and had begun to fill the void left by Marica.

The next day Amos saddled Zara once again, as though all reproaches had been forgotten, and headed straight to Gaia's house without a moment of hesitation.

He found her waiting outside waiting for him as though they had made a date. She greeted him with the eagerness of a little girl, not yet accomplished in the subtle timing of love, and the mischief of a young woman who has already left every trace of innocence behind. "I knew you would come!" she said smiling. Amos feigned offence and replied, "If you don't like it I can easily turn round and go back."

"I wouldn't be here waiting for you if I didn't like it!" she replied promptly.

"But maybe that's only because you like horses!" he teased, enjoying the flirtation. "No!" retorted Gaia bluntly.

Amos was impressed by her unexpected quick spirit. "OK, then no ride today. I'll go home, unsaddle Zara, and wait for you there. If you want..." and with that he spurred his horse into a gallop and headed home. Gaia immediately followed him on her moped. She helped him to put the tackle away and brush Zara down and then also wanted to lead her back into her stable and feed her a good ration of oats. She was pleased and smiling. She went towards Amos with her arms down by her sides and then stopped in front of him. He drew her towards him and held her tightly, filled with a sudden wave of happiness.

Then he let her go and took a few steps towards the well. He had the look of someone troubled by a dilemma, a doubt needing to be cleared up. "Why does all this make me so unreasonably happy?" He sat on the stone wall and Gaia, coming to sit beside him, provided him with a persuasive answer. "I wasn't born to be alone," he thought, "and how much easier and more pleasant life is when it is shared with someone else!"

This thought filled him with a deep sense of satisfaction and well-being.

Gaia was certainly quite different from his classmates, or from the girls Amos met at the university or at the parties he went to. Gaia had a unique way of dressing, behaving, and expressing herself, and he himself felt distant from her way of life; and yet, her spontaneity, her disarming, natural demeanour and youthful freshness, her way of alternating between calm and impetuousness, and her generosity combined with her headstrong will made her good fun to be with and full of surprises. Although she went to school in the city, Gaia had retained her country ways. She bore no trace of the manners or fashions of the city girls and made no attempt, however awkward or successful, to adopt their language and habits. She remained a flower of the fields, a wild animal, a bird on the wing; she was a free and indomitable spirit more suited to living according to nature than constrained by the dictates of conformism and fashion. That is why she loved horses and treated them as companions on her journey, communicating with them through the silent language of her body and her instinct, and that is why she had been attracted to Amos and had loved him without asking anything of him or of herself. She felt entirely unconstrained by the chains of convention and only gave free rein to what sprang from her heart.

Amos got to know her quickly. He soon learned to love the joy she, better than anyone else, could bring him, but at the same time he was troubled by his inability to impose his own will upon her. He did everything he could to try to convince her that she should belong to him. He tried to make her feel wholly and uniquely his, but there was nothing to be done. Every day Gaia would arrive and depart as though that encounter could be their last. Amos had no certainties. Ideally he would have preferred a woman in love who was jealous, faithful, and morbidly attached to him, like Floria Tosca, whereas instead he felt that he had a free-spirited, young, carefree, and rebellious Carmen on his hands. He tried everything he could think of to win her round to his ways, but there was nothing for it.

One day he did not see her: Gaia had failed to keep their regular afternoon appointment. The following day she passed by to say hello, but she did not stay long and left in rather a rush.

After that Amos didn't see her again for some months, nor did he try to make contact with her himself, having learned from his trusted childhood friend Sergio that she was seeing another boy from the village.

Amos found himself once more without a girlfriend to keep him company and to have by his side when going out with friends.

All his friends had their own girlfriends and were not free to spend all their weekends and holidays with him. He buried himself in his books in the hope that at least in his studies he would be successful, but he found it hard to concentrate. Not even Ettore's cheerful attempts to shake him out of his misery came to anything.

He managed to pass exam subjects that were quite difficult, such as civil procedure, constitutional law, and especially commercial law, for which he had spent ages struggling to better understand concepts such as accrued or deferred assets and liabilities in balance sheets. Ettore, to whom all these things seemed crystal clear, had to employ every ounce of patience to try and help him understand these subjects. He could not understand why Amos should have such difficulty, and he was puzzled and helpless faced with his young student's inexplicable mental contortions until one day he surprised him with one of his old theories.

"There are some brains which are so good at self-persuasion that they even convince themselves that some of the easiest things in the world are actually difficult!" he said. "You know that you have to sit a university exam and imagine that this requires some unimaginably complicated mental constructs. Any young store clerk with a very basic education is capable of understanding what goes under the assets or liabilities in a balance sheet. But who knows what strange mental meanderings you are employing here!"

In any event Amos succeeded in getting over that exam hurdle; he prepared and passed others too, and in the meantime he saw Marica again. He had learned from her that she was free again and so invited her to his house, exactly as he had done when they first met. Marica accepted, and to Amos's great delight, they got back together. He was still in love with her and desired her more than anything in the world, or at least as much as one desires and loves whatever one has lost or does not have.

They began to see each other every day again, as though nothing had ever happened between them. This distracted Amos from his studies just when he was preparing for one of the most important and difficult challenges: the criminal law exam. There would be only one more exam after this before the degree. If it went well, as they all had up to now, he would quickly prepare for the criminal procedure exam, and then he would concentrate on his thesis. But now Marica was complicating matters. He couldn't keep her out of his mind even while he was trying to study.

He decided nevertheless to sit for the exam. He presented himself before the examining committee with his usual mixture of nerves and confidence, but that day things went really badly. After only two questions, which Amos answered in an incomplete way, the professor politely suggested that he should come back at a later date when he was better prepared. Amos rose from his seat in disbelief. It was the first time they had ever sent him away from the examination without having even given him a grade. He felt profoundly humiliated and discouraged.

As soon as he got home he phoned Ettore to tell him and to seek his opinion on the matter. Ettore did not seem at all perturbed. Quite calmly he said he would be coming over at the usual time and that they would start studying for the next exam session.

Amos felt somewhat reassured. He went into his study and sank into contemplation for a while. A sort of self-pity took hold of his heart, but it soon gave way to his tendency to laugh at himself, to the point that, when he thought back to his exam and the way it had all gone, he could hardly stop himself from laughing out loud. He immediately picked up his typewriter and threw down some verses in the local Pisan vernacular. Amused by this exercise he began to put his mind to it seriously, and in no time he had completed the story about his dismal university experience that morning.

When he considered he had finished he read over his work with a certain amused satisfaction. This is how he told his story in light-hearted verse:

My Exam in Criminal Law

Dear Mother of God, I'm desperate here,
you know last night I couldn't sleep for fear,
unable to shift my thoughts from that exam,

as boring and sticky as tarmacadam.
You have no idea yet what I went through,
but I cannot rest till I have told you.
I know you will find it hard to believe me,
and you will be inclined to laugh when you hear me,
but had you been there where I was standing,
then you would realize what I was suffering.
One morning I said to myself, "Let's give it our best,
I want to go and study for that new test."
I went to buy the book: but... what a heavy bore...
it was soon apparent I wasn't up to the chore;
as soon as I had started I began to tire,
I swear to you I would have thrown it on the fire
as from the first page it was clear
for me to say, "I have a major problem here!"
A whole pile of arguments and dissertations,
"But this," I said, "is enough to give me hallucinations!"
Moreover it was all about such extraordinary cases!
Weird tales of thieves, assassins, and tarts in laces!...
But somehow I managed to reach the last page,
ploughing through all the miseries of this age
and one day I decided: "I've had enough,
These things are boring me to death."
So I went up before the examiner.
That old bore drove me to the point of dementia:
he wanted to know the crimes of omission,
and in a crime of malice how you establish intention,
the precedents for statutes of limitation...
My back was beginning to give me aggravation.
I wanted to say, "Look here, I'm not a crim!
Of such things I don't understand a thing!"
But impatiently he said, "Come back another time..."
and I nearly gave him the two-fingered sign.
But I thought better of it pretty quick,
for fear the effects of that might stick!

So now as I told you I am here again,
To face the examiner and watch my tongue!
But if you'd like to know the moral of my explanation
regarding the business of education?
Rather than strive for the university's shield,
better stick to the soil and tend the field!

"What nonsense!" Amos thought to himself. And yet those verses had served a purpose because now he felt better and perhaps more inclined to resume his studies for an exam which was actually one of the more interesting ones. After all, in life it is also important to know how to lose.

"Losing with dignity is harder than winning with humility," he thought to himself and immediately looked for his notes in order to get back to work. About one month later he took and passed the exam, and caught up in a strange obsession which urged him on to finish his studies, he immediately turned his full attention to a manual on criminal procedure. He could hardly believe this was really the last exam. The subject matter only really required learning by rote so Amos prepared the material in a fairly short time and was reasonably confident when he went before the examiners.

After a few questions which he answered quite well the professor then asked him to hand over the little booklet in which he wrote the result and then gave him a small affable smile as he took his leave. Amos practically leapt out of his seat and rushed out of the exam room. Once outside he stopped in the middle of the Sapienza University courtyard and thought for a moment. Had he really got to the end of his finals? Could it be true? "Well, then! There's no time like the present!" he thought and with a friend went up to the first floor study of the professor of philosophy of the law from whom for some time he had been waiting to hear the title of his thesis.

He found him quickly and in a good mood. Amos sat down in front of him and, after a good half an hour, left with the title and promising to work hard to bring the professor something to read very soon. The title he was given for his thesis was "Montesquieu's Thoughts on Natural Law and History".

He took no rest. In fact, the very next day he immediately set himself to his task with the faithful Ettore, who seemed full of enthusiasm. However, after their initial attempts, both of them recognised the practical difficulty of writing anything original and not banal on a subject about which practically everything had already been said.

Amos felt so downhearted that for a moment it even crossed his mind to find someone else to write the thesis on his behalf. He immediately felt ashamed of having entertained such a notion, which would have put his entire university career in jeopardy and rendered it entirely devoid of meaning.

Then he considered going to Paris to seek out some rare text or, perhaps, simply to search for some stimulus and ideas. He decided to pay a visit to Dottor Della Robbia, whom he had not seen for some time. That passionate and brilliant conversationalist had often made reference to French writers in general and to Montesquieu in particular. Perhaps he might come up with some helpful suggestion... As it turned out, in Dottor Della Robbia's library Amos did find essays he had never read and had never found anywhere else. He went home in high spirits and full of good intentions.

However, the task of writing and correcting his thesis was a very long and arduous one. Every thought and every sentence had to be discussed with Ettore, and they had to agree before anything was committed to paper. For Amos, who found that the subject matter was not so interesting to him after all, all this turned out to be very laborious and boring.

In the meantime Marica began to complain that she was feeling neglected. It was true enough that in his free time Amos preferred to go off to the farm and take his horse out for a ride rather than remain closeted up in the house or go out in the car in search of the high life. But Marica would get bored waiting for him in the countryside, where she had spent her entire life and from which she longed to finally get away. So for her, the deep love her boyfriend felt for animals, for nature...his passion for the open air, taking long walks along the river or up into the hills, represented the most negative aspect of his character, like a sort of disease that she was not able to cure. Marica really could not find anything which could explain to her why he should not feel the need to go out and have fun mixing with people and not understand her own desire to go out and get others to know and admire her. Instead Amos did everything he could to try and get her to share his own passions, to involve her in his plans and projects and join him in his dreams...

Meanwhile time was passing. Amos's parents began to display their quite justifiable impatience as they wanted him to graduate, whereas he carried on reading his books, playing his instruments, riding his horses, boring his girlfriend, going to bed late at night, cooking pasta, and emptying bottles of wine in the small hours of the night, while everyone else in the house slept or did their best to try and rest...

When he considered he had reached an appropriate stage Amos went to see the professor, and following a long discussion, he was given a date to present his thesis, on 30th April 1985. It was then the end of January so there were only three months to go.

The news raised his parents' morale but did nothing to help his relationship with Marica. There was something between them that was not working anymore. Amos could feel it but he could not, or perhaps did not want to, understand. Marica had changed towards him: she was more cold and detached than before but her young boyfriend pretended not to notice. It was a problem he preferred to live with, just as one lives with a cavity in one's tooth...until one is forced to deal with it.

It was just before his graduation that Amos learned from a close friend that Marica had been spotted in Milan looking a bit too friendly with her new employer. With that news Amos felt a rush of emotion which burned so much it was almost unbearable. Never before had he suffered so much for love.

He took refuge in his study, and in that quiet room he felt wretched, offended, wounded, defeated, humiliated, and for the first time in a long time, his eyes filled with tears. He clenched his fists and tried to hold them back but his efforts were fruitless. Those tears streaked down his face, which he immediately hid in his hands as he broke down sobbing...

After a few minutes he calmed down, feeling a mixture of shame and pity. He decided to go out to the farm. He had no clear idea of what he intended to do, but he felt the need to do something that was not sensible. It was already late and everyone, apart from his mother, was already in bed. He put on a coat and headed resolutely towards the front door and went out.

Taking deep breaths of that cold, late winter air revived him somewhat. The road was empty and so he could walk unconcerned. He soon reached the rough track that led up to Poggioncino; he made his way up the hill and a few minutes later he was at the farm. He stopped for a moment to catch his breath and then headed for the stables.

A three-year-old gelding Amos had recently started riding stuck his head out of the first stable, greeting him with a lively neigh. He stopped, took the horse's head between his hands, and began to speak into his ear with the gentleness of a parent whispering to his child. Amos's mother, who had heard him leave the house and decided to follow him, found him there like this. Amos was so engrossed in that unusual conversation that his mother realised that something very serious must have happened.

She got out of her car and called him but he did not reply. So she joined him and looked at him inquiringly.

"Leave me alone. Go home!" said Amos without even turning round.

"But what is it? What's happened?"

"Nothing, nothing! Don't worry! Go home!"

His mother said nothing more but she did not leave.

Without saying a word she sat on the low wall in front of the stables and waited patiently for him to say something to her.

"Mamma," said Amos, feeling totally exasperated. "I want to be alone!"

"Why?" said his mother.

"Because I was born to be alone!"

"But it's the first time I've heard you say that. In any case, listen: I am not leaving you here alone without knowing what has happened to you."

Amos resigned himself and went back to the car. His mother followed, and in a few minutes they were back in the house, where his father was waiting. He had got up from his bed when he heard his wife leaving in the car at that hour of night.

Extroverts like Amos always have more trouble disguising their suffering than satisfying the curiosity of whoever wants to know more about it. So, as soon as he was back in the kitchen with his father and mother, in whom he could discern a considerable degree of concern, he fought a hard battle with his sorrow and then decided to speak. "Marica is being unfaithful," he said, "so from tomorrow I will be alone again and it's not easy." Then he suddenly turned and left the room. He flew up the stairs and shut himself in his room. He threw himself onto the bed and his mind flooded with thoughts: everything seemed meaningless and pointless, and the future seemed to offer no hope. To start over again with another girl struck him as inconceivable, impossible, totally beyond anything which might be remotely possible or interesting for him. And yet reason suggested that the opposite was true. He knew perfectly well that, with time, this kind of pain passes and is forgotten.

He tried to transfer these ideas from his brain to his heart, but there was nothing for it; his poor heart beat hard, and he was consumed with an uncontrollable desire for Marica, for her fine, young body, which was probably already someone else's. Perhaps Marica had laughed at him and given herself with all her lust and passion.

He did not know how to distance those thoughts that drove him mad, and he remained awake the whole night until his own body finally suggested a way to alleviate his suffering. Then he felt a little calmer; exhaustion took over and he fell into a deep sleep.

At exactly ten o'clock Ettore's voice calling him jolted Amos awake. He suddenly remembered everything and felt sad and alone, but he dressed quickly and went downstairs with the intention of calling Marica to ask for explanations. A furious conflict raged within him between the rancour he felt at the affront and the hope that his girlfriend might have some valid explanations to remove any reason to suspect her.

So, as soon as Ettore had left, Amos grabbed the telephone and dialled Marica's number. Realizing his agitation she rushed to him and followed him into his study. Behind closed doors Amos tore into her with all the venom that he held inside. But that venom, diluted with feeling and passion, produced no devastating effects on Marica, who had time to plan her defence: she had been to Milan with her boss, she admitted this, but it had been for work reasons which she had not considered important enough to report. As for the overly friendly behaviour she was accused of displaying, she said that she was prepared to meet the scandal-monger in person as she had nothing on her conscience and nothing to fear. Amos tried to believe her.

He felt that he wanted her more than ever, and she knew how to play the role of the loving woman ready to do anything to restore harmony with her man. So she loved him with renewed passion and left him feeling a bit calmer and more reassured.

But alone in his quiet house Amos found the right atmosphere in which to reflect: he sensed that things could not have been exactly the way Marica had described. Knowing that cool-headedness was an essential feature of strength, he reasoned that "time would tell; sooner or later the truth will out. One just has to take things calmly." And then he went back and devoted himself entirely to his thesis.

XXII

Amos was still awake when dawn broke on 30th April. He was busy trying to order his thoughts and endlessly rehearsing the way he would begin his presentation. When he heard the cock crow he realized that he no longer had any time left to sleep, so excited and determined, he decided to get out of bed and began to get ready. He heard noises coming from his parents' bedroom. Listening hard, he realised that his mother was already getting up too, so they went down to the kitchen almost at the same time. In reality, Edi, who affected a facade of Olympian calm, was more excited than her son, and, with the air of one who carries on doing everything as normal, she did and said everything possible to reassure him. Amos sipped a cup of hot coffee; then he locked himself in his study and went over his notes until he heard the sound of Ettore's car. Ettore had arrived, punctual as ever, to take him to Pisa.

In the faculty building Amos immediately bumped into Eugenio, his old school friend who was graduating that day just like him. Amos had said he wanted to be alone for the presentation of the thesis, so Ettore went off for a walk around the city, leaving him with his friend. He wished the boys good luck and left promising to come by again later.

The two students began to pace feverishly up and down along the cloisters until Eugenio's turn came.

The discussion started and Eugenio, who was presenting his graduation thesis on canon law, immediately captured the interest of the normally rather distracted and bored examining committee with a perspicacious disquisition on the law governing the validity of matrimonial consent. Some professors even intervened with personal observations or specific questions so the session went on for a long time, but it allowed the candidate to make a good show and graduate with good marks.

Then it was Amos's turn, who was left to talk about Montesquieu and released after a considerably shorter time. The committee was also quite quick to decide his marks: after having called him back, the chairman, who was also his thesis advisor, informed him, in an expressionless tone, that the examiners had been impressed by his work and were awarding him a degree with marks of ninety-nine out of one hundred and ten.

Amos felt as though he was in a dream. In fact, for a while he feared he might wake up at any moment. But he quickly came back to reality when, having left the exam hall, he was literally assaulted by a small group of photographers asking if they could immortalize him. "Dottore, Dottore!... Can we...? Just one shot...! Fantastic... and another one with the porter... it will be a wonderful souvenir. And obviously one with your friend, Dottore!"

At any other time Amos would certainly have hated that ridiculous farce, but on this occasion he played along, almost enjoying it, as though taking part in a dream which he did not intend to leave behind. In the meantime Ettore had returned and was leaning against one of the columns in the portico, observing the scene from a distance with amusement. He was smoking a cigarette and keeping well out of the way of the photographers and the new graduates.

When the group broke up, Amos and Eugenio joined Ettore. They exchanged a few jokes and then the three of them left together. Eugenio's suggestion that they go and drink a toast was met with general favour.

Back home Amos found the family in a festive mood. His father had decided to take everyone out to dinner at a local restaurant.

Eugenio was invited along too, but Ettore declined the invitation, saying he wanted to go home to his wife. "At dinners one eats too much and then feels unwell all night!" he said laughing. "And then old people should stay at home in the evening!" With this he cordially bid everyone goodbye and left.

Just as they were about to leave the house a car stopped in the yard: it was the florist who had come to deliver a bunch of roses to Amos with a card. Once the florist had gone Amos opened the small envelope. It was a gift from Marica. He put the card in his pocket, placed the roses in his mother's lap, and prepared to go out.

That night, lying in his bed, Amos could not sleep. "It's time to take stock!" he was thinking to himself. "I hope my parents are happy. They have suffered so much on my account. They worried so much about my future that they communicated a sense of anxiety to me. I have not achieved anything yet, this is true, but a law degree is an important achievement, especially for them, who so feared I might be sidelined, left behind by this society in which the winners...those who are most efficient...take all. They, gradually, saw me catch up with the others, achieve things, fight with equal arms, hard, loyally, shoulder to shoulder with the best...and it's not over yet. My poor parents!!! They have put so much trust in me and I will prove to them that it is not misplaced. The day will come when I will make them forget all their fears and they will be proud of me."

Amos was caught up in these thoughts and felt elated. He was unable to relax and sleep eluded him, so he got up, went downstairs, and sat at the piano.

Everyone was asleep but the sound of the piano would not wake them. He was sure of that because he was used to playing at that time, and his parents had become accustomed to it by now. At that moment he felt happy and satisfied. Life seemed to be smiling at him and revealing its best aspects. He opened the window and a breath of spring came into the room, warm and fragrant, like a herald of good things to come. He took a deep breath and began to play once more.

The next day Amos received some bad news: Toledo, the expert from whom he had learned the art of breaking in and training horses, had died. That extraordinary man who was so full of life and energy had been struck down by an incurable disease. He felt a sense of dismay and pain which squeezed his heart. "How can certain people die?" he thought and immediately felt surprised by his own thought. "And how quickly people forget about them! But I will never forget him or any of the things he taught me!" he continued to muse to himself, feeling disturbed and deeply moved. Then he cast his mind back to the days he had spent in the heart of the Maremma region surrounded by horses, with that plain-spoken and simple cowherd who would say whatever he felt in his heart. For about ten days he had got up at five in the morning to join Toledo on the small farm where he would break in the horses, and now it seemed that the world would change without him, because men like that never take things at face value and always leave the mark of their original personalities.

For a few hours Amos forgot all about the events of the previous day. His mind was entirely taken up by memories of his departed friend. He could hear his voice in his ears with his proverbial banter. "The earth can even stop lightning", as he would point out to those who fell from their horses, or "You're not afraid; it's just that you lack a bit of courage!" for those who hesitated when trying to mount a horse.

But just as he is incapable of enjoying anything for very long, so a man will fight and force his will to overcome any pain. So that evening the new graduate allowed himself to be tempted out to have dinner with his friends, and after a few glasses of good red wine, his dark discomfort was transformed into a cherished memory forever enshrined in a special place in his heart.

Over the next few days he took some time off to enjoy himself, even though he kept remembering and being disturbed by thoughts of Toledo's death and also the tragedy which had happened recently at the nuclear plant in Chernobyl. He decided to cut his holidays short in order to get down to something useful.

He called Ettore and, slowly, began to prepare for the state bar exam, and at the same time, he began to work in his aunt's office – the same affectionate aunt with whom he had lived for a long period some years ago. It was here that he began his first work experience as a young aspiring prosecutor.

In his free time, however, he still devoted himself to music. He wrote songs, recorded them, and organised expeditions to Milan or Rome to the offices of the various record companies in the hope of persuading some producer to involve him in a project. He still secretly dreamed of becoming a successful singer. If, for as long as he could remember, everyone had asked him to sing...if in all sorts of different situations, in order not to seem rude, he would find himself having to sit at the piano or pick up the guitar and perform, this must surely mean something. But the record producers never found his compositions interesting and said his style of singing lacked originality. Amos opposed those judgements; he presented animated arguments and defended his position, but he got nowhere, and sometimes his behaviour even made him seem arrogant and condescending. Then he would come home bitter and disappointed, and his parents really suffered to see him so downcast and humiliated. His father Sandro would become withdrawn and would always repeat the same thing, not remotely concerned that he might seem monotonous: all it would take would be one TV appearance on an important programme. He would point to the television, and smiling, he would recite, almost as though speaking from memory, "All you need is to get into that little box over there once and that would do it!" But the doors to the television studios seemed firmly closed to anyone who did not already have a recording contract or who was not already known to the general public.

As a young trainee lawyer Amos would spend his mornings at the magistrate's court and his afternoons studying or writing writs of summons or defence briefs. But in the evenings he would go and play the piano in some local bars, and there he felt more at ease. So basically, although he applied himself and worked hard, time was passing, and he was still unable to decide once and for all which path he should take in life. His parents seemed to him to be increasingly tired and concerned. The young graduate realised that his parents were gritting their teeth and carried on getting up at seven every day to go to work in order to allow him every chance of fulfilling his bizarre dreams, and he felt like the innocent cause of all this. It made him feel guilty and, with time, a growing sense of dissatisfaction.

Do anxieties always precede disasters? Who can say! It is often the case, or at least that's how it seemed to Amos, when, one morning, towards eleven o'clock, he heard the phone ring and ran out of his study to answer it. It was his dear friend Luca, who was calling to talk to him about a very sensitive and urgent matter. He would have liked to meet up but Amos begged him to at least give him a clue as to what was up. He immediately sensed the embarrassment of his friend who, after a moment of hesitation, then decided to tell him that he had seen Marica with his own eyes leaving a house in Tirrenia with a guy who had his arm around her waist. Poor Amos felt the blood rushing to his head and his legs suddenly went weak. He thanked his friend sincerely, put the receiver down, and stood there quite still, with his elbow resting on the little shelf where they kept the telephone. The news had knocked him out once again, but it had not surprised him. After all, he had never really harboured any illusions when it came to his girlfriend's fidelity.

However, this time he knew he really had to end things quickly. He pulled himself up straight, dialled Marica's number, and without wasting time with any unecessary preliminaries, he told her that he now knew everything there was to know about her repeated infidelities. Then he announced his intention to end their relationship once and for all. Marica made no attempt to put up any defence; she only asked to be able to see him one last time, and he did not have the strength to deny her that request.

Marica arrived shortly after that. Amos got into her car, and together they headed over to the farm at Poggioncino and parked the car behind the barn. Even before starting to speak she burst into tears. Between sobs she begged to be forgiven, swearing that she would have been prepared to overlook any future indiscretion on his part, but he remained implacable. "How could you imagine that I would tolerate the idea that you had been with someone else while you were going out with me, visiting my house and my family? Do you think I could stomach the idea of carrying on meeting the friends who know everything about us and playing the part of the..." Here, however, he stopped...unable to countenance having to pronounce that horrible word that caused such mirth whenever it was used about others. There was a long pause; then Amos carried on. "Anyway I don't hold any hard feelings towards you. I am certainly no better than you are. I too have been unfaithful to you. It's happened more than once and not always with the same person. So you see, after all, this relationship was bound to fail!"

"But I am prepared to forgive you everything!" she repeated desperately. "I don't even want to know with whom you have betrayed me!" Amos felt really sorry too, but the sting he felt at the loss of his honour was, at that moment, stronger than the pangs of love.

"Let's not talk about it anymore!" he said. He opened the door and got out of the car.

"If you like we could take a walk down to the river," he suggested, leaning against the roof of the car. Marica dried her eyes, put her handkerchief back in her bag, and got out of the car too. That walk represented her last hope.

Perhaps this is what she was thinking when she linked her arm around his and, taking small steps, began to go down the little path that skirted the woods and led to the large flat meadows.

Soon they would be cutting the grass and Amos's father would be bringing back a large quantity of good hay from this place. At a certain point they stopped and sat down. "But you will leave me Lupo, won't you?" asked Marica, remembering the German shepherd puppy Amos had given her a few months earlier. Sadly

Lupo had had problems with the paws of his hind legs due to hip dysplasia, and Marica had lavished all her energy and love on him to help him get better.

Remembering all of this, Marica repeated her question. "Can I keep him with me?"

"Of course," replied Amos, softening to the point that he immediately had to turn away to hide his feelings. "That way you will remember me whenever you stroke him!" he added. Then, to overcome that moment of weakness, he got up and took some deep breaths.

Marica was sad and pensive. Suddenly she looked up and said, "I'm sure that, without me, everything will go well for you. All roads will open up for you as if by some magic spell, and your dreams will soon come true."

Amos smiled sadly. "Now don't exaggerate!" he said softly, and from that exchange he understood that Marica had finally resigned herself to the situation. At that point he thought that the time had come to say goodbye. "Well, let's go back then," he said. "I would not want them to start looking for me and getting anxious!"

Marica got up too, and they retraced their steps back along the shady path in silence, the woods on their left and the valley to the right, the meadows, the fields, and over there in the distance the stream "la Sterza," which had all but dried up by then. The rustling of a lizard running in the grass caught the attention of Amos, who turned to listen and then lengthened his stride. In the meantime a strange thought came to him. "Perhaps these plants will never see us together again and this for reasons which I don't know whether to define as ones of common morals or of habit: the fact remains that, when a woman is unfaithful to her man, in many cases he loves her and desires her even more than before, and yet he must separate from her for ever if he is not to lose his self-respect and the respect of others. And to think that the rules of morality, human conventions, and traditional customs are things that originate and become entrenched for the good of mankind! Yet it is also true that every society, as a result of its structure and for a thousand other reasons, creates its own rules of morality; then the demands of progress or, more simply, of change, lead the more intelligent, the more sensitive, the more enterprising people to break those rules and pay the consequences. However, with their example, gradually, people end up accepting as normal what only a short time ago they would have judged to be absolutely immoral."

He was so engrossed in these thoughts that he did not realize that he had reached Marica's car, and only when she opened the door to let him get in did he come back to reality. Without saying a word he sat down next to her, closed the door, and just a few minutes later he was alone again in his study. As on other previous occasions, once again he felt sad and lonely. He took a book of music down from the shelf. It was a collection Chopin's nocturnes. He opened it and, having run his index finger along the lines, rested it on the piano. He sat there and tried to find some peace in that music. He was reading the score but the notes were not making musical sense in his mind, which was too occupied with other thoughts, so he got up and started pacing up and down his study. He had confessed his infidelity to Marica, but he realised that he had never considered it as such before then. How curious!

Now, however, he had to force himself to be a scrupulous judge: either his behaviour was innocent, and in that case he had to consider that his ex-girlfriend's behaviour was equally innocent, or he had to feel himself as much to blame as she was. The idea that a woman who gives herself to a man does so only for love while a man is able to separate emotions from sex suddenly seemed to him to be perfectly ridiculous and senseless, although in the past on various occasions he had shared that view. In his life he had known and gone out with girls who thought and behaved exactly like their male peers. So he found himself confused, lost in a sea of ideas from which he could not escape. He felt tired and demotivated, so, as slowly as an old man, he made his way upstairs, shut himself up in his room, threw himself onto his bed, and almost immediately fell asleep.

XXIII

After about an hour or so Amos woke up feeling cold and bad-tempered. He went downstairs to the kitchen, where his parents were talking quietly to each other. He could not quite catch what the exact topic of conversation was, but he had the impression they were talking about him. This depressed him even more and made him feel a strange hostility towards them. So he turned and headed for the living room, switched on the stereo system, and listening to music, began walking up and down, contemplating the idea of going to live alone.

"At my age a man should have his independence," he thought. "He should be free to do what he wants without being under anyone's supervision. There is no need to go too far away. It would be enough to have a space of my own. For example, when I feel the need, I could use one of the two small apartments in Poggioncino that Pa has just finished doing up. And soon the house opposite will be ready too..."

Amos was referring to the house his father had started to prepare for the day when he might get married. However, the work was running behind schedule, to the point that Amos had suspected that his father was deliberately going slowly precisely because he had never considered that Marica was the right woman for him. With just a few concise observations, Sandro had expressed his point of view to his son, and he had never broached the subject again.

Now Amos was forced to recognise his father's admirable far-sightedness. While on the one hand that perspicacity had wounded and offended him, on the other it cemented in him, if ever such a thing had been necessary, the profound respect he felt for him and renewed the feeling, until recently denied, that his father could still protect him from life's dangers – childish feelings that in his moments of dark distress offered Amos a glimmer of hope.

While these feelings agitated his heart, he suddenly felt the need to express them to his father. He ran to his typewriter and almost in one single rush began to put down these words: "There's no point talking about it: we will never agree. And I don't want to raise my hopes: there are thirty years between us! Or perhaps you fear that you may no longer find the strength to be by my side should obstacles get in my way? Don't worry. Listen to me: I will have problems and terrible affronts to bear, but... nothing will make me afraid, nothing will corrupt me, nothing in the world will make me forget that I can win... and I want to make it on my own. I know perfectly well that it is difficult for you to justify this desire to fight, to take on impossible challenges. It may seem incredible to you, but the more I think about it the more I realise that... I really am like you, and you have no idea how I wish that your strength should never leave you! So that I could have you here by my side and never, ever give up!"

Amos would let his father have that strange letter once he had told him about his firm intention to start to use the house on the farm. Moreover, taking advantage of a weekend when the Bardi family had decided to go to Lido di Camaiore, Amos announced that he preferred to stay at home but that he would sleep at Poggioncino in the apartment with the front door giving onto the road. Signor Sandro was not particularly happy about this but did not oppose Amos's wish, so soon, Amos was able to fulfil his plan to live an independent life. His mother, for her part, approved the decision, believing that it would be useful for her son. This would surely help him to more quickly and easily get over the unhappy love affair that had made him suffer and become so different from his normal cheery self. Even before leaving for the beach, she cleaned and organized the apartment, making sure it was equipped with everything that had been lacking and promised to finish the job upon her return.

So began a period during which Amos enjoyed a carefree existence which soon turned into wild living, dissolution, and every kind of excess. Cristiano, a young friend who had only recently started university, would always hang out with him. In the evenings they would go to Chianni together, where Amos would play the piano until midnight. Cristiano would help him to set up and dismantle his instruments, and he would keep the cables in order. Then they would eat dinner with the owner of the club, who was a naturally cheerful and gregarious sort. Dinner would inevitably go on until very late and certainly never ended before the flagon of wine on the table was completely empty. Often others would join the group, and on these occasions Amos would suggest that they all come over and spend the rest of the evening at his house. So in the dead of night the whole gang of layabouts, never lacking some lively female company, would move to that place which, although tiny, had everything one could possibly need: a kitchen in perfect working order, a small bathroom, and two little bedrooms with double, wrought-iron beds. No one could ask for better or for more.

By the time everyone went home to bed it was always past day-break. So it would happen that the men who would spot Amos as they headed off to work in the fields in the morning would enquire of him why he had risen so early. He would laugh and reply that his head had not yet even touched his pillow.

So Amos ended up sleeping very little and often skipping lunch. In the afternoon he would saddle his horses or concentrate on breaking in young horses for his friends or aquaintances, because that risky job that everyone advised him not to do was for him the clearest way of demonstrating all his daring and his ability to overcome impossible challenges. In fact, whenever he mounted a young horse for the first time there would always be a small audience around the training pen, and he would feel like the protagonist. He would overcome his fear, and in trying to do everything Toledo had taught him, down to the tiniest detail, he would feel pleased and proud of himself. Those were his moments of glory. Then he would run back to wash and prepare for the evening – or rather, for the night.

Soon Amos's parents began to worry about his health and, perhaps, also his reputation. His mother saw him looking increasingly pale and tired... and then with all those women buzzing around him she was afraid he might catch some kind of venereal disease or worse... At night they could hardly sleep thinking that their son might be driving around in the car with Cristiano, who was also tired and perhaps a little tight...

But a good star was shining over Amos, and his guardian angel was really generous and diligent. So, he would fall from his horse and not hurt himself; he lived a dissolute life and, in spite of this, nothing serious happened to him... he was effectively a single man of no means and yet everyone seemed to love him...

Adriano, in the meantime, had found a job in a bank. He had got married and had a daughter; even so, every Friday, he would come and visit his friend. Together they would write songs; then they would go into the kitchen and prepare themselves huge plates of pasta carbonara. Amos had learned how to beat the egg and fry the onions with garlic and pancetta or "guanciale", whenever he found it in the larder. The two old friends would talk for hours about life, friendship, love... they talked and understood each other perfectly, drinking the good wine produced in the family vineyard and occasionally indulging in a Tuscan cigar. Amos liked to smoke it all and only threw it away when he could not hold the stub between his fingers anymore. He would draw in the smoke without inhaling and blow it out from his lips, but he found the aroma intoxicating, and it helped to ward off his problems and worries, his fears and disappointments.

The more he smoked and drank the more cheerful and talkative he became. He would talk about himself, his dreams, and the reasons why they did not come true. They were reasons which were rooted in the injustices of the world, in the shameful compromises of people who were prepared to stop at nothing in order to pursue their own interests. When his imagination was fired he would talk in perfectly good faith but without ever questioning himself, never identifying his own inadequacies, his own idleness, his own superficiality. In spite of this Adriano would listen to him, with patience and understanding. He would encourage him and Amos, for his part, who considered his friend to be an honest soul, would feel proud of that respect even though he was sorry not to be able to fulfil their joint ambitions.

The idea had become entrenched in Amos's mind that all record producers were obtuse and incompetent individuals, that the directors of the TV networks were corrupt servants of the establishment operating at the behest of the politicians, and that, as a result, it was almost impossible to pursue a career in music based on the old values of honesty, talent, and determination... So full of his own ideas was he that he did not have the slightest notion of the mediocrity and futility of those thoughts. If only he had stopped to think for a moment, he would have realised that such arguments were typical of those who, whether through lack of ability or idleness, never get to the finishing line first.

However, once Adriano had gone and he was left alone in the house, some doubts would start to gnaw at him, and all the euphoria he had felt moments earlier would dissolve like summer mist surrendering to the baking rays of the sun. Then Amos would go to bed, try to sleep immediately, and in the morning, after splashing his face with cold water, a habit of his from his boarding school days, he would think back to the discussions of the previous evening and feel a sense of embarrassment at the way he had exposed his frustrations, his weaknesses, and the least noble part of his character.

Ettore would still come round to see his young friend every day, bringing some book or other with him. Their reading sessions would always give rise to animated discussions. So even during that period of wild living and excess, Ettore continued to be an especially important point of reference for Amos. Without confronting his impetuous disciple too directly, Ettore advised him every day of the need to be practical and never to abandon himself to vain hopes and elusive dreams. He urged him not to neglect his studies as it was on these that he would really be able to found his plans for his future, and these would certainly not preclude the possibility of pursuing an artistic career if that was what destiny had in store for him...

Amos found this attitude really irritating but he had to submit to reality: once again he had to recognise that Ettore possessed a light of reason superior to his own even if he felt that day by day, month by month, there was growing within him an indefinable sense of rebellion against his seemingly hostile destiny. Something told him not to give up, not to lay down arms, not to let those who did not believe in him, who laughed at his illusions, get their way. So he carried on writing songs, singing, going to auditions, and sending recordings left, right, and centre, in the hope that someone might give him the time of day. And every time he would hear the same reply: that being good was not enough, that what was needed was greater originality, a more well-defined and recognisable personality...

Amos rebelled, argued, and protested, but at the same time he understood that something was not working. There was something that needed to be improved and put right. Around that time he had met a young classical pianist, so he decided to take up his piano studies again with him: it would certainly be useful to expand his musical knowledge.

Carlo, his new teacher, had initially refused the job, thinking that Amos would not have dedicated himself seriously enough to classical studies, which always require discipline and self-sacrifice, but Amos had been so insistent that in the end Carlo decided to give this new teaching experience a try, and he quite soon dispelled his doubts. In fact, the two became good friends and established such an excellent working relationship that it went well beyond the normal one between a teacher and pupil: increasingly often Carlo would sit at the piano and accompany Amos while he sang opera arias, and gradually they found they had an understanding which developed quickly into a solid bond.

At first they had a few problems: Carlo played in a very formal style whereas Amos sang too freely, but after a while they found the way to work in harmony. The fine classical pianist discovered a passion for opera, and soon he was able to accompany Amos in any aria without hesitation. He was an extremely talented sight-reader and would place the score on the piano ledge and play, to the great delight of Amos, who was finally able to put his voice and his performing skill to the test without being influenced by the old recordings which he was accustomed to use as a backing to sing over.

These studies restored his energy and enthusiasm. He bought a trailer which he could load up with all his electronic equipment and attached it to the towbar of his father's Land Rover, and this meant he could go and play anywhere: in local nightspots, but also at country festivals, parties, weddings, in hotels, restaurants, and even in town squares...His father would patiently drive him, and together they would carry the heavy amplifiers, speakers, and keyboards on their shoulders. A little after that, Amos would deal with the cables, but soon it would all be set up and ready. Then he would just have time to mop his brow and freshen up before starting to play and sing for two, three, sometimes even four hours solid. At the end he would always feel content and at peace with himself. It felt to him as though that hard work were somehow suitable compensation for the wild and dissolute times he had indulged in, which nevertheless still worried him at some deeper level of his conscience.

One summer evening Amos went with Cristiano and Mario, a Sardinian friend he had been close to for a long time, to the Boschetto, an open-air nightspot where he loved to play, as he enjoyed being out in the pure, fresh air and liked the lively company there. He quickly set up as usual and immediately got to work.

I wouldn't be able to say which song he was singing when Mario went up to him and interrupted him, suddenly, shaking him by the shoulder. Mario was in particularly high spirits, which for him was quite unusual. He leaned over, and taking care to speak softly to avoid his voice being picked up by the microphone only a few centimetres away, he whispered in his ear. "There are two girls who want to meet you and they're not at all bad looking..." Then he stopped, having spotted out of the corner of his eye that the girls had already reached the steps of the small stage set up for the pianist. Mario signalled to them to come up and introduced them to Amos, who, as often happens on such occasions, failed to even catch their names. He held out his hand, said something kind to them, and promised that soon he would take a break and come and sit with them for a while. The two girls said goodbye and went back to where they had been sitting.

Less than fifteen minutes later, Amos was sitting at a table, smiling happily at his two friends and the two girls he had just met, totally unaware of the changes that meeting was to bring into his life. He soon established that Claudia and Elena were effectively very charming and cheerful girls, both very pretty in their summer dresses which showed off their dark, already sun-tanned skin and all the fresh appeal of their youth. Their innocent candour made them confess to being just seventeen years old. Elena was just starting her last year of secondary school while Claudia, who was at the scientific academy, moaned that she still had to put up with another two years of boring school. He enjoyed listening to their girlish conversations, their suppressed giggles, their clear young voices, and with a certain self-assurance he peppered the conversation with banter, amusing questions, quick observations, or understanding comments on their plans and their ideas... He was enjoying it all so much that he didn't notice that he had gone over his normal break time. The owner came up to his table, took a chair, and sat down beside them.

Amos got the message and immediately got up, but the owner quite amiably asked if he wanted to have another drink before going back for the next set. Then, since Amos declined, he felt obliged to say a few kind words to the girls. "Play something for everyone, but take another break soon and come back to these two … they are well worth it!" And he laughed as he pointed to the girls who, to tell the truth, had taken very little notice of him and actually felt somewhat uncomfortable in his presence.

While Amos played, Mario, who had stayed at the table, made enquiries to try to understand which way the two girls' interests lay. Instead, as soon as he took his next break, Amos expressed a degree of doubt regarding whether it was worth spending so much time with two girls who were so young. They seemed to be chaste and innocent schoolgirls and far too well brought up to have any interest in guys of their age, to say nothing of their reputations. And then they should not forget that Elena's father was a well known lawyer! "We'll end up in jail!" said Amos, laughing to Mario who did not share his point of view at all.

However, in reality Amos too was saying one thing while thinking another … he could hardly wait to go back and sit at that table where, just a short time before, the company of Elena and Claudia – their frankness, their simple, straightforward conversation, their fresh, unmade-up faces – had attracted him the way a glass of cool water attracts someone parched with thirst. But when he left the stage and headed towards the table he had so reluctantly left an hour ago, his path was obstructed by people who wanted to compliment him or ask him to sing their favourite song. Then the owner dragged him over to the bar to introduce him to some other people he was particularly concerned to please. The poor musician was frantic to get away, but he was forced to stay there, courteous as ever, fully conscious of the fact that public relations are always important, in all walks of life.

In the meantime Mario had not given up, and during the questioning he had cheerfully inflicted on his new friends, he sensed that Elena had been particularly struck by Amos, by his voice, but not only that. So he jumped up, ran over to his friend, and excusing himself with those present for his rude intervention, grabbed Amos by the arm. He took him aside, and laughing, he announced in his squeaky voice and pronounced Sardinian accent, "I always told you that when it comes to women you haven't a clue! Not the slightest clue!" Amos smiled, bursting with curiosity, and Mario didn't keep him waiting long. "We're not that old, you know! And I really think that you in particular are in with a good chance!"

Amos invited Claudia and Elena to join them for a trip to the beach the next day. When the group got to the beach in Cecina Amos took Elena by the arm and moved away from the others, talking to her more seriously than the previous evening. He asked her to tell him about herself, about her character and her dreams. Then it was his turn to describe himself, presenting a kind of self-portrait. He talked a lot, and never before then had he felt such a need to describe himself in as honest a way as possible, exaggerating his flaws and playing down his virtues. He sensed that Elena saw him as a strong and brave man. He felt her looking at him and thought that perhaps he was hardly worthy of the sweetness and goodness of her gaze, especially thinking back to the unbridled excesses of his recent past, the unforgivable licentiousness for which he now felt quite ashamed. He felt something inside him was slowly changing.

As the sun was burning their skin they wet their heads and shoulders; then they went back to find some shade, and when they were stretched out on the sand next to each other they realised they were no longer two strangers but two people who were made to live together. Their lips joined together in a kiss that for both of them represented the sweetest promise of happiness and peace, irrespective of their difference in age, their very different life experiences, and the difference in their ways of judging things. Elena was attracted by Amos's maturity, his confidence, and his physical strength. He was touched by her fragility, her fears, her lack of worldliness, and her fresh, innocent laughter. Alongside that young girl, who did not try to protect him or mother him but instead looked to him to be guided, advised, defended, and formed according to an ideal of womanhood that they both seemed to share, Amos, perhaps for the first time, felt himself to be the man that deep down he had always wanted to be.

XXIV

A few days later Elena visited Lajatico for the first time. Amos was so keen to take her to the places which occupied a special place in his heart, which held all the dearest memories of his early years, that he decided to show her round the village immediately, even though the burning afternoon sun of late summer made the stifling air almost unbreathable.

They walked around the square and went into the bar on the corner of Via Garibaldi to refresh themselves with a cool glass of water. At that moment all the eyes of the customers sitting at the little tables to drink or play cards fixed their gaze on Elena, whom no one knew or had ever seen before. Their interest was immediately obvious to her, and it even seemed to her that all those people, who had been speaking loudly moments earlier, suddenly started speaking in hushed tones, but this only lasted a few seconds, and then everything went back to normal.

Amos, while talking to Elena about village life a few moments before, had just referred to the nosiness of people who lived there, and he observed with satisfaction the effect that this insignificant remark had had on his young friend. She drew even closer to him, and her smile seemed to say, "You were right again and I love you also for this, because you are always right! Because you know the world better than anyone else ...!"

Then they went out, and proceeding a little further down Via Garibaldi, they crossed the road and went into a little playground area, where they found an empty bench in the shade of one of the tall evergreen oak trees. They felt terribly hot and tired but were happy to be together there or anywhere else; it really didn't matter.

After a long silence Elena suddenly turned to Amos and said, "I want to stay with you forever!" Amos smiled and kissed her. "So do you want to stay with me this evening, prepare something for dinner for example, and . . . " enquired Amos, to whom at that precise moment the afternoon seemed really too short.

"I wish! But what will I say to my parents?"

"We can figure that out later," he replied, fired up at the thought of spending the whole evening with Elena. At last they would be alone, in his father's big house, and it would be like a small taste of that promise of future happiness they both yearned for and in which they had both now started to believe.

"Go and buy something then. Look, over there in the square there are two grocery stores; you only have to choose . . . " continued Amos, taking out his wallet and handing Elena some money. For a moment she was a little uncertain, but then she made up her mind, rose, and headed slowly towards the square.

Alone once more Amos stretched out on the bench, resting his head on one arm. He closed his eyes and abandoned himself to a state of torpor in which reality and fantasy began to blend and become confused, contending for dominion of his mind. Following Elena in his thoughts he saw her walking, looking around, exchanging looks with people, blushing a little from embarrassment, getting flustered, and then looking for the shop. But suddenly he heard her voice calling out to him, so he got up and immediately went to join her and accompanied her to the entrance to the store.

"I'll wait for you here," he said, leaing against the door with his hands behind his back. Inside at last Elena stopped in the middle of the shop to look around and order her thoughts. Perhaps it was the first time she had gone on an errand by herself without having been given instructions by her mother.

Amos was thinking about this when the girl from before came rushing out of the shop. It was Carla, a student from a local hamlet just outside the village. She was a bright and forthright girl with whom he had had a short fling. Amos had ended it about a month before, having begun to suspect that she had been more interested in what he had than in him. He had nothing against her now other than the fact that she had been a little rude towards Elena.

A few minutes later the glass door of the shop opened again and Gaia came out holding a bag full of food. Gaia, who was coming towards him, passed by in front of him, greeting him in a distracted fashion, and then moved away.

Amos was lost in thought when, from inside the little supermarket, he heard a female voice complaining in a loud and irritated tone. "Excuse me, but I put this aside for myself! I'm sorry, but you will have to get another one!" That Emilian accent was unmistakable! Could it really be her? Amos had recognised yet another of his old flames, a girl he had gone out with for a whole summer. She had revealed herself to be so false and opportunistic that he had been left with a sense of deep disgust and bitterness. What was she doing back in Lajatico? Could she possibly want something from him, or did she have it in for Elena who had timidly apologised and given her back whatever it was? While he was pondering these questions the ex-girlfriend from Emilia also came out and left without so much as dignifying him with a glance. "Just as well!" thought Amos.

Then he went into the shop and was greeted cheerfully by the cashier, who immediately called out to Elena, "Look, miss, I think someone is looking for you." Elena turned round and went towards Amos, but in the meantime another familiar voice made him start. It was Marica, who said a quick hello to him as she too made her way out with a load of shopping.

"How odd," he thought to himself. "What are they all doing here together?" Elena was coming up to him holding a little bag in which she had arranged three small sausages. "They were the last ones," she said. "There was a girl in front of me who bought all the others. These were the only ones left. They were there all alone waiting for someone to buy them too so I did. They were the smallest but they might be the best ones! Right?" Amos smiled tenderly and stroked her long hair that fell softly over her shoulders. "I'm just going to look for something else," she added. "I won't be long, just wait for me here." She headed off towards a counter where a short, middle-aged shop assistant, of thin and somewhat sickly aspect, busied herself, nervously slicing bread and arranging perfect displays of pieces of focaccia and triangles of schiacciata with delicious prosciutto ham. Elena asked for some of that ham, and the woman wrapped five or six slices for her, but when she came back to Amos Elena seemed sad. "What's the matter?" he asked. And she replied softly and rather sulkily, "The lady there at the counter gave me ham which was really fatty which a girl before me had refused. But I..." Amos felt such joy and tenderness that his heart wanted to burst. He wanted to console her, to explain that the ham with fat on it was by far the best sort, but he did not know how. "Where does such sweetness come from?" he asked himself. "How can I avoid contaminating such rare innocence? I will marry her, stay close to her, and do everything I can for her so that she will be happy to be by my side and proud of me."

He was thrilled and full of good feelings... but suddenly something happened that rudely interrupted the flow of his happy thoughts: a strange heat on his face suddenly jolted him out of his slumber. Had he really fallen so fast asleep as to have had that peculiar dream?

It was really so and he could hardly believe it. Elena had come back and, finding him asleep, had covered his face with her hands as a joke as she had the habit of doing when Amos didn't seem in a good enough mood, because she knew that her hands had the power to bring a smile back to his face. Elena had immediately lifted her hands to check if he had woken and, leaning over, had pressed her lips to his. That kiss, which put an end to Amos's

dream-induced escapades, had also sealed a secret, unconscious –
but no less binding – proposal. As sometimes happens, that dream
had cast light on everything he felt about his young love which up
till that moment Amos had only understood at an unconscious
level. Bringing together facts, sensations, past and recent experiences,
beliefs, emotions, pleasant and painful memories, and all manner
of other things, that dream had in a certain way brought clarity
into the heart and mind of Amos, who, in effect, did not change
his view when he was fully awake. "I will marry her," he thought
to himself, with the determination of one who decides to take a
vow, and in his heart he felt happy.

That night at dinner Amos thought about his dream again.
Compared to the girls he had known up till then, some of whom
had appeared to him in his sleep like images from an old movie
reel, Elena was undoubtedly the truest, the sweetest, the most in
love, the closest to his ideal companion. Then, as often happens to
those who feel disturbed by a dream, Amos spent that evening as
though it were a continuation of the dream itself and chose that
very occasion to hold Elena in his arms and quite spontaneously,
for the first time, say, "I love you!"

Some days later, sitting on the stool at his keyboards with all his
other electronic gadgetry, Amos played and felt unaccountably sad.
That evening his parents and Elena had come out with him, but
the place seemed to him like a squalid shed, and the bad weather
which raged outside plunged him into a really foul mood. But
perhaps there was another deeper and more serious reason, an
unresolved question which caused Amos such profound unease:
what would happen to him and the family he would soon create if he
did not get down to something better and more secure than the
precarious job he had playing keyboard at the piano bar which,
when all was said and done, provided neither satisfaction nor reasonable assurances for the future? These uncertainties, which he thought
he could also discern increasingly clearly in his parents, made him
suffer and caused him to feel gloomy and hypochondriacal. He
played and sang melancholy songs and could not wait to finish.

Elena, who sat at the table with her future in-laws, unable to take her eyes off him, noticed his disquiet. She left the table and went to sit next to him. Amos stopped singing, and while he continued to play on absent-mindedly, he began to speak to her and make plans for the future, so that, almost without realising what he was doing, he asked her if she felt ready for marriage. Elena was surprised and happy at the same time, so happy that from that moment her youthful enthusiasm knew no bounds.

But the more Elena's enthusiasm and longing to put on that bridal gown and start a new life grew, the more Amos's doubts worried and oppressed him. His doubts had nothing to do with her but with his own capacity to provide for his new family, ensuring its independence and happiness. True enough, Elena was sensible and full of good will and seemed to be prepared to make sacrifices, but he did not want to run the risk of jeopardising their relationship as a result of financial problems or, worse still, his own inability to find fulfilment with a steady and satisfying job. He would start a family only when he was certain he had the material, as well as the emotional, resources to do so without having to depend on his father, which for him would have been the worst form of humiliation.

He decided to speak to Elena about all these things, but she either did not or did not want to understand. On the other hand, a woman in love is drawn to marriage like a weight is pulled towards the ground by the force of gravity. Amos, who had already got the measure of these things indirectly, was now experiencing them himself. So it was that Elena's attitude, undoubtedly in some ways justifiable, but which Amos saw as a lack of understanding, became the first and only source of fierce arguments between them, and this made him suffer more and more every time they occurred. Elena would always provoke him in the same way, repeating the same thing which always made him laugh even when he was trying to be serious: "But when will we be together properly?!" And he would try to defend himself from her melancholy, sing-song entreaty, saying, "Here we go! Now don't you start all that again, I beg you!"

But she would start to set out her ideas as if she had never even heard him, heatedly and with a determination that never failed to astound him.

A whole year went by this way. Elena passed her school exams without particular praise or blame, and soon afterwards, in order to have something to do, she decided to help her sister, who had recently set up a small jewellery workshop where she designed and made her own original pieces.

In just a short time Elena learned how to design her own pieces of jewellery and how to work with precious metals, using the lathe, the drill, the draw-plate, and the laminator to lay out and bend very fine sheets of gold and silver. These were all jobs which, while they made her very tired, really testing her patience and her will, also gave her a sense of satisfaction and pleasure which, most importantly, allowed her to oppose Amos's incomprehensible and incurable sense of uncertainty in the future, which he always used to explain his reluctance to get married. "I have a job. If things should not turn out the way you hope," she would often say, "then we will make do with whatever I can earn. Why are you so worried?"

But Amos was trying to buy time and, meanwhile, doing everything he could in the hope of somehow creating an opportunity for himself, whatever that might be. By now he did not hold too many expectations. Elena was determined to get married and he was beginning to sense a certain unease in his relationship with his parents, who would increasingly plague him with admonitions, advice, superfluous attentions, and warnings with every passing day. So Amos felt the need to make a life of his own, to forge his own path. He felt an unease which did not arouse concern in him as he considered it to be normal. However, one day, after a family argument which had been slightly more heated than usual, he suddenly went quiet and said to his parents, "Once you are a man, you will depart from your father and your mother." Then he moved away, with the self-satisfied air of a judge who has just pronounced a verdict of which he feels particularly proud, or of an oracle who has just revealed the most momentous prophecy.

Amos's life continued, as monotonous and peaceful as ever, notwithstanding his ever more frequent but vain attempts to persuade any recording company to make a serious undertaking to back a project in which he firmly believed. If, since his childhood, everyone had always begged him to sing and he, shy and reserved as he was, had tried to get out of these situations only to eventually give in and become gradually convinced that it was his destiny, then why should it be that the professionals should now be untouched by his singing, by his performance, by that emotion which usually affected everyone else? If they would only have a little faith in him he would have given all of himself to the task, and the results would have surprised them.

Amos was sure of this but he kept on hearing the same thing every time: he sang well, he was good, but this wasn't enough; there was nothing new in what he was doing, the market was going through a bad time, and there was a real need for a wind of change, so what they needed was something more original and modern. This would be accompanied by a sort of judgement, from which he could not escape, and he submitted with the resignation of one who is well accustomed to being overruled, advised, disappointed, as though everyone were naturally more able than he at finding solutions to his problems, at identifying and eliminating the causes of his failures, at moving risks and difficulties away from him. Nonetheless Amos knew that he was not the sort to be easily discouraged. He remembered how as a child he had refused the small toboggan and insisted that he should be put on skis, to the horror or embarassment of his parents and friends; he remembered how he had persuaded his friend Sergio to pedal behind him on the tandem which his father had given him; he remembered how he had ridden difficult horses, in spite of all the recommendations from the so-called experts who, when he would jump down from the horse, would shake their heads with the air of those who know it all and, claiming to want to prudently avoid accidents, would urge him not to ride that animal considered by them to be too highly strung for a less able horseman than themselves. Amos also remembered the day his parents had tried to dissuade him from going skating with his brother, when, in spite of every reasonable concern for his safety, everything went fine for him while Alberto instead had fallen and broken his arm.

He remembered these and many other things which had taught him that "the only thing to fear is fear itself" and "where there's a will there's a way". He was sure he had nothing to fear and felt full of good will and faith in the future. He knew that nothing comes of its own accord, without commitment and a stroke of luck, but he felt ready for any sacrifice and any risk. In his life he had overcome apparently insurmountable obstacles whenever he had been given the opportunity to try. Now, however, he was being blocked on precisely the path that he had always been encouraged to take. It seemed he was not even to consider the world of opera, due to the many problems associated with the fact that he could not see scenes, movements, the conductor's baton, or gestures made by the actors: all of which were apparently insurmountable problems. But Amos sensed that all this could also be faced and overcome. He knew that living in the idea meant considering everything which seems impossible possible ... But who would have joined him in such an endeavour? Who would have been prepared to take such a risk along with him for the sole purpose of proving that nothing is impossible in this world and where there is a will there really is a way? No-one!

With the usual patronising concern, that attitude with which Amos was by now so familiar, everyone would advise him against pursuing his goal, and he was beginning to feel very pessimistic about his chances of winning this battle. On the other hand, he had already learned for himself how pointless and painful it is to embark on battles which are already lost.

Perhaps this was the main reason why until then no better results seemed to be forthcoming from his repeated sorties into the world of pop.

XXV

Despite the fact that, one by one, his dreams were all going up in smoke, Amos continued to strive to achieve his goals. And yet something inside him was changing.

He had enrolled in a post-graduate course in order to take the state law exam and, in his free time, was still recording songs, sending off tapes, and singing in the local bars. In the meantime the competition was becoming increasingly fierce and also cheaper, especially with the advent of computers and synthesizers, which supplied a backing track over which the musicians could just sing along.

Amos was perfectly aware that he could not rely on that sort of work and knew that time was not on his side. He was no longer twenty years old and could not live in a dream-world. However, instead of feeling exasperated, defeated, or at the very least, seriously worried, a calm serenity and a new energy made him feel stronger every day. The idea of doing everything possible and using all his strength to try to improve himself through study and daily work made him feel at peace with his conscience.

Ettore would often say "after the rain the sun always shines", and there was something inexplicable and mysterious upon which Amos based a firm belief that sometime soon a ray of sunlight would appear from under the clouds for him. In the meantime he greeted the success achieved by others with sincere admiration, even in the musical field, and laughed at those who attempted to belittle others' achievements out of a misguided concern that they might hurt his own feelings as a failed and struggling artist.

So life seemed to him simpler and more beautiful. He felt lighter and freer, more open, positive, and clearer in his thinking. Considering his songs with greater objectivity he realized that in effect they did lack a certain originality and perhaps also some force. They were the work of an industrious writer, musically and grammatically correct, let's say, but nothing more. And then his singing lacked something. It could be considered pleasant enough in tone and timbre, but there was some evidence of strain, some tension that in the end left him feeling dissatisfied.

What should he do then? One day, having completed his work, the piano tuner invited Amos to try out the piano. He sat down and played a few scales and arpeggios. Then after having modulated to B-flat major he started to play Schubert's "Ave Maria". Fearing the difficulty of the left hand part to which the score assigned all the accompaniment, when he reached the last chords of the introduction he decided to let his voice take up the singing line. The piano tuner rested his elbows on the piano and listened in rapt silence.

At the end of the piece Amos sprang off the stool and, smiling, praised the piano tuner for his work; then he invited the young man to put his tools away and follow him into the kitchen for a cup of coffee. The tuner seemed pensive. Could he perhaps be struggling to think of something polite to say about his playing? Amos would have liked to spare him the embarrassment, but instead the tuner came up to him and said, "Please excuse my directness, but I feel it my duty to say that with your voice you could really achieve some great results if you put yourself in the hands of a good singing teacher."

Amos was very surprised. It was years since anyone had talked to him about singing lessons. Since he had given up the idea of a career in the theatre even he had stopped thinking about finding a singing teacher. Now, however, that unexpected advice, which struck him as very honest and sincere, made him reflect.

"I know an excellent teacher," he continued, "an elderly retired teacher, who just recently came back to live in his home city of Prato. He spent his life working with the greatest singers of the last fifty years and now gives private lessons.

"If you like I can take you to meet him, since I have to go and tune his piano." Amos said nothing. "Think about it," concluded the tuner. Amos was pacing up and down the room. He suddenly stopped and said, "If you will stay for lunch we can talk about it."

"OK, I'll stay."

A few days later Amos and his mother went to Prato. They parked in Piazza Mercatale and walked towards the Piazza del Duomo. Just a few steps away from the church on their right Amos held his mother back by the arm, struck by strains of beautiful music which he recognized as Albinoni's famous Adagio. But Signora Bardi was in a hurry. It was just before Christmas, and she was worried about the cold and the blasts of icy wind which whipped their faces. They crossed the Piazza and went down Via Magnolfi, keeping to the left, and soon found Maestro Bettarini's house. They went up four flights of stairs and rang the doorbell. A kind lady welcomed them. She was dressed simply but tastefully. She was the maestro's wife. Later Amos learned she had been an opera singer and that now she assisted her husband with the singing lessons.

After introductions and the usual courtesies, the guests were shown into the study. This was a fairly large room with a grand piano in the centre, some sofas, a beautiful desk covered in papers, shelves weighed down with books and scores, and a partition on which were displayed some objects in bronze and silver: a centaur, a chimera, and other mythological creatures to which, to be honest, Amos never really paid much attention.

When Amos went into the study the singing teacher rose from his armchair in quite a spritely way and held out his hand; then, with a slight bow, he introduced himself to Signora Bardi. He was a tall, thin old man whose features still retained the traces of the good looks of his younger days.

Amos briefly explained the reasons for his visit, also hinting at the hopes he held for the future. The maestro listened to him patiently and then sat at the piano. "What do you want to sing for us?" he asked. Amos pretended to think for a moment and then replied, "The aria from *Tosca*. Will that be OK?"

"Which one exactly?" enquired the maestro, smiling indulgently at the insufficient information.

"The second one, that is to say the last one," Amos added quickly, and the maestro, without even seeking out the score, began to play those famous notes which Puccini had written for the clarinet.

Amos sang that aria as well as he could. In any event he gave it his all, and after the last chord, he leaned on the piano, aware of his own agitation in the knowledge that he was now to be judged. In those brief moments he realised that he would finally hear an honest, expert, and perhaps definitive opinion of his voice. If that opinion proved to be a negative one, he decided that he would put his mind at peace. At last now someone would tell him the truth.

The maestro adopted a serious expression and began to speak in the solemn, portentous tone some men use when they pronounce judgements, verdicts, or deliver counsel in situations where it is especially awaited. "You have a voice of gold, my son!" he began. "But," and then he paused for a long time before continuing... "but you do the exact opposite of what you should do when singing. Proper study would not only enhance the quality of your performance, but it would completely eliminate the strain. Your voice would be strengthened and, in short, it would allow you to sing well. In fact, and here I must speak to you quite frankly, what you do now may be impressive to the untrained ear, but to an expert ear the flaws are all too evident..."

Amos listened attentively. No one had ever spoken to him this way before. "So much for that!" he thought, but on the other hand, he had no choice. Basically what the maestro was trying to tell him was that this would not do but there was a way to make it work if he only wanted it to. "And I want to!" he thought to himself.

With her usual efficiency and enterprising spirit, Signora Bardi, who had, in her own way, reached the same conclusions about her son, immediately settled the practical details such as the cost and times of lessons, and then, satisfied that she had made the right decision, she bid goodbye and they left. In the days that followed Amos learned for the first time about the correct way of breathing, about "support", the use of the diaphragm, the various vocal techniques such as "legato", voice placement, colouring, turns, resonance, and a thousand other things that opened up vast, new horizons. But Amos was in a hurry and the maestro reproached him for wanting to rush things. He warned him of the risks associated with an incorrect use of the voice as well its overuse or a bad choice of repertoire. Gradually he introduced him to a world which on the one hand fascinated him, by drawing him back in time to the unforgettable emotions of his early childhood experiences, but on the other hand made him feel intimidated and frightened.

Like a teenager falling in love for the first time, Amos longed to throw himself into this experience with abandon, but he hardly dared believe it was real. He tried his best but at first it just would not come naturally. It took a while before he could sing without hunching his shoulders and straining all the muscles in his neck while holding his head quite still. Even once he had achieved these goals he realized that he had only just taken the first steps. The greater part of the work still lay ahead of him.

The study of singing also imposed a new way of life on Amos. Determined to go the full distance he stopped drinking his father's good wine and adopted a strict diet just like an athlete. As a result he felt better, more fit, and energetic in both mind and body.

There was one last sacrifice yet to be faced, which would be the most difficult for him to bear, and he had therefore decided to put it off for the moment: that of maintaining absolute silence on the days when he performed. This was something Amos had heard about but had always considered to be one of the many myths surrounding the lives of the most famous opera singers. Eventually, however, he would acquiesce meekly also to this kind of punishment, in order to be absolutely certain of doing everything possible for his voice – the voice that with every passing day became increasingly crucial as the one thing upon which he pinned all his hopes for the future.

His moods now became closely dependent on the state of his voice: moments of exhilaration would alternate with others of alarm or discouragement.

When he sang too much and lost his voice he would immediately be gripped by a dark fear which would torment him. He would be riven by doubts and fall prey to a sense of gloomy foreboding and gnawing regret.

He had no intention of becoming one of the many deluded deadbeats. These not-so-innocent victims of their own dreams, suffering from a dangerously overblown estimation of themselves and their artistic talents, so often ended up ruining their own lives as well as those of the people close to them.

But then everything would be fine again because, after a suitable period of rest, his voice would regain its sparkle and flexibility, and Amos's spirits would rise once more.

One day, as he was leaving the house to go to his singing class, Amos met his father at the door. He said, "Just bear with me for a little while longer, Father! I promise you this will be my last try." Then in the car he began to think about the possibility of doing some sort of vocational training to be able to work, perhaps as a masseur, or of trying to apply for a job as a switchboard operator in a bank or an office of any sort. He would turn his hand to anything, as long as he could find an occupation which would provide him with a living so that he would no longer have to be a burden on his parents.

But late one evening a short phone call reawakened all his old hopes. A recording studio in Modena, where he had worked some time ago on a project that he had devised and financed himself, was now contacting him urgently to ask if he would go there to sing with a famous Italian artist. It was for a new song, a duet to be sung by a tenor and a rock star.

It was only a demo but it would be heard by key people in the record industry, and if the project went well, who knows, perhaps Amos might be invited to perform the piece in concert and finally have the opportunity to be seen by those who counted in the music world.

The next morning Amos left early for Modena. With him were his mother, who was always there with him at such times, and Pierpaolo, a young friend who had been helping him for a while now in the modest recording studio of his own that Amos had set up at home.

In Modena he was welcomed kindly and invited into a small office. He immediately became aware of a great flurry of excitement. Everyone going in and out of the place was talking in agitated whispers about the work that was going on in the heart of the studio where some of the most important musicians in the world, under the direction of one of the artists who enjoyed most public acclaim, were cutting an album which was destined for huge international success. Amos allowed himself to be caught up in that extraordinary atmosphere, where everything seemed secret and wonderful. In order to appear active and full of enthusiasm, he asked the first person he came across for the score of the piece he was to sing so that he could study it before finding himself at the microphone. He felt a bit nervous but happy. It seemed as though he were living a dream.

The guy he had addressed smiled kindly. "I don't think there is a score, but don't worry, in a while he will be here in person and he will teach it to you."

If truth be told Amos was somewhat taken aback at this, but he had neither the time nor the inclination to dwell on things too much just then. In the meantime someone had brought him some coffee and struck up a lively conversation, during which no one could hide their enthusiasm and excitement. Signora Bardi urged everyone to be calm, but it was perfectly clear that she was the most anxious and excited of all. She who had always hoped, she who more than anyone had always believed in her son's unique qualities and had helped him to fulfil his dreams, she who more than anyone else had suffered anguish at his failures and the long time that had passed without bringing Amos any rewards for his efforts. Well, now she was the one urging others to be calm without being able to provide the slightest example of it herself.

Suddenly someone knocked at the door which swung open, and a male voice with a marked local Emilian accent announced rather solemnly, "He's coming!"

Amos heard footsteps behind him. The young man at the door moved aside and three or four people came in. Zucchero, the best known and loved Italian rock artist in the whole world, was one of them.

Pierpaolo squeezed Amos's arm and whispered, "We've arrived!" Everything then happened so quickly and easily. Amos sang with gusto and passion, and then he thanked everyone, bade them farewell, and was free to leave.

On the way home Amos and his two travel companions dreamed about what could turn out to be the most thrilling developments following that extraordinary experience. Amos didn't believe any of the things either he or the others said, but he pretended to believe it all. In fact, he had to really force himself to believe it, as up till then he had experienced so many disappointments and frustrations...

He couldn't wait to get home and tell his father all about it. His dear father, who was so quiet and reserved but who would have given anything to help his son's dreams come true.

Amos received no news about the demo for several days, and he made a huge effort to remain calm and relaxed and not to raise his expectations too much. In reality his anxiety was becoming increasingly evident with each day that passed. Was it possible that no one should have noticed him even on that occasion? But one afternoon, just as he was putting on his bathrobe after a hot shower, he was startled by the sound of the phone ringing. He stopped to listen and heard the voice of his dear old grandmother who, with the uncertain tone of someone unsure of having heard properly, was saying, "I'll get him right away. Please wait a moment!" Then he heard her call out for him and he raced to the phone. It was a voice he had never heard before of a man with an unmistakably Bolognese accent who courteously introduced himself. "My name is Michele," he said simply, without further explanation. After all, what need was there of any more than this? In the last few days Amos had heard a lot of talk about him, and he immediately recognized that this was the famed Michele Torpedine, who managed a number of artists including Zucchero. Then, with a gravity which Amos could not figure out at the time, the man on the other end of the phone said, "I wanted to know, and it is extremely important that you answer me in the full certainty of what you say... I wanted to know if you are totally free from any contractual obligations."

Amos promptly replied that he was.

"In that case," said Michele, "I recommend that you do not sign any contract of any kind before my return, before we meet. Probably something has stirred in the heavens and your star is in the ascendant!" Amos was impatient to know more and tried more than once to interrupt that friendly stranger who was talking to him from Philadelphia on the other side of the ocean and who, although he was so far away, seemed so close. Without giving Amos a chance to interrupt, and cascading words so fast that at times the conversation became unintelligible, Michele explained to him that he had had a meeting with the most famous tenor of our times, Maestro Pavarotti, who was a living legend for Amos as he was for so many opera lovers. It seemed that the maestro, having listened to the voice of the young Tuscan tenor with great interest, had expressed a very positive opinion of what he heard, and in fact, Michele continued, he had initially been reluctant to believe the story that Amos was a simple, unknown piano player from a provincial bar. He had almost become angry with Michele, thinking he was being made fun of...as if he would not be able to distinguish better than anyone else a good tenor from an ordinary voice...Michele said other things too but Amos did not even hear them. At the end of the conversation Amos said goodbye and thanked him warmly; then, with his heart in his mouth, he rushed downstairs to tell his parents the good news. He found his mother with Elena in the garden, quietly busy.

He told them everything in a great rush, bursting over with happiness. Then, desperate to share his joy, he said to Elena, "And if things really turn out this way, then you can start to think of a date for our wedding!"

Hearing those words, the two women, who till then had listened to him almost distractedly while they continued with their work, both stopped at once. Each of them had different feelings and concerns. His mother asked him detailed questions about his telephone conversation with Michele, the éminence grise who had been the topic of so much conversation in the Bardi household over the last few days. In her mind this was a man upon whom the whole of Amos's musical career might depend.

Elena instead listened to the conversation as though lost in thought and then timidly shifted the focus of the discussion onto what might happen next, enquiring with great delicacy to know which, in Amos's view, might be the best time of year for their wedding. Amos remained non-committal. Suddenly he felt like a horseman who has just loosened the reins to give his horse his head and allow him to approach a jump in the most natural way.

He was aware of the danger involved in going back on that decision, but like a nervous horseman, he was unable to spur the horse on with the appropriate encouragements: with his heels, his voice, and the participation of his whole body which also included the mind...

But a good intelligent horse that is not afraid of obstacles already knows what to do. So, that evening, Elena won over Amos's resistance, and together they decided that 27th June the following year would be the date of their wedding.

XXVI

The next few months were frantically busy, what with the preparations for the wedding and the building work to restore the family's old Tuscan farmhouse for the newlyweds. In the meantime Amos was also busy attending singing and piano classes and making vain attempts to meet up with Michele to try and firm up an agreement which would have represented the start of his career.

But Michele was unreachable. Like an eel he managed to slip Amos's grasp every time he thought he had tracked him down. If he asked for him at the office his secretaries would reply that he was out or in a meeting. If he dared to try and get hold of him on his mobile phone, which was only very rarely, and he actually replied, invariably the signal would fail or Michele would say that he was busy and promise to call back in five minutes... in which case Amos would be left anxiously waiting for the rest of the afternoon. Afterwards, feeling dejected and mortified, he would try to think up some plausible explanation for Michele's neglect, a hard thing for him to do, being totally uninitiated in the rules of the entertainment business managers' game.

It was quite a difficult period for Amos, but at least he had a concrete hope to cling to.

However, the day of the wedding was fast approaching, and his anxieties regarding how he would be able to provide for his new family were mounting up and making him irritable. So he agreed to sing at a concert organized especially for him in a small but delightful theatre in a village close to his home. Carlo would accompany him on the piano. It would be Amos's first real operatic concert. He knew the risks. His singing teacher had strongly cautioned him against it, but he felt a need to put himself to the test and to give purpose and meaning to his life.

Once he was in the dressing room, he felt gripped by a sense of panic for the first time. He would have liked to have fled, to have feigned some indisposition or perhaps to be genuinely unwell, in order to escape this obligation. But now everything was ready. The little theatre was sold out, packed with music fans from the neighbouring areas who were always keen to hear tenor voices, these being such a rarity these days. So Amos took a deep breath and plucked up courage.

He sang – or more correctly shouted – with the fullest voice he could muster, so that, towards the end of the concert, he felt as though he hardly had any voice left. However, he gave it his all and the ordeal finally came to an end.

He went back to his dressing room and sat quietly, unaware of what was to follow, a very painful experience to which, when he thought about it afterwards, he realized he would have to become accustomed. There was a knock at the door. Carlo, who was with him, went to open up and in no time that tiny room was full of people. Some silently squeezed his hand and left; others seemed to Amos to be burbling about everything and nothing. One rather surly fellow, of middle age and middle height, approached him and asked, "How would you judge your performance?"

The sarcastic tone of this question prompted a prudent response from Amos. "That is not for me to judge but rather for those who sit in the audience and listen!" The man clapped him on the shoulder and said, "Study long and hard before you sing in public, otherwise you will ruin your career!"

An expression of pain and humiliation crossed the face of Amos, who nonetheless had the presence of mind to respond, saying, "I'll follow your advice."

Then in the muddle of his thoughts and feelings he heard a voice saying, "Yet the timbre is very beautiful!" It was the president of an association of music lovers from a nearby town. Had he just wanted to say a few words to console him, or was he expressing his honest opinion? Amos gave himself no peace. Once more he was assailed by doubts, and he felt as miserable as a dog beaten by his own master. "Back to the drawing board!" he thought as he went home. In effect he did have to go back and rethink his plan. That small step was to serve as a warning to him: the path he hoped to take was not going to be either easy or happy. It would be incredibly difficult and fraught with pitfalls, disappointments, and constant conflicting pressures originating from inextricable tangles of commercial and self-interest...

But Amos left that painful experience behind him, and the next day he was back on track. His singing master gave him a stern admonishment too, even threatening to stop teaching him if ever he were to make such a mistake again. Amos promised to be more careful and take care not to put his future at stake.

In the meantime he increased the frequency of his practice sessions with Carlo, with whom he improved his piano technique and exercised his voice. Carlo was a little younger than Amos. He loved his work and above all he loved music, for which he clearly had a notable talent. He had grown attached to Amos, and over time, they discovered that, as well as their passion for art in general, they shared many other things in common: they both loved good food and wine, sports, and good company. Equally neither of them smoked or gambled, nor were they attracted by the false promises of drugs or other such illusory temptations. Instead they both loved life, and together, they lived it to the full while things in general went pretty smoothly. If what Amos and Carlo shared was not yet properly a friendship, it was certainly what could be defined as a rare form of affinity. They understood each other instantly and always found each other in agreement, never having to resort to compromises to make, as they say, a virtue out of necessity. Time would eventually show them how true the words are of the proverb that says "he who finds a friend finds a treasure".

Thanks to Carlo's enthusiasm and patience, Amos made rapid progress with the piano, by far surpassing his teacher's most optimistic expectations. He studied with such determination that he surprised even himself, oblivious of the fact that all that determination stemmed from an unconscious desperation mixed with rage. It was the same urge which drives some athletes when, close to the finishing line, they realize that their immediate rival still has the advantage and so they fear a defeat which is by then almost inevitable.

But studying the piano gave him a sense of peaceful satisfaction. When he felt mentally and physically tired he felt at peace with his conscience.

Ettore encouraged him, occasionally leaving him messages of approval which made him feel particularly proud. Meanwhile time was passing and the day of his wedding was fast approaching.

With Elena's agreement, Amos had decided that the ceremony would take place at the church of Lajatico, his local church. Afterwards they would celebrate with friends and relatives in the big living room at the Bardis' house. From the outset he had insisted that they should have a simple and relatively inexpensive wedding, but day by day, the list of guests inevitably became longer because, even though he had tried to put off making the decision to name the day, once done, he wanted all his friends and family near him to share the occasion. He could not exactly explain to himself why it was, but he could not resist the temptation of adding names to that guest list.

In the meantime phone calls were arriving from the studio where he had recorded Zucchero's song, from that place where all his hopes had been rekindled, which kept Amos in a state of suspense. First it seemed that Maestro Pavarotti had refused to sing a piece of pop music and had specifically recommended Amos to sing in his place; then it seemed he had changed his mind. In the end the maestro had accepted. For Amos, therefore, all that remained was the hope that he might be asked to substitute for him alongside Zucchero at the concerts where surely the maestro would not perform.

Amos was very disappointed but there was one thought that came to his rescue. Who could know whether perhaps, when all was said and done, that umpteenth disappointment might not turn out to be a really lucky break? The fact of performing a melody made famous by being sung by such an important artist as Maestro Pavarotti, the best known tenor of his day, the most charismatic figure in the world of opera, would undoubtedly have attracted comment and comparison from which he only stood to gain. This idea didn't completely console him but it certainly helped to soften the blow.

"Obviously then this is how things must be," he thought to himself. "Then so be it!" And some verses from Dante came to mind: "Thus it is willed where will and power are one; enough, ask now no more".

One morning Amos left for Bologna with his father in an attempt to meet up with Michele. He had decided to go and wait for him at the entrance to his office until he agreed to grant him a minute of his precious time. When he got there a secretary met him and welcomed him kindly. Michele, unbelievably, was actually there for once, closed up in his office and busy with an important meeting, but surely he would have agreed to see him. Amos waited patiently. He was so nervous that the hour or more that he spent waiting there seemed hardly more than a minute. Suddenly the door opened and Michele immediately came towards him.

"At last I have managed to meet you!" said Amos, smiling and happy.

"Really," replied Michele. "We're always terribly busy and especially right now with Zucchero's record about to be released... But don't you worry, we'll find the time for our projects too. I'll do everything I can to take you on tour. Unfortunately now I have to run to the airport as I am already late."

Michele glanced at his watch quickly and then took Amos's hand and shook it, saying, "It was a pleasure to meet you. We will certainly see each other again soon." He also shook the hand of Signor Bardi, who had not even had time to say a single word. "Please excuse me!" he said again, then grabbed a raincoat hanging on the coatrack and rushed off down the stairs.

Amos and his father stood there immobile, almost in disbelief. They had travelled so far, driven for an entire day and all for this. Could this be true? Was this all they could do?

They said goodbye to the secretaries and slowly took their leave, defeat written on their faces. On the way back they did not speak much, each one sunk in his own thoughts, trying to find a way to make the best of it.

Amos thought about Elena, who was waiting at home. Elena who cared little about the outcome of that journey, Michele's promises, and the indifference of the record companies, because she accepted Amos just as he was, with the virtues she saw in him and the vices to which she was blind. Soon they would be embarking on a series of meetings with Don Carlo, the parish priest of Lajatico, to prepare for their marriage, and just as one thought drives out another, that idea took hold and fully occupied Amos's mind, giving rise to new sources of concern which presented themselves in the form of a subtle anxiety like a pain. In fact, Elena had agreed to present herself as a believer, but her father had instilled in her an anti-clericalism and an antipathy for organized religion which, although not a strongly held position for her, was nevertheless fairly evident. During the period they had been engaged Amos had taken part in numerous discussions at Elena's house on the subject, always fully respecting everyone's opinions, of course, but each time the discussions became more animated and heated than the last.

Thinking over it, Amos was sure he had not succeeded in awakening even the shadow of a doubt in his fiancée. That was the only flaw in the almost total devotion Elena had always shown towards him from their first meetings.

"How can I make her understand the need, the importance, and the joy of marrying reason to faith? And if the most rational minds, the most refined intellects of all humanity have accepted that reason should yield to faith, how and why use and waste our miserable intelligence in pointing out the inconsistencies in the behaviour of our priests and the futility of religious functions, in deriding the credulity of simple folk rather than devoting oneself to an act of intellectual humility and professing that poverty of spirit preached by Jesus of Nazareth in the Sermon of the Mount? Elena is a simple girl, ten times, no, one hundred times worthier than I! I know that I am a man without virtue who seeks it with all my strength but never attains it because I am not strong enough, and I agonize over my inability to be what I would wish to be. Perhaps this is the reason why I am not able to persuade her."

Amos was so immersed in his thoughts that he didn't even realize he had got home. He felt so exasperated that instead of sitting down to dinner he called Adriano on the phone. "I've just got back," he said, "and I'd like to talk to you. Could you come over?"

Adriano jumped into his car and in little more than half an hour he was there. Amos immediately gave him a quick rundown of the events of the day, finding it painful and unbearably tedious to have to tell his friend about yet another failed undertaking. Instead he dwelled on the thoughts that had disturbed him during that last part of the journey home.

He went into the living room ahead of his friend and began to pace up and down, talking as though to himself in a state of feverish agitation. Adriano sat on a sofa and settled down to listen patiently. "In a few days time I will lead a woman who loves me to the altar," began Amos. "We are in agreement between ourselves, but in church she will be at my side as she was when we went to the theatre, when I took her there for the first time so that she could discover and love the world of opera. She will listen to the priest absent-mindedly, she will make the sign of the cross, recite the Lord's Prayer, she may even receive the holy communion, but all without being convinced of the mystery of the Eucharist. And she will do all this for me, just to make me happy, while I am assailed by doubts and find myself in the grip of a terrible turmoil so that I can no longer tell right from wrong!" He paused. Adriano said nothing. Probably rather than seeking a solution to his friend's doubts, what he was searching for was some word of comfort. "Anyway," resumed Amos, "Elena doesn't deny the existence of God. Who knows, perhaps, in her own way, she is looking for him! Perhaps she is closer to Him than I who..." Then, sitting down next to Adriano he smiled and added, "It must be God's will! I suppose that is really all one can say!"

When the Bardi family went upstairs the two of them moved into the kitchen, closing the door behind them in order not to disturb anyone, and forgetting his bad mood, Amos resumed the role of cook that he loved to adopt on such occasions, and soon they had a piping hot plate of pasta alla carbonara in front of them. He opened a bottle of red wine, and between one glass and another, the conversation took a lighter and easier tone.

When Adriano left late that night, Amos ran up to his room, quickly undressed, and lay down on his bed completely immersed in his thoughts. There was something in his life that was causing him to feel a sense of disquiet and dissatisfaction, something that had nothing to do with his lack of success in his working life but rather an indefinable spiritual confusion which left him bewildered and lacking any solution to all his existential problems.

"Life goes on," thought Amos in the silence of his room, "one day after another without leaving you the time to grasp its meaning, without any chance of appeal, just like that, without any, at least apparent, reason. Maybe you are free to judge it, love it, or hate it, to be suffocated by remorse or allow yourself to be consumed by vain regrets! But what does all this mean?

"Just one thing is certain. The only thing that never leaves you, that can help you to live when you heed it and to liberate you if you haven't neglected to listen to it, is your conscience. It is the only thing that distinguishes man from other living things and brings him closer to God. It is the only thing that makes this life worth living and lends nobility to man's existence. It is a man's conscience that allows him to make his mark, as a plough creates a furrow, which will remain as testimony for the loving memory of posterity to judge. Oh sweet enchantment, oh secret happiness, oh paradise...such is the gift of an unsullied conscience, which I do not possess!"

Amos was lost in these delirious thoughts. His best friend's company had lifted his spirits and the wine had added to the effect. Then his thoughts became confused, clouded by an increasingly dense fog, and soon he fell into a deep sleep.

XXVII

Time flies, and it certainly flew quickly for Amos and his family, who were all busy making all the necessary preparations for 27th June, which was fast approaching. On that great day – a day so full of significance that everyone who experiences it feels as though they are reaching the winning line – Amos woke up in his family home for the last time. That evening he would be leaving, but he woke calm and rested and got ready without having to rush so that by the time he left his room and went downstairs it was nearly lunchtime. But that day no one took issue with this. On the contrary everyone was delighted to see him so happy and relaxed. After he had eaten a frugal meal he noticed a certain increase in the tension around him which soon developed into confusion and then degenerated into a commotion, or at least that's how it seemed to him. He instead felt as though he were being directed by a will which was not his own, acting like a robot or like an animal in the middle of a herd, who, for reasons unknown to him, is driven in a given direction, forced to run, slow down, stop, and then start running with all the others again, and all without questioning why. Part of the time he felt ridiculous; in other moments he managed to really immerse himself in the role of the protagonist which was assigned to him on that day and which meant that he, more than anyone else, had to shoulder the responsibility for the success of the celebrations.

Finally, when Amos had been persuaded that it was time, he agreed to go upstairs to get dressed. He put on the suit that had been purchased specially for the occasion, and when he was ready he took his place in the car with his parents, and they made their way to the church in Lajatico. Once there he rushed off to find Don Carlo, whom he found soon enough in the vestry. "I want to confess," he announced resolutely. So the parish priest made everyone leave, but instead of leading Amos to the confessional he sat down next to him in a friendly way and invited him to unburden his heart of remorse and to free his soul of sin. It was a brief but intense discussion during which Amos, struggling to overcome his reluctance, embarrassment, and personal pride, came out, almost in a single breath, with everything he knew he had to say. Then, having received absolution, he went back into the church to make sure that the musicians had arrived, that his friends with cameras and videocameras were well placed and not getting in the way of the priest – in short, that everything was proceeding well. Finally he went off to find Adriano, who had accepted his invitation to be best man.

Elena was not late. At exactly five o'clock she was in front of the church. Amos went towards her, took her by the hand, and together, their faces radiating that special happiness that fills the hearts of lovers who are about to fulfil their dream, or, more real-istically, their shared life plan, they entered the church to the accompaniment of Mendelssohn's famous Wedding March and went up to the altar followed by the festive procession of family and friends.

"I, Elena, take you, Amos, to be my lawful wedded husband, and promise to be faithful, for better and for worse, in sickness and in health . . . " Amos was startled hearing Elena uttering those words. His lips spread into a smile. A strange thought suddenly came to him. Who knows if his fiancée had ever considered the enormity of that promise that he too was about to have to pronounce out loud to her in a few minutes time! Why was this solemn undertaking so necessary, one that was so hard to keep?

But her voice, so sure and serene and perhaps just a touch nervous, which inside the church sounded mysteriously deeper and more serious, that voice which was so familiar to him continued, "...and to love and honour you for as long as I shall live!"

Amos tried to drive those inappropriate thoughts from his mind, and in order to make this easier, he concentrated his attention on the sound of his own voice to make sure it did not sound trite or insincere. So, in a serious but humble and unemphatic tone, he too, rather hurriedly, voiced his promise. After having said his part he suddenly felt rather light-headed and dazed, then Adriano gently nudged his arm, Elena smiled at him, and he felt calm again. Outside the church the newlyweds were taken aback by the number of townspeople, acquaintances, and curious onlookers who had gathered to see them, and it took quite some time before they managed to reach the car.

The reception had been organized to take place in his family home just as Amos had always wanted, the house he had grown up in, and to which he was so attached. His family and all his closest friends were there, and they all made sure that everything went well. Verano, the pastry chef, who had always been a great friend, had prepared a splendid wedding cake with various tiers, topped by an excellent meringue, Amos's favourite, and with other delicious layers below. Luca and Giorgio had organized an amazing fireworks display, while other neighbours helped serve at the tables.

The festivities went on into the small hours. After saying goodbye to the last guests, the newlyweds finally retired to their own house, where they had decided to spend their wedding night. Elena was very happy, and as she entered her new bedroom, she was so moved she struggled to find words to describe her joy, but failing in her efforts she simply came out with, "It's exactly what I always dreamed of!"

The next day they left for a brief honeymoon: a cruise of the Mediterranean, stopping off in Spain and Tunisia, then returning to Italy, stopping in Palermo and Naples before disembarking in

Genoa, their point of departure. The trip was very interesting and exciting for both of them because neither Amos nor Elena had ever been on a cruise ship before; moreover, Amos loved the open sea, the mystery of that infinite expanse of water, that infinite space where the imagination can wander free...

At night he would go out onto the small balcony of their suite, rest his elbows on the railing, and stay there for hours, lost in thought, filling his lungs with the clean sea air which would make him feel inebriated and almost dizzy. Every time they left the ship, the first thing he would do was to run to find a phone to call home for news of his parents and Michele, who had promised to do all he could to take him on tour with Zucchero. It was the only thing he hoped for, the thing he most wanted. However, when he called from Naples in the hope of hearing some good news, the by now familiar voice of one of Michele's secretaries informed him that for the time being everything was on hold. Zucchero had decided to release the video of his duet with Maestro Pavarotti instead of performing the piece live. The young lady asked him not to call anymore. If there were any new developments she would personally take it upon herself to let him know.

Amos felt his world collapse around him and he withdrew into a gloomy silence. Elena was upset by this too as she could not find any way to console him. Nor were the words of comfort and optimism his father and father-in-law offered, when they came to Genoa to bring them back to their lovely home in the country, of any use. There was nothing to be done. Even at home, surrounded by his friends, Amos continued to be serious and downcast.

Elena would leave very early in the morning to go to work and return at dinner time. Amos would be left alone. He would skip lunch, practice his piano and singing, and see Ettore, who would drop by to visit every day, and they would read something together. To Amos Ettore seemed completely unperturbed and this amazed him. "Is it possible he should have nothing to say about the situation I find myself in?" he thought to himself, and he could not find a moment's peace.

He spent almost a whole year in that state, carrying on doing the same things as usual. But day by day his dismay was giving way to resignation, resignation would give way to calm, and gradually this allowed him to recover his energy, his will to do things, his faith in himself and others. Winter came. Amos was very worried by the thought that he might be forced to ask his father to help him to provide for his family, so as soon as Elena went out to work he would immediately switch off the heating and put on an extra heavy wool sweater. He did everything he possibly could to economize, imposing frugality upon himself as a form of discipline, and this new habit gave him a strength, a capacity for application and sacrifice, that he never knew he had.

Elena wanted a baby and she would bring the subject up increasingly often. To be honest, Amos had never had a particular desire for children; still, the idea of a son intrigued him. But how could he bring a child into this world without having first made sure that he would be able to provide him with a life of freedom and opportunity? And so he continued to put Elena off and try to dissuade her from the idea, although with every day it became more and more of an obsession with her, just as the idea of getting married had been a while ago.

He would spend entire days alone, and it was during this period that he also succeeded in imposing the rule of silence on himself as an essential discipline for a singer. All the most celebrated opera singers had adopted this practice, and he could not be an exception.

His first attempts were very difficult, especially when he determined to be silent in the midst of other people. Instead, when he was alone, the silence had a voice that not only never tired him out, but also had the ability to calm him and to provide him with a sense of well-being.

The fact of not being able to interject and have his say, of having to submit to the opinions of others without being able to reply and to express himself, was a real hardship for him. But those early harsh criticisms and first disappointments he had suffered, plus the increasingly real fear of seeing his dreams go up in smoke, all added to his strength and determination.

No one understood the need for that extravagance, so instead of encouragement he found everyone merely laughed at him and urged him not to bother. This is why Amos spent most of his time completely alone, between the walls of his own house, where the silence caressed his spirit and spoke to him in a reassuring tone. "Try to give your best, to be honest in judging yourself and others. Listen to your conscience, and carry on without losing heart because good will and hard work will always be rewarded in the end!"

Amos paced up and down in his room, smiling at the almost childish simplicity of those ideas. "Those are the things our teacher used to say, that my grandmother would lecture me about when I was little, and that the catechism teacher would reiterate..." But still the voice would speak to him, advising that "although to you these things may seem banal there is more simple truth in them than you will find in the obscure and high-flown speeches of politicians, in the confused and abstract pronouncements of the bureaucrats, in the presumptuous and fatuous words of men of science, or worse, in the cynical and sinister rulings of the men of the law..."

In a letter to his singing teacher Amos wrote, "I can't thank you enough for having recommended to me the discipline of silence. It certainly helps the voice but it is of even greater help to the spirit. When I am alone silence teaches the spirit to know itself better and it also gains a better understanding of others when they direct noisy torrents of words at each other. How many pointless absurdities, how much foolish nonsense is said in the course of any conversation, and how many important things are instead missed because we have not listened hard enough either due to fear of not having said enough ourselves or of not having been sufficiently persuasive! How many things I have learned, Maestro, and how many surprises the music of silence must still have in store for me!"

Amos derived enormous satisfaction from his singing lessons and from the development of his voice, which in some way compensated for all the worries he felt about his lack of achievement in other areas. Whenever someone would invite him to emerge from his solitude and enjoy himself a bit, he would smile and reply that he was very happy with his life and did not need anything, and he would think to himself, "An artist's worth is in inverse proportion to the extent of his needs, his demands, and his whims, because a true artist is nourished essentially by his art which alone is enough to make him happy and entirely fulfilled."

Besides, what would he have gained from becoming rich? Amos believed that, in his frenzied race to acquire wealth, a man begins, it is true, by possessing the indispensible, then the useful, and eventually the superfluous, but he is never satisfied and so money becomes, first, dangerous, then actually damaging, if not for him, who usually cannot even find the time to spend it, then certainly for the members of his family and especially the youngest ones.

Somehow that winter too, which for Amos was one of the longest and coldest he could remember, passed into spring. In the meantime he had completed his study of Bach's famous Sonata in D minor, transcribed by Busoni for the piano, just as he had promised himself he would. It was a surprising result, although his playing was still far from perfect. With the arrival of spring he decided to allow himself a romantic interlude, finally tackling Liszt's Nocturne No. 3, better known as the "Dream of Love". He threw himself into it with joy and passion. In no time he had learned it by heart and then concentrated on perfecting the more complicated passages.

One day he was completely immersed in the study of a particular cadenza when he heard the phone ring. That interruption was really the last thing he needed. He got up reluctantly, but nevertheless ran to answer the call as usual, and he could hardly believe his ears when he recognized Michele's voice. "I have some good news for you," he said quickly. "This time I think I've done it. Get ready to leave towards the end of May for a tour of Italy, in the major soccer stadiums."

Amos was speechless. Should he believe it or not? Probably better not to! But he immediately called his wife, then his parents, bursting with ill-concealed elation.

Suddenly a thought came to him that stung like a poisoned dart: just in that same period in May there was going to be a very important singing course held by a famous Italian soprano who had warmly invited him to take part. So what was he to do? What should he give up? What kind of sadistic destiny had it in for him in this way? These were his first opportunities, the only really important steps for his career, and he was immediately being forced to choose between them.

Desperate, Amos thought of Ettore, in order to get his advice, but then, knowing him so well, he could immediately predict his reply. "In cases such as these," he would have said, "the best advice that one can give is not to accept advice from anyone." So he called his father and calmly explained the situation. Signor Bardi sighed and he too seemed to be gripped by the same consternation. Then he said, "Amos, I think that you will have to make your own decision because no one will take the responsibility of deciding for you. At times like these everyone is alone." Then he passed a hand through his son's hair, a gesture which filled Amos's heart with tenderness.

Now Amos was no longer thinking about himself but about his father, who he knew would have shed his own blood to see him happy and fulfilled. "Poor father!" he thought, and immediately felt a need to console him. "Well! Listen, two opportunities are better than none!" Then, reasoning to himself he thought, "If I don't win this battle I will be forcing my father to work for as long as he has the strength to do it. No! This isn't right! If things turn out badly again I will look for any job at all. I will work as a switchboard operator, a masseur, I will try for a job as a bank clerk, but this situation has to stop once and for all!"

Women, it has to be said, are often more practical and efficient than men. So it was that Edi Bardi and Elena had no hesitation in advising that Amos should opt for Michele's proposal, which would produce immediate and concrete results. There was no comparison. The other idea was expensive and held out only promises. Upset and embarrassed, Amos thus resolved to call the famous and kind singer to inform her immediately of his decision to decline her offer and embark on that other adventure, without concealing from her any of the reasons that had pushed him in that direction. Somewhat peeved and in a reproachful tone of voice she listed the opportunities that in her view he was throwing away forever, but in the end she seemed resigned and, with a certain cool detachment, said goodbye.

The days passed and to Amos, who lived in terror of the possibility that there might be a change of plan, they seemed never-ending. One performance at the theatre in his local town was all that lay between him and the date of departure. Once again, for a moment, he feared the worst. At the rehearsal Amos accidentally fell from the stage onto the first row of seats, but fortunately he was only slightly bruised. The following day, accompanied by Elena and feeling almost as incredulous as he felt happy, he left for Bassano del Grappa where, for the first time, he would sing a duet with Zucchero in what was considered the high spot of the concert.

Amos was to sing the part which the public knew from the masterful performance of the most celebrated tenor in the world. How would the almost fifteen-thousand-strong paying audience react faced by such a disappointing substitute?

This is what poor Amos wondered, full of apprehension, before appearing on the stage, sitting at the grand piano, on a moving platform. But the public almost always likes something new. So the first tremulous notes from the unknown tenor were received by a genuine ovation. By the end of the piece the audience seemed to have literally gone crazy. Fifteen thousand deafening voices were crying out, even drowning the exaggeratedly loud sound from the enormous amplifiers, and, the next day, on the entertainments page of a major daily newspaper, a headline appeared which was to remain impressed forever in the memory of the entire Bardi family: "Amos Bardi does not leave us regretting the absence of Maestro Pavarotti".

Filled with emotion and almost moved to tears, Amos had finally won his first, real battle.

XXVIII

Evidently something was moving in the heavens, and the stars were shifting in Amos's favour. In the meantime, unaware and incredulous, he proceeded along his own path, which by now consisted of strongly rooted principles and a tangle of doubts to which over time he had become so fondly attached as to prefer them to any deceptive certainty. His path was also paved with hopes, but he allowed himself these only if they were grounded on the solid base of his own will, his own capacities, and his own dedication and hard work.

Zucchero's tour was a real triumph. Amos left the stage every night to a deafening, almost intoxicating ovation which filled him with joy. In his dressing room he would find Elena waiting for him, also in a state of happy disbelief. In a little less than a month they travelled the length of Italy, from north to south, in a bus loaded to bursting with musicians and baggage, without even the comfort of air conditioning. And yet Amos had never felt better. In fact, he was dismayed at the bad attitude displayed by some of his colleagues who were wilting and irritable from the heat. For him it all felt like a wonderful dream, and in fact, occasionally he worried that he might wake up at any moment and find himself back in his own bed at home with all his old problems. Instead he was really there on tour and was even being paid a salary which was enough to cover his needs for a whole year. He felt full of a boundless energy which astonished him as much as anyone. He was always raring to go and keen to get on well with his travelling companions; he was never sleepy, and at night he would ruminate on the question of the strange relationship between his past and his future. He tried to examine what his destiny might hold and could not forgive himself the negative views he had held up till then. But after all he had been patient; he had never given up and never completely lost his optimism. Perhaps this was why destiny was now beginning to reward him.

It turned out to be a really hot summer. Sometimes Amos would get up from bed and open the fridge. Then, overcoming temptation, he would close it again and make do with a glass of water from the bathroom tap and continue with his nightly meditations.

"How unjust I am!" he thought. "I wasn't content with my life when instead it protected me from every danger and spared me from those easy victories which not only do not pay but actually cost one dear. What a fool I've been."

Everyone quickly became Amos's friend. Zucchero himself invited him to dinner on several occasions, and once, when Zucchero was due to appear on a very popular TV show, he did not refuse Amos's timid suggestion that he might replace the keyboard player who had fallen ill the day before. Zucchero thought about it for a moment but then agreed, and in fact, he even decided to perform the same song that he had sung with Amos in a duet during the concert tour. So for the first time the doors of television opened for Amos. This is what his father had always hoped for, and it was also what Michele needed in order to understand if, and to what degree, the camera loved Amos and whether he had charisma on the screen.

Once again the song was an outstanding success which surpassed all expectations. Everyone agreed, especially the next day when the viewing figures were published which showed that the number of spectators who had tuned in to see Zucchero and his young friend sing had shot up the ratings to register the most unexpected peak.

A few days before the end of the tour Amos received some news which made him feel both totally thrilled and also apprehensive. A master class held by the famous tenor Franco Corelli was due to be held at the Press Club in Turin... Could it be true? Was it possible that Corelli himself, in person, would hold a class with students and talk to them about singing? Amos could hardly believe it but his parents assured him on the phone that it was true. There would be a selection process conducted by a jury of experts, and then the maestro would arrive. Amos was persuaded. Delighted and impatient, he begged his parents to enrol him for the course and began to prepare himself psychologically to face all the obstacles he would encounter before his meeting with the man who, more than anyone else, had spoken to his heart and moved him to tears with his extraordinary voice.

The last day of the tour was probably the most emotional for Amos because it took place at the municipal stadium in Florence, finally back in his own region of Tuscany. His friends had all come to see him, and there were also many people from his area whom he did not know personally but to whom he felt great attachment. In the dressing room with the other members of the group he felt his heart beating fast. When he got up on stage, in the middle of all that uproar, he heard his name being yelled out.

Someone wanted to communicate their affection and be, in some way, closer to him. At the end of the concert he was able to hug his family again at last. He had not seen them since the day he had left for the tour, and that evening he went back home, but just for one day. He only just had time to repack his suitcase before leaving again for Turin, this time without his wife, for the first time since his wedding, to limit the cost of the trip. He arrived in Turin late at night, accompanied by his father, who would leave again the following morning, and immediately went to the small convent where a friend had found him lodgings. The room was small and bare, quite different from the big hotels he had been used to during the tour, but he did not care. He was thinking only of the moment when he would meet his teacher, and that was all he needed.

In the morning, after his father had left, Amos made his way with the other hopefuls to the course at the Press Club for the first audition. He had decided to stay on even if he wasn't selected; at the very least that way he would be able to hear Maestro Corelli's words and his precious advice. When it came to his turn he went into the large hall in the grip of such tension that it was clearly visible in his face. He leaned on the piano and without further ado launched into the famous aria from Francesco Cilea's *Arlesiana*, "Il Lamento di Federico".

After completing his piece he left the hall with his head bowed, with the pianist, and calmly prepared to wait for the results of his first audition. Out of approximately one hundred candidates, only twelve young singers would be chosen to take the course. It was a really ruthless selection process which would be decided that night.

Amos felt he would burst with joy when he heard his name among the list of the successful candidates read out by the president of the adjudicating committee. Maestro Corelli arrived a few days later by train. Having run out of patience, Amos and another course participant went to meet him at the station. The maestro and his wife were among the last passengers to get off the train, or so it seemed to Amos who, when he finally stood before him and was able to shake his hand, really thought for a moment that he must be dreaming. They loaded the maestro's bags into the taxi cab, and then the two young students respectfully took their leave and ran back to the Press Club, where the master class with one of the most celebrated singers of the century would soon begin.

When Maestro Corelli made his entrance into the great hall which was packed to overflowing with fans, journalists, photographers, and young singers, a thunderous applause accompanied him as he walked over to a podium near the piano. The maestro crossed the floor quickly, placed a hand on the piano, and took a bow. He made no introductory speeches. It was clear he was embarrassed and would have preferred to have been anywhere but there, being stared at by all those people who hung on his every word, impatient to hear him speak.

"Who would like to sing first?" asked the maestro. There was a long silence. Everyone looked at Amos, being by then aware of the love and admiration he had for Maestro Corelli as well as his unusual ability to imitate him. But Amos did not move; in fact, he tried to make himself as small as possible. A girl in the first row got up and went over to the piano in a determined fashion. She greeted the maestro and announced that she would sing an aria by Puccini from *La Rondine*. She handed the music to the pianist and began. Her performance was shaky, her voice small, unsteady, and laboured, especially on the high notes.

When she had finished, Corelli seemed very embarrassed and hesitant. "Do you have a singing teacher?" he asked her. She nodded. "And does such a teacher take money from you?" added Corelli, staring at the floor, as though talking to himself. The poor girl's eyes welled up with tears and she ran back to her seat covering her face.

The maestro was visibly mortified. He must have certainly regretted what he had just said, but by now it was too late, so, to disguise his discomfort, he made a sigh and announced, "I would like to hear a tenor." The fellow who had gone with Amos to the station and who was now sitting next to him took Amos by the arm and thrust him forward. Amos tried to resist this but Maestro Corelli had spotted them, recognized him, and invited him to sing. Amos did his bidding. With his heart in his mouth he took a couple of steps and sat at the piano. In a somewhat confused fashion he announced that he would sing Rodolfo's famous aria from Giacomo Puccini's *Bohème*, and he suddenly heard a sound which he just about recognized as the first note of that piece. As if in a dream, he now found himself singing for his idol, his hero, and he felt completely at a loss. He sang without the slightest consciousness of what he was doing, and when it was over, he was struck by the silence in the hall, which shook him awake again the way a sudden shout rouses a man from a deep slumber. Seconds passed which seemed to him like hours. The maestro approached him slowly, rested a hand on his shoulder, and said, "The voice is very beautiful, you know... I think I could give you some useful tips."

Amos listened, hardly able to believe his ears. He regained his composure and was able to reason with a degree of calm once more. His voice shook as he thanked the maestro, and then he politely asked permission to go outside for a moment. His shirt was soaked with sweat and he needed a drink of cold water, but he was thrilled to have passed the test and now felt he was on safe ground. He ran to the men's room, removed his shirt, wrung it out, and put it back on again. It was shamefully crumpled but what could he do about that? He drank some water and slipped quietly back to his place in the hall.

Corelli was in the middle of saying something, but when he saw him he stopped and called him over again, inviting him to sing his aria once more. This time, however, he stopped him after each phrase and discussed the singing technique. He gave very short examples and asked Amos to repeat this or that phrase following his suggestions regarding technique or interpretation, and this continued for the whole lesson. At the end Amos was exhausted, but happy.

On his way out he was stopped and complimented by Signora Corelli in a way that gave him the confidence to ask if he might pay the maestro a visit at home when the course was over to have private lessons from him. This way Amos would also have the chance to develop a personal relationship which for him was extremely important. Signora Corelli unhesitatingly reassured him regarding the good impression he had made on her husband, saying that she was sure that he would be happy to offer him his personal attention.

The master class concluded with a concert performed by the five best students. Amos sang the same aria that he had worked on in great detail with the maestro during those days, and the following day, an interview with Maestro Corelli was published in a local Turin newspaper, in which he discussed his impressions on the standard of the course participants and other reflections on the subject of opera singing... The maestro said that he was pleased with the interest displayed by all those young singers and mentioned that he had been particularly struck by a tenor by the name of Amos who had thrilled him with his performance because his voice was full of pathos, so sweet and sad, that it really moved the audience. Amos could hardly believe it when another of the course participants read him that article shortly before they left. Like a child, he snatched the paper from his friend and clutched it to his breast, swearing to himself that he would keep it forever.

In such a short time his life had been radically transformed. From that monotonous, lonely existence to which he had resigned himself he had suddenly been thrust into a life of continuous excitement. He was still young, strong-willed, and full of energy and enthusiasm, and not only did the whirlwind of events not worry him, it regenerated him, or, to be more precise, it brought out everything that up till then had remained hidden in his way of being and of presenting himself to others.

When he got home he found a message from Michele asking him to go to Milan the next day for a meeting with a record company that had shown a strong interest in him following his success with the Zucchero tour. Then there was a distinct possibility that they might finally come to an agreement representing a solid commitment on both sides to undertake an interesting project. Amos did not need to be told twice. He immediately left with his father and Elena for Milan, where he was able to meet the president of the company, whom he had tried to contact several times in the past without success.

He was shown into an office which seemed to him very large and bright. The president, a very distinguished and professional lady in her middle years, invited him to sit down and immediately heaped him with praise, telling him how she had felt the first time she had heard his warm and expressive voice. She said he had given her goose bumps and had soon convinced her that something had to be done so that everyone could hear that voice. She was prepared to get to work immediately – in fact, she had already talked to the songwriters she regularly worked with and had a song ready for him, an extraordinary piece, which, in her view,

Amos could present at the Sanremo Festival. He smiled and covered his face to hide his emotions: how many failed attempts, how many dashed hopes and humiliations...and now suddenly it seemed someone had turned the page.

Amos had always liked to refer to himself as an optimist, but he was still not accustomed to believing in so much good fortune, and he did not dare to believe it. However, he liked the song, and what is more, it seemed to be very well suited to his voice. It was not long before the recording was done and it was such a success that it took everyone by surprise. Michele too was delighted. At last a record company had listened to him and he couldn't wait to show everyone who had closed the door in his face that he, with his infallible instinct and enthusiasm, had got it right once again. The record company's enthusiasm was contagious even when it came to an old hand like Michele.

In no time at all everything had been arranged. Any difficulties were smoothed over, even the contractual details which are usually so tricky; the record company, as is always the way in these cases, imposed its own rules.

For his part, Amos, with a real effort of will, setting aside his principles and everything he had learned in many years of hard work and study, complied and decided to treat that adventure, which had only just begun, as no more than a great game which should not be taken too seriously.

In November of that year, Amos found himself in Sanremo, among the newcomers competing in the festival. He felt totally ill at ease in the midst of all that chaos, all that excitement and ambition, and kept to himself, mostly shut in his hotel room with his wife, Elena, who never left him for a moment and did her best to keep him calm in her tender, affectionate way.

Still he was tense and inexplicably withdrawn. He was especially nervous of the vote which would be cast by the popular panel, the members of which were almost all young. What would those kids, accustomed as they were to music genres which were louder and more modern, have made of his calm and pure voice and his somewhat old fashioned way of singing? But, in the quiet of the night, those fears were faced down and conquered by a sensation, which was hard to justify in any rational way, of being safe from any harm and navigating in a calm sea with a good wind driving him towards his destination.

The candidates were asked to present a previously released and popular song. Consequently Amos had no hesitation as to the choice of what to sing: he would perform the song which had brought him such good fortune up to now, singing both the part originally sung by Zucchero and the tenor's part, which was known to the public thanks to the voice of Maestro Pavarotti. Surely – at the very least – this would give it a surprise element, and the extreme versatility of his voice might favourably impress the jury. Already during the afternoon rehearsals, everyone had noticed the reaction of those who witnessed Amos's performance, and he felt more relaxed.

That evening he was one of the last to perform. The audience had already had its fill of music, voices, and new faces and hardly paid attention as he went up on stage. Indeed, the people listened to the very popular presenter's introduction rather distractedly, and someone even guffawed with derision when he announced that Amos would be performing both Zucchero's and Pavarotti's parts, on his own. Then the orchestra struck up and immediately Amos's voice resounded, full and strong, throughout the hall. Surprised and curious, everyone then sat up and took notice. After a few bars, Amos's voice changed register, completely transforming its timbre and intonation, and a thunderous, unstoppable applause spontaneously rose up from the audience. Meanwhile, in a small private room in a hotel not far from the theatre, Michele with his colleagues and some friends watched the show on television with bated breath. Some of them had tears in their eyes, some could hardly hold them back, and Stefano, one of Amos's most ardent supporters, was so tense it almost made him feel ill. At the end of the song the whole audience stood up and submerged the orchestra's last notes in thunderous applause and delirious cries. He had done it. Even Amos felt convinced that victory was his, and to be honest, he was no longer so worried about the jury's verdict.

In the three months leading up to the festival, Amos had gone back to his usual way of life, except with a little more impetus. Now he felt he was fighting for a more concrete opportunity and no longer for a remote chance of success. He was infused with a new energy and an uncommon self-confidence took hold of him to the point that he had an uncanny feeling that, from then on, everything he undertook would immediately turn out well. But how could he or should he explain this sudden turn of events in his life? There were no clear, rational, understandable reasons for it, or in any event, none that Amos could find. A few days after this, Amos began to record his first album in a studio in Bologna. It had not been easy to find songs which suited his voice, but a certain amount of material had been put together. He threw himself wholeheartedly into the project, and in a short time it was possible to develop a fairly good idea of the nature of that album which would prove so decisive for his career.

One day, while Amos was practising a piece on the piano, a businessman from Reggio Emilia, a friend of the owner of the recording studio, who happened to be there by pure chance, heard his voice from a distance and stopped to listen, as though transfixed by the sound that he was hearing for the first time. He made some enquiries and was told that it belonged to a young singer called Amos who was competing in the Newcomers category at the Sanremo Festival and was recording an album. Quick as a flash, Signor Monti, a man of great intelligence and acumen and an extraordinarily successful entrepreneur who was also a generous patron of the arts, without even asking to meet in person the artist who had so impressed him, begged his friend to persuade that young talent to perform in concert at the theatre in his city of Reggio Emilia, promising he would be accompanied by a good orchestra and conductor. He said that he would personally bear all the costs and take care of everything required for the organization of the event, and with that he said no more on the matter that day.

To sing in a traditional theatre accompanied by an orchestra was something Amos had always dreamed of. Signor Monti had to work really hard on his extravagant project: at the theatre they warned him that not even a famous tenor would be able to attract an audience of more than three hundred people, so what hope was there for an unknown songster from the provinces who was just preparing to take part in the festival . . . But Signor Monti was not the kind of man to go back on his word. Smiling, he assured them that the concert would have a full house, and inviting at his own expense friends, acquaintances, and his company employees to hear what he by now, without fear of contradiction, claimed to be the finest voice ever heard, he kept his promise with a box office sell-out such as that theatre had not seen for a long time. Thanks to his extraordinary powers of persuasion everyone flocked there. So every part of the theatre was packed to the great delight of Signor Monti and the consternation of those who had doubted the successful outcome of one of his projects.

Everything was ready while Amos, shut up in his dressing room, nervous as ever, vocalized a bit and had the impression that his voice was not at its best. His hands were freezing, and he was in a cold sweat under Elena's apprehensive gaze and his mother's desperately helpless gaze. Suddenly there was a knock at the door and a voice echoed down the corridor: "on stage". Amos made his way towards the back of the stage, his legs almost too weak to carry him; then he began to sing and undoubtedly gave it his best shot. The public responded with warmth and affection, but his voice was not yet supported by a diaphragm of steel or a solid technique, so at the end of the concert, in spite of the applause and the handshakes, Amos felt that things had not gone as well as he and his generous friend, Signor Monti, had so fervently hoped.

XXIX

February arrived in the blink of an eye. In the Bardi household there was a constant ferment of activity to prepare for Amos's departure until one fine morning a car came to Poggioncino, sent by the record company to take him and Elena to Rome, where he was to appear on an important TV show in advance of the festival. That morning the family was together just as generally happened on special occasions. Signor Bardi waited for Amos, who came downstairs with his case and a rucksack; he helped him put his bags in the trunk of the car and then gave his son such an emotional hug that Amos was quite surprised. Edi Bardi, who probably felt more emotional than her husband, chose to play the part of the courageous woman who remains impervious to external events even when they are out of the ordinary, so she said goodbye to the couple with studied cheerfulness. Amos was so familiar with her ways and he felt a rush of tenderness for her. "Poor Mamma!" he thought. "Who knows what she is feeling right now and how hard she tries to be strong to give me courage!" He got into the car quickly to control these feelings, closed the door, and tried to distract himself by adjusting the position of the seat.

In Rome there wasn't even time to drop the bags at the hotel or freshen up. The driver went straight to Parioli, where he dropped Amos and Elena at the theatre and left. A young woman then showed them into the dressing room. She brought mineral water, offered them coffee, and then explained that Amos would be called for make-up in a few minutes time, as indeed turned out to be the case. "Why the long face?" the make-up artist asked Amos, who clearly hated all that attention to his features, the smell of the greasepaint, and the sticky face powder. And to think that the young woman had only been asked to add a touch of colour…just something very light! "No, no! Don't worry!" laughed Amos. "It's just that I'm not used to it, and to be honest, I find it rather embarrassing…" At last the curtain went up and the TV host began to introduce his guests. When it was Amos's turn he stood up, and when invited to sing, he performed one of the tracks from his first album. It was an Italian version of an old South American hit, a simple, catchy tune to which he lent all his own passion and youthful energy. The audience burst into loud applause even before he had reached the end of the song. From his seat in the back row of the audience, Michele could hardly believe what he saw, and he had to confess to himself that even he could not find a logical explanation for such a staggering outcome.

After the show another car was waiting to pick up Amos and Elena to take them to the main station. The driver, a rather corpulent fellow who wheezed and gasped and made them feel somewhat anxious, urged them to hurry to avoid missing the train. He was a jovial, loquacious character who wanted to know all about Amos's plans and promised to watch the festival on television and to support him. Amos smiled but he had quite different things on his mind.

Once at the station, they collected their tickets and ran to the platform where the train was just about to leave. Carrying rucksacks and with tickets in hand, they hurriedly searched for the sleeping car where they would spend the night. Amos wanted to ask someone for information to save time, but the platform was practically deserted, and they were a long way down it by this time. The train was so long that the idea of walking back its entire length to ask was distinctly unappealing, and, in that moment of nervous exhaustion, Amos felt as though he had been abandoned and that he was running for a train more or less the way we race towards our fate: alone and defenceless.

In the end, however, the two disoriented travellers managed to find their places. They were so hot that the air inside the train seemed quite unbreathable. They placed their bags up on the racks and Amos immediately stretched out on his bunk bed. Although it was too small for someone of his size it nevertheless felt quite comfortable. Elena lay down on the bunk below his, and they both stayed there in silence, not because they had little to say to each other, quite the contrary, but perhaps they had so many things to share, too many sensations to put in order, and silence was the easiest and most effective way to express things which sound banal and inadequate when put into words. The silence instead was like music and they both had a need for that music.

Amos tried to sleep but he was too agitated: his mind was flooded with memories; he heard voices both close and more distant in time, words which encouraged him and others that upset or intimidated him, demonstrations of affection and commiseration… and he had the strange feeling of going towards a place from which he would be able to reply to all of them, but he did not know whether he would emerge defeated or victorious. His personal pride was locked in combat with common sense, and once again he heard Ettore's voice warning him that "things should never be taken too seriously!"

Meanwhile the train rumbled monotonously on its way. By this time no one was speaking inside the carriage. The ticket inspector had already passed by, advising the passengers to lock themselves into their compartment before going to sleep to avoid any unpleasant surprises when they awoke. The train made a great many stops, and Amos was already awake when, in the depth of that cold, wet winter's night, he heard a loudspeaker announce that they were in Pisa station. "I could get off here, in my city, and decide for myself which direction to give to my life! Why do I feel that I wouldn't have the strength to do it? Why do I laugh at the idea and do nothing, curled up in this bunk and letting myself be taken wherever it decides?" The train left again almost immediately. Amos turned over onto his other side. A sudden exhaustion finally got the better of him; he closed his eyes and fell asleep.

XXX

When the train stopped at Sanremo station, Amos and Elena were among the first to get off. Outside there was bright sunshine, and a light sea breeze blew the last traces of sleep from their faces. The night, the cold, and that dark sense of solitude and discomfort were now behind them.

The train was already about to leave again when a friendly young woman came towards them, greeting them cheerfully. It was Delfina, who worked for the record company and had the job of looking after Amos for the duration of the festival, organising his extremely full working days. "You just have time to drop your bags and freshen up and then we will start the radio interviews; I think there are three of them, so that makes four with the press interview," she said, laughing with satisfaction at her own work.

Amos was overjoyed. All that work was a blessing. Too bad there was not more! He felt great, on really top form, and he wasn't going to let anything get in his way. The test everyone was waiting for was about to take place. His life's dream, the one everyone had encouraged him to dream of ever since he was a child, was about to happen. He was completely aware of this and yet he felt calm; he took some deep breaths of that salty air and prepared to do his very best.

Unknown to him everyone was now talking about him as the likely winner of the festival, but none of the professionals in the music industry seriously believed he stood a chance of success in the charts. "He will cause a certain excitement on stage," they said, "but he won't sell any records." Only Caterina, the president of the company, really believed in him. She had bent over backwards to persuade her own colleagues of her cause, fighting tooth and nail to support the project, with her passionate temperament and tenacity as a former artist. She and Michele together had done everything possible; now they crossed their fingers and waited to see how things would work out.

Meanwhile Amos got to work, and gradually, he made his name, not just as a singer, but also as someone who was truly committed to always giving the very best of himself without any need to put up a front or hide behind pointless barriers made up of platitudes and banalities. After all, he was a product of the countryside and was the result of that solid tradition which, thanks to Ettore, had become even more deeply rooted within him.

He always answered journalists' questions with his true opinions because that was the easiest and safest course of action. During a press conference one of their number had launched a stinging attack of the "Newcomers" category at the festival which, in his view, had presented nothing new or original at all, and this journalist had invited every participant to provide some justification for his or her presence at the event which remained the single most important such event on radio and television. This was clearly a provocation, an embarrassing question which everyone answered with difficulty and a degree of clumsiness. When it was his turn Amos replied unperturbed, "To tell the truth I have always concentrated on seeking what is beautiful rather than prostituting myself by courting the new..." He had not even completed his answer when a burst of applause rose up to greet that elegant defence. The next day almost all the Italian daily newspapers, which always dedicated a lot of space to the country's most popular song festival, quoted Amos's answer. One of them published this headline on its entertainments page: "Bardi speaks out: a few words and he is already a celebrity". And to a famous journalist who made a harsh criticism on television of the festival and the weak quality of the songs, citing Amos amongst others, he replied, "Who knows, perhaps he's right; in any case there are people who do and others who criticise, and I prefer to chance my arm among those who do."

In the meantime the tension was increasing, and you could feel it in the air wherever you went. Amos was curious and tried to get the measure of all this while at the same time remaining outside the fray. Everyone was either excessively irritable or excessively generous and helpful, either excessively loquacious or excessively withdrawn and quiet; no matter what their behaviour, it was always excessive. Obviously they were all trying to maintain some composure, to appear calm and in control, but every gesture and every conversation betrayed an ill-concealed state of agitation. The only thing anyone talked about was the festival, the gossip and rumours about what was going on behind the scenes, as if during that period there had been nothing else important going on in the world. Amos saw that exaggeration for exactly what it was and in a way he laughed at it, but slowly, inevitably, he too felt drawn into it, caught in the trap and contaminated by that heated atmosphere. Then he would retreat to his room and try to think about something else and wonder what Ettore would have advised him to do.

Who knows what Ettore made of his young friend's adventures! Undoubtedly he carried on with his usual life in Lajatico, quite calm and unperturbed. Since Amos had left he had not heard a word from him. That was a good sign; it meant that Ettore was confident that he was fine and had no advice to impart... But Amos spent a lot of time wondering what Ettore might be thinking, and that mental journey made him feel calm and secure as the days passed and the final competition approached, that fateful last Saturday in February when more than twenty million television spectators would sit in front of the TV set and remain glued to it until the end of the show. They would all hear his voice, see him, and make their judgements. And it was precisely those twenty million people who, in the space of just a few minutes, would decide his fate. He knew that perfectly well but he tried to think of other things.

On Friday his parents, aunts, and uncles arrived in Sanremo. Amongst them was the uncle who had accompanied Amos onto the stage for that memorable day when he won the margherita d'oro. His closest friends had chosen to stay at home and watch the festival on television. Amos thought of them often and he knew – he could feel – that they were with him, sharing his hopes and fears. Adriano and Verano would certainly have been watching the TV together, their hearts thumping with excitement, but in his hometown of Lajatico everyone would have been rooting for him. In fact, in La Sterza they had set up an enormous industrial hangar with a huge screen, and hundreds of seats had been set out for the occasion.

Amos did not know it, but his heart was beating at the thought of all those who were close to him in spirit and who shook with nerves and suffered with him. As for the others, he didn't give them a single thought – all those who had made fun of his aspirations and his failed attempts or who had even attempted to put him off. He did not give them a single moment of his time, so convinced was he of the need to think positively at all times and especially at important moments such as these.

At last Saturday came. Amos spent the day alone in his room in the strictest silence. When Delfina went to call him she was amazed to find him so far removed – at least apparently – from the crazed atmosphere that prevailed outside his room. Amos had not even switched on the TV to watch the show, which had started over an hour ago. It was already late and they had to rush to the theatre. A taxi was waiting at the hotel entrance. Amos sat in the back with Elena, Delfina got into the front seat and immediately gave instructions to the driver. The traffic was terrible. There were people lining the pavements, everyone wanting to catch a glimpse of the artists up close and shouting out every time they thought they spotted someone inside the luxurious cars that passed by.

Once out of the taxi Amos made his way through the crowd. No one knew him well enough to recognise him yet and he ran straight to his dressing room. He just had time to vocalize a little and then it was his turn. Elena was by his side gripping his arm tightly. Caterina was on the other side and she too was visibly tense: after all the battles she had fought to defend this project, which was objectively quite far from the norm and outside the range of the commercial fashions of the day, she too was preparing for that important moment and was not managing to keep as calm as she would have wanted.

Elena was silent. She was gulping in an attempt to swallow the knot in her throat that felt as if it were choking her. When she heard Amos's name called and realized that she had to let him go, a thought suddenly came to her. "I have always been at your side; I have loved you and am ready for anything with you! But what can I do now other than stay here and wait and suffer? Now everything is in your hands. Go and whatever will be will be. Now go, my darling!"

Seated, or more precisely, curled up, in one of the first rows, Edi Bardi was experiencing feelings which were not very different from those of her daughter-in-law. In cases like these, conjugal and maternal love have a lot in common; they are both painful and absolutely sincere. Edi too felt an anguished sense of impotence when she embraced her son with her eyes as he sat at the piano and placed his fingers gently on the keys. She felt an urge to adjust his hair and to fix his shirt collar, to undo one of his jacket buttons perhaps, and to remind him to hold his head up straight and to keep calm; for a few seconds a very short but intense prayer occupied her thoughts. She clenched her fists, bit her lip, and then she just sat back in her seat, completely still, as though totally deprived of strength or will. Only her gaze remained luminous, fixed stubbornly on that single point, onto which her big blue eyes seemed to project rays of hope, joy, energy, fear, passion, and agitation.

Amos, meanwhile, had started singing with the passion he always brought, with his way of identifying totally with the music that made his performance uniquely true. He sang and thought only of giving his best. He began the first verse delicately, almost timidly, but then he gave the refrain his full voice, finding all the strength and warmth he could muster, and the effect was immediate: a thunderous applause rose up from the audience. Behind the scenes Elena and Caterina stood watching him on a monitor, and they dared not take their eyes off that image for fear they might no longer be able to contain the intensity of their emotions.

By now Amos felt calm and secure. He gave every word such impetus and energy that even he felt amazed, allowing him to adopt such a masterful way of changing tone that the audience went wild: some cheering out loud, others getting to their feet, and by the final high note, which the conductor held for an unbelievably long time, they were all standing. The applause and the cheers were deafening. Many people had tears in their eyes and the presenter had trouble restoring order.

Backstage Amos immediately found Elena who, almost without saying a word, headed towards the dressing room. On the stairs she suddenly stopped, and grabbing the lapels of Amos's open jacket in both hands, she buried her face in his chest and started sobbing. Caterina, who was following a few steps behind them, witnessed the scene. Carrying on her way she reached the stairs, gently stroked the hair of her new artist with her hand, but did not stop, perhaps in order not to disturb that moment of intimate emotion that held something so romantic and rare.

Shortly after this Amos and all the other contestants were taken to a different floor of the building where they were to await the final results of the votes. They were led down a narrow corridor with many doors on each side leading into poky little rooms, one for each contestant. In his room Amos found just one chair. He sat on it and Elena sat on his knee. Through the plywood walls that separated those little compartments, Amos could hear the sound of an acoustic guitar. It was his neighbour playing to pass the time and to release the tension which naturally increased with every minute. On the other hand, there was nothing to do and above all nothing to say. Every word sounded useless and ridiculous. Every so often there would be a cheer but these were just false alarms. Some time passed and for everyone concerned it seemed never-ending.

Suddenly there was a knock at the door: it was Barbara, one of Delfina's colleagues who worked for the same record company. "Come," she said, smiling, "we have to go upstairs right away." "What for?" asked Amos, a little stunned and impatient. "What! Don't you know anything?" she said almost in disbelief. "No!" replied Amos. "They told me to wait here for five or ten minutes but by now it's been..." Barbara interrupted him. "You've won, Amos! You've won and no one has told you! We have to rush upstairs immediately. They sent me to fetch you!"

For a moment Amos thought he was dreaming. A feeling of lightheadedness threw him, and he couldn't think of anything to say, but then he pulled himself together. "Then let's go," he said calmly. Around him were all the other contestants, and he did not want to upset anyone with foolish displays of exuberance. He took Barbara's arm and walked towards the stairs followed by Elena. Everyone shook his hand and congratulated him. Upstairs he was stopped by reporters from three of the most important news agencies. "Just give us a quick impression, Bardi... what do you feel right now?... and who are you thinking of?" "What do I feel?" replied Amos. "I really could not explain it, but my thoughts go out to all my friends and to all those who share this great joy with me... to all those who are physically far away but very close to me in spirit..."

Meanwhile millions of spectators were glued to their television sets, anxiously waiting to hear the name of the winner. In the midst of all the confusion Amos thought he heard the host say, "In tenth place is..." He strained to hear but couldn't catch the name of the contestant. With considerable difficulty he made his way through the people towards the backstage area. He moved a heavy curtain aside and took a few more steps forward. By now he was behind the scenes and from there the host's voice could be heard quite clearly. "In seventh place..." and he paused to raise the tension and hold the audience in thrall.

Amos thought about his parents, who would still not have known anything yet and in that moment were suffering painfully, caught between hope and fear, but he could do absolutely nothing for them. He imagined them in their seats with beads of sweat on their foreheads and ice cold hands, their throats dry, and with tears in their eyes... But in reality Sandro Bardi had got up and gone to stand with his shoulders resting against the wall at the back of the theatre. He was waiting like that, with his hands behind his back, avoiding catching the eye of the people who were all focused on the stage.

After announcing the contestant who achieved third place, the TV host, an old hand, interrupted his flow. He paused for a long time and then called his assistant and asked her to guess who the winner might be. Meanwhile some technicians ran to move the piano into the position where it had been for Amos's performance. His father noted all those movements and felt a little reassured. After the announcement the winner would certainly have to sing his piece again, so according to that logic, the winner must surely be his son. He felt a moment of disorientation which lasted for an instant, and then at last Amos's name rang out throughout the theatre, accompanied by a truly overwhelming ovation from the audience. Sandro Bardi tried to applaud with the others, but then he turned towards the wall, as though trying to find a way out, to be alone with himself to fully savour that moment which seemed so incredible but instead was completely real. So many battles, so many disappointments, so many worries for the future of that son of his who he had always felt had been born to sing but who had seemed unable to find the way to transform that great passion into something which could earn him a living! And just when they were about to see their last hopes fade, everything had happened as though by magic! At that precise moment the audience was on its feet, applauding Amos, the winner of the Italian song festival. It was enough to drive one mad with joy, but, seeing the wall in front of him, Sandro Bardi came back to his senses and turned suddenly to look for his wife. There was no knowing where she could have gone. A man who had been observing him carefully came up to him and, placing one hand on his arm while indicating Amos, who was by the piano, with the other, said, "If I'm not mistaken you are the father!" Signor Bardi nodded, slightly embarrassed. "Congratulations! My name is Angelo. I am a hairdresser and I have been doing your son's hair these last few days. I already love him like my best friend."

Amos thanked everyone who had worked for him; he praised the other contestants who had been less fortunate than him on that occasion, sang his song again to great general acclaim, and then posed for the photographers. At least an hour passed in this way before he was able to go and hug his parents and friends and then only for a few minutes. He just about had time to grab a bite to eat and was immediately rushed to various radio studios which had been specially set up for the purpose, to give one interview after another until five in the morning. There were a couple of TV appearances in the afternoon of the following day, and then finally Amos headed for home, where a really big surprise awaited him. When, in his father's car, he reached the area by the bridge of the river Sterza, there was an enormous banner greeting him: "Thank you Amos for an amazing performance at Sanremo." Beyond the bridge a crowd larger than any that had ever gathered there before prevented the car from advancing. The whole village had come out to welcome and celebrate its new hero. Everyone was touching and shaking his hand. They shouted out unintelligible things to him while Sergio, his childhood friend, who was strong as a champion fighter from ancient Greece or Rome, protected him from the overzealous fans. It was a truly moving and totally unforgettable demonstration, a spontaneous display of affection which only someone fortunate enough to live in a small town can really understand. Needless to say Amos was deliriously happy. Yet, he was fully aware of the fact that, basically, although everything had started, nothing had really happened yet.

XXXI

For some time Amos feared that he would wake up from that wonderful dream and find himself in bed with all his old problems and the apparently insurmountable difficulties that he had faced for so long. In reality many aspects of his life had changed in a very short space of time. Now everyone was talking about him, some claiming friendships with him which had never really existed, or telling stories about themselves and Amos together which were entirely the product of their imaginations. Amos always found these very amusing and often he would laugh till he cried. Many practical problems, or at least the most immediate ones, had been swept away by that unexpected turn of events from which he had emerged a winner and a true star. His private life, however, was gradually becoming public property. The thin veil that protected it became thinner by the day and this made Amos unhappy, as did the attitude of the people around him who seemed unable to behave as naturally with him as they had always done in the past. Now he felt himself constantly under observation and also perhaps treated with undue respect. It wasn't that people were false towards him, but they lacked the spontaneity that he was accustomed to and which he couldn't do without. Sometimes he felt as though something incomprehensible had made him different in the eyes of others, and privately he hoped that time would bring things back to normal. On the other hand, the professional commitments that took him far from home were increasing daily.

Elena went with him almost everywhere. She was happy but at the same time apprehensive about that sudden transformation in their lives. Amos tried to reassure her. He told her that marriage was supposed to bring serenity, the most precious gift which everyone should do their utmost to safeguard. One evening, coming home after a long day at the recording studio with Carlo, he found her waiting for him outside in the courtyard. It was well into June by this time, and it was lovely outside in the evenings, but her unusual solicitude struck him as a little strange. Also Elena seemed particularly cheerful: she accompanied him into the house arm-in-arm, and only when the door was closed behind them and with the air of someone who cannot find the right words to confide a secret did Elena reveal to him that she was expecting a baby. She was radiant, happy in a way he had never seen her before. From the kitchen came a mouth-watering smell, and there was even a bottle of champagne in the fridge to celebrate the special event. Amos was happy too in his own way but he was mostly happy for his wife. If truth be told he had never had any special liking for children and especially not for infants. He would certainly love his own children, but he could not imagine how or how much, and he was curious to experience for himself something which he knew full well was totally life-changing for everyone. In any event, Elena's joy was contagious, and Amos never held back from sharing it as she began to involve him in her innumerable projects: the preparation of the baby's room, the things to buy, the small modifications required to make the house safe for the baby.

In the meantime Amos was preparing to make his debut in the role of Macduff in Giuseppe Verdi's *Macbeth*. It was being staged at the local theatre, and this gave him great pleasure: somehow it seemed to him like a sign of destiny and, above all, a real challenge to all the sceptics who had repeatedly and unhesitatingly claimed that it was impossible for a blind person to tread the boards of the stage. He was reminded of Goethe's words: "To live in the idea means to consider the impossible as possible". He studied hard and when the rehearsals started he earned everyone's good will by his diligence: he was always the first to arrive and the last to leave, he took heed of advice and did everything possible to please the conductor and the director and to avoid being a hindrance to his colleagues.

The tickets sold like hot cakes. Amos found an atmosphere of warmth and also of recognition developed around him, and he felt, quite naturally, very moved and full of a sense of responsibility. In the dressing room he vocalized a bit in his heavy wool warrior's costume, and a few minutes before curtain up he was already bathed in sweat. It was September and still very hot. The theatre was filled to capacity. His was not a major role but to him at that moment it seemed insurmountable. He knew that he had to pay close attention to his colleagues' breathing in order not to miss his cue for the ensemble sections. He knew he could not allow himself a moment's distraction: calm and total concentration were essential to avoid making a hash of things on stage. He was fully aware of all these things, and he felt the full weight of responsibility for this debut, but of one thing he was certain: in the depth of his soul he had everything it took to identify completely with the hero who finally succeeds in making good triumph over evil and to act the part in the most credible way. It was a role he loved unreservedly, and the audience understood that immediately. When he went on stage surrounded by three ballerinas, symbolising Macduff's tragic memories of his sons who had been killed at the hands of a pitiless tyrant, Amos thought about his unborn son and felt profoundly moved. His voice contained all the sadness of a man who has suffered and fought a mighty struggle, and at the end of the aria, even before his voice fell silent, suffocated by emotion, a deafening ovation filled the theatre, confirming the success of that venture. Until just a few months ago he had been playing in piano bars, performing for distracted listeners. He dwelled on that thought for a second, and his heart filled with a feeling of pure gratitude.

Around the same time he was invited by Maestro Pavarotti to be a guest on a television show, on which they would sing a duet together. The invitation had been made by phone one evening. Amos had already gone to bed and when the phone rang he woke up with a start. He heard a voice say, "Good evening, I am Luciano Pavarotti..." At first, still half-asleep, he thought it was a joke, but then he recognised the unmistakable timbre of the voice of the most famous tenor in the world, and he had to acknowledge the reality of this unbelievable moment. Only a couple of years before, at the end of a concert, he had tried to approach the maestro to shake his hand and congratulate him, but it had proved impossible as the security guards would not let him pass. How was all this possible and why? Now he asked himself these things and in the meantime carried on without worrying about the tiredness and discomfort that the sudden changes in his life and the abrupt detachment from the past invariably caused him.

At the beginning of October Amos's record company asked him to go to the studios in Bologna to record a new album. He was seriously worried about the choice of songs. He knew that it was absolutely essential to have at least one song that went straight to people's hearts, otherwise the album would never be a success and all the hard work put in till then would have gone up in smoke. On the other hand, what could one do? Record companies have commitments and contracts have to be honoured; all he could do was record, put his soul into it, and hope.

But there were to be more surprises that year. In fact, towards the middle of December he was invited to take part in a Christmas concert at the Vatican in the Sala Nervi. It was a great honour to perform there alongside famous artists from all over the world – an extraordinary sign of recognition. Once again Amos gave his all, and the audience that filled the hall gave him a wonderfully warm reception.

A few days later Elena and Amos went off alone to Stockholm, where he was to take part in a New Year's Eve concert. This proved a truly unforgettable experience. The problems started right away, outside the airport, due to what was effectively a communications problem: Amos spoke very little English then, and he had the impression that his hosts, who quite understandably spoke not a word of Italian, hardly spoke English either. Everything, including the simplest things, became difficult and laborious, although everyone was very kind and generous. Furthermore, it was freezing cold and Amos feared for Elena's health. By this time she was seven months pregnant and had a big belly. He thought of Italy and of all his friends who would be gathered together to celebrate New Year's Eve, and he felt sad and lonely in a way that had rarely happened before. So much so that on the evening of the concert when he was in his dressing room he felt a distinct need to cry, but he was ashamed of his weakness, so he plucked up courage and went out on stage, although the expression on his face was more that of a condemned man than of a rising star.

He went back to Italy as happy as a boarding school student coming home for the holidays and immediately set to work. The Sanremo Festival was coming up soon and it was a risk Amos had to take, however reluctantly. The song he had recorded was undoubtedly interesting, quite different from the regular fare and one which made no concession to what was in vogue, but in his view it was too refined, rather too elegant and lacking that impact that was so necessary in these situations when everything depends on those five minutes. "This song," he said to Caterina and Michele, "is good for a long-distance race, but what we need is a piece which is right for the one-hundred-metre dash..." "But we haven't got anything better," they replied, "and it's a beautiful song; you just have to believe in it and give it all you've got. On the other hand, you can't stand back and watch; you can't miss an opportunity like this one..."

So Amos resigned himself to his fate. Perhaps things just had to be this way, he thought, and it was pointless to try and go against the tide of events. It was better to swim with the current, taking great care to avoid accidents on the way... and so he did. He left for Sanremo on a cold, wet February morning in a car specially sent to Poggioncino to take him to the "City of Flowers". It was just like the previous year, but this time he went without his family. Elena had considered it prudent to stay at home for fear she might have ended up giving birth in a hospital where she did not know anybody. Amos would have preferred to have her with him: according to his calculations there was plenty of time to go and come back before the happy event, but he raised no objections. He only urged his wife to be careful not to expose herself to any risks and never to be alone for any reason at all, and then he left.

From the start, his stay in Sanremo proved pleasant and less arduous than expected. Adriano and Pierpaolo, a young musician Amos had become friends with, and his parents were there with him. His performance was on the evening of 21st February. He put in his best effort, but there was no doubt his concentration was not the same as it had been on the other occasions, and then, as he knew full well, the song was not one of those that immediately captivate the audience, so when the votes were cast he was not even in the top ten. It was exactly as he had feared. In first place, in the interim results, was a young singer who was also one of Michele's stable. Amos was well aware of the consequences of such a situation: Michele would undoubtedly have dedicated all his efforts towards that new promising project, shelving his own. It was terrible. Everything could fail from one moment to the next and end up in nothing. Then he would have to start all over again from square one, to the delight of his detractors and all those who, for the past year, had been forced to bite their tongues for having spoken too soon. How much criticism would he have to suffer now! His detractors would smirk and speak out, saying, "I always said he would not go anywhere, that it was just a lucky break..."
All these thoughts whirled around Amos's mind and tormented him while, in effect, Michele was hardly ever around. The situation was therefore objectively critical. Amos was downcast but he had not lost his fighting spirit. On the other hand, what could he do now if not try to set out on a damage limitation exercise? He ran

back to his room and asked not to be disturbed for any reason. He had to rest and not think about anything in order to regain his peace of mind. What would Ettore have recommended to him? Would everything really go back to how it was before? Is the weight of defeat so crushing? Buried in these dark thoughts, Amos slowly fell asleep.

Suddenly a sound startled him awake and he heard his mother's voice. "Why did you wake me?" An expression of annoyance was imprinted on his features; he was about to make a gruff response when he heard his mother repeating, "He's born, he's born! Everything's fine...it's all fine!" He sat up on the bed. "Calm down, I told you everything is under control! Elena is fine. Now you get some rest and don't worry about anything else. Forgive me, but I had to tell you right away." She kissed her son and left the room, closing the door behind her. Amos could not get back to sleep. An endless cascade of thoughts kept him company. A new life had come to grow up in his house. How would this child be? It was the first time that he was struck with this question. He realised that he could not possibly wait till the end of the festival before going to meet his son, and he also felt a certain remorse for not having been by his wife's side at such an important time for a couple. Who knew how much she had suffered and how she had missed him, accustomed as she was to always having him close to her...

Suddenly he remembered the festival and felt a sort of pang in his heart: his position in the ranking was really desperate. What a fine mess, just at the time when he should have honoured the birth of his first-born with a great success. He was overwhelmed by a deep sadness, and woe betide anyone who told him that he should be happy and that the happy event was worth so much more than winning a festival...How empty and false are those words! A father must be a good example to his son; he must fight to win: whatever we do, we must give the best of ourselves, providing others with a model of moral rectitude; only in this way can one man's victory soon become a victory for all. But precisely for this reason one has to find the strength to put aside all those pointless concerns and concentrate one's energy on the task in hand. So, as he searched for inner peace, Amos prepared himself, as he had the previous evening, and went up onto the stage feeling motivated and full of good intentions. However, even this did nothing to improve his position in the ranking. Amos was sitting at a table in a restaurant with his parents when the results of the votes were brought to him. His stomach immediately clamped shut and he stopped eating. He turned to his father and said, "I have to get back to Elena. I have two free days and I can't stay here..." Signor Bardi knew right away that it would have been pointless to try and change his mind. After all, Amos's wish was entirely legitimate, and he agreed to take him to the hospital in Volterra where Elena had given birth and where she was to remain for a few more days.

Amos did not say a word on the way there. He was in the grip of a gentle turmoil and did nothing to fight it. He was afraid of not loving his son, of responding with indifference to the first physical contact with that creature who had only just emerged into the light of day, and he was anxious at the idea of the upset he would have caused Elena, towards whom instead he felt a new emotion of tenderness and gratitude. As he stepped towards the small room with two little beds in it and in-between the tiny cot, he felt his heart beating fast. He took some deep breaths, just as he did before going on stage, and went in. He understood the reasons for that racing heartbeat very well, but he couldn't do anything about it. He went up to Elena's bed and embraced her timidly as though afraid of hurting her. Huddled up in that hospital bed, she seemed to have suddenly become very fragile. He asked her how she was and then remembered the baby, and forcing himself to feign an interest that in reality he did not feel, he went up to the cot and cautiously searched out the baby. The little one was sleeping peacefully. Fear of waking him could have provided Amos with an excellent pretext for delaying the first contact with his son, but a strange curiosity won over his hesitation. He held out his hands, and with a gentleness which he would never have imagined himself capable of, he lifted up his son and held him to his chest. A vaguely sweetish smell, mild but clearly defined, the smell of new-born babies, introduced itself into his nostrils and all around. Amos breathed it in deeply and for the first time in his life he felt as though intoxicated by it. He touched the baby's cheek with his lips, and when he finally started to say something he found he was alone with his wife in that little hospital room. The others had all gone out to allow him to give free rein to that complicated tangle of sensations and emotions which are the most intimate, the deepest and most indelible ones within a family. In those brief moments he understood that a new meaning, a new form of love had put down deep, ineradicable roots in his heart. Everything had happened so fast and in such a surprising way. Now he felt like a new person who, in that different situation, had recovered the ability to understand what was truly important, and he now placed the apparently weak and tiny creature, of whom he was the father and for whom he would not hesitate to lay down his life, on the highest rung of his hierarchy of values. The doctor allowed him to spend the whole night with Elena. To Amos this felt like a favour worthy of eternal gratitude. He said goodbye to his father and lay down on the empty bed with the little one on his chest, promising Elena that he would set him back down in the cot before he fell asleep. But Amos was not sleepy and the little one seemed to be listening to his heart beat. It was a new emotion, a deep and mysterious one which grew with the baby's every small movement, with every small cry. Next to him lay a woman who had brought a child into the world, and he, Amos, was the father of that creature. This thought struck him as so enormous and so complex as not to be able to fit inside his head, and yet it was so. He thought and occasionally gently stroked the tiny face of that little angel with its delicate little body, almost as though testing its consistency. He whispered sweet words with no meaning but lots of feeling until he had the impression that the baby was asleep. Then, lying very still on the bed too for fear of waking him, he slowly began to compose some verses which summarised in some way the sensations and thoughts of those unforgettable hours:

> While, like a giant, proud and happy,
> I hold my little one in my arms,
> and his tiny, innocent body,
> fragile and alive like a little bird,
> is pressed against my breast,
> quiet and safe, half-asleep,
> for a few moments, almost sweetly
> my destiny appears as in a dream.
> So I see myself old and resigned,
> sitting there, by the fireplace,
> awaiting the night as fearful as a child
> to hear him suddenly return
> with the gift of a smile,
> a word, a kindness,
> and like a promise that consoles,
> the immense joy of a caress...
> Then I awake and have already forgotten,
> but within me my enraptured soul
> tells me that the newborn child
> is already worth more than my own life.

For a few hours he forgot all about the festival, the problems regarding his career, and his future: an indefinable sense of gratitude towards the whole world, a sort of emotional exhilaration completely overcame him. He got up slowly from the bed and began to pace up and down the room with the baby in his arms.

"There is a man to whom I owe most of the little I know," he thought. "A man who taught me that it is better to do than to say; that it is better to doubt than to have unshakable certainties; that it is more important to try to be, rather than to strive to have.

"I will give this child his name, Ettore, so that I will think of him often even when he will no longer be with us." Pleased with this idea, which he was sure Elena would agree to, he went to the cot and put the child down. Then he stretched out on the bed and tried to rest for a while, aware of the ordeal awaiting him over the next few days.

XXXII

In the early hours of the morning Amos left for Sanremo again. He was very sad to leave that room but he was summoned by his sense of duty.

On the night of the final he felt in perfect form and also found the calm required for a good performance. The audience was beginning to know and like his song. He got a very warm reception, and he managed to considerably improve his place in the ranking but even then could not get past fourth place. For Amos this was a great disappointment, perhaps something that should be realistically considered as the beginning of an unstoppable decline. But what could he do about it? He had to put a brave face on it and give it his all as he always did. Now there was also a child to raise who would certainly look to his father as an example, so it was absolutely imperative that he redouble his efforts.

Without neglecting his own studies, Amos threw himself into the promotion of his album, travelling ceaselessly all over Europe, with Carlo always by his side, vigorously fighting off exhaustion and the boredom of the interminable hours spent waiting in airports or in the dressing rooms of television or radio stations. Elena waited for him at home with the baby, and she seemed happy, conscious of the importance of all those trips which left her feeling fearful and alone. However, around October they went on a long concert tour together which took them to Belgium, Holland, Germany, France, and Spain. The show was very original: a large orchestra played symphonic pieces and then accompanied famous singers in a variety of different musical genres. The audiences in those countries seemed to particularly enjoy this type of concert, and every night was a box office sell-out.

Amos's record company had somehow managed to get him onto that extraordinary tour, and to general surprise, after the first few performances, Amos began to sell an impressive number of records in all those countries. This led to a period of enormously hard work which forced him to travel around the world for almost three hundred days of the year. However, the results of these efforts proved to be truly incredible, and one would not even dare announce them if not supported by the knowledge that this is a story which is essentially true and rivers of ink have already been used to describe this success in the press all over the world.

In a short time Amos's albums began to sell out everywhere. In Germany, for example, the CD producers had to work all weekend in order to satisfy the huge rise in demand to levels which, according to the staff, were unprecedented. More or less the same thing happened in France just a couple of months later and then even in America, where the barriers holding back artists who performed in a language other than English had always been practically insurmountable.

So what was happening? Everyone was asking themselves the same question, including Michele, who lost no time and dedicated himself once again to Amos's project, abandoning everything else he had been working on recently to concentrate all his energies on his singer's career, which seemed more like an extraordinary fairy tale with every passing day. Topping the record charts all over the world in pop as well as, and especially, in the classical music charts, Amos was greatly in demand: on the one hand the record industry claimed him for the promotion of his albums, and on the other hand, the most prestigious theatres and concert halls in the world were clamouring for him to come and perform, offering mind-boggling fees to which, realistically, it was very hard to say no, especially for someone like Amos with his country upbringing and who, until very recently, had been afraid he would not be able to provide for his own family...

And yet, in spite of this euphoria, Amos's overwhelming success, and the change in his economic circumstances, he made a great effort not to significantly change his lifestyle and especially to avoid changing himself. In his heart were always his family, his friends, his people – the same people who had awaited his return from the festival and who had welcomed him with the huge banner which said, "Thank you Amos for an amazing performance at Sanremo." He would never forget that.

All over the world Amos remained open and direct in that typically Tuscan way, always modest and respectful but never subservient. Perhaps this was the combination of qualities which endeared him to the Holy Father and to the president of the United States, who, after having met him for the first time, repeated their invitations for him to perform for them. Who could say? Amos asked himself the same question without succeeding in finding any answer other than the one he would occasionally give to journalists, which was ironic but, in a certain sense, also vaguely religious: "Thus it is willed where will and power are one".

Time passed quickly and events followed on from each other at an almost unsustainable pace, each one more incredible than the last, so that it would really be impossible to describe them all and at the same time expect the reader to believe everything to be true. As a consequence of this change in his life and the increasingly relentless pressure of his professional commitments, Amos was forced to give serious consideration to the need to move to a place which would be more convenient for his travel requirements. The purchase of a new house, the first which was really his own, would also solve the problem of how to invest his first earnings. So, after a long and complicated search, he decided to buy a fine house on the border with Versilia, just a stone's throw from the sea and with a view of the Apuan mountains as backcloth to that incomparable work of nature. Moreover, in that place he would finally be removed from the allergens which had been such a problem for him in his youth.

It was during this period that Elena became pregnant with their second child, another little boy, to whom they gave the name Andrea. This time Amos managed to be with his wife for the happy event, and he was delighted to share that new experience, so painful before as it was joyous after the birth itself. The press rushed to spread the news, which would be embroidered with the most curious details which were a mixture of truth and complete invention. Now he was a famous artist and Amos was not best pleased with this state of affairs, but he had by this time accepted the fact that he no longer had a private life as such. Nevertheless, this was one of the happiest times in his life, in spite of the physical and psychological strain and the occasional health problems affecting some of his nearest and dearest. He felt the wind in his sails; he clenched his fists and gave thanks for being alive and for the great satisfaction life brought him. He dedicated his thanks to his parents, who had done so much for him and worried so much, suffering in silence, fearing that he would not find fulfilment and would never find a path to match his good will and his qualities.

If truth be told there was another thing which also worried Amos a great deal: the constant battle with his voice, which was not only reluctant to comply with his demands but would also behave unreliably, presenting him with different problems on a daily basis for which not even the most distinguished teachers could provide any ready or effective solutions. He also needed to resolve the even more thorny and important question of the top notes that he feared he could no longer achieve. One famous teacher had jokingly tried to encourage his efforts by saying to him, "With the beautiful mid notes, which you have, you can sing bel canto, but it is with the top notes that you make your fortune!" As a result he felt extremely frustrated. He would not be able to carry on singing pieces which did not include very high notes for very long. Soon he would find himself in the firing line and be demolished by the critics... The consequence of all this was that he was worrying about his voice night and day with a maniacal intensity. Sometimes he would try out a high note in the middle of the night while his family slept peacefully. On the other hand, he would never manage to get to sleep while tormented by a niggling doubt about his vocal ability, or driven to try out a new vocal position which he felt compelled to test immediately. Elena would wake up with a start and be angry, although, knowing her husband, she was well aware that reproaches and sulking would be to no avail. Amos was ready to apologise and be sincerely sorry, but he knew he could not promise that the same thing would not happen again, perhaps even the very next night. But with time, determination, and a good dose of luck those high notes came to him. The first ones were small and not well supported, but they improved daily and surprisingly fast so that soon this became the most secure part of his range.

After this he had to deal with the matter of producing seamless transitions between the various registers, but this task was certainly less difficult for him than the previous one. The path may have continued to be an uphill struggle, beset with hazards and difficulties, but now he was beginning to see a glimmer of hope which gave him strength and courage. After all, he would certainly not give up now that his career had finally taken off after so many vain attempts...

One day he received an invitation to perform at a concert in Bremen in Germany, to celebrate the one hundredth anniversary of one of the most famous and prestigious record companies in the world, Deutsche Grammophon. Amos was honoured by such an invitation, so he decided to accept, and soon the appropriate agreements were settled by both parties. He phoned Ettore to see if he could be persuaded to go with him. It was a long time since he had last seen him, and he felt a strong need to spend some time in his company, to hear his opinion on so many things that had happened recently on which he couldn't get a clear perspective himself. From their meeting he would finally be in a position to understand if, and to what extent, his success might have altered him as a person and affected his lifestyle. In other words, Ettore, frank and direct as he always was, would undoubtedly have assisted him in carrying out a kind of examination of his conscience which Amos felt he really needed in order to feel calmer and more at peace with himself. Perhaps he felt this way because deep down he was not happy: all that money which had forced him to change his ways; the occasionally harsh clashes with the people he worked with, the agents and record company representatives; the attacks in the press, by critics – Amos found all this extremely exhausting and disappointing. He would talk it over with his old friend, who he was sure would be a great help.

Ettore accepted the invitation immediately. He loved to travel and was delighted to have the chance to see Amos in person rather than on a TV screen. He arrived at the airport, punctual as always, dressed as usual in jeans, a sweater, and sneakers. As agile and fit as a man in his prime, the way Ettore carried his seventy-six years was truly enviable, and yet Amos noted a slight change in him that caused him some concern. It seemed to him that at certain moments Ettore was absent or at least distracted, as though his mind were elsewhere and not totally focused on the here and now. Amos was worried and he thought for the first time about Ettore's age. How would that confident, unassailable man who was as healthy and strong as an oak cope with illness or doctors (of whom he had never had need in his life) or hospitalization? Could Ettore also be pondering the very same thing? Was he gradually losing interest in the things of this world? Amos immediately tried to chase that strange thought away; it was a beautiful sunny day and quite hot and this put him in a good mood. During the trip, however, Ettore returned to his old self, unstinting in his advice; he did not spare his young friend the odd paternal reproach for which his disciple was nonetheless sincerely grateful. On the plane a flight attendant touched him lightly on the shoulder to get his attention. "Sorry, Mr Bardi, can I have an autograph?" she said in English. So Amos opened the tray-table, took the card and the pen from the young woman, and wrote "Cordially yours" above his signature. The woman smiled broadly, put the card and pen back in her pocket, and then held Amos's hand between hers and shook it warmly. "Oh, it's very kind of you! Do you know, all my family loves you!" "Thank you, it has been a pleasure for me!" Amos replied in English to the young woman who had still not let go of his hand. Ettore, in the meantime, had opened his newspaper. Once the flight attendant had left he turned to Amos in a joking tone. "Hey, Count Vronsky, did you take her for Anna Karenina perhaps? Remember," he added in English, "you have a family, two children..." "What are you saying?" Amos quickly parried in English. "Oh nothing, nothing... only I know you very well!" continued Ettore, still in English. After all, he had been the one who had taught Amos the first rudiments of that language, and now he was pleased to see his progress. "Don't worry," concluded Amos, laughing.

In Bremen Ettore attended one of Amos's performances for the first time, and at the end of the concert he came to congratulate him, shaking his hand warmly. Who knows what Amos would have given to know exactly what sensations were felt by that lion-heart of a man, sitting in the audience, when he saw him go up on stage next to a famous conductor, to perform for all those expert music lovers who lived for music and were able to make hundreds of discerning comparisons and hard judgements. Who could know if once again Ettore had found time to observe all those concentrated faces and to analyse them with his usual sharp insight, or whether he had abandoned himself to the music, listening with emotion and feeling profoundly moved? Amos would never know.

XXXIII

On the day of his fortieth birthday, Amos, surrounded by all his dearest friends, had many reasons to celebrate and be happy. In just a few years he had achieved incredible goals which honestly were quite beyond his wildest dreams. He was top of the charts all over the world, both for classical and pop music; he had dozens of platinum discs, prizes, and awards coming at him from all directions and theatres and concert halls competing for him to perform there, to the great joy and disbelief of Michele, who could not believe his eyes when he sat at his desk and read the offers that came to his office from all over the world.

Amos, in spite of everything, had remained the boy he always was, and he loved to share his success with his friends: Adriano, Verano, Carlo, Luca, Giuliano, old Monti (which is what he called the man who had fallen in love with his voice after hearing only a few notes of music and who, at his own personal risk, had created false documents in order to arrange his debut at the Valli theatre in Reggio Emilia)...Even Sergio was there, a tennis coach Amos had befriended recently, having found that they shared a similar approach to the world and with whom a friendship had developed which was as precious and clear as Bohemian glass.

All his friends had accepted his invitation, and his birthday party was among the best he had ever had. Verano had been in charge of the food and Signor Bardi had brought his excellent wine: no one that night gave the slightest thought to diets. Jokes, songs, and funny stories went on until well past two o'clock, when the partygoers began to wilt and the first guests began to leave. Before his father left, Amos went to him and said, "My cousin Giovanni has asked me so many times to go on his boat with him, and I have never found the time to do it. Tomorrow morning he is free and the weather is promising. What do you say to a day out in the boat?" "Call me around nine and I will tell you," said his father, with a quick glance at his watch. Then he left too.

As soon as the alarm went off, Amos jumped out of bed and dressed quickly. Elena followed him, although she was still very sleepy, and ran down to the kitchen to prepare some milk for the children. Little Ettore slept so soundly in his parents' big bed that no noise disturbed him.

Amos waited impatiently for the agreed time when he could call his parents to go out on his cousin's boat. When it was almost time, just a few minutes before nine, he dialled his parents' number and waited. The phone rang but no one replied. After five or six rings he finally heard his mother's voice and immediately sensed that something was wrong. "So," he asked energetically, "are you ready or are you still lounging around in bed?" There was a pause, then his mother sighed and, in a faltering voice, said, "Amos, unfortunately I don't think you will want to go out on the boat today!" "Why?" asked Amos, by now clearly agitated. He knew his mother well and was able to read her state of mind from the tone of her voice. He was immediately alarmed by her words and her tone and during those terrible moments he thought of all his loved ones. What could have happened to whom? The children, fortunately, were there with him under his vigilant care, and Elena was downstairs in the kitchen. His thoughts turned to his father, then to his brother, but his mother interrupted them and said, "Yesterday afternoon, Ettore fell from his bicycle and hit his head on the tarmac." Then she stopped, as though unable to find the words to continue, and Amos felt as though his face were on fire, while a sudden weakness in his legs forced him to sit down on the edge of the bed, next to his son who was slowly waking up.

"And then what happened?" asked Amos, almost shouting into the receiver. "I'm sorry...it didn't end well!" said his mother, knowing the pain her son would be feeling.

For a few minutes they remained silent. Amos was stunned. He felt as though everything was spinning around him, and he was completely disoriented. All of a sudden, as he recovered his reason, everything became clear: Ettore was dead. He would never see or hear him again. Passing on from this life, Ettore would no longer be there to counsel, encourage, or comfort him. All of that was gone forever...

Without saying a word, with a hysterical gesture, Amos slammed down the receiver. He jumped up and ran towards the stairs like a madman, shouting, "Elena! Elena! Ettore is dead!" In his desperation poor Amos was shouting without realising the panic that he was causing in his wife as a result of their choice of the same name for their child.

She, meanwhile, was downstairs in the kitchen pouring hot milk into the children's decorated mugs. When she heard her husband's voice she put down the saucepan and tried to make out precisely what he could be shouting so hysterically. Suddenly Amos's cries struck her forcefully. She felt a terrible stab in her heart and an excruciating pain in her stomach, her eyes filled with tears, and a desperation that she had never felt before overcame her so that she almost fell to the ground. She mustered what strength remained and ran up the stairs like a robot. She crossed the hall, went into the bedroom, and, racked with sobs, threw herself onto the bed next to little Ettore, who was staring at her in wide-eyed terror. "Ettore! Ettore!" cried the poor distraught mother, only gradually beginning to realise that her son was alive and well. She clung to him with all her strength like a madwoman. She pressed him to her breast and then looked at her husband, who had covered his face with his hands and was on his knees on the bedside mat. "Are you trying to kill me! I thought I was going to die!" she yelled through the tears which seemed to be choking her.

"Why are you crying, Mamma?" asked Ettore in a small voice, visibly upset. "Who has died? What was Daddy saying before?" Amos got up and ran to the boy, who had freed himself from his mother's embrace and was sitting on the pillow, observing his parents with a puzzled air. Poor Amos took him into his arms and began to speak to him tenderly in a soft voice. "Do you remember Ettore? That good man who had the same name as you? Do you know he is no more?" "Daddy, what does it mean that he is no more?" came the reply from Ettore, who was at the age when children ask a million questions. "No, I made a mistake!" said Amos, overcome with emotion. "He is and always will be, but we will just not be able to see him anymore, but we will be able to remember him and keep him in our hearts! All right?" "All right, Daddy, all right, but I haven't really understood what you mean, Daddy!" the little boy said and quickly ran off.

Amos shut himself in his study, sat at the desk, and began to think: Ettore's death seemed absolutely inconceivable to him. How could such a stupid accident have cut short the life of such a strong man? Amos had never contemplated the idea that Ettore might die. For him that man was invincible, perfect, and as eternal as an idea. But he was gone, perhaps after having done everything he set out to do. On his last trip with Amos to Bremen, perhaps he had told his young friend the last things that needed to be told: a kind of moral testament which Amos would never forget.

XXXIV

Amos reached the church square with his spirits in a state of disarray, gripped by a desperation which became more unbearable with every passing minute. He gritted his teeth, clenched his fists, breathed deeply, and tried to find the strength to avoid breaking down in tears. Elena walked by his side in silence, avoiding looking at him. Amos was aware of his brother, Alberto, on his other side and behind them were Adriano, Verano, Carlo, Giuliano... all his old friends who never let him down, especially in life's more difficult moments.

When Amos entered the church of Lajatico, a church which held so many joyful memories for him, it was already full of people gathered together to pay their last respects to Ettore. The coffin was there, at the foot of the altar, and inside it lay a body. Amos felt a cold shiver run through him and a wave of dismay filled his heart. The heat, the heady smell of incense and flowers, and the solemnity expressed on the faces and in the voices of everyone around him almost made him faint. He looked for a space in a pew and sat down.

The funeral began but Amos could not concentrate. With his head bowed and his face in his hands he followed his own train of thought which brought back memories, both recent and from the distant past, and he was only jolted back into the present when the priest started to talk about the deceased. At this point he was startled into listening with attention. The parish priest spoke about Ettore's life and his Christian journey, but everything he said was so remote, so lacking in life or truth that it struck Amos as almost offensive. "What is he saying? Who exactly is the priest talking about?" he asked himself. "Can he really be talking about Ettore?" Did he know him so little? Or could he not forgive him for the fact that he had not seen him often enough at the Sunday Mass? And yet Don Carlo always had a good thing to say about everyone! Amos's heart was full of uncontrollable indignation, and he began pondering the need to intervene with a eulogy himself, before the funeral mass was over, in order to bid farewell to Ettore with the love and emotion that he deserved, saying the things that needed to be said in the way they needed to be said. "I will speak from the foot of the altar, near the coffin, next to him," he thought. "And I will talk about him to all these people who loved him as I did, who like me received something from him that they will never forget: advice, assistance, or a good word!" He had stopped listening again and was lost in his thoughts, which were now entirely focused on planning what he would say.

"Dear friends," I will say, "I hope you will forgive my need to speak to you briefly about the man whom we all wish to recognize, today more than ever, with love and gratitude. The religious aspects of this ceremony have already been dealt with by our priest. I, as a lay person, instead feel the need to attempt to describe the extraordinary human, moral, and intellectual qualities of this man so that no one will forget him and nothing, nothing at all will be lost of all that he has left to us. Today, in this church, conquered by an emotion that fills our eyes with tears and puts a catch in our voices, we bid farewell to a man who is departing on a long voyage, but is there any reason to cry for a man who departs as dead? Those who have walked by Ettore's side on the path of truth, humility, and goodwill, of daily commitment towards others, so close to the teachings of Christ the Redeemer, of the risen Christ, cannot and should not think of Ettore as a man who has left us forever but as a companion who continues to walk by our side and to comfort us with the clarity of his ideas and with the kindness of the good words he always had for everyone. Am I perhaps being blasphemous if I ask you to rebel, to rise up in arms against the insane idea of this death? Well! I implore you, once the remains of our brother are closed up under the shelter of a tombstone and an epitaph, I beg you to forget this unhappy day. Forget this day and remember him, continue to make him live amongst you, in your houses, in your conversations, as surely you will have already done a thousand times while he was away on one of his many long trips to so many parts of the world. After all, what has happened really? Something has broken, something broke in Ettore, his body has fallen. So what? These are things that happen, just as hair falls and nails break. Over forty years every human body is transformed and becomes something completely different and unrecognizable. And does anyone despair because of this? No! Of course not! So why despair so much today if substantially nothing has happened? Everything in this world perishes, so let the body perish too! It is not worth more than beauty which, as a famous poet said, is like the 'shadow of a flower'. It is certainly not worth more than power which is like 'a trumpet's echo lost in the valley'. No! Absolutely not! The only thing that is important is that the idea of what he was, of how he was, of what he has left of himself in us should remain intact, and then we will have lost absolutely nothing! Because the idea, only the idea 'wins over fleeing time and barbarous silence'..."

Amos's heart was swollen with that feeling of courage that makes men launch themselves into the fray of battle, disdainful of the tremendous risk that awaits them. In any case the sudden idea of speaking to the assembled faithful and in some way snatching Ettore from the arms of death by consigning him forever to the memory of those who had respected, loved, and emulated him gave Amos some respite from his despair and restored him to a state of calm. He was about to get up to go towards the altar when he heard a chant which brought him back to his senses quite suddenly.

It was the sad, solemn chant which often accompanies the dearly departed on their last journey: "*in paradisum deducant te angeli*..." The coffin, carried by four young men from the town, passed by him in that moment, and the people started leaving the pews to join the mournful procession.

His eyes filled with tears, big hot tears that streaked down his face as sobs shook his chest. He had said none of the things he wanted to say, or better, cry out, and now it was too late. He slipped into the middle of the crowd like a stranger and slowly followed the procession to the small cemetery just a few hundred metres outside the village, among the dark green cypresses of his beautiful Tuscany.

XXXV

A few days later Amos left for a concert tour of the United States. With him were Carlo, Michele, and his excellent secretary, Cristina, of whom Amos was very fond and whom he admired greatly for all the patience and effort she put into her work. The Americans loved Amos fanatically and were waiting for him with open arms. The concerts were a sell-out at all the venues from the very first day the tickets went on sale...

Amos's story, though, ends here. Everything that followed is by now in the public domain as a result of all the attention the media have devoted to his story from the start. It is better to end with some passages from Amos's diary to allow him to conclude his story in his own words.

1st October 1998

I am leaving with death in my heart, but I leave, nonetheless, full of life and hope. I am alone, without my family, and I know I will miss them a great deal. But I take Ettore with me...he will be there among the people I will meet, with whom I will speak or simply shake by the hand, and that will be a great comfort to me...

5th October 1998

The American people seem to love me. The audiences at my concerts are fantastic and no words can describe the warmth that welcomes and sustains me. If only every one of them knew the fear I feel as I go on stage, if they only knew my anguish, my silences, my loneliness...

7th October 1998

I have the very disagreeable impression of having been turned into a money-making machine and being treated accordingly. I have become the focus of large and conflicting interests. I am afraid and I am ashamed of being afraid, because a man who gives his best should never be afraid of anything, not even of making a mistake...

9th October 1998

I have discovered that I am the innocent cause of a battle between two powerful organisations, as well as the undeserving target of their artillery fire, but some saint will come to my aid or else I will withdraw in orderly fashion. After all, I have already been very fortunate: I have what I need to live, and above all, I still know how to live with little.

12th October 1998

Today I was very moved: arriving in Boston I found a huge crowd waiting for me at the airport, and I found that the city authorities had proclaimed today Bardi's Day: a holiday in occasion of my concert, but to what do I owe such benevolence?

15th October 1998

I can still hardly believe it. This morning I was received by the mayor of New York, who awarded me a big glass apple, the symbol of the city. He is a true lover of opera and in his speech he praised the qualities of my voice. Then it was my turn to speak, and in my faltering English, I said, "I have always been convinced that life is really a wonderful mystery. Meeting you today, Mr Mayor, and meeting so many of the people who live in this country, has only served to confirm this idea of mine. As an Italian I promise to do my utmost to be worthy of this honour, honouring my country and all those who had to leave it."

In any event, however hard I try, I really cannot explain to myself the reason for all this attention.

One day, who knows, I may decide to write a book that tells the story of my life, to satisfy the curiosity of my children and my grandchildren, to pass the time which, in the dressing rooms of theatres and television studios, really seems never-ending, or to reveal, after the fact, the arcane secret that drove a blind boy who was born and bred in the remote countryside in the region of the Maremma towards such ambitious goals as to surpass the limits of the wildest imagination.

20th October 1998

Tonight I will be singing again so I must spend the whole day here, shut in this anonymous hotel room, without exchanging a word with anyone to rest my voice and maintain its quality. But all in all it is fine this way because I am tired, tired of travelling constantly, tired of charts, battles, contracts, tired of the press that says whatever it wants about me without the slightest concern for the hurt that can cause, tired of the critics who turn their pitiless and sterile artillery fire on my success. Clinging to their principles, forgetting that no one is the repository of absolute truth, they ignore the facts, but principles crumble while facts remain. That is how I think of my fate, and no one can imagine how dear to me, in the solitude of this room, is the music of silence.

XXXVI

Ten years on...

We left Amos in the midst of the turmoil of events relating to his artistic life, and we return to find him where we first encountered him at the beginning of this story: sitting patiently in an armchair in a dressing room with his computer on his lap, waiting for the appointed time for his performance.

How many things have happened within a period of time which has passed by in a flash! So many ambitions fulfilled, so many trials, so many painful losses, and so many precious memories impressed upon the soul of a man, who, with the trust of a migratory bird, continues to make his way towards his destination, using every last ounce of his strength to work so as to leave his mark in the very best way.

His hair has turned grey and no longer covers his shirt collar, but his smile and his expression have not changed, and these clearly convey his peace of mind and unshakable optimism. And yet, just when we interrupted our story, at the time of Amos's spectacular rise to stardom, which was so richly constellated with fabulous achievements, dark clouds which did not augur well began to gather in the skies above him.

Amos's much loved father, Sandro, had been afflicted by an incurable disease, and his condition began to worsen. On Amos's return from a very important Easter concert broadcast by a German TV station, he found his father lying in a hospital bed entirely bereft of strength or will. He embraced him and tried to say a few words which he hoped would cheer him up. "The whole audience stood up, Pa, and Maestro Maazel was very happy." The patient just about managed a smile and raised his hand to stroke his son's hair but said nothing. Amos felt his heart squeeze. He felt an urge to cry and, with his tears, to wash and purify his poor father's body to remove the disease that consumed him, but tears were not enough for such a task, and after all, those who are suffering need smiles, hope, and courage.

"Do you want me to stay here with you, Pa?" he asked, when the time came to leave. And he heard that dear voice reply weakly, "No! No! You must go, I am happy to know..." He became a little confused and then added, "Just call and tell me how you get on..."

Amos gave him a big hug and kissed his forehead, and as his lips formed that kiss he had the feeling that this would be the last time, the last embrace, the last breath, the last precious memory of his father. He felt Sergio's hand on his shoulder affectionately drawing him away and his friend quietly saying, "Let's go, Amos, let's go!"

Sergio was very sad too. The suffering felt by one's close friends is highly contagious. With huge reluctance Amos left his father and slowly made his way from that room where he would never see him again. His legs felt heavy and his will crushed by the weight of the cruel destiny which took him far from that bedside and far from that life that was about to reach its end.

He was suddenly overwhelmed by a flood of recollections. They were fond memories of a happy childhood: his father's gentle touch, his reluctant admonishments, his precious, passionate teachings; his values, the ideals he had gently made his own; the winter evenings by the fireplace and the summer nights in the country lanes looking for fireflies, or under the moonlight, in the freshly ploughed fields...

He thought and walked robot-like towards the waiting car, to an airplane that would take him away...As he thought he vowed to himself, "I will take your name all over the world. You will see me run, fight, you will see me fall, but you will be proud of me. Every evening I will tell you about my journeys and my concerts, just as I have always done, and your smile will always give me the strength to carry on to my next task." He could feel the understanding of his friends, the suffering of his mother, whom he had left there, faithfully and heroically close to the man she had loved all her life, and suddenly, in a way that had happened very few times in his life, he felt very sad and alone.

A few days later he received the call that confirmed the accuracy of his previous painful sense of foreboding. He heard the voice of his brother, Alberto, telling him that their father had died. He was in Rome at the time. It was the 30th April 2000. Amos was preparing for a concert the following day – a very important concert which he was to perform, accompanied by the orchestra of Santa Cecilia, before the Pope. He wasted no time. He immediately called for the car, gathered up his luggage, and raced home.

Amos spent the whole night next to the coffin. His father was there, but he was no more. He stroked that cold forehead and could not believe that this body had belonged to the man who had brought him up, loved and supported him. Suddenly he had a very strong feeling that his father was somewhere else, or perhaps everywhere else, probably actually there, in their midst, anywhere, in fact, rather than contained within those remains which seemed so foreign to him, like a statue made of wax or of cold clay.

His mother kept coming and going and spoke to her poor husband's body as though he were alive. Amos felt himself freeze with dismay. His mother should be looking for Sandro where he had gone! Not there! She could and should speak to him with her heart...but all those words addressed to a stranger!!! No! She should not be doing that. In the morning he was exhausted but had no wish to lie down and rest.

Suddenly the phone rang. Someone answered. A few minutes later his mother came to tell him that they were expecting him in Rome, that he absolutely had to go, and that a police helicopter would be coming to pick him up to get him there just in time for the concert. Amos felt disoriented and incredulous. How could that be possible? After such a night and after feeling such pain! How would he be able to sing? How could they possibly expect him to manage something like that?

But his mother and Alberto encouraged him. "Your father would be happy. He will be with you ... " He understood that once again the forces of destiny would get their way. Destiny is a whirlwind that countenances no opposition; it is a powerful wind and we are like reeds that must yield and give way to it.

He gathered up all his strength and left for Rome with Alberto and his friend Adriano, who didn't want to leave him in such circumstances. He just had time to change his clothes when he was called onto the huge stage which had been set up for the occasion before an enormous crowd in the midst of which was His Holy Father Pope John Paul II. There were several moments when he felt as though his throat would let him down and that his voice would irretrievably give way, but he forced himself to be calm. He told himself not to think of anything other than those notes. He asked his heart to be cool, his soul to move away from there, his thoughts to go away ... and for some mysterious, incredible reason it worked.

Those dark clouds in Amos's sky had begun to clash furiously as they were buffeted by that sudden squall; the storm had begun. The first frightening downpour had left its mark, but as Amos was to find out, the turmoil had only just begun.

One day the Financial Police suddenly descended on his house with two flying squads; nine members of the Military Police found him alone at home. In just a few hours they had gone through everything with a fine-tooth comb, every cupboard was thrown open and investigated, every drawer opened and emptied out, the contents of every computer scrutinised ...

Initially Amos was caught somewhat off balance and felt shocked and embarrassed, but he soon calmed down and responded in his natural, spontaneous, and almost cheery way, his curiosity aroused by these events, which struck him as quite unreal. When Sergio arrived he found his friend deep in what seemed to be a friendly chat with the captain. "May I go now?" asked Amos politely, adding, "I have something to attend to and the house has never enjoyed such levels of security!"

The captain courteously explained that his presence was required and that he could not leave, at least not for the time being. So Amos responded, laughing, "Then I am under house arrest!" Everyone joined in the joke and the atmosphere became more relaxed. The police then left the house and headed off to the offices of Signor Martinelli, the accountant, so Amos saw no more of them for a long time. Nonetheless, he felt quite perturbed by that first experience.

During that same period Elena and the boys were vacationing in the mountains, but on this occasion their departure had not been a very peaceful one. For some time the young couple's relationship had been rather rocky. Elena displayed a degree of resentment towards her husband's career. She was irritated by his long periods of absence and the constant visits made by his colleagues. She had first met him in a local bar where the kids hung out in the evenings, and the last thing she could ever have imagined was a frenetic life such as this, requiring such commitment and so charged with responsibility. Elena had dreamed of a simple and quiet life with a husband who would always be there, instead of which she found herself splashed over the front pages of the press and forced to put up with interviews and being constantly ambushed by photographers and journalists. For her all this was too foreign to her nature, too hard, too much. Gradually she grew more distant from her husband, from his public and private life, from his friends, and from his ways, which were becoming less and less tolerable to her every day.

It is not unusual for the fulfilment of one dream to shatter the remains of another: Amos had fulfilled his dream, indeed reality had far exceeded it, but now he was being presented with a hefty bill to pay. Amos had not noticed, or perhaps he underestimated the problem. What is certain is that he was taken by surprise when he heard the cleaning lady call him in a state of alarm and fear: a gentleman had turned up, whom she took to be a bailiff, who had handed her an important document which worried her. It took only a few moments for everything to become very clear: Elena was asking for a separation. In a few days Amos would have to leave his home, the house for which he had made so many sacrifices, the house which held all the sweetest memories of his children's first steps and first words...

An unfair, anachronistic law would exile him from those four walls. From that day on a heavy iron barrier would be lowered between him and his little ones. He felt the shame of the court order, the locks of his house being changed, the unnatural and evil ban preventing him from seeing his children if not according to the times and ways dictated by a judge.

What was the point of achieving success and a degree of well-being if the price to be paid was so high and required such enormous sacrifice, effort, and endless trials? It all suddenly seemed senseless.

Amos felt a sense of rage and desperation which accompanied a feeling of impotence and insecurity he had never experienced before. He did not cry, he did not pretend, he did not go mad, but his lips no longer spread into that familiar broad smile, and for the first time he lost his unbridled enthusiasm for life, for music and singing. He became quiet, pensive and sad.

He bought a small property a few yards from his house and set up home there. His mother rushed around in a loving frenzy to purchase all the basic necessities for him: a bed, a table, a sofa. There he received the first visits from his bewildered and incredulous sons. There he tried to dig down deep within himself to summon whatever vital energy he had left. Like an exile he resigned himself to organising this new life, and it was not at all easy. Nonetheless, day by day, month by month, the optimism that had always been part of his nature, the instinct for survival which comes to the fore in difficult times, and love, the love for everything that is good and beautiful about the mystery of life – all these things combined, as we will see, to revive a dead soul.

One May morning he awoke feeling the warmth of a ray of sunshine, and after so much distress he felt heartened. That ray of sun rested on his arm like a warm hand delicately wishing to shake him from his torpor. He grabbed his computer, switched it on, and feverishly poured out these words:

In the deepest sorrow, love,
just there the seed of the greatest happiness
puts down its roots
and all reason for anxiety and torment dies.
So despair not, at least,
until your sky turns clear and fine.

It was like saying, "No, I will not put up with this! It cannot be like this. It cannot end this way. This is not how one should give up ... for the sake of my children, for my mother, my poor mother, who has fought, hoped, at times despaired, and then tasted the fruits of countless sacrifices! I have to face life with a newly found passion. I must rediscover the irresistible will to learn, to live, and to love!"

He jumped up quickly, almost wildly, from his bed, got ready with a bit more care than usual, and went out into the open air. That was not just the beginning of a new day, it was more like the start of a new life.

XXXVII

A few days later Amos received a call from his manager. He ran to the phone and immediately recognized Michele's voice imparting the following instruction in his usual agitated tone: "Get in the car and rush here, near to Ferrara. Tonight there's a really important event on. There will be politicians, show business types, industrialists... You'll find out the rest for yourself, but hurry because I have sort of promised that you would attend and that you would sing something. Nothing too demanding obviously, just a few pieces with Carlo providing the accompaniment on the piano, and then it's a party... and what a party!... Trust me." Amos tried to put up a certain resistance but all his efforts were in vain. Meanwhile outside it was raining, or rather it was bucketing down, and he was expected to set out in that foul weather to attend an extremely stupid and boring gathering of jumped-up, self-important local types, or something of the sort. It was a ridiculous endeavour. Perhaps it was an enterprise that suited Michele in order to further some personal scheme or other.

Amos planned to duck out of this expedition. He would find some excuse... or better, to hell with excuses, he would simply say the truth and stay at home where he was warm and comfortable. But hadn't he determined to fight that state of apathy and deadly indolence and move on to a new life? Hadn't he promised himself that he would live a real life once more for everyone's sake? Then perhaps he should go after all; he should fight his lazy inclinations and get to grips with the bad weather and his own natural aversion for frivolous, social occasions... and that is what he did. He asked his friend Sergio to be his driver; they passed by Carlo's place to pick him up and raced off towards Ferrara.

It rained almost all the way, and once they reached the Po valley they also found themselves driving through thick fog, but they didn't allow this to dampen their spirits. They were in open countryside when the metallic voice of the satnav device interrupted their conversation. "You have reached your destination!" it announced as Sergio turned up a narrow, muddy lane and, a few metres further on, entered the driveway of a fine, well-maintained, and elegantly decorated eighteenth-century villa.

Amos was shown into a hall on the ground floor where a grand piano was already in place on a small stage specially set up for the purpose. The tuner had just completed his task. He greeted the new arrivals respectfully and asked Amos to try out the instrument. Carlo introduced himself, sat at the piano, and began to play. "That's perfect, thank you," he said after he had completed a very short piece, at which point the piano tuner took his leave.

The three friends were left there alone. Amos did a little vocal practice for a while and then started chatting about this and that with Sergio. He was asking his friend what impressions he was formulating about the evening that lay ahead of them when he was interrupted by Luciano, the sound engineer, another faithful member of the crew who had been helping him for years by now. He too had been invited along by Michele "just to be on the safe side". There was nothing to record, nothing to amplify, but you never know what might come up... And anyway Luciano was a jovial fellow who was always good company, so it was appropriate for him to be among the guests.

"Hi, Amos," said Luciano, "how are things? Was the drive all right in this downpour?... Listen," he continued, "I have to introduce you to an amazing girl." And he laughed cheerfully as was his way.

The girl came towards the singer and held out her hand. "It's an honour to meet you, Maestro! My name is Vanessa."

Amos shook her hand. "The pleasure is mine, but please let's not be formal; after all, we are more or less the same age!" he replied laughing, not having the slightest idea that in fact, he was more than twice her age. Then he asked, "Where are you from?" "From Ancona," came the prompt reply. "Ah...the birthplace of the greatest opera singer!" Vanessa thought for a moment and almost automatically responded, "Would that be Beniamino Gigli?...Mmm no...Franco Corelli. That's right, Franco Corelli!" she said, quickly correcting herself..."Of course it's Franco Corelli. Gigli is from Recanati, how silly of me..."

Amos listened to that sweet and sensual voice...that very young voice...saying things and suggesting others, a voice that had been speaking to him for just a few minutes and yet felt to him as though it had been speaking to him forever. Suddenly he sensed that she was about to leave. Instinctively he took her hand and held it tightly in his own, and then he brushed her naked arm as though wishing to leave an impression of a caress and let her go.

A few minutes later a young journalist came to introduce herself and to ask if Amos would kindly grant her a short interview, and he distractedly agreed.

Meanwhile the party guests had slowly gathered to hear the famous singer perform. When everything was ready Carlo came up to Amos and asked, "Which piece do you want to start with?" Amos reflected for an instant and, smiling, he replied, "Tonight I would start with 'Enchanting Eyes'", and together they went to the piano.

"Oh beautiful enchanting eyes, oh beautiful eyes so strange and deep!..." (Oh, begli occhi di fata, o begli occhi stranissimi e profondi!...), Amos sang with rapture. Rather than tired he seemed revived by the journey and by that extremely long and rainy spring day. He amazed his audience as he ended the song with a note which was loaded with emotion and passion as he sang the phrase "...but give me love!" (...ma datemi l'amor!).

In the meantime Vanessa was standing right at the back of the room, leaning against the wall. Amos did not know, nor was he ever to find out, what she was thinking then or what was going on in her heart. She, for her part, was unaware of the fact that at that moment she was the muse inspiring the artist who had shaken her hand for the first time just a few minutes ago. She listened to that piece which she knew well, smiling at life, at her very young life, with the innocent trust which is the prerogative of youth. She listened to that song and the ones that followed, allowing herself to be lulled by the sweetness of those melodies that she had so often heard sung to her by her father; then, at the end of the short concert, she disappeared into the crowd and left the room.

Amos was cheerful. After so much heartache and so much up-heaval in his life, that night he felt rather more restored than usual. He sat down to dinner in a small room set aside for his group of friends and began to mull over the events of that curious day. Suddenly his thoughts turned to Vanessa. With a firm movement he pushed his plate away and called for Sergio. He turned to him and whispered in his ear, "Where do you suppose that girl from Ancona has got to? The one Luciano introduced to us... How would you like to go and check if she's still around and, if she is, ask her to join us here?" Sergio immediately got the picture. He smiled and quickly set off on his mission.

It was not an easy search. There was great confusion: people coming and going with plates of food, some drinking toasts, others flirting with the guest seated next to them, some attempting to smooth their way towards the politician of the moment, others seeking to insinuate themselves into the favour of this or that magistrate or powerful businessman, and so on... But Sergio did not give up and in the end he was rewarded. He saw the young woman disappearing into another room and called out to her. Slightly surprised by this she stopped. "Amos asked me to invite you to join us downstairs." "Amos? Who?"... Vanessa was about to say when she suddenly remembered. She smiled. She had managed to avoid yet another gaffe by a whisker. "He asked for me?" she asked with some dismay. "Fine, I will come right away," she added without asking further explanations. With that she came downstairs and sat next to Amos, who immediately took care to make her feel at ease. He chatted about this and that with the natural spontaneity of those who are accustomed to such situations, but he could do nothing to prevent the looks that focused on the girl and, as he was perfectly aware, caused her a degree of embarrassment.

At a certain point, while adjusting his napkin on his knee, his hand encountered Vanessa's under the table, and, without thinking twice, he took hold of it. It was cold and delicate. What a beautiful hand!

Hands had always held a special fascination for Amos and he had held many in his life! Although he gave no credence to the notion that the lines on a person's palm could reveal their future, he was sure that hands could very quickly tell a great deal about the person holding them out to him, the hand being a doorway to the soul. Amos was quite convinced of this and in that moment of contact he searched for all the messages that a hand can send out in coded form. Suddenly he felt overwhelmed by a wave of love and tenderness. In that moment he wished he could be alone with Vanessa and be able to tell her everything his heart was urging him to say, but the language of the heart is encrypted; words are not enough; they sound small and inadequate to the task. A heart speaks directly to another heart and rejects intermediaries. And anyway they were not exactly alone there.

So Amos let go of Vanessa's hand. He tried to regain some composure, to assume a natural expression, and very quietly he asked her, "Do you have to go home tonight?" "No," she replied, "I am staying here till tomorrow morning, and the next day I have to take an exam at my university." "Well, in that case, if you like, you could stop over at my place and tomorrow I can take you to the station..." he suggested.

Vanessa thought for a moment and then ventured timidly, "If it's not too much trouble..." "Not at all, and you will keep us company on the journey which was so boring on the way here."

Amos and Vanessa talked, brushing against each other occasionally, almost as though they wanted to bring their souls closer together, while destiny, that most sublime, most illogical, mysterious, and divine of artists, prepared a more extraordinary masterpiece for them than they could ever have imagined before now. Vanessa had accepted the invitation, so they had to make a move quickly. There was no longer any reason to stay, whereas there was a real risk that she might change her mind, or that they might encounter some set-back...

Amos hurriedly finished eating, bid everyone goodbye, and left the house. Outside it was still raining. He sat in the front passenger seat next to Sergio, who drove, while Carlo sat in the back next to Vanessa.

There were some comments about the party guests, and then the conversation turned to literature and poetry. Amos was surprised at how well-read the girl was... perhaps she was not as young as she seemed...

Eventually they also talked about music, and Amos pushed a button in front of him, and turning to Vanessa and laughing, he asked, "Do you recognize this voice?" "This is the voice of someone from your home town. He was my teacher, you know, and if I had never heard his voice when I was a boy perhaps I would not be a singer myself today, and then perhaps you and I might never have met!" She understood, and thinking back to the moment when they had first spoken to each other, she smiled. This time she would not get muddled up.

Now in the car they all listened to the music in silence. The voice of Franco Corelli filled Amos's heart, just as it had done so many years earlier, with that masterly performance of the "Improvviso" from *Andrea Chénier*: "Colpito qui m'avete, ov'io geloso celo..."

That voice, that music, heightened Amos's emotions and probably also those of Vanessa who, to Amos's astonishment, began to sing quietly along with the recording. So she also knew the opera, thought Amos to himself. She certainly was quite an extraordinary girl. He became thoughtful for a while and then suddenly asked, "Excuse my curiosity, but how old are you?" "Twenty-one," she replied quite simply. "Twenty-one..." thought Amos to himself... "that is really very young, too young. She is less than half my age... hardly more than a child, even if she has the maturity of a woman. Perhaps I have been foolhardy. Perhaps I shouldn't have invited her..." but, as everyone knows, it's easy to say things with the benefit of hindsight. In the meantime they had left the Emilia Romagna region behind them. That stretch of motorway, which was unusually empty, snaked around the Tuscan side of the Apennines. By now they were approaching Florence, which was already visible over there in the distance. Corelli was still keeping them company: "Come un bel dì di maggio, che con bacio di vento e carezza di raggio..." Amos smiled. Perhaps destiny, that great master of ceremonies, had also thought up this artistic detail for his plan. It was indeed the month of May. Chénier had written those last verses of his short life on his shirt cuffs in his own blood. Listening to those sublime lines, Amos instead felt as though he was experiencing the first day of a new life, and this was not so far from the truth. In his soul, which had been tried and tested by so much suffering, the pain of those verses was being miraculously transformed into joy.

They reached the house filled with a lust for life which cancels out all weariness, problems, and afflictions and gives new impulse to dreams, hopes, inspiration, and passion, which makes couples eager to exchange stories and hungry for words, even small insignificant things spoken only to fill uncomfortable silences. When they fell asleep, overcome with exhaustion, the sun was already high in the sky, lighting up the splendid backcloth of the Apuan mountains.

Love and joy often go hand in hand. That meeting was a meeting of souls. From that moment on Amos and Vanessa would never leave each other's side. They would travel the world, face difficulties of all kinds together; they would discuss, plan, sing, and play like two adolescents embarking on life. Because love is also able to perform these miracles.

Conclusion

To the patient reader who has got this far I owe a few explanations. You will surely have understood that the main aim of this book is my desire to represent, at least approximately, who I am and, above all, my state of mind today, my view of life, as well as to tell whoever may be interested about the world of show business seen from behind the scenes, from the dressing rooms and the corridors of the television and radio studios.

I have given myself a different name and did the same for certain others who populate these memoirs. I did this on the one hand so as to be able to recount certain episodes with the most scrupulous regard for historical truth, and on the other in order to respect the identity, and above all the privacy, of those people who are mentioned without having expressed a desire to be so. In this way I have been able to tell the sin without naming the sinner. Instead, in the case of a few famous people, I have used real names in the certainty that they will have no cause to reproach me. Now it only remains for me to take my leave with apologies, thanks, gratitude, and the hope – allow me this small sin of vanity – that I might have stolen a little of your time from its urgent flight, and spared a moment of boredom and idleness.

Andrea Bocelli

Dear Parents,
Dear Veronica,

I hope you will receive this odd composition that I dedicate to you with all my heart as a testimony of the profound recognition of the love and understanding with which you have always surrounded me and for the faith you have placed in me. In these pages you will easily recognise episodes and aspects of your life that I have decided to describe: I wanted this story to be rooted in truth, albeit partial, inasmuch as it is essentially mine, that nevertheless springs from a mind which has done its utmost to clear away all the prejudices and preconceptions that might have irretrievably compromised what little good there may be to be found here. Because, just as it is dedicated to you, so it is dedicated to my children, the primary reason for my existence, in place of many, pointless lectures which I know, in spite of everything, I will not manage to hold back from at some time in the future.

How hard I have striven, and continue to strive every day, to elicit from the world, from the society in which we live, which is so complex and contradictory, some secret formula or miraculous prescription to reveal to my sons as a safe remedy to protect them from the difficulties and challenges of life, which are as frequent as they are inevitable. Yet nothing, nothing comes to me! Nothing absolutely certain, absolutely good or just! Nothing at all other than some brief thoughts, some innocuous reflections, from which have sprung a few basic convictions that have allowed me to live a tranquil life dedicated to the pursuit of an inner peace that, aside from some moments of quite ordinary difficulty, has never left me.

What better opportunity than this could I have found to leave my children the advice which springs spontaneously from the bottom of my heart, never to lose the ability to look to the future with optimism, to develop faith in themselves and above all, faith in others, upon which, more than anything else, will depend all the best that life will be able to offer? They will read these pages when they are older, and they will see me perhaps as a nostalgic old man who is incapable of understanding their problems, enclosed within a shell of old memories, as out of touch and irrelevant as an expired lottery ticket.

Here then is the reason for this book, in which I have tried to describe the joy and the good fortune of a man who, in the course of his life, has learned to fight hard with the intention of embracing his ideals but never considering himself to be the repository of absolute truth and always with doubt close at hand.

With the passage of time, just as I have learned to think before making judgements and to weigh matters by listening to my conscience before believing anything, so, one by one, all my certainties have crumbled, giving way to nagging doubt. But doubt is the vestal virgin dedicated to the sacred fire of human intelligence, and so I accept it, despite the fact that this logically implies that I cannot take for granted the very ideas which I occasionally believe and which from time to time I take pains to expound.

Human intelligence, like the tremulous flame of a candle in total darkness, casts light only a very short way over the path ahead of us. Further on and all around us looms the unknown. So man advances slowly and cautiously along the part which has just been lit, choosing only the spot upon which he places his foot, and this ability convinces him that he is master of his fate.

Paying careful attention to where one treads and deciding the exact spot may be useful, but this is certainly not enough to influence our destiny in any significant way. Each of us advances in a direction which is decided from the time of our birth. It is in that direction that we take our first uncertain steps and in that feeble light that we try to make our way and overcome obstacles, moving on as quickly as possible.

I think that humanity, considered as a whole, seems like an immense, disorderly procession which advances chaotically, piercing the darkness with the light from innumerable tiny flames, towards a destination which is as distant as it is unknown, as sought after as it is incomprehensible . . . In other words, human life, the destiny of each one of us, sails on the frailest of vessels riding the current of a stream swiftly all the way to the sea. At the helm, each individual tries to avoid collisions or shipwreck, but can do nothing to turn back or stop for a moment of rest . . .

If the inescapability of the events which mark the fundamental stages of mankind constitutes for me a deeply rooted belief, thanks also to the illu-minating reading of great masterpieces of literature, it is also true that over